Praise for *A True Cowboy Christmas*

"Readers willing to brave the emotional turmoil like a frigid winter day will be rewarded at the very end with Christmas warmth and love." —*Booklist*

"Get yourself a cowboy for Christmas this year!" —*Entertainment Weekly*

"*A True Cowboy Christmas* will fill you with many emotions. . . . This is a good Christmas theme story-line, where love overcomes even life's toughest, beat-in lessons." —*Fresh Fiction*

"Crews hits the mark by concentrating on personal development and internal struggles, minimizing outside drama. The story flows smoothly, is loaded with charming characters, and is full of wit. These mature, thoughtful, caring protagonists will win the heart of any romance fan." —*Publishers Weekly* (starred review)

"Full of emotion, humor, and small-town charm. Caitlin Crews delivers everything I want in a cowboy!" —Maisey Yates, *New York Times* bestselling author of *Claim Me, Cowboy*

"Caitlin Crews writes cowboys you'll swoon over, heroines you'll root for, and families that will grip your heart." —Nicole Helm, author of *Cowboy SEAL Redemption*

D0092810

Secret Nights With a Cowboy

CAITLIN CREWS

St. Martin's Paperbacks

First published in the United States by St. Martin's Paperbacks, an imprint of St. Martin's Publishing Group.

SECRET NIGHTS WITH A COWBOY

For information, address St. Martin's Publishing Group, 120 Broadway, New York, NY 10271.

www.stmartins.com

ISBN: 978-1-250-62549-6

Our books may be purchased in bulk for promotional, educational, or business use. Please contact your local bookseller or the Macmillan Corporate and Premium Sales Department at 1-800-221-7945, ext. 5442, or by email at MacmillanSpecialMarkets@macmillan.com.

Printed in the United States of America

St. Martin's Paperbacks edition 2020

10 9 8 7 6 5 4 3 2 1

1

Rae Trujillo did not wake up on a regular weekday morning at the end of another one of Cold River, Colorado's chilly Octobers prepared to turn her life inside out.

Again.

She woke up grumpy. Outraged that her alarm had jolted her out of another night of too few hours of sleep. And furious that, as ever, she was her own worst enemy, because why did she keep doing this?

It felt brutal every time. Like she kept punching herself in her own face, but did she ever learn her lesson? No, she did not.

But it was far too early on a shivery Thursday to think about the epic disaster that was her endless—and endlessly complicated—relationship with Riley Kittredge.

Besides, Rae knew by now that by the time she staggered outside and crawled into her trusty old pickup, she would be good to go. If not exactly singing a happy tune, certainly awake enough to handle the drive into town. But the waking up part never got any less shocking when she'd only gotten home a few hours before.

Because whatever else she was—and sure, there was a part of her that enjoyed it when people thought the worst of her, because the truth was a sharp little knife she kept to herself, and after all this time, she could admit she sometimes liked the cut of it—she was first and foremost an idiot when it came to Riley.

"And lying here brooding about it doesn't help," she muttered into her pillow.

She sat up and swung out of bed. Long years of experience in exactly this idiocy meant she'd laid out her clothes the night before. All she needed to do was stagger into them without making herself think about anything. Especially her life choices. Then she headed downstairs to perform a face dive into the strong coffee that was the only thing that ever made her feel remotely human at this hour. With or without her two whole hours of sleep.

Rae tiptoed through the dark old house, once a small farmhouse and now a collection of meandering updates various ancestors had made. At least one for each generation since the first Trujillo had showed up on this land, long before the English settlers came west. She moved silently down the stairs because her grandmother claimed she woke at the slightest sound, and the last thing she wanted to confront at this hour was Inez Trujillo in one of her states.

No one wanted Inez's lacerating commentary on anything and everything but *especially* about the ways in which every person she'd ever met had disappointed her.

Especially Rae, who Inez had once called her favorite—but Rae had opened her big mouth and ruined that a long time ago. Now she tried to appease her grandmother like most people did, because it was easier.

Rae made it to the main floor and headed for the lit-up kitchen where her father, the earliest riser because he liked to be out in the greenhouses well before dawn, always left a hot pot of coffee behind him when he left the house. Things she was not thinking about included: Riley.

Always and ever Riley. And the many choices she'd made about him and because of him that had led to her living in her parents' house now that she was inarguably *in her thirties.*

Not adjacent to them. Not newly thirty. But *in them.*

But no morning-after yet had been made any easier by beating herself with the shame stick. And she was so busy trying not to do it today that it took her longer than it should have to realize that when she walked into the kitchen that smelled marvelously like her father's preferred dark roast, she wasn't alone.

"Good morning to you too," rumbled her older brother, Matias, sounding obnoxiously *alert.*

Possibly he'd learned such things in the Marines. Where he had also learned how to transition from the sweet, funny boy she'd always hero-worshipped into the too-quiet man who'd come back changed, with too many secrets in his dark eyes.

Rae wanted to growl at him but restrained herself. Because she was a lady.

She shuffled across the floor to the coffee machine as if it were some kind of shrine and treated herself to a large, steaming mug, adding in an overly generous pour of cream. Then she savored that first sip.

Okay, she thought. *I* might *live.*

This time.

Only when her synapses were firing at last did she turn around, lean back against the counter, and allow herself to take in this strange appearance of her brother in the usually empty kitchen.

"What are you doing awake?" she asked in a far sweeter tone of voice than she'd been using on herself so far today.

"Long day ahead," Matias drawled.

He lounged back in his chair, too big, really, for the

kitchen table their mother mostly used as her office. Right there in the middle of the most-used part of the house, because Kathy Trujillo was not one to suffer or toil in obscurity. She and Inez had that in common.

Though they would both have acted deeply appalled at any suggestion that they were alike.

"It really will be a long day," Rae agreed. "Since you're starting it before dawn."

Matias let a corner of his mouth drift up in a vague approximation of a curve. Rae and her younger sister, Tory, firmly believed he practiced that in his mirror. "You really do wake up on the wrong side of the bed. Just like when you were fourteen."

That was maddening. Rae assumed it was meant to be. Accordingly, she smiled sweetly at her brother as if he'd said something *marvelous,* secure in the knowledge that he found that equally annoying. Balance was important.

She concentrated on draining her first cup of coffee as if she were on a mission, then went back for more. Matias was not drinking coffee. He was sitting in that chair that was on the verge of too small for his big frame, still and watchful.

More so than usual, if she wasn't mistaken.

"But really," she said when it was clear that he planned to keep that up, and because he normally didn't get up for hours yet. Who would if they didn't have to? "Are you doing a shift in the shop?"

It would be news to her if he were. And maddening in a whole different way, because if he were planning to go open the family floral shop in town, she wouldn't have to and could still be asleep right now.

"I don't have a shift today." Again, a ghost of a curve on his mouth. "Do you see me wearing the red shirt of shame?"

This time, when Rae smiled, it was a real one. "I do not."

She looked down at herself, representing the family business in the required uniform of the Flower Pot, the retail arm of the Trujillo plant and flower operation. It was, at best, frumpy. A trim red shirt with a collar, tucked into dull khaki pants, and aggressively comfortable shoes. Plus a green apron while actually in the shop.

No one wore the uniforms—the uniforms wore them.

But their grandmother claimed she loved those uniforms and had *designed them especially,* so the uniforms stayed. Who would dare complain? Certainly not Rae.

She waved a hand over her outfit. "My shame, on the other hand, is sadly all too evident."

As she said it, she really hoped that was not the case. Or not *all* her shame, anyway. That would be awkward.

Matias rose then, as silently as he did everything else. "Have fun with that. Wrap it up in a bouquet and call it a seasonal special. You're good at those."

Rae did not care for his tone. She was more than *good* at putting flowers together, whether for bouquets or bigger arrangements. She was an artist, thank you, even if no one else ever used that word. Sometimes she thought the flowers were the only reason she'd survived her train wreck of a life so far. They saved her day after day. But even if her life had been perfect, she would have been sick of Matias and the rest of her family acting as if they did all the real work with the corporate and industrial clients while she *played with flowers* in the cute little shop in town.

Not sick enough to say anything about it, of course.

The squeaky wheel in the Trujillo family did not get the grease. It got in trouble if it was lucky, and if not, iced out.

She knew that all too well.

"Everybody likes a little shame in their bouquet. It's the secret ingredient." Her tone was light, but she frowned at him. "If you don't have to go into the shop, why on earth would you be up at this hour? It's inhumane."

Her brother stopped in the kitchen doorway and looked back at her, stoic and stern suddenly. Great. That expression usually meant a lecture or some other form of his disapproval was incoming, the way it had been with regularity since he'd come home.

Rae braced herself.

"I'm moving out," Matias said.

That was not what she was expecting. "What? Since when?"

"Since I spent the last eighteen months making my favorite outbuilding livable." He nodded toward the darkness outside the windows. "By the river with a view, and best of all, a solid three-mile drive from here."

"How did I have no idea you were doing this?"

Matias eyed her, and she wished she hadn't asked. "Because you're the expert on ignoring things you don't want to see and pretending all kinds of things aren't happening when they are. Aren't you, Rae?"

Ouch.

But then, it wasn't a surprise. Matias had come back from serving his country to find his little sister's marriage to a friend of his in disarray and had not been happy when she'd refused to tell him why. When she was feeling charitable, she suspected his harping on the topic was how he expressed love.

She was not feeling charitable at why-do-you-hate-me o'clock in the morning. "Is that supposed to be a dig? I don't even know what you're talking about."

"Of course you don't."

Rae took a big pull from her coffee. "I'm happy for you that you're moving out, I guess. Not really sure why that's making you hostile."

"I'm not hostile." Matias's dark gaze, unforgiving and shrewd—she blamed it on the Marines because she missed the boy he'd been—moved over her. "What I am is a grown man. Who's been back home for just over two years and can't handle living with his parents any longer. I would have moved out before the end of the first month if I hadn't decided to work on the cabin."

"Yay?" Rae offered, draining the rest of her mug and then taking it to the sink so she could wash it the way she knew her mother preferred. And could therefore avoid the otherwise inevitable tirade about how Kathy was not the family servant.

Better to do the things that made the loudest people in the family happy than suffer the fallout if you didn't. Another Trujillo family truth Rae had learned the hard way.

Was there anything she *hadn't* learned the hard way?

"Meanwhile," Matias said from behind her as if he could read her mind, "you've been hiding out here for how long now?"

Rae froze, only realizing that she'd gone too still when the hot water became uncomfortable. She slapped the faucet off and took much too long examining her skin to see if she'd managed to hurt herself. And wondered how her brother had zeroed in on the very thing she'd been thinking already this morning. "I'm not hiding anywhere."

"You have your own house. Why don't you go live in it? And if you don't want to move back in with your husband, why are you wasting away here? Get a life, Rae. Seriously."

That was hideously direct. No one referred to Riley as

her husband anymore. Not in her hearing, anyway. She couldn't remember the last time someone had dared.

Rae felt . . . winded.

"The question isn't why *I'm* moving out." Matias's voice was dark and condemning and aimed straight at all those messy places inside her. As if he knew that he was setting off a seismic event, deep where she kept the sharp blade of the truth. It took every scrap of her self-control to keep from showing him how much it hurt. "It's why you don't seem to want to move out."

"What is *wrong* with you?" she managed to ask. "Did you wake up this morning and think, *I know, I think I'll take a swing at my sister*? What did I do to you?"

"The real question, Rae," Matias said in a voice she might have called something like sad if he wasn't being *awful,* "is why are you so comfortable here? Is this really what you want for your life?"

Rae was still turning that over—and over and over—in her head hours later.

She'd fumed all the way into town. First on her drive out through their property to the already-bustling greenhouses, where she'd loaded up on the day's fresh-cut flowers. Then the solid thirty-minute drive into town that provided a person with entirely too much time to think. No matter how loudly she cranked up her music in her rattly old death trap of a truck.

She'd tried to lose herself in the best part of the day, saying hello to the plants and flowers inside the shop while arranging the day's new flowers in the windows to best catch the eye of anyone happening by. Sketching out the daydreams she'd had about the centerpieces she'd make for the town's Harvest Gala the night before Thanksgiving, because even though she hadn't heard from the organizers yet, the Flower Pot always provided the gala with gorgeous pieces its attendees could bid on. And then she settled into the day's orders, many of which needed to be ready for deliveries starting at nine.

Normally, it was her favorite part of the day.

The Flower Pot was an institution in the Longhorn Valley, and Rae took immense pride in being part of her family's long history here. She also just really loved the flowers. She could always lose herself in the colors and scents. She could slip out of time and think about nothing but the shapes different flowers made together, or the way their colors blended, or the way the fragrance of the sweetest blossoms could come together to make a magical perfume all their own.

Flowers were pure joy on stems. People could come in, pick up a few flowers, and be happy.

Maybe flowers couldn't *solve* problems. They sure hadn't solved Rae's. Still, they always made her *feel* as if, at any moment, they might.

But all she could think about today was her stupid brother. And his typically unsolicited commentary.

And your house, a voice inside her taunted her. *And your husband.*

Rae didn't like to think about that house too much. And she had spent far too much of her life thinking about Riley already. Surely, at some point, it had to stop . . . didn't it?

Not if you don't stop it, that voice retorted.

Stupid voice.

Meanwhile, deep inside, the secret she kept and intended to keep forever seemed to burn hot and bright as if it were new.

She was still wrestling with it when her shift ended. She waved goodbye to the teenage employees who weren't any younger than she'd been when she'd started working in the shop, but looked impossibly young to her, anyway. Babies, really. It was scary to think that she'd been their age and already planning her doomed wedding, God help her. She tried to shake the Riley-ness of it all off as she pushed her way out of the flower shop's lovely, humid grasp and onto the street.

Outside, the October air was crisp with a hint of snow from the impressive Colorado Rockies that rose all around the little town of Cold River. Rae paused outside the shop to zip up her insulated jacket before the chill got too deep into her bones, then shoved her hands into the pockets. She loved fall. She loved the golden aspens and the sturdy pines that seemed to smell better with snow coming in. They'd already had the first few snows this season, leaving the mountaintops painted white and the briskness in the air that made it clear winter was coming in. And hard.

Rae had always found the slide into the dark and cold exhilarating. She loved the upcoming holidays. She loved the bright lights in all the windows that fought back the longest nights. She loved pumpkin spice everything, walls of shiny, bright red poinsettias, and the same Christmas decorations they'd been gathering to put on the tree on Christmas Eve in the old Trujillo house since before Rae was born.

And it helped that her favorite season was right here in Cold River, where she could walk up Main Street and see the holiday things she loved reflected in the window displays. Currently Halloween, soon Thanksgiving, and then all Christmas, all the time. Her hometown looked like a postcard. It was the perfect Western town, and she usually liked to remind herself as she walked that she was lucky that she got to live here, even if her ex—or whatever he was—did too. The Flower Pot was down near the frigid river that had long ago given the town its name, right by the road that wound its way through the mountains toward Colorado's fancy ski resorts. Normally, Rae loved the walk up the length of the old street and its perfectly preserved, weathered brick buildings, many with the old galleries that cried out for a high noon.

But today, she couldn't seem to concentrate on the familiar old places that had been here her whole life, mixed in with the new boutiques and restaurants that everyone agreed were a breath of fresh air in a town so remote. The more of that fresh air, the more often Cold River was a weekend destination from Denver, two hours of treacherous mountain passes and questionable roads away.

People who lived here didn't waste a day with relatively mild weather when winter was on the way. Everyone was outside. Rae smiled and nodded as she passed folks she knew along the street—which was almost everyone, to some degree or another. The colder it got, the more the weekenders faded out and the locals remained. That meant Rae either personally knew everyone or she knew of them, and it was always easier to smile when passing them on the street than it was to handle the fallout of anything that could be construed as rude.

She was not always extended the same courtesy, because people knew her too and had their opinions.

And maybe she took a little bit of pleasure in smiling the widest at the people who she knew judged her the most harshly, like Lucinda Early, reigning town dragon.

Still, she was grateful when she finally made it up to Capricorn Books, Cold River's only bookstore that was currently run by her friend Hope, and Hope's sisters. The Mortimer family had been selling books here for three generations.

Rae pushed through the door, the entry bell chiming

above her. She expected to find Hope where she usually was, half hiding behind the mountains of books she liked to keep stacked on the counter as a barrier and an ever-expanding to-be-read pile. Instead, her friend's voice floated from farther back in the store, indicating she was engaged with a customer.

But this bookstore was Rae's second home. She, Hope, and their other best friend, Abby, had spent half their lives here. When they'd been younger, Hope's mother and aunt had run the place, and the three girls had whispered their secrets into each other's ears in the depths of the stacks. Both Abby and Rae were from longtime Cold River families who lived outside of town in opposite directions. That made afternoons after school here in the bookstore convenient for everyone. Their families could pick them up at their leisure, later in the evening, and the three of them took their firm school day friendships and made themselves more like sisters.

Because she considered herself family, Rae rounded the counter—taking care not to accidentally tip over any of the stacks of books—and made a beeline for the big, oversize armchair that sat behind the desk. It was currently occupied by Orion, a cat of enormous size and what Rae assumed would be a fearsome temper. If he could ever stir himself to display it.

Instead, he merely gave her a baleful glare and refused to move from the high back of the chair.

That was where Hope found her when she walked back to the front of the store with her customers in tow and a small armful of books. Hope began ringing up the books with a single raised eyebrow in Rae's direction, but Rae knew it wasn't because Hope was surprised to find her here. It was never surprising to find Rae here.

When the bell jangled behind her customers, Hope

came and dropped down onto the wide arm of the chair. And then all that was missing was Abby, who would historically have taken the other arm. The three of them had spent years jumbled up like this. *Lying there like a heap of puppies,* Hope's mother had said.

But Abby had a different life these days. Though she was still a manager at Cold River Coffee, just around the corner, she didn't spend the kind of time she'd used to hanging out in town with her oldest friends in the world. She had a husband now. A teenage stepdaughter.

And a baby who'd turned one at the end of August.

A baby Rae loved so much it hurt.

It actually *hurt.*

"Your mood is way too loud," Hope said after a while.

"Matias is moving out of the house," Rae informed her. "Apparently, this whole time he's been home, he's been remodeling one of the outbuildings to his specifications. Whatever that means."

"How enterprising. If I wanted to renovate an outbuilding, my only option would be that terrifying shed out back. Not really worth braving the inevitable spider situation." Hope shuddered.

"Living in town cuts both ways, I guess. No agricultural chores or barn duties, depending on what the land is used for. But no outbuildings to choose from, either."

"Better still, when winter comes, no getting snowed in on the wrong side of the pass."

"Is that in the plus column?" Rae asked. "Because I seem to remember you complaining that it wasn't fair when Abby and I would miss school when the passes were closed, but you still had to go."

"That was sheer injustice," Hope shot back.

Rae reached up and tugged out the tight, professional ponytail she wore at work, rolling her shoulders while she let her hair down. And the longer she sat in this familiar chair, in this place where she'd always felt far more comfortable than in the house where she still lived, that gnawing, insistent knife-edged thing inside her seemed to throb.

"Abby has her own family now," she said softly, pretending to study her close-cropped nails that she always meant to spice up with a manicure, but never did. There was no point when she spent so much of her time with her hands in dirt. "She spent her entire life mooning around after Gray Everett, with literally zero hope of him ever noticing. Much less marrying her. Now she has his baby."

Hope sighed happily. "It never gets less amazing, does it?"

"But what are *we* doing?" Rae asked, swerving her head around so she could really look at Hope. And too aware she was talking mostly to herself. "It's a big joke, I know. You're eternally single. I have a complicated past. But here we still are. Alone. Both of us still living in our mothers' houses."

"My mother does not live in said house, thank you," Hope said indignantly. "It's completely different."

"But your sisters do. It's not like it's your house, is it?"

"I'm not the one in this chair who's living with her parents, that's all I'm saying."

Rae rubbed at her face. "My baby sister lives all by herself in an apartment in Austin. Matias apparently built himself his dream house. I was the responsible, grown-up one, once upon a time. Yet I still live at home, forced to endure the endless hundred years' war between my mother and grandmother. It's against the natural order of things."

Hope shrugged, her expression carefully blank. "Then move out."

Because Hope wouldn't call Rae out the way Matias had. They'd passed that point years ago. Rae had made it clear what she would and wouldn't talk about, and her friends had acquiesced. But today, it was like this pretending—just like Matias had accused her—had infected her pulse. And was pounding around inside her limbs, making her feel edgy and uncertain and *wrong*.

"I could do that," she said quietly. "But if I move out of my parents' house and I don't move back into *his* house . . ."

Her stomach knotted, her throat was much too tight, and she couldn't finish the sentence. She felt winded again, the way she had when Matias had walloped her with this in the kitchen.

Beside her, Hope's eyes widened almost comically. "Are we . . . talking about him? For the first time in more years than I can count?"

Rae wanted to tell her everything. But then, she always did. One of the reasons she didn't like to talk about Riley was because she always wanted to unburden herself, at last. To take that sharp-edged weight she'd been carrying all this time and share it. When she couldn't.

If she hadn't told him, how could she tell anyone else? The more time passed, the less she could imagine ever telling anyone. And the more she took it as a badge of honor, really, that people made all their assumptions about her when they had no idea what had really happened.

Not her friends, who loved her unconditionally and staunchly, even if they didn't understand. But Riley's family, who she'd loved so much, who no longer spoke to her when they could avoid it. Her family, who had also stopped asking why, but had never quite treated her the same, either, and were always so *disappointed*. The whole freaking Longhorn Valley, who were more vocal and openly judgmental about the things they didn't understand, like Lucinda Early and her pointed *sniff* on the walk here today.

Threaded through it all were those secrets she'd decided to keep a long time ago. And the newer ones she told herself she regretted in the light of day.

What if you told them at last? a voice inside whispered.

But if Rae knew anything, it was that telling secrets was a risky business. And mostly not worth the trouble.

As far as the world was concerned, pretty much nothing Rae had done since she'd married Riley Kittredge a month after she graduated from high school made sense. She'd decided she could live with that.

That didn't mean she had to live like *this*.

"Okay, then," Hope said mildly as the silence dragged on. "We can maintain the silence for another ten years, no problem. Whatever you want. You know I'm fully ride-or-die in this and all things."

Rae cleared her throat. "I'm not actually sure my personal life can be salvaged. Or solved. Or . . . anything, whether we talk about it or not."

And Rae was sure that she could see, swirling between them, all those things they never talked about. The suspicions she knew her friends had about her actual relationship with Riley these days. Their real opinions about how Rae had handled herself then and now, and no doubt a great many theories about what she should do about it all.

But Hope didn't say any of that. She waited.

And when Rae didn't say anything else, she leaned in and pressed her shoulder against Rae's. "Maybe it's time to fix it, Rae, whatever that looks like. Maybe it's finally time."

The shop door opened, and Hope got to her feet, already smiling at whoever had come in.

Rae stayed where she was. She wished Abby were here,

because Abby was always so calm. Filled with the kind of quiet strength that made you think, if you were next to her, that it was actually your strength, too. Rae could use all the strength she could get, since she apparently had none where it counted.

And the more she thought about Abby, the more she thought about Abby's sweet little Bart. It had been getting consistently harder to think about anything else ever since he'd been born, but now he was less a squiggly baby and more of a *person*.

Yesterday, Abby had come into the flower shop with Bart to preview his Halloween costume, an adorable lion that made him so happy he'd screamed with delight, and something inside her had shifted. And ached.

Oh, how it ached.

And now it seemed to bloom, straight on into something sharp and bright.

I want that, something in her declared.

Loud and clear.

Cutting straight through the mess.

Not Bart himself. Not Abby's rancher husband, as remote as one of the mountains. But her own version of those things.

She wanted the same things she'd always wanted. A crowded, cheerful house filled with family who loved each other as passionately as they argued with each other, one never overpowering the other, so it was all part of the same bright tapestry.

As bright as all the flowers that filled her days.

The opposite of her own family and their endless battles and silences, in other words.

But if she wanted those things, if she was finally ready to move on the way she should have a long time ago, she knew what she had to do.

The trouble was, she had never wanted to do it.

"Why do you look like you're plotting a war?" Hope asked when her customers had left with cheerful bags of books.

"Just a little war," Rae said softly, though it made that knife buried deep inside her slice at her. Deep, then deeper still, when she would have sworn there was nothing left to cut. "Just a tiny little war, hardly worth mentioning."

Hope smiled back at her, big and brilliant, but Rae had the feeling that neither one of them believed that. Not for a second.

And later that night, she gathered up her courage and headed out into the foothills to face her demons.

Just the one demon, really.

Riley Kittredge, the boy she'd married, then left a hundred times, yet couldn't manage to stay away from.

Until now, because Matias was right.

It was high time Rae let go, moved on, and got herself a life.

2

Even before the rattly old truck pulled into view, Riley Kittredge knew who was coming up his drive.

It was after eleven o'clock at night on a Thursday. It could only be one person.

He lived a long way out from town in the foothills of the Rockies, in a clearing carved out of the woods on the twenty acres that were his personal part of the land that had been in his family since the first Kittredge had settled here way back when. There were no neighbors aside from his own family members—none within miles—and nobody *happened by*.

Folks had to be looking for him to find him.

And one person in particular always knew exactly where to find him.

Riley had only gotten home maybe a half hour before. He'd had dinner with his sister, Amanda, and his best friend, Brady—who was also Amanda's husband—in the small carriage house they lived in down by the river in town. It was tucked back behind the barn he'd helped them renovate so Amanda could turn it into a kind of celebration of the local goods of Cold River and Colorado. That his baby sister had gotten together with Brady was something that had bothered Riley a whole lot when he'd caught them kissing last year, but he now viewed the two of them as meant to be. No one was more surprised than he was, but there was no denying they worked.

As pretty much the reigning expert on relationships that didn't work, Riley should know.

When he'd filled up on about as much newly wedded happiness as he could choke down, they'd all walked up from the river that wound through the town to the Broken Wheel on Main Street. It was the nicer of the two bars in town, complete with decent food, live musical acts, and half of Cold River there to watch your every move on any given evening—a favorite local sport. The Coyote, by contrast, was housed in what had once been a bordello, was as dim as it was loud, and though everybody might know you there too, no one tended to talk much about it the next day.

It had been a night like any other. Right up to and including Riley's ex sitting at a table with one of her best friends, Hope Mortimer, acting as if he weren't in the same room. Or even on the same planet.

When both of them knew that even though Rae had moved out years ago for her own mysterious reasons—reasons she'd never explained to his satisfaction and he'd come to doubt she ever would—she'd be showing up later.

Because she always showed up.

The old truck pulled into the yard and stopped. Or maybe died at last, not that Riley was supposed to care about things like her safety in that rolling disaster any longer. She cut the engine, and there was nothing but the quiet of the thick October night this far out from civilization. There were stars up above, the rush of wind through the evergreens, and the scent of potential storms in the mountains high above. Another winter coming in fast, and here the two of them were, playing the same game.

Every time, Riley told himself that this time he wasn't going to let her in. Every time, he assured himself that *this* time he was going to put an end to it.

This time, he was going to lay down the law.

But he didn't do that.

You never do that, he mocked himself. *You never will.*

He walked to his front door and yanked it open. Then stood there, waiting.

Rae took her time getting out of her truck. Riley liked to think she was filled with as many second thoughts as he was, or maybe even more, since this entire situation was how she wanted it.

But then, Riley was really good at making himself the martyr, he acknowledged with a little dark laugh he would have concealed if she were closer. The truth was, he'd always been perfectly capable of putting an end to this. He never had.

So he stopped thinking about who was to blame and settled in, leaning against his doorjamb and folding his arms. And waiting to see what version of their little dance was on the menu tonight.

Sometimes he thought he was a glutton for punishment. Other times he thought he was a genius, because he had all the heat and none of the hassle.

Either way, here he was again, standing outside in the cold. It was bracing, though not as truly cold as it would get once November rolled in and sank its teeth in deep. The Longhorn Valley sat high in the Colorado Rockies and took its seasons seriously. There was no messing around, no creeping into late autumn bashfully. Sometimes the inevitable snowstorms waited there, up on the peaks, for winter to start. Other times they howled down in the kind of serious winter preview that forced him to use ropes to get from his front door to his own barn.

And sometimes the kind of storm that blew in was Rae Trujillo, who climbed out of her truck while he watched. She slid to the ground with that same compact grace that had gotten him in trouble in the first place.

She was always the same kick to the gut.

They'd known each other their entire lives. They'd been buddies when they were small, according to the photographs, but that had changed as they'd grown. The two years Riley had on her had seemed like more and more of a vast, unconquerable distance. They'd gotten less and less comfortable with each other, which Riley could trace directly to the day that little, tomboyish Rae, all of twelve years old, had turned up at a church picnic with brand-new curves.

At a worldly, sophisticated fourteen, Riley had found the sight impossible to handle.

So he hadn't. It had taken them three more years and a lot of adolescent drama to get together. Scenes in parking lots. Intense conversations when she was too young to date and he was supposedly dating someone else. When he'd been a junior at Cold River High, one of his classmates had tried to take her to the prom, and it embarrassed Riley to this day that such a provocation had made him snap. He'd shoved Stephen Crow into a bank of lockers, shouted something filled with a young man's testosterone, and had taken her to the prom himself.

Though it had taken months to convince her deeply unamused parents that he, one of the Kittredge boys renowned for the kind of behavior parents of teenage girls weren't likely to view favorably, could be trusted to take her out at all.

He had married her a month after she'd graduated high school. He'd built her this house. He'd figured they'd have the rest of their lives together. On nights like this, he thought he should have been more specific about *how*.

Four years into their marriage, she'd left him for the first time. It had taken her a solid two years to leave him for good. Meaning she'd finally moved out at that point. Back to her parents' house, where she'd stayed ever since.

He'd been pretty sure that was the end of it. He'd gone down to Denver to spend a little time with Brady, who'd lived there then, a long way from the mess. And when he'd come back, he'd been home all of twenty-four hours before Rae showed up at his door.

Just like tonight.

And more nights than not ever since.

She walked toward him, holding his gaze the way she always did and as unreadable as ever. She climbed up to his porch, then stopped as if she couldn't see the clouds her breath made on the cold air. Or as if she liked the clarity of the cold in the face of the confusion between them. Like he did.

But then, if either one of them really wanted some clarity, they wouldn't keep doing this, would they?

"Pretty sure I told you I was done last night," he said, not moving from where he stood, leaning up against the door like he planned to physically bar her from coming inside.

More games, he was well aware. All they did was play these games.

Some nights he enjoyed them.

Rae looked like a delicate, snappable twig of a thing, when he knew she was anything but. Her brown eyes were silky and huge and had always made him foolish. These days she liked to keep her wavy, black hair in a

knot on the back of her head instead of the loose curtain down her back that he preferred, which he personally thought she did deliberately to annoy him. And it
was always the same sweet torment to look more closely
and see those curves that had wrecked his world at fourteen. They were even better these days, especially since
he knew exactly what to do with them. Sometimes Rae
dressed to accentuate her perfect hourglass shape. Other
times she wore slouchy clothes that hung off of her and
hid the way her waist nipped in—but he knew. He always
knew.

This woman had been making him stupid for most of
her life. She still did.

"You always say that." Rae folded her own arms, less
to mirror him than to proclaim her own willingness
to fight—oh yeah, he knew every single step in every
variation of this dance of theirs. "If you suddenly started
meaning it more last night than ever before, you're going
to have to make that clear."

Like always, he felt his pulse begin to kick and that
familiar, uncontrollable fire begin to build in him. Like
always, he felt edgy and dangerous and a lot like he
might die if he didn't get his hands on her. Because that
was the one place they were always on the same page.

"One of these nights you're going to show up here and
I'm not going to open the door," he told her, very darkly,
because he was sure that must be true.

One day, that had to be true.

"I think about that all the time."

"I don't think you do. Why would you?" He laughed.
Not nicely. "You get everything you want."

"Do we have to do this?" She looked almost tired
then, he thought. Or something heavier, for a moment
there beneath the porch light he would have turned off,

wouldn't he, if he hadn't assumed she would turn up. But sure, this was all her fault. "How many times do you think we can have the exact same conversation?"

"You tell me, baby. It's been years."

She sighed, staying where she was. "Come on, Riley."

And that was . . . different. Normally, Rae was only too happy to jump into the fight, any fight, her blazing temper at the ready and more than capable of matching his own. Sometimes Riley thought that was the whole reason she came here.

Well.

That and how they handled the fighting, historically. One flame led into another, and they always let it burn.

But tonight, she didn't move closer. She didn't defend herself. She didn't throw the same accusations at him, setting that merry-go-round of theirs into motion.

Riley wasn't sure he'd ever stopped to think about how much he relied on the flare of temper and injustice to make the usual spark between them blaze. And he couldn't say he liked how that realization settled in him. He was supposed to be a grown man. Yet when it came to Rae, he might as well still be a profoundly stupid teenager.

"Did you come here for a serious conversation?" He pushed away from the doorjamb, wishing—as usual— that she wasn't the prettiest thing he'd ever seen. "You never come here to talk, Rae."

She studied him a moment. "I know you think this is easy for me. It's not. It never has been."

"Every time, the same game," he said in a low voice. "Show up at my door. Pick a fight. Poke and prod until we're all over each other, like always. I keep thinking that one day, you'll just ask for what you want. One day."

Riley wasn't being entirely fair. Everything he'd said

was true—but he was no saint. He also did more than his fair share of poking and prodding when he felt like it.

And he usually felt like it.

"I've spent a long, long time trying to figure this out." Rae didn't say that angrily, which made the back of his neck prickle. "And I want to blame you for not being everything I want, because you've always been the only thing I knew how to want. But that's not fair."

That sounded a lot like a goodbye.

But they didn't do goodbyes.

"I can't help you figure this out," Riley growled. "You've never seen fit to clue me in on what's been bothering you. For years."

She frowned as if she wanted to argue that, but . . . didn't.

Something cold introduced itself to Riley's spine, then tracked its way down the length of his back. He kept going. "You told me we had problems that couldn't be solved. That's it. Care to update that?"

"Maybe what I should have said a long time ago is that I have problems that you can't solve. But I've never known how to say that."

"You said it fine."

It wasn't lost on him that this was maybe the most honest they'd been in years. Honest when not shouting at each other, that was. There had been a point, back there somewhere, where he'd veered between two extremes. Either assuming that he needed to let her work it out in her own time—whatever it was—and therefore accepting this for what it was whenever she turned up. Or so riled up about all of it that he knew if he even opened his mouth to ask one question, he'd tear down his own house with his hands.

Funny thing was, time marched on all the same.

"I don't want to fight with you," Rae said in that same soft way that made every alarm in his body start to howl. "I'm so tired of fighting with you, Riley."

Normally, they would have poked at each other enough that they would have been tearing off each other's clothes by now, staggering inside, sometimes not making it to the bed at all the first round.

Some years, Riley told himself it was that kind of passion that mattered most. That it would be the thing that saved them in the end.

But tonight he felt strung out on the softness in her, far more deadly that her temper. Because he knew what to do with a fire. He knew how to let it burn and take them both into the white-hot center of it until neither one of them could move, much less fight.

Softness, on the other hand, just might kill him.

But Rae didn't continue. And following an urge he would have denied if they'd been sniping at each other, he reached out to smooth his hand over her hair until it rested there, curled around her neck. He let his thumb move over her jaw.

And watched, something in him scraping wide open and raw, as her eyes filled with tears.

He had seen her cry too many times to count. He liked to pretend he was immune, but he wasn't. What he was, he knew, was good at playing this game of theirs because it was all he knew. Their families had taken sides. Their friends knew better than to ask direct questions. Sometimes Riley thought their secret wasn't much of a secret, but no one brought it up, so he figured it didn't much matter that they weren't as "ex" as they pretended they were in public.

He knew that it was generally assumed that he was the way he was—grumpy on a good day, according to his siblings—because he was bitter.

Riley knew better. It wasn't that simple. But it was easier to let them think that.

Rae's mouth moved then, as if she were about to say something, and he had the strangest sensation suddenly. Some kind of premonition that because she wasn't fighting tonight, she was actually gearing up to take a much bigger swing at him—

He told himself that was silly.

But he went with his instinct anyway, leaned down, and covered her mouth with his.

And like everything with Rae, it was too good. Too *right*. The way it had been when they were just kids. The way it had been every time since.

Every time he kissed her, it was like he could remember every other time he'd kissed her too. That first time, her very first kiss, out behind her family's flower shop. The day he'd kissed her to claim her as his wife, standing up there feeling so grown up in front of everyone they knew and loved. And all the other ways he'd kissed her since then.

To say goodbye. To ask her to come back. To do the begging he refused to do with words. To convince her, compel her, even confound her if that was what it would take.

He had kissed her a million times, and it still wasn't enough.

It was never enough.

Riley could feel the cold air all around them, but her mouth was warm. Hot the way she always was. He took the kiss deeper, angling his mouth as she surged against him the way she always did, gripping his T-shirt in her fists.

Because another truth was that he might not be able to resist her, he never had been, but she was equally unable to resist him.

Some years that felt like balance.

But tonight there was this. Only this. His other hand moving so he could hold her face where he wanted it. So he could kiss her over and over. Drawing it out. Finding that fire that was always between them, making them both burn.

He would usually haul her up against him and carry her inside. Or not bother going inside, depending. Tonight, he didn't do that.

Tonight was different, and Riley didn't like it.

It wasn't until he pulled back and they were both breathing heavily, their foreheads touching, that it occurred to him that this was a whole lot like the way they'd kissed during those years before they'd gotten married. When they'd been dating and he didn't want to push her into anything and they'd taken breaks like this, panting and delirious and so wild for each other it had actually hurt.

He was amazed that he could want anyone this much. Still.

And it took him a moment to realize that tears were pouring silently down her face.

"Tell me what's wrong." He tipped her face back so he could use his thumbs to wipe her tears away. And he gave in. "Just once, baby. Tell me."

He could feel her shaking. She closed her eyes.

And it occurred to him that maybe he didn't actually want her to answer the question.

That if he'd really wanted an answer, he would have demanded it years ago.

That if some part of him weren't afraid to know the real reason why she'd left him—or *sort of* left him—he wouldn't have put up with all this in the first place.

But like most things where Rae was involved, it was too late.

It was always too late.

He'd felt a distinctly similar sensation at that church picnic a lifetime ago when he'd been fourteen and completely incapable of handling what was happening to him, because of her. It was lowering to realize that where she was concerned, a part of him was still that fourteen-year-old.

Rae straightened her shoulders. She lifted that stubborn chin of hers. The way she looked at him was as sad as it was determined, and it sent a kind of iron spear straight through him. Because she normally hid that part.

They'd been playing this same game for a long time, and he'd spent each and every one of those years wishing that it would change. But now that it was, on a Thursday night that had been otherwise unremarkable, Riley wanted to stop it. Whatever it was.

He wanted to keep things as they were. Messed up and frustrating and maddening, but familiar. Theirs, somehow.

"Riley," she said, a lot like she was saying her vows, though he knew instantly that this particular vow was not going to lead anywhere he wanted to go. "I want a divorce."

3

The moment she said it—actually *said it, out loud, to him*—Rae felt dizzy. Her stomach heaved, and she thought she might actually throw up right there on the porch with the October wind slapping at her wet face. And some part of her wanted that.

She wanted to crumple. She wanted to give in, now, before she even tried.

Because her heart hurt so much her ribs ached, and a panicked voice inside her kept telling her that this half-life of theirs was better than no life—

This is long overdue, she told herself sternly. *This is what's best for* both *of you.*

Riley didn't let go of her. His hands—always a little rough, always so strong, and so familiar—tightened, but that was his only reaction.

And for a moment, Rae took comfort in that.

Even though his eyes had gone so thunderously dark it made her shiver. And as she watched, everything about him . . . changed. She was suddenly entirely too aware that he was a huge, tough man towering over her, that he could tear her apart with his fingers if he liked, and that she had never, ever, seen him look quite this . . . scary.

But if she knew anything in this life, it was that Riley Kittredge would never, ever hurt her. Not physically. He would hurt himself first.

She tried to swallow, though her throat was like chalk, and tried again. "I want—"

He dropped his hands. "I heard you."

Rae missed his hands, instantly. And his voice . . . *ouch*. But she'd known that this would be messy.

Everything with Riley was messy. Always had been, probably always would be, whether they divorced right now or limped along the way they usually did for another decade.

All she was doing was cleaning up her mess. Their mess. Whether he appreciated that right now or not.

The look on his face made her breath catch. It did not look remotely appreciative.

And her throat was still much too dry.

"You want a divorce," Riley said.

Eventually.

They called him the most dangerous of the Kittredge boys, though none of them were boys or particularly approachable or *safe*. Rae had always thought that was funny. But tonight she finally saw it.

Did she ever.

"We both know that this isn't healthy," she said, working overtime to make her voice sound even. And not to end the sentence with a question mark, because she wasn't asking him. "I'm not sure it ever has been."

"I must have missed when *healthy* became a goal."

"We got together too young and held on too long."

That line had sounded particularly good in her head. She'd repeated it to herself, out loud, on the long, all-too-familiar drive from her parents' place to his.

She expected Riley to explode. She expected his temper.

They'd always fought like kids who didn't know any better. Loud and mean. Saying things that were better left unsaid. Throwing things. Making threats and ultimatums and generally behaving like idiots with each other, because that was how they'd fought when they were teenagers.

It hadn't been until Rae's friend Abby had gotten married to Gray, an undisputed adult complete with a teen daughter, that Rae had understood that it wasn't necessary to burn down the house every time they disagreed. That some people—with far healthier relationships than her secret marriage to her ex—actually didn't *try* to hurt each other.

Some conflicts were actually resolved, and then the people concerned grew closer and loved each other more. Imagine that.

Maybe that was where this had started. Maybe that was when Rae had begun to understand that continuing this insanity was legitimately bad for both of them.

She braced herself for Riley to yell at her, but he didn't.

That was worse.

"This has never been healthy," he said, sounding more resigned than angry, which didn't fit a single narrative she'd imagined about how this would go. "It's been an adolescent mess from day one. And 50 percent of that is you, baby. You think you're going to be healthy out there on your own? Great. Have fun."

Rae watched, astonished, as he turned and stalked back inside. She half expected him to slam the door in her face, but he didn't. Instead, he headed for the bottle of whiskey he'd left on the coffee table. The bottle of whiskey he liked to swig when she was around, because he'd once said it was the only way he could handle her.

That comment had caused a knockdown, drag-out fight that had ended with the two of them winded and wrapped around each other in bed, with some embarrassing holes in the wall besides.

But tonight there was . . . nothing.

When she'd expected fireworks.

You can't possibly be disappointed, she lectured herself. *Maybe he knows this is the end of the road too. Maybe he's* grateful *you brought it up first.*

Rae did not feel grateful. She felt . . . painfully bloated with a fight she'd expected to have but wasn't having, after all. More than anything, she wanted to run away. Just . . . literally turn and run, drive out of here, and pretend none of this had ever happened.

The way she'd done so many times before.

Tonight, she was changing the script. She was doing the thing she'd been too afraid to do. For years. She sucked in a ragged breath. She tried to keep her hands from curling into fists. Rae followed him inside, easing the door shut behind her. She leaned against it once it was closed, watching Riley warily.

He took a healthy swig from his whiskey bottle, his eyes glittering.

But he didn't say a word.

Normally, when she was in this house again, she was otherwise engaged. She didn't have time to look around the place and remember that it had been hers too. Or she avoided thinking about such things, because she came here in the dark and she left while it was still dark, always. That was how she'd pretended she'd forgotten that she'd helped him build this house that summer after he'd graduated high school two years ahead of her, knowing with every nail and every swing of a hammer that she would move in here one day and live here. With him. As his wife.

Despite herself, Rae remembered how happy they'd been at first. How overwhelmed with the sheer joy of it all. That they were married and could live here, wallowing in that attraction that had been like a pulse inside her almost as long as she could remember, and it was . . . perfectly acceptable.

You know better than to let memory lane take you down, she told herself.

She made herself look around. She made herself soak in all the details of the house they'd furnished together, piece by piece. He hadn't changed much of anything. A new throw on the same old couch. New scratches on the coffee table they'd liberated from a yard sale in town and hauled back here, bickering all the way about why they needed a table for a beverage Riley had maintained would never be drunk on or near it.

Rae was surprised he hadn't chopped it up into kindling years ago.

Because he always thought you'd come back in the end.

She couldn't pretend she didn't know that. Even when he was standing across the room, studying her as if she were the devil.

"This still feels like my house," she said without thinking.

And regretted it when that glare of his went molten hot and furious. Or maybe she didn't regret it, exactly, because her pulse kicked over into high gear. Her cheeks felt hot. And between her legs, as ever, she felt the same rush of greedy excitement.

But Riley didn't explode.

He did not come at her. He did not shout. He did not throw that whiskey bottle against the far wall. She didn't rush at him. She didn't throw the bottle herself. He didn't haul her up against him, his mouth hard and perfect and always so demanding, then cart her away down the hall to the bed she still considered hers—

Focus, she ordered herself.

If she had to think about this house and all the dreams she'd indulged in here, surrounded by walls she'd helped put up, it was only fair to think about the nightmares too. That one lonely and terrible night she'd never been able to talk about, and had only that glowing-hot blade wrapped up tight, deep inside her as an unwanted memory. The way everything had changed after that, because she had.

And how did you tell a man that you'd become a ghost right before his eyes when you couldn't tell him why?

"Are you actually, deliberately, trying to drive me insane?" Riley asked.

Conversationally.

That was new. And not . . . un-terrifying.

"I am not."

"If this still feels like your house, why do you want a divorce?" he asked. Not unreasonably.

"I shouldn't have said that."

His mouth twisted. "Which part?"

She couldn't seem to do anything but sigh, standing there against the door as if it were the only thing holding her up.

Riley let out a dark laugh and muttered something that she was glad she couldn't hear. She told herself it was a mark of her seriousness tonight that she didn't demand to know what he'd said. Maybe that was growth.

He took another shot, letting the whiskey bottle dangle

from his hand when he was done. And yet still *not* giving into the temper that was stamped all over him.

Which meant they were both standing here. In this tense, layered silence that felt louder than all their fights put together. It made her chest feel so tight she wanted to cry—really cry, this time.

But it also meant there was no other option but to just . . . *gaze* at him.

That was a luxury Rae hadn't allowed herself in ages. She couldn't do it in public, because the entire town was always watching the two of them, spinning out theories as to how they'd gone wrong. And she never did it here, because everything between them was always a flash flood, a sudden thunderstorm, a mad blizzard. There was no *gazing,* there was only surviving it, then slinking off into the night again.

But tonight, she was facing things. Including this.

Him.

Riley Kittredge in all his glory.

The bracing, inescapable truth of the matter was that if Rae were forced to paint a picture of what the perfect man looked like, she would draw Riley. Any version of him. The hot-eyed teenager he'd been, too knowing and just this side of insolent. The boyfriend he'd been, holding her hand as gently as he'd kissed her fiercely, and never pushing her for anything she didn't want to give—and then only laughing when she'd tried to push the boundaries they'd agreed on. The brand-new husband who had carried her into this very house, laid her down in the bed they'd picked out together, and taught her every last thing her body could do.

And tonight, he was all of those versions of himself and more, all grown up in a T-shirt and jeans, bare feet, and that hard, glittering look in his dark eyes.

He made her heart *do things* even when he was furious with her.

He was dangerously beautiful. His hair was dark, his eyes were darker, and his mouth was a straight-up problem. He was big and lean and had been born to wear the cowboy hat she didn't have to look for to know was hung up just inside the kitchen. Riley was a man who worked with his hands and his whole body, day in and day out since he'd been a kid, and she knew that every inch of him was fashioned out of hard slabs of muscle, powerful and determined.

She knew his hands were gentle and firm, demanding and soothing. She knew he was as good at calming all his high-spirited horses as he was at making her body perform each and every one of his darkest desires, until they were her desires too. He had taught her how to kiss. He had taught her the kinds of things a couple could do way out in the woods in the back of a pickup truck without breaking any promises that might have been made. He had taught her that she was the prettiest girl alive, and he had made her a woman, and she didn't know who she was without him. She never had.

Riley Kittredge was the perfect man.

But he couldn't be hers.

And it was far past time she faced up to that.

"Okay," he said, still almost laughing in that way that wasn't remotely amused. "I guess I'll bite. I can't seem to help myself. Are you going to tell me why you want a divorce now? Tonight?" The grin he aimed her way was like a knife, a jagged rip right through her. "It could be anything, after all. Anything or nothing and me the last to know."

Rae had practiced for this. The whole drive here.

"We should have divorced years ago."

"But we didn't." He slammed the whiskey bottle back down on the coffee table, and the look he gave her then . . . smoked. "Have you met someone else, Rae?"

He might as well have punched her in the gut.

She was outraged, when she shouldn't have been. "Of course not. We're still married."

"I didn't forget. I'm not the one who has a problem with that. Historically speaking."

"I've never been with anyone else. You know that." And she was finally doing this, so she asked the question she'd never wanted the answer to. Thanking the heavens above that her voice didn't go all squeaky and vulnerable. "Have you?"

That grin of his made him look like a pirate. Not an entertaining one.

"If I were with other people, Rae, I certainly wouldn't let you waltz in and out of my front door in the middle of the night every time you felt the urge to scratch an itch."

"Good," she said, and meant it. "Make it ugly. That will help."

But what she actually felt was relief, down to her toes.

"Just tell me what you want."

"I already told you. I want a divorce."

It was harder to say *again*. This time in the light. Where she could see him and she could remember everything too well, and she now understood why the cowards of the world preferred to either send a text or simply disappear.

Why would anyone do this?

Yes, yes. She knew it was the right thing to do. But knowing that didn't take away from her desire to sink into the floor and just . . . go away.

"Why?" he asked again, his voice the crisp sort of demand that made untamed horses leap to do his bidding. "Why do you want a divorce now?"

Rae felt the same urge to leap but repressed it.

She was not a horse.

And she was horrified when she realized she'd almost said that out loud.

"I'm not a kid any longer," she said instead.

She saw his eyes flare at that, but he didn't say anything. All he did was continue to watch her, looming there across the room, dangerous and for some reason more in control of his temper than he normally was.

And she knew she owed him an explanation. She wanted to do it right this time. She wanted to do at least one thing right.

Her stomach twisted, but she made herself keep going. "I look at Abby. She's settled now. And happy. Happier than she ever believed possible."

"So were we."

His voice was quiet. Not an accusation, and that somehow made it worse.

Rae's eyes burned. "That was a long time ago. We were different people."

"If you say so. But fine. Please keep telling me about how happy your friend is. And how that has something to do with you showing up here in the middle of the night, wanting a divorce." He made a very male sort of noise. "Instead of what you usually want when you show up here."

"You're never going to give me what Gray gives Abby," Rae said, her voice cracking a little bit. "If you're honest with yourself, you know that."

"I do know that," Riley shot back at her. "Because I'm not a cattle rancher, praise the lord. I'm a Kittredge, not an Everett. I didn't have a previous, tragic marriage, aside from this one. I don't have a teenager. And my father is a challenge, but he's not a mean drunk like Amos Everett was. Also, he's alive. Oh, and most of all because I'm not Gray Everett and you're not Abby Douglas."

There were a lot of things Rae could have said to that. So many ways she could have explained what she meant. But she'd made her choices a long time ago. She didn't know if she would make the same choices now, but that was the funny thing about time. It only went in one direction, and there was no taking it back.

She cleared her throat as best she could. "I thought you be happy about this. You're the one who always says you want to stop playing games."

Riley shook his head. "I don't even know why I'm surprised."

"Great," Rae said then, a little more hotly, because it was easier to lean into her temper. It had always been easier. That and a dose of self-righteousness with some martyrdom thrown in and she was good to go. "Then it shouldn't be a big deal, should it?"

The way Riley looked at her then made a prickling, shivery sort of thing start at the back of her head and snake its way down her spine.

Rae chose to ignore that. "The good news is, we're the only ones who know that we're not divorced already."

"Yeah. Good news."

"And there's no need to divide anything up," she continued brightly as if she could neither see nor hear all that darkness that coiled around him.

It was what made him who he was, and she'd always thought it was the real reason they called him dangerous. Rae knew him best, which was to say completely and not at all, and she knew it was because of this. That clear signal he gave off that if he wanted, Riley could shake the mountains apart with a single look.

Or maybe just her.

She ordered herself to focus on the necessary details, because she needed to leave. Before she forgot how, the way she often did. "I'm not going to try to take anything from you. Not this house, not your horses, nothing. I certainly didn't bring anything to the table. So."

"So," he repeated.

One single syllable that shouldn't have exploded inside of her like buckshot.

It seemed like a lifetime spread out there between them. Their lifetime. The roller coaster of it that she could still and always feel in the pit of her stomach.

He never made it easier . . . but this wasn't the time to talk about that. He stood there like a wall and wondered why she couldn't talk to him. She'd always been undone by that dark, brooding glare of his. Particularly when she was younger and could seem to do nothing at all but cry, which only made him angry . . . and around and around they went.

But there was no point debating any of that.

Because they had. And gotten nowhere. Ten thousand times or more.

"It's coming up on midnight," he pointed out, gravelly and too intense, and if she wasn't mistaken, *daring* her. "What's your plan? Are we going to have a divorce like our marriage? You want to go out and make it legal and then still show up whenever you feel like it?"

"Is that what you want?" she found herself asking, though she shouldn't have.

It was this cabin, maybe. The warmth from the stove that sank into her bones and made her forget herself. All their history, soaked into the floorboards and making the walls seem bright when she knew it was because he repaired them. Every time one of them did something foolish, he patched it up like it had never been.

But Rae didn't want patches and lies and pretend.

She wanted a life.

He was shaking his head. "When has what I want had anything to do with this?"

"Yes, of course. What a saint you are, Riley. Burdened with this messed-up relationship that you have no part in."

She really needed to stop doing that. She had *promised* herself that she would stop doing that.

"If the shoe fits," he replied, almost in a drawl.

And their usual patterns seemed to shimmer there between them. Their history and their routine and *them.* She could surge forward, let her temper get the best of her. She knew he would meet her. They could fight, they could make up, and they would end up right where they always did.

Rae knew the journey would be amazing, because it always was—

"No," she said then, as much to herself as to him, "I want to be done."

"Rae. *Why.*"

It was a demand, not a question. And the way he belted it out made her wonder whether or not her knees could do their job.

Whether she could really do this after all.

"Because." She held his gaze because she owed him that much. "I want a life. You should want that too."

"What makes you think I don't?"

Rae wanted to shout at him. She wanted to throw all their history in his face, again, as if that could change their future. She knew it couldn't, or it would have. She wanted to sob, but that never worked—because he was the only one who ever managed to make her feel better.

"You deserve that life," she managed to say. "So do I."

He was quiet, though that didn't make him look any less brooding or dangerous. His mouth formed that thin, hard line, and she hated that. She hated all of this.

"Rae . . ."

She hated that most of all. Her name in that mouth when she'd never been any good at resisting him.

"We're going to get a divorce," she told him, maybe a little too fiercely, while her eyes burned all the more. "We're going to move on. We're going to live wildly happy lives, Riley. The way we said we would when we were in high school."

"Rae."

"Just not with each other," she managed to get out.

Without breaking down, though she would never know how she did it.

But if she stayed even a second more, she would crumble. She would dissolve into a puddle, or she would throw herself at him—to punch him, or kiss him, or *something* to shift the intense weight of these feelings inside of her. And if she did that, he would do what he always did. He would pick her up. He would soothe her and seduce her the way he always did, and much too easily.

He would carry her into their bedroom, lay her down, and for a little while, make them both forget.

Rae couldn't let that happen.

Not again. Not anymore.

So before he could do something with that thundercloud on his face—or she could do something with her traitorous heart—she turned around, wrestled the door open, and finally threw herself back out into the blessedly cold night.

It wasn't running when she'd done the thing she'd come to do. It was a strategic retreat.

Better still, it was a step forward.

At last.

And for the first time in as long as she could remember, when Rae gunned her engine and peeled out down that long dirt drive, she didn't look back.

4

"I need to move out," Rae announced the next afternoon, after she'd spent her day in the back office of the Flower Pot balancing figures, tracking shipments, dealing with the relay service that funneled orders to them from outside Cold River, and all the other parts of running a flower shop that she loved a lot less than the flowers themselves. All while absolutely not obsessing over the fact she'd actually, finally asked Riley for a divorce. "I need my own place. Or not my family's place, anyway. And if I'm moving out, why not closer to work?"

Rae was sitting with Abby and Hope in the comfortable back office of Cold River Coffee. Hope and Rae were taking turns holding a passed-out Bart while Abby worked on her own paperwork as the longtime manager of the coffeehouse that was considered an institution in the Longhorn Valley.

"Really?" Abby blinked as she looked at Rae from behind her desk. "You're going to move into town?"

"Apparently, there are apartments over the Coyote," Hope said with a smirk.

Because Rae's former sister-in-law, Amanda—who had worked for Abby here in the coffeehouse for years and was now Abby's sister-in-law—had moved into one

of those apartments last fall. A move that had scandal-
ized half of Colorado and had somehow led to Amanda
getting together with Brady Everett, Gray's youngest
brother.

Once upon a time, Rae and Amanda had been close.
Amanda had told her everything. Rae had been her
older brother's girlfriend and then his wife. They'd been
family—until Rae had moved out.

But Rae wasn't going to trot out her list of losses.

Not today. Today was about moving on.

"There have to be places to live in town that aren't
connected to the Coyote," Abby said, shaking her head at
Hope. "I heard Theresa Galace rents out that little renovated cottage behind her house from time to time."

Little Bart fussed a bit, and Abby extended her hands
as if to pluck him away from Hope—who only frowned
and adjusted how she held him. Bart was a sturdy, adorable
little boy who still conked out like an infant and was happy
enough to be carted around by his mother and her friends.
Until he wasn't.

He made Rae's *heart hurt*.

"Obviously, Hope and I can't comment on the urge
to move out," Abby said, shifting in her desk chair. "I
only moved once, and not only was it from the house I
grew up in to my husband's house, his house is next door.
There are some miles from door to door, sure. But it's
not really the same thing as *moving out,* is it?"

"I like to think that I've lived in two homes," Hope
said, rocking Bart as she held him. "The house I grew
up in that my mother and aunt ruled with humorless iron
fists, and the more relaxed house my sisters and I now
enjoy." She considered that. "Relatively more relaxed."

"It's the same house," Rae couldn't help herself from
saying.

"The same walls," Hope agreed. "But believe me, a different house altogether."

"Anyway," Rae continued as if they'd never gone off on these tangents, "I think it's time. Past time."

"Does it make sense for you to move all the way into town?" Abby asked. "I know the shop is here, but all the greenhouses are way out in the far valley. You'll spend your entire life on the road."

Rae shrugged. "I already do. And also, Matias can do the greenhouse-to-shop run more often. It won't kill him." She looked back and forth between her friends, who were both looking studiously blank, and sighed. "I want to completely change my life. Make it absolutely unrecognizable from anything it's ever been before."

She'd kind of expected *girl power* cries and perhaps the odd parade, but again, her friends . . . paused.

"That sounds a lot like a midlife crisis," Hope said after a moment.

"It sounds amazing," Abby contradicted her, a little bit sternly.

Rae eyed Hope. "Thank you, *Abby*."

"You might as well get a shiny little convertible and a twenty-year-old, blond girlfriend," Hope continued, her eyes gleaming. "That always ends well."

Rae slumped in her seat, her heart kicking at her. "I'm not having a midlife crisis. Possibly because I'm not *middle-aged*, thank you, Hope. I don't want a convertible or twenty-year-old girlfriend. I just want to feel . . . different." It shocked her how hard it was to say that. And then to keep going, when she was so used to tamping everything down and keeping it to herself it was almost a reflex by now. "Like this is the start of a brand-new me."

Abby smiled. "I like the sound of that."

"You can be brand new in a sweet little convertible, though, can't you?" But Hope laughed as she said it.

Rae found herself sitting up straighter. Almost as if she'd thought her friends would slap her down. Almost as if she'd wanted them to argue her out of this. But she shook that off. And prepared to tell them at least some part of what she should have told them all along.

"I decided what my life was going to be like when I was fourteen years old," she said, carefully and deliberately, here in the confessional of the back room of the coffeehouse. Even though it made her a little light-headed. "Work at the Flower Pot. Or out in the greenhouses." She sucked in a breath and reminded herself that this was a day of joy and truths—hard or otherwise. That meant she had to stop pretending a huge chunk of her life hadn't happened. "Marry Riley Kittredge."

She wasn't surprised to see Hope's and Abby's eyes widen. They looked at each other for a long moment. Then they looked back at her, their expressions notably bland.

"It's okay," Rae made herself say, because it needed to start being okay. Right now. She was *making* it okay. "We can talk about it. Him. *Riley.*"

It was like stripping naked to just . . . say his name like that. It reminded her of back in high school when he was all she'd talked about, ever. When it seemed everyone she knew, and certainly her best friends, were as involved in her relationship as she was.

She'd found it hard to shift away from all that *discussion* when her marriage was good. And then, when it wasn't good, there was a part of her that had almost been embarrassed that she'd let everyone down by not being the perfect happily-ever-after story she was supposed to be. Today, everything felt a bit like a bruise. She told herself that was growth.

"This feels like a trap," Hope muttered.

Abby didn't say anything.

"So. Uh." Rae cleared her throat and tried to ignore the commotion in her stomach. And the way her heart was pounding at her. "*Riley* and I are getting divorced."

Then she sat there, trying not to squirm. She might have actually imploded from the strain of all that stunned silence had Bart not started fussing again. Little Bart, who had caused this without even knowing it, simply by existing. Rae found her hand on her belly without realizing she'd moved it.

It was a relief when Hope stood, transferring Bart to his mother so Abby could soothe him. It took the tension out of the room. Or delayed it, anyway.

But then the little boy was snuggled on his mama's lap and everything was quiet again, and Rae couldn't think of a single reason she hadn't made a run for it while she could. It was one thing to grandly decide that she intended to change her life and start by talking about the one subject she'd always, vehemently declared off-limits. It was something else to actually *do it*.

"So, to clarify," Hope began in an overly calm voice that put Rae's teeth on edge. "This whole time . . . you've still been married to him? You didn't get divorced years ago?"

There were approximately five million ways she could answer that question. Rae opted for the most direct answer, ripping off that Band-Aid. "No."

Hope looked at her for what seemed like a very, very long time. Then she looked over at Abby.

"Pay up," she said, and cackled.

"I don't believe this." Abby groaned. "I was *sure* she kept the divorce secret because she didn't want to give all the gossips more ammunition."

"My money was on a secret marriage the whole time," Hope crowed. "Come on, Abby. With the books you read all the time? You should have known better."

Abby shook her head sadly. "I'm deeply disappointed in myself."

Rae, meanwhile, couldn't decide if she felt outraged or stunned or something in between as her two best friends in the entire world continued to laugh. At her busted-up marriage. Abby dug around in her desk drawer, pulling out a ten-dollar bill. She slapped it down on her desk, and Hope swiped it up triumphantly.

"I *knew* it!" she cried again.

"Are you kidding me?" Rae asked. A little more stung than she was prepared to admit. "You *bet* on my *life*?"

"Just because *you* didn't talk about you and Riley doesn't mean *we* didn't," Hope replied, looking completely unbothered as she settled herself back down on her side of the couch.

"But now that you're talking about him again," Abby chimed in, clearly reading Rae's expression and swallowing down her laughter, "you can tell us what happened yourself. No need for us to speculate."

"Or place bets?" Hope asked. "Come on. Double or nothing that the two of them—"

"I don't want to talk about Riley," Rae interrupted her with as much dignity as she could summon. "Not because I can't, or won't, but because that's the past. I want to move on. I don't want to be trapped by decisions a fourteen-year-old made. Just like I don't want to live in a house where I constantly have to negotiate the peace between two bitter women who don't want peace when I've finally decided to stop fighting. No more fighting."

Her mother and grandmother had already been at it when Rae had come downstairs that morning, set up in their battle stations in the kitchen where, she knew, they would stay all day. Sniping at each other the way they'd been doing ever since Rae's father had brought Kathy home to meet his parents.

She'd poured her coffee into a travel mug and had gotten out of there. Fast.

"Your grandmother's terrifying," Hope said, sobering. "Legitimately."

"I like to think of her as more . . . incapable of showing her affection in productive ways," Abby said gently, ever the peacemaker.

Rae rolled her eyes. "That's very kind. But you know that doesn't fit. Inez Trujillo has never been *affectionate* a day in her life."

"She and your grandfather were married for a thousand years," Hope ventured. "Surely that suggests a little bit of affection? I hope?"

This was another topic Rae didn't talk about. But wasn't that the point of her new start? It was time to talk. *Especially* about the things she never talked about. It was time to do the things she never did.

Floral design was all about balance. Proportion and scale. Harmony and rhythm. She could do wonders with a selection of stems and vases, drawing the eye where she wanted it to go and creating compositions that were all about creating joy. But the minute it was her life she ought to be arranging artfully, she retreated.

That had to stop. Might as well be now.

"They hated each other," she said baldly. "They only stayed together for the business."

Rae had never just . . . *said* that. No one in her family said it. They didn't have to—everyone knew. It was one of the family secrets no one was supposed to discuss. As she'd learned. The hard way, naturally.

"I don't know that I thought theirs was a love story for the ages," Abby said slowly. "But I didn't think they *hated* each other."

"My grandmother is a woman of deep and abiding grudges," Rae said. "She and my grandfather never divorced, when they probably should have. Some of my earliest memories are of walking back and forth between their separate houses delivering messages because they refused to speak to each other, right there on the same property." She tried to smile. "I'm not supposed to talk about that. Do you remember when I got mysteriously grounded in sixth grade?"

"*Yes.*" Abby sounded as if it had happened last week. "We were all supposed to go on the class camping trip together."

Hope nodded. "Abby and I were forced to share a tent with *other people,* Rae."

Rae reminded herself that she was not retreating, no matter what. "I was grounded because a teacher called home, and you know we always had a very strict policy on calls from school. Whatever the reason they're calling, you're wrong. And in trouble."

"You never did anything bad in school." Abby looked mystified. "None of us did. Ever."

"Mr. Thessaly was concerned because I'd written an essay about my grandparents for our family tree presentation. He wanted to make sure my family was aware of the things I was planning to say to the class." Rae smiled faintly at Abby's and Hope's expressions. "You know, stuff like the kinds of things my grandparents shouted at each other at a regular Sunday dinner."

"I never liked Mr. Thessaly," Hope announced. "His chin was very suspicious."

"My parents sat me down and explained that I couldn't share private family things with other people," Rae continued, because she didn't want to start thinking about an old teacher's *chin*. Because if she did, she knew she would use it as an excuse to stop talking about this. And then maybe never would again. "Then they told me I couldn't go on the camping trip because they really wanted me to understand the point they were making."

"Rae." Abby looked warm and sad at the same time. "I can't believe you didn't tell us about this then."

"We would have camped out in your backyard in solidarity," Hope agreed. Her eyes narrowed. "Why *didn't* you tell us about this?"

"I wasn't just grounded from the camping trip," Rae told them. "I had to redo my whole presentation. That very weekend."

She had been as outraged as an eleven-year-old on the cusp of twelve could be. What was being done to her was *wrong*. Surely everyone could *see* it.

Rae had wanted to *make them see*.

"A grave injustice was done to you, Rae," Hope said solemnly, though there was laughter in her gaze. "I'm glad you can talk about it. Twenty years later."

"At Sunday dinner," Rae continued softly, "I made my case. It was a school project. We were *supposed* to share intimate stories about earlier generations. And I knew my grandmother could be harsh about things, but she'd always loved me best. She said so. I was sure she'd take my side." She swallowed, and it was funny how painful it still was, two decades on. And how dry her throat was. "She did not. Instead, she didn't really speak to me. For nine years."

Rae had never wanted to disappear more than she did then. She felt clammy. Maybe some part of her expected her entire family to materialize in front of her and condemn her all over again. It took a few intense moments to understand that . . . nothing was happening. She was fine.

Abby blinked. "What?"

"*Nine years?*" Hope sounded flabbergasted.

She was *fine*. "Not a word. Not at my grandfather's funeral. Not at my wedding. She just glared." Rae rubbed at her chest. "I didn't tell you because, you know, I couldn't. I figured I'd already said more than enough."

And she'd learned a valuable lesson, hadn't she? People made a lot of bold claims about truth setting them free, but that wasn't her experience. At all. Truth was dangerous.

Better all around to keep it to herself.

So she had. She'd swallowed down all kinds of truths. And the blade buried inside her reminded her why every time she thought about telling the *really* ugly stories.

"But she's talking to you now." Hope was shaking her head like she couldn't stop. "I've *seen* her talk to you. In an ice queen kind of way, now that you mention it, but I always thought that was just the way she is."

"Flowers." Rae had to clear her throat. She didn't know what to do about how fast her heart was beating. "I got good at flowers, and she wanted to take credit for that, you know, since designing arrangements was always her thing."

"Flowers," Hope echoed. "Rae. That's not okay. You know that, right?"

"Oh, I did it to myself," Rae said, a tight smile on her lips. "Ask anyone."

"Your grandmother is a very sad woman," Abby said then, staunchly. "I feel sorry for her."

"I do not," Hope retorted.

"Anyway," Rae said. "I'm ready to move out."

"I think this is great," Abby said, lifting her brows at Hope as she said it. "A fresh start."

Hope leaned forward and swiped a pad and pen from Abby's cluttered desk.

"Operation New Rae," she said as she wrote the same words in huge block letters on the top of the pad. "We start right now."

"We?"

Hope eyed her. Imperiously. "You want to change your life, and Abby and I are here to be your wing women. What's number one?"

Rae didn't have to overthink it. "Move out of my parents' house."

Hope dutifully wrote that down. Then she got a speculative look on her face. "That one I think we can solve pretty quickly. You know we have room. You should move in with us."

"With you?" Rae asked, startled. "And . . . your sisters?"

"Sadly, they both live in the house too." Hope sighed. "In all their state."

Hope's sisters were named Faith and Charity, naturally. Faith was the oldest and had never had any use for Hope's ever-present best friends. Charity was the youngest and had veered between following them around and loathing them, often in the course of an afternoon. Still, Rae had to imagine the Mortimer sisters in whatever state would still be better than the endless Inez and Kathy show.

"I . . . would love to move in with you," Rae stammered out. "I've always wanted to know what it's like to live in town."

"Right?" Abby smiled. "It always seemed so fancy."

"I think you know it's not fancy at all." Hope laughed. "It's a rickety old house behind a bookshop, that's all. But you know we have spare bedrooms, you're welcome to one, and best of all, you can move in whatever you want."

"Don't you have to . . . ask permission or something?" Rae asked.

Hope's gaze gleamed. "No."

Rae took that to mean Hope didn't feel she should *have to* ask permission, which probably meant she should, at the least, run it by her sisters. But she also knew how stubborn her friend was, and figured that was a Mortimer family issue. And she knew all about family issues.

As far as Rae's own issues went, she felt a bit dizzy. It was one thing to say she wanted something. And something else entirely to have it offered to her five seconds later.

Everything was moving so fast. She thought about the look on Riley's face last night. The way he'd watched her from across the room, intense and brooding and—

But she had to let go of him.

Moving on meant . . . actually, finally moving on. It had to.

"What else do you want?" Abby kissed Bart's head, her eyes dancing. "At this point, I feel like anything is possible."

"A good divorce lawyer?" Hope asked. Then frowned at Abby's expression. "What?"

Rae thought about Riley again, no matter how she told herself not to. He was in her, like it or not. All their years were part of her, like it or not.

And the worst year was that knife that still drew blood, deep inside her.

There before her in Abby's arms, Bart was sleeping heavily with his face nestled into the crook of his mother's neck. His little cheeks were red and flushed, as if it were hard work. And Rae had spent enough time around him to know that he certainly wasn't some perfect angel of a child. He was a perfect little boy, was what he was. Stubborn, willful, adorable, and more often than not, sticky for no discernible reason. He liked mud, dirt, sitting up on the saddle with his papa, all kinds of machines, and making an earsplitting sound that could set the livestock off on a stampede and deafen multitudes.

And yet.

"I want a baby," Rae announced. Just throwing it out there, that wildfire longing she'd been denying for much too long.

Once again, her friends stared back at her, wide-eyed.

Rae met their gazes. She made herself sit still. She would keep herself from fidgeting, she would not run away, and she would wait to see what happened now that she'd gone ahead and put it out there. Bold, unvarnished.

For years, she'd been sure that if she said it out loud it would kill her, and yet here she was, still breathing. If a little quickly.

"You always said you didn't want children," Abby said softly. "Any children, ever. You were absolutely positive."

"I was a kid myself." Rae's voice was unsteady, and she hated it. She knew better. Show vulnerability, get hurt. Her grandmother had taught her too well. She cleared her throat. "What does a fourteen-year-old know about how she's going to feel when she gets older?"

But Abby was right. Rae had been more than positive she didn't want children. She'd been certain and stubborn, and like most things, once she decided on something, there was no telling her otherwise.

Yet however little she'd wanted children, Riley had wanted them even less. He'd been dead set against the very idea. He'd always shaken his head sadly when another person they knew announced a pregnancy or brought a child into the world. Like he was mourning their loss while everyone else was celebrating.

I have too much family already, he'd always said. *No need to add more Kittredges to the existing mess.*

Rae really had to stop thinking about him.

Hope was tapping her pen against the pad. "How do you want this baby?"

"What do you mean? The usual way, I guess?"

"Do you want to adopt the baby, or do you want to actually have the baby?" Hope asked with exaggerated patience. "If you want to adopt, excellent, let's start thinking about the paperwork. If you want to have the baby yourself, are you thinking an anonymous donor through a lab? Or are you thinking about something more traditional?"

Until five minutes ago, Rae hadn't been thinking about this at all. But oddly, having questions fired at her in Hope's cool voice . . . helped. It made her feel settled. It made her think about what she wanted, not what she'd lost.

"The traditional way, I think," she said, testing the words as she said them. "Which I guess means . . ."

Abby made an encouraging noise. "If you mean fully traditional, that would mean a husband. But maybe that feels a little out of the flame, into the fire for you right now."

"Only in your version of marriage." Hope laughed at Abby. "Not everybody jumps right past the whole dating part, straight into the marriage, and hopes for the best."

"Maybe they should," Abby said loftily. "I recommend it."

"There's a no-flame, no-fire, happily lukewarm middle ground, Abby."

"The problem is the modern-day version of dating involves all that online stuff." Rae wrinkled up her nose. "And I think I'd rather die alone, fighting with my mother and grandmother, until the end of time."

Hope rolled her eyes. "There's no need for a dating app in Cold River, Rae. You sweet little innocent. You can just stand out on Main Street and look one way, then the other way, and see who's around. Cell service is iffy, anyway."

Rae couldn't keep the vaguely horrified look off her face. She told herself it was because she couldn't imagine the trials of modern-day dating whether it was on her phone or out in the street. She told herself it was because she had only ever dated one man her whole life. That was why she felt like there was a stone inside her, weighing her down. Change was good, but no one said it wasn't hard.

She made herself smile brightly. "I guess I should go out onto the street, then. Maybe throw a rock and see what I hit."

"But I'm the weird one," Abby murmured.

"No need for rocks," Hope said grandly. "I have personally made a study of all the reasonably attractive single men in Cold River. One of them is your brother, Matias, of course."

"Ew, Hope."

Hope shrugged. "Sorry. He's hot. If scary."

She did not look scared.

"Please don't make me think about you and my brother," Rae begged her. "Ever."

Hope leaned back in her seat, grinning. "Moving on. There are your brothers-in-law. All those Kittredge boys, just waiting around for some enterprising woman to claim them."

"She's not looking to date one of her in-laws," Abby chided her. "Come on."

"And even if I wanted to, which I luckily do not," Rae said dryly, "they all hate me. And Riley would kill them. So."

There was a pause, and it took her a moment to realize it was because she'd said his name. Just said it out loud like it was nothing. Like she said his name all the time and hadn't forbidden it to be spoken in her presence for literally years.

You might as well be Inez, she thought, slightly dazed.

It wasn't only the flair for flowers. It was the silent treatment too. Maybe their execution had been a little different, but wasn't it all the same in the end?

God help her, but Rae did not want to be like her grandmother.

"First, we have our bad boys," Hope was saying. "If we weed out the actually scary ones, we're left with two reasonably bad selections."

"What's *reasonably* bad?" Abby asked.

Rae considered. "I'm guessing . . . not currently in prison?"

"Wyatt Hall," Hope intoned. "Rumored to have done a great many bad things, but yet still manages to run that shop of his. Last I heard, he's not only capable of fixing any engine that comes his way, no matter what vehicle it comes from, but is more than capable of using that same magic touch on the women of his acquaintance."

"When you say *Wyatt Hall,*" Abby said slowly, "are you referring to *that* Hall family . . . ?"

"Hope. I don't want to date bad boys." Rae made a face. "And I certainly don't want to date a member of the Hall family, who would probably rob me in my sleep. And anyway, I thought they were all in various prisons?"

She was being dramatic. But only slightly.

"A common misconception." Hope waved a hand. "But no, not all of them."

"Artificial insemination is looking better and better by the second." Rae tried to imagine kissing Wyatt Hall. Touching him. Letting him put his distinctly un-Riley-ish hands all over her. She gulped. "This is a farming community. How hard could it be? Everybody breeds livestock left and right."

"Tate Bishop," Hope said, ignoring her. "A former bad boy who's now done very well for himself."

Rae actually considered that one. They'd known Tate in school. He'd gone through a rough spot, then had disappeared, and had come back to Cold River about a year ago. Since then, he'd established himself as one of the new crop of young entrepreneurs who'd either come to Cold River or come back to Cold River, and were committed to reviving and elevating the local economy. His microbrewery was due to open next summer.

"Noah Connelly," Hope continued, nodding at Abby. "You might know him as the gloriously grumpy chef who is also Abby's boss, owner of this very coffeehouse where we find ourselves sitting today, but perhaps you've forgotten that he is also a single, good-looking man."

"That's actually true." Abby sounded almost surprised. Probably because the only man she'd ever really been aware of was Gray Everett. Rae could relate. She'd only ever seen Riley.

They all sat quietly for a moment, listening for the telltale signs of Noah and his mood, out there in the front of the coffee shop. He liked to slam his pots and pans around, all the time, but no one complained about it. Because the grumpier he was, the better his food tasted.

And also because he looked a lot like a Viking.

"And since you don't want any of the more questionable characters lurking around here, I would say that the other single man you should think about is Jackson Hale."

"Does Jackson date?" Rae asked. "I thought he just loomed around in the Broken Wheel, talking about beer and investment opportunities."

"He doesn't *loom*," Abby protested. "He owns the place."

Hope smirked. "Also, have you looked at him? He definitely dates."

Rae had looked at him. But she hadn't *looked* at him. When she conjured up an image of him in her head, sure, she could see that he was good-looking . . . though it didn't really land.

You have your Riley filter on, she reminded herself. *You're going to need to turn that off.*

Hope opened her hands as if she'd performed a magic trick. "That's off the top of my head. I'm sure that if I put my mind to it, I could think of more. This is Colorado. There's no shortage of gorgeous, outdoorsy types wandering around. And if that's not what you want, no problem. We can go down into Denver and find you a city slicker."

"What I don't understand is why, if there are all these eligible men milling around this town, you're still single." Rae eyed her friend. "This isn't more of that Mortimer family curse nonsense, is it?"

"An excellent question," Abby said.

"What makes you think I don't have my own secret

life?" Hope asked lightly. "Like you've apparently had for the past, oh, six years?"

"Not racing to file for divorce isn't the same thing as having a secret life," Rae said, aware that she sounded all the more self-righteous because she was lying.

And only once she'd said it did she recognize the fact Hope had maneuvered the conversation away from her apparently deeply held belief that all the women in her family weren't simply alone—they were *cursed* to remain alone.

"Everyone's entitled to their secrets," Abby said calmly. "I have my own secrets."

Hope and Rae both turned to her. Abby stared back.

"You do not," Rae and Hope said at the same time.

Abby laughed. "Well, I could. I'm no longer the vestal virgin of Cold River. I don't walk around like a billboard of sadness these days, thank you very much."

"I think that's me," Rae said, and she'd meant that to be a joke. To be funny, poking fun at herself and her situation in her life, for that matter.

But that wasn't how it came out.

"Not anymore," Hope said with conviction in her voice. "There will be no more billboards. No more sadness."

"No more curses?" Abby asked.

Hope ignored that. "No more wafting around chained to the decisions we made a thousand years ago for no good reason."

"Amen," Rae said then, fervently.

She was sure it would all be smooth sailing from here.

The first day of her new life was going beautifully. She'd admitted the past—or parts of it, anyway. She'd set the wheels in motion to divorce Riley and move on, and it was okay that it hurt, because it should. He had been her whole life even when she was pretending otherwise.

She'd even told her friends things she'd never said out loud before.

"Here's to a brand-new life," she said, smiling at her friends and feeling . . . almost light now. And sure she could handle this storm she'd put into motion. "How hard can it be?"

5

"I get that it's your goal in life to brood yourself to death," Riley's older brother Jensen said a few days after Rae had dropped her bomb, in his usual too-loud, too supposedly amiable way. Riley knew perfectly well Jensen did it deliberately, because everything was a show where the second-eldest Kittredge was concerned. "But you're starting to scare the horses."

The colt Riley was currently grooming, a glorious quarter horse descended through the stellar bloodlines that made the Bar K one of the premier quarter horse operations in the West—if not the world—tossed his head. Then snorted as if he found Jensen as irritating as Riley did.

"Maybe they smell all those fires on you," he replied, not bothering to look over to where Jensen was lounging at the door to the stall as if he were on a break. On a beach somewhere instead of here in the middle of the Rockies at the tail end of a frigid October. "And shouldn't you be running off? Something must be burning somewhere."

"I'm real sorry that saving lives offends you, Riley," Jensen said piously.

In the next stall over, Riley heard their youngest brother,

Connor, laugh out loud. Though it was hard to tell at who. Probably both of them.

"Do you need something?" Riley asked, leaning back from the colt to study his brother. Jensen looked the way he always did. Big, tough, and deceptively lazy. "If you're looking for something to do, there are always stalls that need mucking out. I know it's not as flashy as fighting fires and bragging about it, but it still needs to get done."

"Do you hear that, Connor?" Jensen asked, pitching his voice to be even louder than usual, but not shifting his gaze from Riley. "Stalls need mucking out." At Connor's inevitable, profane reply, Jensen laughed. "Next time, be born sooner, little brother. Problem solved."

Riley couldn't quite keep himself from grinning when Connor appeared, glaring at Jensen on the off chance he was kidding. The bland look Jensen presented him said he wasn't.

"Stalls," Jensen ordered, nodding down the line. In the kind of hard voice he only used on Connor, because it was entertaining all around to treat him like he was still a kid.

He wasn't. But Connor still muttered something predictably filthy, the way he would have if he'd still been fifteen instead of twice that. It only made Jensen let out that booming laugh of his again as Connor stomped away.

"Maybe we shouldn't torture him," Riley said, mildly enough. "One of these days, he really is going to stick a boot where he keeps promising you he will."

Jensen looked wholly unconcerned with that prospect. "He can try."

"Not that I'm not entertained. But you should know I'm going to be just as entertained when he does it."

"This sounds like a whole lot of younger-brother

whining to me," Jensen observed, his gaze gleaming. "I think we all know the order of supremacy around here, Riley. Or are you suddenly confused about that?"

Riley was not confused about much. Just the one over-arching thing he was trying his best not to think about. As usual.

"Grandpa, then Dad," he said. "That's the order of things. You're nowhere in that lineup. Probably because you take a five-month vacation every year."

"Two things." Jensen shoved his cowboy hat back on his head and made a production out of lounging there. "One, only you would call smoke jumping a vacation. It makes me worry about you, Riley. Truly it does. And two, you better not let Dad hear that you think Grandpa is still in charge around here. He might actually . . . react."

"He *almost* frowned at me the last time I said it." Riley rolled his eyes. "It was chilling."

Jensen laughed at that, not that it was all that funny. It was just life out here on the Bar K. Donovan Kittredge might as well have been one of the mountains that rose around them. He was about as chatty and communicative. Riley and his brothers had grown up crushed under the weight of all that silence. Donovan didn't fight. He simply disappeared, there in plain sight, leaving nothing but his mountainous disapproval. Meanwhile, their mother, Ellie, had spent the better part of their childhood battering her head against Donovan's silence, poking and prodding until she got a reaction.

Their oldest brother Zack had taken the same tack with Donovan, which was probably why he'd found himself a different career path and was now the sheriff of Longhorn County. He'd walked away from the Kittredge family business, leaving the ranch to his brothers. The first firstborn Kittredge son to turn his back on the Bar K since the beginning.

Riley wasn't the only one of his brothers who found the memory of their mother's tears hard to forgive.

Donovan reacted rarely. But when he did, it had always been terrifying. Not because he broke things, handed out beatings, or anything like that. Instead he was . . . quietly devastating. A few well-chosen words that would inevitably cut whoever he was talking to in half.

Riley was older now. He tried to tell himself that it wasn't surprising that a laconic man like their father had been unprepared for four rowdy sons, close enough in age to present endless opportunities for fireworks over . . . everything.

Zack had yelled. Jensen had attempted to make everyone laugh instead. Riley had brooded, and Connor had shouted until everyone had laughed at him, as the youngest brother. Which was when he punched things. Walls, the table, or more foolishly, one of his older brothers.

It had been tense or it had been chaos. They'd all been sure their parents would break up, and Zack had actively agitated for it.

Instead, Ellie and Donovan had gone ahead and had Amanda, who was a solid ten years younger than Riley. And whatever their relationship was behind closed doors—a great mystery to all—they had remained a united front ever since. Something that usually only frustrated their sons more.

As ever, thinking about his parents made Riley deeply, ferociously glad that no matter what other mistakes he and Rae had made over the years—and they were legion, clearly—they'd always agreed on one thing. No kids. No carrying on the family drama.

This meant, among many other things, that there

weren't innocent children caught between them now. It felt like cold comfort this morning, he could admit. But it was comfort all the same.

"I have a new buyer coming in this afternoon," Jensen said as Riley made his way out of the stall. Finally getting around to his real reason for being there. "It's that hotel guy from Jackson Hole who's been sniffing around. Wants to make horses the centerpiece of his new program, blah blah blah."

"You need me in on that?"

Jensen nodded slowly, a considering look on his face, which always amused Riley, because it showed the truth about his entertaining big brother. Ask anyone in Cold River about Jensen Kittredge and they'd talk a lot about high school glory on the football field, his bigger-than-life personality, that laugh of his. Happy-go-lucky. Carefree. Possibly not smart enough to realize that parachuting into active fire zones looked a lot like a death wish.

The reality was that Jensen was the businessman of their generation. Between them, Connor and Riley were sheer magic with horses. Connor had an eye for breeding lines and was already building a reputation as the man to watch. Riley had inherited their mother's ability to train, gentle, and gain the trust of any horse she encountered— and his clinics for problem horses were usually filled up months in advance, despite his reputation for what the more polite called *bullheadedness*. Jensen, meanwhile, knew profit and loss, expenditures and acceptable risk like a farmer knew how to till a field but, better still, could sell pretty much anything to anyone.

And in his spare time, yes, jumped out of planes in various Western states to battle forest fires—a pastime that might be a death wish dressed up like heroism, but still required a lot more attention to his physical fitness than folks seemed to think. Something they'd know if they were ever foolish enough to work out with him when he was training for his season. It was exhausting.

"This guy has a regional chain of hotels," Jensen was saying now. "Or is heading in that direction, anyway, and looks legitimate. I think the way to play him is to make him think he's getting one over on us salt-of-the-earth, honest country folk."

Riley didn't bother to sigh. He knew this game. "I'll be there."

"Two o'clock." Riley expected Jensen to walk off then, heading back to the office part of the stable complex where he spent the bulk of his time. But instead, he stayed where he was, that considering gaze of his suddenly all over Riley.

"Something going on with you?"

Riley turned to stone. "What would be going on with me?"

"Offhand, I can think of a number of things. Want me to count them?"

"About as much as I want to get kicked in the face by an ornery horse."

He headed out of the stable toward one of the corrals, where one of his consulting cases waited. A bad-tempered Arabian filly whose owner didn't want her spirit broken but needed her a whole lot calmer than she was now.

"You know." Jensen's voice was . . . careful. It made Riley stop walking, it was so unusual. Though he didn't turn back to face his brother. "Anytime you want us all to stop pretending we're blind to certain things, just say the word."

"I don't know what that means."

"You do."

Riley turned slowly. "Is this like how I pretend I don't know about your nights at the Coyote and all the girls you like to take home? Because I'm actually okay with that. I'm not your Cub Scout leader."

"I don't have to go to the wrong side of town to find a girl to take home," Jensen said with a laugh. "But I also don't pretend that's not what I'm doing when I'm doing it."

Riley stared, stone straight through. "Again. No idea what you're getting at."

Even as he said it, he wondered what he was doing. He and Rae had maintained a code of silence when it came to their personal business, but it wasn't something they'd ever set out to do. It had just happened that way. He knew he shouldn't feel this sense of loyalty to her when she obviously didn't feel the same.

But he couldn't do it.

Riley had grown up with parents at odds, and there had been a lot of years of a lot of external opinions, delivered at potlucks and church picnics and sometimes in the form of pointed prayers. He remembered that much too well. Then he and Rae had started dating while they'd been in high school, which meant there had been a lot of other people not only invested in their relationship but only too happy to share their thoughts. With the two of them and with half of Cold River.

He'd never talked about his marriage when it was good. Why would he talk about it once it went bad?

"Okay, then," Jensen said amiably, sounding every inch the superior, know-it-all big brother. That was so irritating that even if Riley had wanted to unburden himself, he wouldn't have. "You don't know what I'm talking about. Fine. Meet me at two o'clock."

"I planned on it," Riley replied. "I never miss an opportunity to watch folks treat you like you're dumb. It feeds my soul."

"Noted," Jensen replied with a big smile that maybe

only a family member would see was far edgier than it appeared.

Riley felt slightly better about things as he went out to introduce himself to the horse he already knew wanted to stomp on him and rip him to pieces. Something he wished Rae had made clear a million years ago, because in retrospect—knowing that it would all end up where it had the other night—surely, it would have been better to avoid the whole thing.

And if his chest hurt as he climbed in the corral and started murmuring at the unimpressed Arabian waiting for him, he knew it was only because he didn't know how to think about his life without Rae.

"If I could have," he murmured to the filly like it was a little love poem, just for her, "I would have."

He'd made incremental progress with the high-strung beauty by the time he finished his session. After he was done with her, he was thinking about heading out to see if any of the hands needed help with the fences that had gone down over the weekend, thanks to a spicy little wind that had rattled Riley's own house as it blew.

But out in the yard, he found his parents. Ellie was standing by the side of Donovan's truck, talking to him through the open driver's-side window, though the day hadn't warmed up any.

Riley had seen them this morning in the ranch kitchen, where everyone grabbed coffee and daily ranch jobs were allocated. Any new crises that occurred, the way they always did on days that ended in *Y,* were handled as they cropped up.

He walked toward them, trying to read *something* into their body language, but there was nothing to read. Donovan was a slab of granite. And Ellie had made herself into a kind of walking snowdrift.

"Thought I might help with those fences," Riley said when he drew near. Donovan's gaze slid to him, dark and unreadable as ever. He nodded. Or the Donovan version of a nod, which was more suggestion than fact.

"Good talk," Riley muttered when his father drove off.

Ellie gave him a cool look. "You might ask yourselves where all your stubbornness comes from sometime, Riley. It isn't me."

"Of course it's you," Riley told her. "You're the one who stayed."

But his mother didn't respond to that.

Which left Riley turning it over in his head while he drove out into the vast acres of land that were as much a part of who he was as his own bones. He helped wrestle some fences back into place. He ate the lunch he'd packed himself in the front seat of his truck, watching snow-storms dance over the eastern range and keeping his window cracked so he could smell winter rushing in. Then he dropped into Jensen's meeting to quote outrageous prices, deadpan, that Jensen could then undercut in his role as the charming, supposedly more clueless brother.

When his day's work was done, he declined his brothers' invitation to go have a few beers in town. He didn't think the storms in the east were coming for them just yet, but all the same, he tried to race them home.

But when he got there, he didn't go in the house. He eyed the front porch, freaking thrilled that he could now add another memory of Rae to the mix. There were already too many ghosts in those walls, all of them her fault, and now there was the divorce thing, hanging there—

You're going to have to burn it down, he told himself. *That's the only way you're going to get her handprints out.*

He headed for his barn instead of his whiskey bottle, saddled his favorite horse, and headed out.

Because there was only one thing in the world that had ever made him feel as free and as right as being on horseback, and the trouble with Rae was that those good times never lasted. And now she wanted to end these not-so-good times that were all they had left?

He took his favorite trail up behind his house, into the woods and then out again, on a ridgeline that dropped him between the Rockies on one side and this valley of his on the other.

The view always settled him, and today was no exception.

Riley liked feeling as if he were the linchpin between the two. He'd felt that way his whole life. He'd always been more of a peacemaker in his family, back during the wars, as he and his brothers liked to call it. Zack and Donovan had always been butting heads. Jensen had been the comic relief. For a long time, Connor had been the baby, and he was always the squeaky wheel.

It had been up to Riley to sand the edges off, if he could. He'd always found a way, though it had left him nothing *but* edges. And it was only out in the familiar grip of the land that he ever found himself again.

He resented the fact that now, when he looked out over the sweep of the Longhorn Valley, all he saw was Rae. He was trapped somewhere between the brooding, careless mountains, a valley filled with history he was personally related to, and the land that had made them all, one way or another.

And still, all he saw was Rae. Brighter than the stars had ever been.

No matter what she did.

Riley didn't like the fact that Jensen knew—or suspected, anyway—the truth about what Riley's relationship with his supposed ex had been all this time. He didn't like that his brother seemed to think he should unburden himself, because that meant Jensen thought Riley needed such a thing. It brought back memories of high school, and other kids asking him questions about things they shouldn't have known the first thing about as if it were *their* lives. Their fights. Their feelings.

He knew it was part of living in a small town and working in his family's business. His life wasn't so much under a microscope as it was just . . . a part of everyone else's life too. It wouldn't occur to his brothers *not* to get all up in his face and deep in his business, because they figured it was their business too. Because he was.

There was a reason Riley had chosen to build his own house almost as far as it was possible to get from the central ranch house and still be on Kittredge land. And why that spot happened to be way out in the foothills, far enough out of town that it discouraged most visitors from making the long drive.

But he knew, sitting there with his horse beneath him and this land he loved all around him, that he wasn't actually mad at Jensen.

He wished he were. That would be easier.

The truth was that he'd expected her to skip a night, but to come back. Because she always came back. He hadn't thought much of it when she hadn't turned up on Friday night. She was making her point, he'd thought. But then Saturday and Sunday had passed too, and Riley had woken up this morning with a slight headache and a host of unpleasant truths crouched over him like they might smother him if he wasn't careful.

The biggest and hardest to accept being that despite

what he'd thrown in her face last week, he'd never really considered it a burden to play these games with her.

Oh, sure, he liked to pretend. Rae liked to tell him he was a martyr, and he couldn't fully deny that. This wasn't what he'd wanted. This certainly wasn't how he'd expected his marriage to turn out.

But he'd never expected her to end it.

He almost laughed at that. The horse stamped its feet and made a kind of laughing noise for him, so Riley murmured the usual soothing words until he settled.

Tonight, he was having trouble settling himself, and he couldn't blame the coming storms the way he wanted.

All this time, it turned out he'd been hopeful, after all. Optimistic that all these years were leading somewhere, though he would have denied it right up to last Thursday. And since neither one of them seemed to be any good at letting go of each other, he'd always figured they'd end up together—one way or another.

Because what was the point in moving on? Riley might not have the kind of experience Jensen had. He and Rae had gotten together young enough that his so-called reputation in high school seemed kind of silly in retrospect. But he and Rae had always been magic. When they weren't fighting. When they weren't breaking up with each other. When they were together, and especially when they were naked, they were golden.

Where did she think she was going to get something better than that?

Riley knew there were some who assumed there had to be someone else in this equation. They generally thought it had to have been Riley who'd done something terrible, because why else would Rae leave him like that? Moving back into her parents' house and maintaining her silence about what had made her do such a thing.

One time, he'd overheard two local ladies at a potluck discussing when and how he could have cheated on her.

Deliveries, Genna Dawson said staunchly over a plate of her own taco cups. *Those Kittredges are always driving all over the place, delivering those horses. Who knows how many women they have out there?*

I thought they always did those deliveries in pairs, replied Whitney Morrow, a little bit archly, as she shoveled in her shepherd's pie.

You can't really believe that the Kittredge boys would sell each other out. Please, Whitney. That's not how men are.

At the time, Riley had thought that was funny, especially because his plate was full of both shepherd's pie and taco cups, as well as his first helping of old Martha Douglas's famous pie. And also because their individual stock deliveries involved more than one brother because that meant they could drive straight instead of stopping off to sleep along the way. Meaning there wasn't that much room for the kind of shenanigans the two ladies thought they were carrying on out there.

There was another vocal group of people who blamed Rae. After all, she'd always been so sharp. Assertive. Not sweet and shy and afraid to speak her mind, the way some were. *Maybe it was only to be expected,* Riley had heard more than one person say, *that she couldn't keep her man.*

He'd obviously found that even funnier. In the sense of not being all that funny, really, but that certainly hadn't stopped him from throwing it in Rae's face when they fought.

Still, Riley really had thought they were heading toward *something.*

For years, he'd let her do as she liked with this. With

him. Leave, come back, leave again. Move in, move out. Show up, ignore him.

Riley had told himself that she needed to get all this out of her system. Whatever *all this* was.

But that only worked if they'd been headed in the same direction.

It wasn't that Riley was any kind of a pushover. He'd just been prepared to wait her out. But if she thought she was done, maybe it was high time he shifted from waiting to something a little more active.

Just to clarify *his* feelings, which he couldn't help but notice Rae hadn't asked about while she was busy blowing things up.

Riley had barely noticed the shift in the weather, but he certainly felt it when the first snowflakes began to fall.

Winter is coming, he thought as he rode back down the trail, faster than he'd come up. Here in these mountains, the cold season was brutal. And endless.

And he, by God, didn't intend to spend another one in limbo.

One way or another, this thing with Rae needed to end. She wasn't wrong about that.

But Riley had a different solution in mind.

6

Rae's alarm came as brutally early as ever the following Monday morning.

The difference being, she'd actually gone to bed at a reasonable hour the night before. And for the first time since Thursday, didn't kick off her day by sobbing in the shower.

She had to count that as a step in the right direction.

When she was in her truck in the frigid, early morning, driving that old, familiar country road into town, that step seemed more and more like a huge, momentous jump with every mile she covered.

"You can do this," she told herself and the night still holding on out there on the other side of her windshield. "You're *already* doing this."

It was still dark when she made it into Cold River. Main Street gleamed against the last of the night, not yet done up in the Christmas lights that made it really sparkle as the year wound down, but bright all the same. This was just a regular end-of-October predawn morning, fall taking a firm grip but not standing in the way of the usual order of things. She could see the usual early-morning crowd in Mary Jo's, ranch hands and truckers and the like gathered in the sturdy, unpretentious diner for the cheap coffee, huge platters of food, and no-nonsense, gray-haired waitresses who called them all by name. Rae knew that if she drove down to the other end of Main Street, she would find Cold River Coffee open too, with its far fancier espresso drinks and baked goods. Because this was a rural mountain town and folks took their coffee and their breakfast seriously before they headed off for a long day of hard work, no matter what form.

Flowers were not hard work, she thought as she let herself into the shop, because the things she did with them made her happy. She'd spent the better part of her Sunday refining her sketches for the Harvest Gala and planned to play around with some of her ideas once the morning rush of orders was handled.

The Flower Pot itself, on the other hand, was harder because it was a small business in a small town, subject to the whims of tourists and weather and the local economy like every other shop on Main Street. Even if everyone in the family regarded it as the not very serious part of the *actual* business. It was an outpost. A gesture of goodwill, according to Inez, because the Trujillos' main business was more corporate. Their greenhouses delivered directly to Denver and cities even more distant. They developed seeds and plants to the specifications of their corporate clients, like hotels and office complexes. Rae's father didn't have a green thumb, he liked to joke, but a deep green spreadsheet.

Rae, on the other hand, had spent the wide swathes of time when she was ignoring the state of her marriage digging deep into becoming a real florist so she could take the Flower Pot to the next level. Not just being the Trujillo family member of her generation who spent the most time in the retail shop but an actual florist. She'd considered a degree in horticulture, but had decided she had all the information she could possibly need at home.

And yes, it was possible that when her grandmother condescended to speak to her again because she'd done some centerpieces that the ladies Inez lunched with had praised, Rae had decided to lean into the part of the family business she'd always liked best.

Over the years, she'd branched out from the prearranged compositions that her family had been using for the Flower Pot's traditional arrangements since the dawn of time. She could do those in her sleep, and did. They went hand in hand with the required uniform.

But what she loved was making her own.

She'd started doing flowers for local events after those first centerpieces, and the more she did, the more she was asked to do. Unique, onetime flower arrangements, not the identical large-scale installations to make a chain of hotel lobbies look the same that were her family's bread, butter, and chief calling card.

Art that was all the more beautiful, to her mind, because it wasn't meant to last. Because flowers were happiness when happiness itself was thin on the ground, and Rae found she spent more and more time looking for ways to spread that kind of happiness around.

No matter how many spreadsheets her mother and grandmother brandished at her or how many times Matias muttered about having to take over her shifts when she had events.

Rae took a big, deep breath once she was inside the shop. All those different blossoms mingling together to make something better, deeper. Potting soil, humid air, and all that glorious green no matter how cold and dark it was outside. Then she busied herself with her usual shop-opening tasks. She carried in the flowers she'd gotten from the greenhouses. She fired up the computer and the register, checked the list of the day's flower deliveries, and made sure the preordered arrangements were ready to go.

Only when those were done did she put on some music and busy herself with her own ideas. She put together a few bouquets and bigger arrangements of the newest, freshest flowers from the greenhouses, some for clients and some to beguile any walk-ins. Then she started playing around with her Harvest Gala concepts, making a mental note to remember to call and confirm the centerpieces and the raffle. A formality at best.

Some hours later, the cold sun was up outside, and she straightened from her work table, feeling pretty close to marvelous. Her music was pumping, and if she said so herself, she not only had a pretty fantastic selection of flower arrangements prepared and pretty, she'd made some fun decisions about her gala compositions too. A little bit of whimsy and a whole lot of heart, if she got it right.

Maybe, just maybe, there was one thing that fourteen-year-old Rae had gotten right.

Because there was nothing better than watching people come in and pick up something that made them smile. Or gaze happily at the flowers she made into centerpieces and wedding bouquets. She took great pleasure in her window displays and in the warmer weather, letting those displays spill out onto the sidewalk so that her storefront was always bursting with all the bright and cheerful flowers she could find.

At the moment, she was rocking a harvest theme. Pumpkin spice bouquets, orange and yellow and black for Halloween this weekend, and the more broadly based seasonal bouquets without her jack-o'-lantern and black cat motifs. She would shift all of that over to Thanksgiving soon and start laying in the poinsettias and the tiny pines she could use as her own little Christmas trees.

The rest of her family like to sit around and talk drearily about corporate this and chain contracts that. But Rae was never happier than when she was making things with her hands. The brighter and more cheerful, the better.

She was so entertained with her own creations today that she took an extra moment or two to look up when she heard the bell ring to announce a new customer. She kept her smile on her face as she lifted her head . . . then froze.

Because it was Riley.

Darkening the door of the flower shop that he had basically pretended had been wiped off the face of the planet years back.

He was dressed in his typical workday uniform. Jeans and boots with a Henley beneath his heavier barn jacket to keep the cold away. His cowboy hat left his face in shadow, but she didn't need a bright light to see that dark, considering gaze she knew so well. She felt it deep in her bones.

She always did.

And Rae could tell herself that she was turning over a new leaf. Starting a new life, making changes that were long overdue. She could believe that with every particle of her being. But her heart still spun around at the sight of him. She still felt that bubbly, giddy thing that had doomed her from the start. From way back before she'd understood what that feeling even meant.

As ever, she found herself forced to consider, at length, the mesmerizing line of his jaw.

Move on, she ordered herself. *Let go.*

She forced herself to keep that smile on her face, because there was a point when people were holding on for no other reason than the fact they'd been holding on. When the hope they could make sense of all the years they'd invested far outweighed any hope that they could work it out between them. She and Riley had passed that point a long time ago.

You're doing the right thing, she told herself. *No one ever said it would feel good.*

"Looking for a pretty bouquet?" she asked the way she would ask anyone. Even though she tended to know the people who came into the shop and, better still, usually knew who they were buying flowers for.

Of course, thinking about *Riley* buying flowers for someone made her stomach feel trembly and sour.

But by God, she would keep that smile on her face if it killed her.

"I hear you're moving out," he said, his voice raspy, a dangerous thing.

Not because he sounded threatening in any way. But because she was a danger to herself. Even now, hearing his voice made her . . . foolish.

The smile ached a little. "How could you possibly have heard that?"

"How do you think? Faith Mortimer told Jensen last night in the Broken Wheel. He couldn't wait to tell me over coffee." But instead of humming with fury and intensity, Riley sounded almost . . . *friendly*? That couldn't be right. "I guess congratulations are in order."

"I don't know how to respond to that." Mostly because she was looking straight at him and he *looked* like Riley, but nothing he was saying was something he would say. Ever. "You know I can't stand all these Cold River games of telephone."

Most of the games of telephone she'd ever heard about herself cast her in the role of villain. And she took a certain pride in refusing to wilt off in shame because of them, sure. Her grandmother's silent treatment had taught her a lot of things, but one important one was to always sail around, head up high, and smile brightly in the face of judgment.

Happily, that also helped her out in retail.

"Seems simple enough," Riley drawled. And she thought there was a more recognizable flame flickering beneath the words he chose, but in the next moment, it was gone. Leaving only that *friendliness* she didn't trust at all. "You're either moving into her house or not."

Rae found herself clearing her throat and crossing her arms, a lot like someone who was uncomfortable. She decided that she was most certainly not uncomfortable. Because she had no reason to be uncomfortable.

Maybe you're disappointed? But she ignored that voice.

"What makes you think where I live is any of your business?"

Riley's mouth crooked. "Try again."

She didn't know why that made her flush. Or she didn't choose to investigate it too deeply, because there was no point. "As a matter of fact, they have a spare room, and I'm planning to make use of it."

Rae braced herself for the inevitable explosion. Because if history had taught her anything, it was that Riley had definitely not turned up in the flower shop because he was interested in maintaining any kind of peace. She prepared herself, keeping her smile in place and reminding herself that this—right here—was *why*. This scene that was about to blow up the way scenes between them always did was *exactly why* she was divorcing him all these years after leaving him but not really leaving him. She should have done it long ago.

Because fighting and making up was . . . fighting and making up. It wasn't a *relationship*. War and sex wasn't putting down roots, it was tearing them up. It wasn't Corinthians. It was a long, extended game of pretend.

She should have been smart enough to see that long ago. But now she would—

"I think that's great," Riley said.

And then, impossibly, grinned.

Rae didn't even try to keep her smile on her face then. ". . . what?"

Riley didn't cross his arms over his chest. His hands were not in fists, his mouth was not in that stern, unforgiving slash. And it was entirely possible that under the brim of his hat, he . . . wasn't actually glaring at her.

She felt winded.

She didn't know what was happening.

"It's great," Riley said again when she'd started to tell herself that she'd imagined it. Because she must have imagined it. "You always wanted to live in town. Without the commute, maybe you can spend even more time doing what you love." He jerked his chin at the arrangements she'd spent her morning on. "You have a gift."

"Who are you, and what have you done with Riley Kittredge?"

That grin widened. "You and Hope under one roof, though. How's that going to work? Are Hope's sisters ready?"

Rae couldn't control her face. She could feel the shapes

it was making, but she couldn't seem to do anything about it. "Did one of your brothers hit you over the head this morning? Do I need to take you to the hospital?"

"Nothing's wrong with my head. I can be happy for you, you know. I've known you my whole life. Is it really a stretch?"

Rae blinked at him. Maybe she was also making a face. "Yes."

Riley pushed his hat back on his head, giving her an unreadable sort of look. And not the kind of unreadable she was used to from him. Instead of a storm, this seemed to be something far more . . . considering.

It reminded her, vaguely, of how he looked at the horses that people brought him to fix. Or *teach,* to use the word he preferred. He spent a long time watching them move before he did a single thing that could be construed as training, and there was absolutely no reason that notion should send heat spiraling through her. When she should have been offended.

It felt new. That was the most disconcerting part of all.

"You said you were tired of fighting." He was still studying her. "You want to move on, and I get it."

If he had announced that he was picking up and moving to the center of New York City, something that was as likely to happen as him growing six new heads, she could not have been more surprised. "You do?"

"I should have put a stop to this a long time ago. I blame myself for letting it drag on like this."

"You blame yourself," Rae said, stunned. "You blame *yourself.*"

Only when she said it did she realize she was echoing him. She snapped her mouth shut.

"We've always had a hard time letting go," Riley said. Conversationally. As if it were perfectly normal for him to be lounging about in the Flower Pot, talking about his feelings. Or their relationship. Or any combination of the two. "I want to deny that, but I can't."

"I'm obviously having an out-of-body experience." Or a stroke. Or maybe she was actually already dead. That made more sense than this. "I thought that was just, you know, something people say. But no. There's the me who knows you, who knows nothing that you're saying makes any sense. Then there's the me who's hearing you say it. And they don't go together."

"That sounds medical, baby," he observed, still grinning, and Rae couldn't be expected to handle that kind of provocation, could she?

She was used to surly Riley. Grumpy, brooding, storming around with a thousand chips on each of his shoulders. He'd always been an intense guy, but the breakdown of their marriage had cranked that up to high. And it was easy to beat herself up over *that* Riley. To make pronouncements to herself about how she needed to walk away from *him*. Because nobody needed that much angst in their life.

It was easy to convince herself of her own commitment to stepping away from *the tragedy*. To embrace light. Happiness and joy and all kinds of good things that didn't involve a brooding cowboy who never smiled.

So of course here was Riley, grinning ear to ear.

It felt a lot as if she'd been dropped headfirst into a vat of boiling water and everything in her was bubbling along, hot and red and out of her control.

"Why are you smiling at me?" she demanded. "Why are you smiling at all? I forgot you even had teeth."

His grin changed then. "No, you didn't."

Her entire body flashed about fifteen degrees hotter, just like that.

Rae surged forward, not caring that she was still wearing her gardening gloves, that her apron and likely her face were smudged with dirt, and that there had been a time in her life when she would have died of embarrassment if Riley Kittredge had seen her like that.

But today, all she did was point her finger at him from about a foot away. It was the next best thing to hauling off and hitting him, which she knew better than to do. Because putting her hands on him, in any fashion, usually made him laugh. And then led to other things, all of which were over now. Because they had to be over.

"Don't you dare come in here telling me you want me to be *happy,* or offering me congratulations, or whatever psychotic thing you're doing."

"That hurts my feelings, Rae."

"It does not."

It didn't. She was closer now—a tactical mistake she couldn't remedy without making it worse—but she could see that gaze of his much better. His dark eyes were alight with amusement, and that same rush of giddiness threatened to undo her.

"I don't know what game this is, but I want no part of it," she told him. She didn't thump him in the chest, but she sure thought about it. And she could see that he wanted her to do it—which was why she didn't. "I don't know what Faith told Jensen. Or if that bears any resemblance to what Jensen told you. But I have no intention of backsliding, Riley."

He looked no less amused. "Fair enough. Nobody likes a backslider."

"You've been an addiction since I was practically a kid."

"Since we were both practically kids," he corrected her, the way he always did. "Let's not make it creepy just because you want to move on and pretend this never happened."

She felt her fury ebb away at that. Or maybe she only wished it were fury, because fury was a rush. That flash of certainty and passion that wiped away everything else, and it was a lot preferable to the sensation that took over her body when it was gone.

"There's no pretending it never happened. But this is a detox program. I'm going clean and sober where you're concerned, and I have no intention of falling off the wagon."

His mouth crooked again. "The more you say things like that, the more convincing it is."

"I'm not the one who turned up at your place of business, offering Trojan horse congratulations. You're the one who isn't convinced, Riley. Not me."

Riley laughed, which was as shocking as anything else that had happened today. So deeply shocking Rae couldn't really process it even as it was happening. And especially not when he looked at her with all that laughter still in his eyes and across his face, like memories she refused to let herself fall into. She *refused*.

"You're reading me all wrong. I genuinely want you to be happy."

"If you want me to be happy, you would respect that I'm going cold turkey and not show up here all . . . smiley."

"I understand the urge to cut off all contact." And again, her stomach flipped around at the sight of that considering expression he aimed her way, shot through with entirely too much laughter. What *was* that? "But I don't think that's the right move."

"You don't. Let me guess. You think the right move is if I come over—"

"Oh no," he said, and suddenly that dark gaze was a little too intense. "That's done. I think you're right, Rae. It's time we move on."

"I am . . . really glad you see my point of view on this."

She decided she didn't sound desperate. Or wounded. Just rightly, understandably baffled.

"Here's the thing." Riley leaned a little closer as if he were confiding in her. As if he weren't a big, edgy, dangerous cowboy, but someone far more innocuous. When every alarm inside of her was ringing wildly and she was as incapable of cutting off this bizarre conversation as she'd ever been when it came to ending anything with him. "What do you know about moving on?"

That surprised her. Or it surprised her more. "Nothing. Obviously."

Again, that disconcerting grin. "Neither do I. I figure we should help each other out."

"You think you and I should . . . help each other move on? From each other?"

Her voice went up way too high, but she couldn't care about that because he was grinning again, and that . . . did her absolutely no good.

"Everybody needs a wingman, Rae. And I've been with you for so long, I wouldn't even know how to go about picking someone new. Would you?"

She felt as if he were rummaging around inside her, deep down, so that all she could do was . . . wheeze a little bit.

"Picking someone new? We're talking about . . . Are you really talking to me about *dating*?"

For a moment, she saw something entirely too male in that gaze of his, and it made her catch her breath. Even if it were shuttered in the next instant and disappeared behind that grin that was making her skin . . . prickle.

"Don't worry, Rae," Riley said. Riley, her soon-to-be-ex-husband, but still, *her husband.* "It's not going to be a one-way street. I'm going to help you too."

7

"No," Rae said flatly. With an undercurrent of panic. "Absolutely not."

Riley grinned down at her, enjoying himself. Almost too much, maybe, but he liked it. He'd almost forgotten what it was like to *enjoy* Rae when they weren't both naked. "It's actually the perfect solution."

"How is it a solution?" That was definitely panic in her voice, he thought. With a great deal of satisfaction. "It sounds a whole lot more like a three-ring circus. And I have no intention of being Cold River's newest dancing bear, thank you."

"No one would ever confuse you for a bear, baby. You're too little."

"*And* you have to stop calling me *baby,* Riley. It's a relic from the past that needs to be buried and forgotten."

"By the past, you mean . . . Thursday?"

Rae didn't like that. She stiffened, there in her cute little uniform that had been making him happy as long as he could remember. Something he opted not to share with her today. Instead, he watched her ponytail bob around with the force of how passionately she was trying to convince both of them that they needed to divorce. Now.

"It's over," she declared, and she sounded very certain. But that was Rae. She was always certain. That didn't make her right. "We are over. And believe me, I understand that this feels new and uncharted, because it is. But that doesn't make it any less real."

Riley could have argued. But if these years had taught him anything, it was that arguing got them nowhere. If he wanted to change things, he had to do something new. He figured she might have come to the same conclusion— but he didn't intend to go about it the same way.

So he grinned at her some more, because he could see it was making her edgy.

And he could admit that he liked that just fine.

"Understood." He kept his voice calm. Almost soothing, which made her eyes narrow. "I can't promise the wrong words won't slip out now and again. But this is why approaching it as a united front is better."

He could practically see the words *united front* hanging over her head in a word balloon, and she didn't much care for them.

She even sputtered a little. "You . . . you can't really think that we're going to try dating other people *together,* can you?"

He only grinned wider.

Rae huffed out a breath. "We can't do anything together, Riley. We've only ever been good at one thing, and it's not like we can do that in public. Which is why we've spent all these years pretending we were completely broken up, remember?"

Riley didn't intend to let her sidetrack him into discussing his take on what they'd been doing. Though everything in him tensed. He forced himself to keep on grinning. Happy-go-lucky, as if he were a different Kittredge brother altogether.

And because it clearly flummoxed Rae. Her confusion was written all over her, and if he wasn't mistaken, making her tremble a little too.

Good.

"Tell me how you think this is going to go down," he invited her. "You're going to go on out one night, to the Coyote or the Broken Wheel."

She sniffed. "I will not be going to the Coyote. I want to date, not get wasted, forget my name, and do God only knows what in somebody's pickup truck."

"I had no idea you were so informed about the way a typical Friday night goes down over there. Learn something new every day."

"No judgment," Rae said in her most judgmental voice. "If that's the kind of thing you're after, you are now free to do it exactly as you please."

He didn't allow himself to linger on unhelpful visuals of the two of them doing exactly as they pleased in that dive, and not with each other. It would only make him . . . testy. "Right, but how?"

"The usual way, Riley," she snapped. "Do you need me to draw you a diagram?"

"What's 'the usual way'?" he asked with exaggerated patience. "Do you know? I don't think you do. You don't know anything about dating, hooking up, or random pickup trucks. Want to know how I know that? Because the only person you've ever dated was me, and look how that ended up."

He could see that pulse in her neck that he'd been studying for years go wild as her chest rose and fell much too fast. Her eyes darkened.

Riley figured he could chalk that up as a point to him.

"This is not a productive conversation," she said after a moment.

"I'm not fighting with you, Rae. I'm talking about reality. You go out all dressed up cute and a little bit tipsy, trying to hit on people we both know, what do you think is going to happen?"

"I don't know. Kismet?"

"The first thing that's going to happen is that they're going to panic," Riley said quietly.

She flinched at that. "Thank you. What a compliment."

"Baby. Come on. They're going to think that if they even look at you the wrong way, they're going to have to deal with me. Because that's the way it's always been. You've been mine so long that nobody knows any different." Somehow he kept his grin in place, like this really was nothing more than a friendly chat. Instead of a strategy session. "A pretty significant barrier to your new social life."

He could see that pulse rocketing around there in her neck. He knew too many things about her and how she worked, as ever. What that flush on her cheeks meant. Why she kept worrying at her lower lip, a nervous habit he didn't think she even knew she had.

"I . . ." She stopped. Swallowed. "I did not think of that."

"What do you think would happen if I decided to cozy up to someone in a bar one night?" he asked reasonably. So reasonably it made his ribs hurt. "They'd pick up the phone and call you. Right then and there. Just to let you know, out of the goodness of their heart, what I was up to. Or they'd drop in here the next morning to buy some flowers and accidentally mention it."

"No one actually talks to me about you, Riley. Or they didn't." She shrugged, her expression defensive. "People don't think of us as one unit anymore. As far as they know, we've been broken up for years."

"Rae. No one thinks we're broken up." He laughed when she scowled at him. "You know what people who break up do? They date other people, sooner or later. Something neither you nor I have done since high school. Where, as I recall, I went to one movie—"

"It wasn't the movie, Riley. It was that you lied."

"And that I went to that movie with the captain of the girls' volleyball team. You can talk about the principle of the thing all you want, but I think we both know the real problem was Kelly Adler."

Rae's eyes glittered, even as she assumed a saintly look he recognized all too well. "Kelly Adler is a perfectly nice woman. She buys flower arrangements for her poor mother in that nursing home every week. She's one of my best customers, in fact."

"You make her mother spite arrangements, and you know it."

"I'm not doing this." Rae stiffened as if it had only then occurred to her they were slipping back into their old patterns—up to and including a fight they'd been having since before they'd started officially dating in high school. "See? I can't be around you for thirty seconds without backsliding. You need to leave."

"Yes, ma'am," Riley said, and even thumbed the brow of his hat as emphasis. "I'm not trying to make things harder for you. If this is what you want, I'm trying to support you while we do it."

"And somehow, I just don't believe that."

Riley lifted his hands in an over-the-top, exaggerated gesture of mock surrender that only made her scowl at him more.

"Are you . . . pretending to be Jensen? Is that what's happening here?"

"Not at all," Riley said. Though he had been. He

wouldn't do that again. "I really thought you and I could bury the hatchet. I heard everything you said to me on Thursday, and I don't disagree."

She looked surprised, maybe. Possibly sad, though she cleared her throat and that part went away. "That's something, anyway."

And for a moment, there were no games. There was nothing but the two of them, stark and gleaming bright, the way they always had been. Too much to handle at first. Too much to handle later. Always too much, and one way or another, all they'd seemed to do was make it worse.

He'd never wanted anything more than to step forward and put his hands on her. He wasn't sure he could take that dark gaze of hers, glittering then as if she were fighting off the same compulsion—

The door to the shop opened behind him, and the spell was broken.

"You have to go," Rae said again in an undertone— even as she flashed a professional smile at the trio of women who'd swept in, Aspen or Vail written all over them, bringing in a blast of cold air from outside. "Don't make this harder, Riley."

"I'm not making it anything." Riley made himself keep on grinning. "Don't take my word for it if you don't want to, Rae. Get on out there. Date up a storm. See what happens."

"That had better not be a threat, because I will—"

"Baby. People don't want a drink at a bar to turn into a complicated tangle with your ex. That's all I'm saying."

"You could start untangling things by erasing the word *baby* from your vocabulary."

"I could. But what you need to worry about isn't what I will do but what all these shiny new dates of yours *think*

I might do. Is the risk worth the price of a beer? You tell me."

He could see she wanted to argue with him. He could see her turning over all the small-town politics in her head.

Just like he could see when she got his point and didn't like it.

There was no need to beat a dead horse, Riley figured. He turned and headed out of the Flower Pot, in a significantly better mood than when he'd walked in.

A couple of days later, Riley found himself kicked back at his usual table at the Broken Wheel. The remains of his dinner sat before him, because this place specialized in excellent hamburgers and the truffle fries that every cowboy in the Longhorn Valley mocked, then devoured. Him included.

The particular faces around the table changed depending on the season, or life, but it was all usually the same sprawling cast of characters. Brady and Amanda were there tonight, Brady looking on fondly as Amanda talked to his brother Ty's wife, Hannah. Ty Everett himself sat on the other side of his wife, looking like the cocky, famous rodeo star that he'd been back before he'd gone and gotten good and stomped by a bull and come on home.

"How often do your mother and aunt let Jack stay over?" Amanda was asking Hannah. "You must love a little toddler break."

"Not often enough," Ty drawled.

Hannah grinned at him. "Settle down, sugar. I could have made this a girls' night."

But the way Ty grinned, hot and a little lazy, Riley figured there hadn't been much danger of that.

Across the table, all three of his brothers were arguing

good-naturedly about football. Or possibly over the current jukebox selection, it was hard to tell. Over at the dartboard, Matias, who'd eaten his food quicker than the rest, was making what should have been a happy-go-lucky bar game look almost militaristic as he hit bull's-eye after bull's-eye.

If it had been anyone else, Riley might have said something, but he and Matias treated each other . . . gingerly.

They'd been friends, or close enough, all their lives. But Matias had come home from the service to find his sister living back at his parents' house, stubbornly refusing to discuss her marriage.

What did you do to her? he'd demanded the first time he'd seen Riley.

Which was, to his credit, when he'd driven over to Riley's house within the first forty-eight hours of his return.

Nice to see you too, Riley had growled in yet another front porch confrontation.

He had half a mind to rip the whole thing out, chop it to pieces, and see if not having a porch led to fewer fights on it. Though somehow, he figured that if Rae wanted to fight with him the way she always did, they'd end up squabbling out there in the dirt all the same.

And a man had to draw some lines.

Riley hadn't mentioned any of that to Rae's older brother, who had still looked every inch the battle-tested Marine, like his return to civilian life might take a while to settle on him.

What did you do? Matias had asked again, and there wasn't a single hint of the guy Riley had grown up with before him then. No trace of that Matias. There had only been the soldier, the wars he'd seen in his gaze.

I wish I knew, Riley had replied, holding that gaze. *You're going to have to ask your sister.*

She says you grew apart.

Then you have your answer, Riley had replied.

Matias had eyed him. *What I'm trying to figure out is if I need to slap some sense into you or not.*

You're always welcome to try, Riley had drawled right back.

He and Matias stood there another while. Then the other man had let out a low noise that could have been approval or irritation. Both, maybe. *Would rather have a beer.*

They'd gone ahead and had a few beers, talking about very little of substance, and that had been their truce ever since. Beer was fine. Having a hamburger or two was good. Riley wasn't sure he'd turn his back on Matias Trujillo in the dark, but the good news was, there was no blood feud between their families because of his messy marriage.

"You look alarmingly pleased with yourself," Brady said from beside him.

Riley took his time looking back at his best friend. "Just enjoying my life. I didn't realize it was a crime."

"Not a crime," Brady said with a laugh. "But also not you."

Riley considered that. "I'm evolving."

Brady laughed even louder. "Why do I doubt that, somehow?"

Riley leaned back, prepared to offer a long, inspired defense of his personal evolution—otherwise known as a crock—when he heard the door to the saloon open up behind him.

And he knew who it was immediately without having

to look. Because he was looking at Brady, which meant he could see his sister on Brady's other side. He watched Amanda's expression change, the way it always did. Her eyes lit up, then clouded, and then her expression tightened.

Because she loved Rae. But she didn't forgive Rae for leaving him. And she had to fight through that same cycle of emotion every time she saw her. It was the sort of thing that, if Riley allowed himself to think about it too much, would kick him right back into his temper. Right where he didn't want to go. Not tonight.

Especially not when he turned to look over at Rae himself.

It was always a kick straight to the gut. He accepted that. But tonight, it was more like a sucker punch.

She was flanked by her two best friends, who he figured she'd brought along to stand sentry over her bad choices. There was Abby, tall and serene on one side of her. And Hope, just as tall but crackling with that usual electricity of hers. But all Riley really saw was Rae in the middle, dwarfed by her friends in size and yet far brighter.

She'd really gone for it, he thought, in a desperate attempt to remain calm. Her hair was down, wavy and dark and gorgeous, just the way he liked it. She was wearing that smoky stuff around her eyes that made her look sultry and edible. Her lips were enough to make a grown man cry, and he knew how she would taste, and he had to shift a little in his seat to deal with it.

But that wasn't the heart attack.

The heart attack was when she shrugged out of her coat, revealing the skimpy little dress beneath it. Spaghetti straps. Way too much skin. And if he wasn't mistaken, which he might have been because he was potentially having an aneurysm, a hem that *only just* saved her from indecency. It was impossible not to take a moment—or ten—to really appreciate the sweet sweep of her legs, entirely too much of which were visible, in shoes that were completely inappropriate for a mountain town with winter barreling in.

He was dimly aware that his table had gone deadly silent.

"You're the sheriff," Jensen muttered darkly to their oldest brother. "Do something."

"Like what?" Zack replied in a similarly dark voice. "I can't actually arrest a grown woman for wearing a dress when she feels like it."

No one looked at him. Directly. But still, Riley knew that they were all braced and ready for him to go ballistic.

Over by the door, Rae and her friends seemed frozen, telling him that they were waiting for his reaction too.

The entire bar seemed to be collectively holding its breath, waiting to see how badly Riley was going to take this.

Exactly like you told her this would go, he congratulated himself.

And instead of flipping the table or causing the scene everyone expected, he grinned. Wide and friendly and a little bit pleased, like he was *delighted* to see Rae dressed hotly and sweetly and aimed at him like a loaded gun.

That was almost enough to distract him from the sight of his wife in that dress, a sight he planned to cherish forever, because every single person at his table and within his eyesight looked . . . terrified.

"He's going to kill us all," Connor muttered.

"You okay?" Brady asked from beside him.

"What's the matter with you people?" Riley asked with a lazy drawl that carried and made everyone at the table frown at him. Except Zack, who squinted at him in what looked like a professional assessment. "Haven't you ever seen a pretty girl in a dress before?"

Connor groaned. "We're doomed."

Riley looked around and saw pretty much the same reaction all over the bar. Matias stood frozen by the dartboard. A tableful of folks Riley knew, though not well, were as wide-eyed as if they were family members. Behind the bar, Tessa Winthrop's mouth had actually dropped open.

When he looked back to Rae, he could see that while Abby and Hope stood on either side of her as if they were fully prepared to do battle in their own ways, Rae herself looked more . . . fragile.

And he couldn't have that.

There was only one thing on this earth that should make Rae Trujillo emotional, and he was it.

"Maybe we should go outside," Jensen said conversationally, his gaze narrowed on Riley. "Take a walk, cool off."

"Knock yourself out," Riley replied. "I'm good."

When he stood up from his chair, he felt like it was high noon in one of the old Western movies his grandfather loved so much and he was the gunslinger. Every single eye in the place slammed to him and stayed there.

Including Rae's.

Riley grinned again, though all that seem to do was freak everybody out more.

Deep down, he could admit that he didn't hate that. He had a reputation as a dangerous man to push, and he couldn't say he minded it. It was a pity that the only person around who really dared push him was the one he needed to stop pushing back.

Or stop pushing back in a way she would recognize, anyway.

He took his time ambling over toward the door, his grin only widening when he saw the way Hope moved slightly forward as if she were ready to throw herself bodily between Riley and Rae if necessary. Even Abby, renowned all over the valley for her trademark level-headed sensibility, looked at him in a way he could only call . . . a warning.

At other points in his life, he'd loved the fact that his woman had two fierce defenders, ready to stand up for her no matter what.

"Maybe you should walk away," Hope suggested.

Riley took that to mean that his grin was faltering a little bit at the edges. But that was okay. He could let his temper simmer as long as he didn't let it burst free, because letting it loose now would be a disaster. Not only a disaster but all the proof Rae thought she needed. He knew better.

This was a long game, and he was going to win it.

"You look great," he told Rae.

Her eyes were too big, and he could see the uncertainty there. That fragility he didn't like, because it was too close to her hurting. That was unacceptable.

She cleared her throat. "Um. Thanks?"

Riley flashed his grin at Hope, who only raised a wary brow. Then at Abby, who smiled back, because she always did—but she didn't move away from Rae's side.

"Let me buy you all a drink," he said.

And he actually laughed when all three of them gaped at him as if he'd tried to hand them something horrible. Like, say, a bouquet of skunks.

"Are you kidding?" Rae asked, her voice little more than a breath.

"Of course I'm not kidding, Rae," Riley said, injecting a faintly disapproving note into his voice as if he were shocked at her behavior. Instead of delighted. "That's what friends *do*."

8

This was obviously a bad idea.

Rae was wearing as skimpy a dress as she'd ever worn thanks to Hope's younger sister's questionable wardrobe. She was actually *wearing it out in public* even though that much exposed skin was pretty much the exact nightmare she'd been having since she was a child. And Riley was there the way she'd feared he would be.

Or had hoped he would be, maybe.

But unlike the way it had gone down in her head, he was . . .

Grinning.

Laughing.

And if the ringing in her ears wasn't warping things, he was calling them . . . friends.

"*Are* you friends?" Hope was demanding with a challenging sort of laugh. "That's news to me. Normally, there's a lot of sulking in corners, glaring, and dire mutterings."

Because of course Hope would just *say* that. Rae expected Riley to react to that with a blast of all that leashed darkness he was so good at throwing at her. At everyone.

But he didn't.

"That's not a very nice way to talk about Rae," Riley

replied instead with a sort of lazy, indulgent edginess spiraling all around him. And winding tight in her.

How could she hold on to what she was feeling when it kept changing? When it was like a kaleidoscope that Riley was twisting over and over, so that every time she thought she was looking at something, it shattered into a thousand pieces of something else?

Over and over again.

"We probably shouldn't stand here," Abby observed mildly. "Everyone is staring at us."

Riley gestured for them to precede him toward the bar with an exaggerated courtesy that was a whole other problem. Especially because Rae was also wearing ridiculous shoes to complete her *announcement* of an outfit. She would die before she let anyone see that they were too high for her. Sadly, she might also die when she tripped and slammed her head into the floor.

But everyone she'd ever met was *watching* her. That meant she had no choice but to brazen it out. Since she'd gone ahead and made this choice down the block in Hope's house, where it had seemed *delightful* and *fun* to get all dressed up and remind everyone that she was alive.

Consider this dress your new dating profile, Hope had said.

It seemed a lot less delightful and fun now that it was happening and Riley was *right here,* but Rae didn't intend to slink off into the night. She launched herself toward the bar instead, hoping her legs would figure out what to do while she moved. Hope stayed by her side, hopefully prepared to catch her if she started to tumble, while Abby fell back to talk with Riley.

Like this were a normal night and they all usually hung out together.

"Where's that man of yours?" Riley asked.

Rae couldn't see Abby grin, but she could hear it in her voice. "Gray Everett in a bar in town on a Thursday night? Has the world ended?"

Riley's laugh sounded appreciative. Rae hadn't seen or heard of him laughing in years, and now there were *different kinds* of laughter?

"How exactly did you end up with the oldest young man in the Longhorn Valley?" he asked Abby.

"There are compensations," Abby replied, more laughter in her voice.

Rae knew she'd hit a low point when she felt what she was embarrassed to admit was actual jealousy kick around inside her then. Jealousy. Of *Abby.* Who was so in love with her own husband she could hardly see straight, but even if she hadn't been, was one of Rae's best friends of all time. And would never, ever betray her.

"Where did you just go in your head?" Hope asked when they made it to the bar. "You look like you saw a ghost."

"No ghosts," Rae said, angling her head toward Riley as he came up behind them, all saunter and smile. "He's entirely too real."

"We are not here to wallow in Riley Kittredge," Hope said. Fiercely. And not exactly under her breath. "I have absolutely no qualms telling him to go away."

As she said that, Hope got a certain gleam in her eyes that came before she *Hoped out.* Which was kind of like hulking out, but much prettier. If with the same potential for destruction.

Rae had to think that as entertaining as that might be in the moment, it would only make things worse overall. Not that she could think of any way to stop Hope from doing as she pleased. No one could.

Riley, having known all three of them for their entire lives, didn't consult them on their choice of beverages. He ordered from Tessa, then stood back, leaning against the bar with that same genial grin all over his face.

It wasn't any less disconcerting here than it had been in the flower shop the other day.

"As a friend," Riley said, amiably, lounging there as if he were someone else. Someone deeply unconcerned with what was happening around him, when the Riley that Rae knew had always been burning with intensity no matter what he was doing or who he was with. "It's my duty to tell you that if you keep scowling around the place, you're probably not going to get the results you're after."

Rae only then felt what her face was doing. She tried to correct it and scared the hiker-type standing a few feet away.

"As *her* friend," Hope retorted, "I think maybe it's the looming presence of her mean and bitter ex that might stand in the way of her progress here tonight."

Riley shifted that dark gaze of his to Hope, still holding on to his grin, though Rae watched it change. Taking on that edginess that made her whole body shiver in awareness.

Hope did not look like she was shivering.

"As everybody's friend," Abby said then, in a far more conciliatory tone, "I think the thing to worry about here is whether or not we're putting on a show. Right now, I would say yes, we are." She smiled placidly when everyone looked at her. "And I'll point out this is certainly not going to convince anybody that you two are just friends."

Rae wiped her face clear of whatever expression she was wearing. And for his part, Riley shifted so he was less aggressively *leaning,* and looked . . . Well. Still not that simmering, male darkness that she knew best. Almost approachable, really.

She told herself that the way her stomach twisted around at that had to do with this new enterprise of hers. The short hem and high heels. The invitation she was trying to extend. Not with him.

Because one way or another, Rae was determined that for at least five whole seconds strung together, she would think about something other than him.

This was admittedly harder to do when he was standing in front of her.

Almost as if he were . . . waiting.

Abby and Hope struck up a completely different conversation then, this one about all the new boutiques and shops and restaurants that had opened in town over the last couple of years. A conversation they'd had with each other pretty much every day of those years, so it was clear the purpose of it was to rope in Riley. So the three of them could carry on having a congenial night out with friends while Rae stood there at the bar baring more skin than she thought she'd ever expose at this time of year— or ever—and trying to look casual.

She folded her coat and put it on a barstool, making a slight production out of it for Hope's benefit. Since Hope had threatened to rip it off her if she didn't remove it once inside and that would not be remotely *casual*. When Tessa came back with their drinks, she smiled her thanks and then turned back around so she could look out over the bar as if this were a normal thing she did. As if she were dressed like this purely to gaze around in what she thought—*hoped*—was a compelling sort of way. At the Broken Wheel's so-called scene that she'd witnessed a million times before. But never quite from this perspective.

She ignored her brother, who she could see eyeing her from his place over by the dartboard, where he liked to quietly terrify anyone paying attention with his skill and accuracy. Because Matias never liked to point out his own accomplishments when he could perform them, right there in plain sight, for everyone to see and fear.

There were the usual tables of the usual groups of locals and scattered tourists. There was the group that had been hers, once upon a time. A mix of Kittredges and Everetts and an empty chair that she knew was her brother's—because he'd made it very clear that he wasn't picking sides. By then picking sides.

And not her side.

A claim she knew he would dispute. But still.

There were families with kids, many of them eating out here in town before taking the long drive back out into the valley, the way Rae and her parents had done as often as not when she and Matias were younger. But it was right at that hour when the families would start to leave. Soon there would be a different sort of dancing than the few indulgent parents with toddlers out there now, on the dance floor in front of the tiny little stage where there were sometimes live bands. Lucinda Early was out there now, two-stepping sedately with her husband, George. Because even dragon ladies were sweet sometimes. Tonight was a quiet Thursday in the last gasp of October, so the only music came from the jukebox. And the same way there'd been as long as Rae could remember, there was the typical group of teenagers clustered around it, out-cooling each other with their selections.

Once, that had been her over there, hoping to impress Riley Kittredge if she could just pick the right song—

But she wasn't thinking about him.

Rae had to kick herself then. Because she wasn't here to admire all the things she usually liked to pay attention to in the Broken Wheel on a comfortable, forgettable evening. She wasn't here to wax rhapsodic about Cold River and all the people she loved who lived here, no matter how tempting that was to do every year come fall when there were fewer tourists and more of the real folks who made this place what it was.

Possibly because reminding herself what she loved about her hometown outweighed the whispers about her.

Either way, tonight she was here to *scope out the talent,* according to Hope. A phrase that had made Abby laugh uproariously, back behind Capricorn Books in the Mortimers' ramshackle old Victorian house that an enterprising new shopkeeper at the dawn of the twentieth century had bought from a catalog to assemble for his brand-new bride.

Rae had not laughed along, mostly because she was the one who was going to be expected to perform said scoping, and she hardly knew what that meant.

Or worse, she knew exactly what it meant and was horrified at the prospect.

That sounds very romantic, Abby had said.

Tonight is not about romance, Hope had declared. *Tonight is about* prospects *and new beginnings. It's time to remind the good people of Cold River about your assets, Rae.*

You mean the family greenhouses?

Hope had smiled in that serene way of hers that was, first of all, not all that serene and, second of all, was actually more like bloodcurdling when you knew her well.

I do not mean the greenhouses, she'd replied. *I mean your body. Which is usually in those sad khakis and that Izod shirt that is not doing you any favors.*

I can't help my uniform, Rae snapped back, every fight she'd ever had with her parents about how ugly it was ringing in her head.

Your uniform is fine in the shop, but it is not fine on an evening out, Hope had decreed.

And that was how Rae found herself dressed the way she was, which had the unexpected benefit of being so outside her comfort zone that it was too much to actually process. She had no choice but to look as relaxed as Hope had ordered her to pretend she was.

Beside her, the little knot of her two best friends with the man who seemed to think they could be friends after all their tangled history looked animated. But Rae was an expert on Riley's surreptitious glances. And it turned out that she was capable of picking them out of any mess. Or knot.

She knew each and every time that dark gaze of his tracked over her. Over all of her exposed skin that she'd known full well he would appreciate.

She could *feel* his appreciation.

And her body reacted to him the way it always did. She felt herself shift as she stood, because she felt looser. Brighter. Softer, straight through the middle.

You're supposed to be looking at literally any other man, she reminded herself tartly.

The fact that she wasn't actually looking at Riley seemed like splitting hairs, really.

One of the doors in the back that led to the kitchen swung open, and she saw Jackson Hale come in, carrying trays of freshly washed glasses. He had been on Hope's list of potentials. Rae remembered when he'd first come to town and all the buzzing and carrying on about an attractive new single man on the scene when so many of them had grown up here and were known a little too well.

I know people grow and change, Hope had said once about another man they'd known as a kid. *But the problem is, if I know he was a nasty little bully in fourth grade, there's some part of me that assumes that when things get tough? That nasty little bully is going to come right out again.*

Jackson Hale could have been horrible in fourth grade for all anyone in Cold River knew, but there was no way to find out. Rae fixed her gaze on him dutifully. He was tall, and though he was dressed in jeans and boots like every other man in town, he didn't wear the typical plaid or flannel shirt. Or even a T-shirt. He wore the kind of thin sweater that highlighted the excellent shape he was in and also hinted at the much fancier life he'd lived before he'd come here.

His gaze—moving around the saloon much the way Rae's had, though she figured it was likely different when a person owned the place—found hers. And unlike every other time she'd happened to catch the man's eye, Rae didn't smile distantly and look away.

She held his gaze, though it made her pulse pound in what she told herself was *not* a kind of horror. Then she made herself smile.

Jackson's gaze sharpened as he slung the trays of glasses onto the end of the bar. And Rae watched, a strange sensation whirling around inside of her, as his gaze lowered to take in her outfit. Then rose again even more slowly.

And her smile faltered because she didn't have the slightest idea what to do next—

But Jackson looked slightly to one side of her. His eyes widened. Then he walked away, disappearing into the back again.

Riley.

Rae clenched her teeth tightly. Then, not paying the

slightest attention to what he might have been discussing with Abby and Hope at that point, she hooked her hand around his elbow and yanked him toward her.

It was only after she'd done that—after he'd let her do it—that it occurred to her that putting her hands on him with that kind of familiarity wasn't exactly helping her cause.

"What did you do?" she asked him.

"Listen, baby, Hope and Abby can talk all they want about progress and moving into the modern age, but you're never going to convince me that Cold River doesn't trade as much on nostalgia as—"

"I don't care what Cold River trades on."

Rae searched Riley's face, that strange sensation she'd felt while she was looking at Jackson blooming inside her. She thought she understood what it was now. A kind of uncertainty.

She wasn't used to feeling anything like it.

"You can't stand here," she told Riley flatly. "You scare men off."

Riley's grin made her pulse do a very different sort of dance. "Men don't scare that easily, Rae. If they want something, they usually figure out how to get it."

"Whether they want it or don't want it is something that is impossible to determine when you're right next to me. Looming over me. You might as well put a dog tag on my neck and yank me around on a leash."

She chose not to notice the way his dark eyes gleamed at that.

"I have no intention of looming over you while you flirt with other men," he said a little too quietly.

Not for the first time, Rae wondered what she was doing. Moving on was a great idea. It was long overdue. She knew that. She believed that.

But no one said she had to do the moving on *here*. Right under Riley's nose.

She could move literally anywhere else and not have to deal with this. Or with him.

"You want to be friends," she said, wishing her voice were little bit steadier. "But I don't think . . . I don't know . . ."

"It seems to me we have two choices." Riley grinned again, and she told herself that was better. Because maybe it wasn't the Riley she knew, but maybe she'd never really known Riley all that well. If she had, surely this wouldn't have happened. Any of it. "With all of our history and all of these years, we either have to be blood enemies or best friends, Rae. We've done the-enemies-in-public thing for a long time. I'm tired of it. The only way forward is as friends."

"We've never been friends."

"So we figure it out." He shrugged. "We're already broken up and on the road to divorce, right? That was the hard part. This should be easy."

And this time when he aimed that grin at her, she forced herself to return it.

But deep inside, something shivered.

A lot like foreboding.

The following night, Rae found herself at her usual place at the table in the dining room in her parents' house, ordering herself to do the thing she'd promised herself she would. To rip off the Band-Aid, make her announcement and make it real, right here and right now.

Because it was one thing to say it the back of the coffeehouse with her friends and then basically sit there, giggling about boys, the way they had in high school. It was something else to go out in a party dress and act like a single girl—even if there had been a little too much Riley all over her debut as a dateable option. It was something else again to change her whole life.

She knew. She'd done this before.

But a yawning sort of pit threatened to open up inside her at that thought. She did her best to clamp it down, poking at the meal in front of her even though her appetite had fled.

"I can't imagine what would possess anyone to dedicate all their time to ungrateful groups of women who will never return the favor," said her grandmother, supposedly discussing charity groups and well aware that Rae's mother dedicated huge swathes of her time to a great many of said groups. Because she could never resist a dig.

Rae's mother sniffed. "It's not for everyone, I grant you. There are always those who are far too busy imagining themselves above everyone else. The fact is, Inez, those sorts wouldn't be welcome." A point to Kathy.

Rae did her best not to sigh, as that would only draw fire.

You have to stop hiding here, she told herself then. *Before you become just like them.*

But she didn't announce that she was moving out, because that would draw more fire. And she couldn't help but wonder what would happen if she didn't say anything. If she just left. Moved out under the cover of darkness. Would her mother and grandmother stop taking shots at each other long enough to notice?

She offered to do all the dishes as soon as it was feasible. Not because she was such a great daughter but because it was the quickest means of escape. And she wasn't entirely surprised when her father came up beside her, carrying a few dinner plates. He set them down on the counter and smiled at her in the reflection of the window before them.

The dark eyes she'd gotten from him seemed to pry straight into her, even through a reflection.

"Something on your mind?" he asked.

This was easier, Rae thought, because her hands were in the sink and there were suds up to her elbows. She didn't have to make eye contact with her dad—the only member of her family who'd ever been able to read her at a glance.

"Nothing bad." She shot him a quick smile before returning her attention to the sink. "The time has come for me to make a few life decisions, that's all."

"Happy to be an ear if you need to talk those through."

Rae had a sudden pang of something like hope. Fantasy, maybe. Because she knew exactly what he wanted to hear. He'd given Riley a hard time when they'd been kids trying to date, but the truth was, he'd always liked his daughter's one and only boyfriend. More than liked him. Rae knew that nothing would give her father greater joy than for her to announce that she was heading back to try to work things out, save her marriage, make it work.

She could remember, too clearly, how disappointed he'd been in her not just the first time she'd come home. But the time she'd come home for good.

Nothing will ever make me love you less, Rae, he'd told her. Steady and solemn, which made it worse. *But I didn't raise you to be a quitter.*

It still burned. There in her throat like a sob.

"I need to get on with my life," she told him now. "Hope has a spare room in her house in town. I think I'm going to move in. Change things up a little bit."

She could feel the burn again, and she didn't have it in her to look over and actually confirm whether or not he was looking at her in that same way he had when she'd moved back in. Then again, she didn't need to. She could feel it.

She swallowed, hard, against the lump in her throat.

"It's not that I don't like it here," she began when he was quiet.

"You're a grown woman, Rae. Of course you don't want to live with your parents."

She couldn't help herself then. She snuck a look his way, but he wasn't looking at her. His gaze was trained on the door to the dining room. When she shut off the water in the sink, she could hear her mother and grandmother, engaged in yet another one of those conversations of theirs—nothing more than endless battles for supremacy.

"I love living with my parents." It wasn't entirely untrue. They weren't the real problem. Kathy was lovely when Inez wasn't around. "And I'm pretty sure that Hope and her sisters spend all their time bickering too."

Her father laughed, then reached over to squeeze her shoulder. Just once. In as gruff a fashion as possible while still being affectionate. His trademark.

"All the comforts of home," he said.

There was no reason that Rae should find herself lying awake later that night, staring at her ceiling while she turned that interaction over in her head again and again. Her father had given his blessing. Wasn't that what she'd wanted?

And maybe it was only because it was there in the dark of her old bedroom that she could admit to herself that there'd been a large part of her that wanted him to argue. To ask her what on earth she was thinking. To treat her like a child so she could have railed against him. Fought back like he was still trying to give her curfew or keep her from dating Riley, the way he had way back when.

She tossed and turned, ordering herself to go to sleep and yet unable to find a comfortable position.

All she could think about was Riley. The many times they'd had a fight, there on his front porch, because that was the best way to make something happen. Because if they fired their little jabs at each other, they could blame what always happened next on their tempers. One passion leading to another and nobody's fault.

Was that who she was? Determined to fight no matter what—and especially if it seemed to do nothing but hurt her? Just like the two women she shared this house with?

God, she was turning into them before her own eyes.

If you had the courage of your convictions, she told herself—while the only thing she could seem to see was Riley's face—*you wouldn't need someone to argue with you. You would just be sure.*

For once in her life, Rae wanted to be *sure.*

But no matter how many times she told herself that no matter what she felt, she was doing the right thing, she lay there until dawn.

Wide awake and looking for answers on the ceiling where she knew there were none.

9

The old warehouses and barns that lined the river were a testament to a different era in Cold River and had been abandoned as long as Riley could remember. Until his best friend had gone ahead and bought them up, which had been Brady's way of putting down roots in a town he'd thought had wanted nothing to do with him.

They'd stood empty until a year ago, when Brady and Amanda had gotten together. Brady had given Amanda one of the old barns, and Riley's little sister had gone from working in a coffeehouse and a bar to starting her very own budding enterprise. A pretty impressive upgrade, Riley and his brothers had been forced to admit.

Riley parked his truck out in the gravel lot, peering up at the old barn that he'd helped renovate and the little carriage house behind it that Brady and Amanda lived in these days. For reasons she had never explained to his satisfaction, Amanda had chosen to call her new business the Lavender Llama. Though there were no llamas inside, unless the local yarn section counted, and the only lavender around was in the local specialty teas she sold and what she'd told him were called *sachets*.

During her first summer of operation, she'd rolled open the big barn doors and let all the local artisanal goods spill out. But when Riley walked in this morning, he was glad the doors were shut tightly against the mean November wind, coming straight down from the ominous peaks up above with a bitter kick.

He blew on his hands, taking in the rush of warmth and heat from inside.

He could admit that he'd been skeptical about this whole plan. And everything else having to do with his baby sister and his best friend, granted, but he'd come around. Still, it was one thing to support their wedding. He and his brothers had all kind of figured that it had to be a shotgun wedding when it happened so fast. But Amanda showed no signs of being pregnant even now, so he supposed it had just been love all along. It was hard to keep being mad about that, though Connor sure seemed to want to hold that line.

It was this idea of Amanda's that Riley had continued to have reservations about, but he'd been wrong about that too. The place was packed today, when it was an off-season weekday and he'd expected it to be empty. Amanda had filled the barn with various nooks and crannies, wide tables and little cupboards that made the goods she featured feel a lot like treasures. She'd gotten so busy over the summer that she'd had to hire help, and he saw that she'd kept that up even though this was the dawn of the lean season.

Riley had to admit that while it would never have occurred to him to create a specific place where people from around the Longhorn Valley could display their various passion projects and small business goods—from local honey to hand-dyed yarns, hand carved wooden tables to delicate wrought iron pieces of art, handmade candles and even clothes—Amanda's barn had already become a go-to destination. The tourists certainly couldn't get enough. But the locals came here too, because it was easier to stop by in town than drive all over the valley or wait for the seasonal farmers' markets to find the same items.

He wandered into the thick of things, where he found his sister rearranging a display of handcrafted microbrews from a variety of local beer enthusiasts. There was a new gallery for artists that hadn't been here the last time he'd come in, a lot of funky-looking pottery along one wall, and it took Amanda a minute or two to look up from what she was doing and register that he was there.

When she did, she grinned. "You came."

"Yes, ma'am," Riley drawled. "Ready and reporting for duty."

Amanda straightened, looking around the shop with a practiced eye. Riley didn't know if she actually looked older these days or if he'd finally adjusted his thinking away from how he'd always pictured her—as the infant in the family, forever, that he'd helped raise with the rest of his brothers. Or maybe he was retroactively making it work, because it was the only way he could make sense of the fact that she was married to his best friend when she was a decade younger.

If his parents had wanted to teach their sons a lesson about consequences and proper precautions, they'd succeeded in spades. Riley loved his sister, but he had no interest in raising *more* babies. Changing diapers at ten had cured him of any urges in that direction, thank you.

"You don't have to 'report for duty,'" Amanda said, wrinkling her nose at him. "You're so dramatic. I just need someone to sign off on the events the Bar K is offering this year."

"I was under the impression we were offering whatever events you wanted us to offer," Riley said dryly.

"You said so at Sunday dinner just yesterday, when you announced you were taking over the Harvest Gala. See? I pay attention."

Amanda grinned as she led him back toward the register. She waved at her employee as she passed and smiled at the folks in line. Then she led him into her office, a stark contrast to the artful jumble of things outside. Here, everything was remarkably neat and organized, from the desk to the shelf near the back door Riley knew led to her cute little house. She took him over to the wall that faced her desk and looked to be nothing more than a huge whiteboard. Filled with names and businesses and whatnot, all written out in Amanda's careful handwriting that reminded him of his mother's.

"Are you sure you want to do this?" Amanda was looking at him with entirely too much *knowledge* in her eyes, in case he needed a reminder that the baby of the family wasn't a baby at all these days. "You used to say that if you never had to teach another riding lesson again, you would die happy."

At some point Riley was going to have to accept that just because *he* had dismissed his little sister as being too young to understand their family's dynamics, that didn't make it true. She'd clearly been paying close attention for years.

"I didn't want to *only* teach riding lessons," he said, remembering the years before he'd built up his clinics and clients, when Donovan had thought his ideas were crap and he needed to *be realistic* and do what he was told. Not his favorite set of memories. "For a while there, that was all Dad thought I had to offer."

Amanda shot him a look, so Riley bit his tongue. Because he might not have much use for his father, but Amanda had different parents from the rest of them. She was the miraculous accident that had kept the family together, and maybe that was why they were all so protective of her.

Not that he planned to say that out loud.

He cleared his throat. "What I don't understand is why, when you have a new husband and a new business and a whole new life, you would take on an event like this on top of it."

The annual Harvest Gala took place at the Grand Hotel, Cold River's fanciest Old West landmark, a throwback to the days of robber barons and copper kings. The gala took advantage of its setting, using the hotel's historic prominence and current glossy luster to lure as many donations from its attendees as possible. All in the name of preserving Cold River's historical character and buildings, many of which were designated landmarks and all of which fell under the purview of the Cold River Heritage Society.

Riley couldn't think of anything he'd enjoy less than having to deal with that particular cross section of officious busybodies.

But Amanda only laughed. "Someone has to be in charge of it. And it's not that bad. Most people have been offering the same auction items for so many years in a row, it's really about collecting all the items and figuring out how to present them."

"Just because someone has to do it doesn't mean it has to be you."

"I choose to take it as a vote of confidence that the Heritage Society thought that I should run things. I'm the youngest chairperson in the gala's history."

Riley snorted. "Or all the people who've been around forever were smart and flatly refused."

Amanda took her time turning back from the whiteboard where she'd written ANNUAL GALA in big letters across the top. And had different columns for raffles and silent auction items, not to mention a long list of various goods and services. Then she studied him for so long that Riley began to feel faintly uneasy.

"What?"

"You're clearly in a mood." Amanda crossed her arms. "Is it Rae?"

Riley ran his hand over his jaw. "Why would my ex-wife have anything to do with my mood?"

"You tell me. But I should tell you that you were seen entering the Flower Pot the other day."

"I was *seen*? Is someone spying on me? I hope they have better things to do than watch me go about my business. And I really hope the spy isn't you, Amanda."

"You never go into the Flower Pot. Who would you be buying flowers for? Mom? She would drain all the fun out of that by lecturing you on how unnecessary it is to give anyone a present, ever, for any reason. Don't you remember Mother's Day?"

"We have a grandmother."

"Oh, please. Grandma would be insulted. Store-bought flowers for Janet Lowe Kittredge when she can grow her own?"

Riley had no argument for any of that. It was all too true. His grandparents lived in the house they'd built when they'd decided to turn the ranch over to Donovan and Ellie to run, across a pasture from the main house and surrounded by Kittredge land. Grandma would hate a bouquet—and not be shy about explaining why.

Amanda's eyes were gleaming. "You in the Flower Pot was questionable enough. But then there was the Broken Wheel."

"Not that it's any of your business, but Rae and I have come to an understanding," Riley said in an attempt to cut this off. "You don't have to go around pretending that you don't know her, the way you've been doing for years."

It was Amanda's turn to stiffen, then act like she hadn't. "I don't pretend that I don't know her. I just don't linger."

"Call it whatever you want. Rae and I are good. You want to be good with her, have at. If you don't, that's your choice." He frowned at her. "And why are we talking about her when we're supposed to be talking about me donating riding lessons?"

Amanda rolled her eyes. "Do you really think that's going to work? You make statements and we're all supposed to forget your entire history together?"

Riley stared at her. Stonily.

Eventually, Amanda sighed. "Do you want to offer single lessons or a series?"

"I'm here to support you, Amanda. Whatever that looks like."

Amanda laughed. "Point taken, big brother."

She didn't ask him about Rae again, but he was still relieved when Brady showed up a little while later. After Amanda had extracted a promise for a series of five lessons as well as a separate group trail ride, as soon as weather permitted. An investment of time Riley definitely wouldn't have made if the gala were being run by Marianne Minton, the way it had been the last few years. The forbidding widow of one of the town's few decent lawyers hadn't known how best to extort Riley or the Bar K. Not the way his kid sister did.

"I was going to come out to the park next," Riley said, lifting his chin in Brady's direction.

"Good," Brady replied easily. "I was just heading out there now."

And Riley headed out to wait for his friend in the main part of the barn, because he might fully support them, but that didn't mean he needed to stand around watching Brady stick his tongue down his little sister's throat.

When the two of them emerged a few minutes later, Amanda looked flushed and Brady looked amused, and Riley stopped imagining anything else right there. In a hurry.

"Ride with me," Brady said as they went outside. "Unless you're in a rush to get back?"

"Not today. Jensen is sweet-talking a new boarding client who wants us to put up his entire stable over the holidays. He prefers to do it when I'm not around, if you can believe it."

"Not much of a sweet talker, are you?"

Riley didn't quite grin as he swung into Brady's truck. "I try."

His best friend laughed. "You do not. You like being *known* for being bullheaded."

"It weeds out potential issues before they become problems." Riley was more than fine with being called bullheaded. "What's not to like?"

Riley settled in as Brady drove him out of town. Over the pass into the cold fields where Kittredges and Everetts and the old Douglas farming family had been tending the land for generations. But instead of heading toward the Everett ranch house or the Bar K, he headed toward his park.

Brady had always had a lot of big ideas, unlike Riley, who had lived and breathed horses since he was small. It had only ever been a question of *how* to work with horses. There had never been any *if*s. But Brady had been different. He'd gone off to college in the city. He'd made something of himself. And these days, he was the kind of dreamer who liked to have a business plan in hand. After his father had died and left the family ranch to Brady and his two brothers, it had taken him a while to convince his older brothers that his ideas had merit, but he'd done it. The park was the first time they'd agreed to let him do his own thing. Brady wasn't walking away from the ranch that required the combined work of all of the Everetts and their families in one form or another, because that was a lot of black Angus, but his park was adjacent to it.

Literally.

Brady and Amanda had gotten married out here on a rock overlooking the river on a pretty April day. Since then, Brady had transformed the little piece of Everett land that he'd claimed as his own. He'd spent spring whipping it into shape before summer came and campers made their way up from the city. He'd put in campsites and marked out hiking trails, and he was only getting started.

Riley couldn't help but be impressed. Especially when he'd never had those kinds of dreams. He'd always known exactly who he was and what he wanted. And nothing on that list had changed since he was seventeen.

Not one thing.

"Are you really going to build a hotel out here?" Riley asked when they stop by the main entry. Currently, it wasn't much more than a kind of ranger station, where guests could check in, pay, then head on in to enjoy what had been, until now, a private piece of the beautiful Colorado landscape.

Brady shrugged. "People paid three times the going rate for private campsites here, with the guarantee that there would be no noise or neighbors, because we have enough space to spread them all out. We don't allow RVs. And there's the option of a site with a cabin to keep the elements out. I have to think that if I offered a higher-end experience, people would want to pay for that too."

"Imagine paying to *camp*," Riley said with a laugh.

Brady laughed too. "I know."

Because they'd grown up out here. The land was part of who they were. They'd slept beneath the stars more times than Riley could count. They'd lived their lives out in the elements, born to big skies and mountains that claimed whole horizons.

Brady drove them through the entry, waving at his man at the counter, then heading deeper into his park. Riley was still staring out his window at the Rockies, towering in the distance with winter already sprawled across the peaks like a crown. "There are campgrounds all over the place. It's all national forest land in the hills."

"Not everybody is as comfortable in the great outdoors as we are," Brady said as he drove. "There are a lot of people down in Denver who like living there because it's close to the outdoors without actually being inconvenient about it. My park gives them the opportunity to have the best of both worlds."

"I'll admit I thought both you and Amanda were crazy. Shows what I know."

Brady smirked. "Very little as I recall. Since birth."

Riley invited his best friend to perform an unlikely anatomical feat. Brady declined. Then they spent an enjoyable hour or so saying very little while they went from cabin to cabin, closing them all down for the winter and making sure the small, spare structures were likely to remain standing when the heavy snows came in. Soon, by the look of the distant whitecapped peaks.

When Brady headed back toward town, Riley lounged

in the passenger seat of the truck and watched the night come in early, falling like a curtain over this land their ancestors had fought and died for. And somehow felt more at peace than he had in a long while.

"So," Brady said as they started to climb the hill toward town.

"No," Riley replied, not even looking over him. "Stop right there."

"*Friends?* Really?"

"I'm not having this conversation."

That didn't appear to concern Brady much. "On what planet are you and Rae Trujillo friends? You've never been friends. You've never been anything close to friends. Do you remember the last time you decided you were going to be *friends* with her?"

"I remember the time I said I wasn't going to have this conversation. Literally five seconds ago."

"You don't have to say anything, Riley. I remember fine. It was fall of our junior year. You got together with Andrea Fields at homecoming. A dream come true by any measure. But what did you do?"

"Andrea Fields." Riley couldn't help but appreciate the memory. "She only dated seniors. Until me."

"You mean, until you decided that you should really lean in hard to your *friendship* with your freshman buddy in study hall."

"Rae was an excellent student."

"Not really the point. Remind me what happened between you and Andrea Fields again?"

The inarguably succulent Andrea had dumped him unceremoniously for a graduating senior. But what Riley remembered about that time wasn't Andrea Fields. It was Rae. Cute, maddening, fascinating Rae.

It was always Rae.

"This is all ancient history," he said. "I think you might have been more into Andrea Fields than I was."

"Everyone was more into Andrea Fields than you were," Brady retorted. "I know this because everyone else would have actually been with Andrea Fields instead of what you did, which was spend all your time with your supposed platonic freshman *friend*."

"If I wanted to go to a high school reunion, I would do that," Riley replied. "I don't."

His best friend sighed.

"I don't consider myself a dumb man," Brady said as they reached the crest of the hill, where Cold River was spread out before them in the early dark, glittering like a bright jewel. "But it surprised me how quickly a smart man can turn dumb in the face of a certain, specific provocation."

Riley rubbed at his face and prayed for deliverance. "Are you . . . talking about my sister?"

"You're smart about a lot of things, Riley," Brady replied quietly. Too quietly to dismiss. "But Rae Trujillo has never been one of them."

Riley was reckoning with that parting shot when Brady dropped him back at his truck, leaving him to his own devices. What he should have done was drive straight on out of town. Jensen had left him a couple of messages about work issues, but nothing that couldn't wait. There was no reason that Riley needed to call him back, or stick around town in case he came in for the evening, or even head out to the ranch to hunt him down.

And there was definitely no good reason he should find himself in the Broken Wheel, ordering himself a beer and a burger when he had a perfectly good house out in the foothills and a fridge full of food.

He already had the beer and was waiting on the burger

when someone stood next to him. With such silent intent that he knew it was Matias before he looked over.

"Beer?" he asked his brother-in-law. Or former brother-in-law, depending how he looked at the thing.

Riley found he did not want to look at anything.

"Won't say no," Matias replied.

Jackson—who Riley had liked well enough until he'd had his eyes all over Rae—slid Matias a beer at Riley's signal, kept a wary distance from Riley, and retreated back down to the other end of the bar.

And for a while, Riley and Matias stood there in a companionable silence.

"I just moved my sister into the Mortimer house," Matias offered sometime later. Riley said nothing. Matias took another pull of his beer. "Seems like information you might want to have."

Riley reminded himself that this was all part of the plan. The plan that had come to him when he was galloping back down the trail out on his property, trying to outrun a snowstorm. He'd failed, of course. Because no one could outrun the weather. Not when it had a mind of its own like it did in these parts. It would do what it liked, and did.

By the same token, he'd tried arguing with Rae for years. It was time he took a different tack.

She wasn't wrong about things needing to change. What she was wrong about was how to go about changing them.

Riley had meant every word he'd said to her in the Flower Pot. Well. Almost every word. She wanted to get out there and try to date and do her level best to move on. He had every intention of helping her. Not because he had any interest in seeing his wife date some other guy. But because he didn't think she was going to care much for the experience.

If he told her that right now, she wouldn't believe him. It was something she was going to need to face on her own, and he was more than happy to do what was necessary to help her face it.

But that didn't mean it didn't bother him that she'd moved again. And was now under yet another roof that wasn't his.

It ate him up.

"Thanks for keeping me in the loop," he said to Matias, trying to sound at peace with it all.

But clearly failed, because the other man laughed. Then clinked his bottle of beer against Riley's before sinking back into blessed silence.

It took Riley longer still—the length of his meal, a couple of conversations with friends and neighbors who happened by—to accept that he wasn't there for any good reason. That he should take himself home before he did something stupid, because his *good reason* was apparently unpacking boxes at her friend's house down the block.

You have a long drive and an early morning, he reminded himself. *Like always.*

He pushed out into the night a little while later. It was cold enough outside, now that the sun was down and the dark had gripped on hard, to make him stop for a moment, brace himself, and reconsider his options. Riley blew out a breath and saw the cloud of it in the leftover light from the Broken Wheel. Then he shoved his hands in his pockets and walked down the block toward his truck.

He wasn't stopping at the bookstore, closed at this hour, but he could admit he slowed down a bit. If only to torture himself. Then laugh at himself.

Then he really did stop. Because in the little slice of

an alleyway that ran between the bookstore and its near-est neighbor, long ago done over into a walkway that led back to the house behind Capricorn Books, there was a figure near the lamppost that stood sentry halfway down. Trying to juggle a stack of boxes. And failing.

Riley watched for a moment, battling a whole host of feelings at the sight of Rae and her heavy moving boxes. The evidence, once again, that she wanted a life that had nothing to do with him. Or them.

Those feelings weren't going anywhere, but he didn't see the point in indulging them.

"Need a hand?" he asked, his voice loud in the still-ness of the cold night.

Rae jumped, sending all the boxes she was trying to juggle crashing to the ground. She whirled around to face him, slapping a hand over her chest as if her heart were clawing its way out from beneath her ribs.

"You scared me," she said, and she sounded it.

Riley expected he ought to feel guilty about that.

But he didn't.

"Those boxes look like they weigh more than you do."

He thought he deserved a pat on the back, at the very least, for the friendly tone he used. Downright neigh-borly, in his opinion.

She didn't look particularly convinced, out here in a too-light sweatshirt like she was gunning for hypother-mia. "I'm fine."

Riley had been moving toward her as he spoke, and now he stopped, a foot or so away. "You don't look fine. You look like you can't carry them all at once."

"Are you just . . . hanging around in alleyways look-ing for heavy things to carry?"

She sounded irritated. Riley took that as a victory. He

bent down and picked up all three boxes easily, then jerked his chin toward her new home.

Rae walked in front of him, her reluctance evident in the way she held her shoulders so stiffly.

"I had a burger at the Broken Wheel," Riley said as he carried the boxes down the path. "I wouldn't have come in the alley at all, except I heard a commotion. To be honest with you, Rae, I thought it was raccoons."

"*Raccoons,*" she huffed out. "Please."

"Scavengers. Instead, I found you."

"There's vermin everywhere, Riley. A sad fact of life."

Riley made it to the house and set the boxes down on the side porch. Then he stood back, studying Rae in the light that spilled out from inside another house she intended to live in without him.

Not a helpful thought.

"Since when do you have dinner at the Broken Wheel?" she asked him. "On a random weekday?"

There were a lot of ways he could have responded to that question, but what he chose to do was grin at her. Slowly. "I'm a single man, Rae. I have to get out there, don't I?"

He watched with a sense of satisfaction and something a little bit brighter and a whole lot more intense as she processed what he might mean by that. The sweatshirt she was wearing had a collar that went to her chin. And he knew it was a nervous tick of hers when her jaw tightened, against the top of the zipper, like she was biting back words.

Really, it was all the pat on the back he needed.

"You sure do," she said, sounding overly cheerful. Forced, even. "Were you on a date?"

He only looked at her, still grinning, until she flushed.

"You're right," Rae corrected herself quickly. "That's none of my business. I hope you were on a terrific date.

I'm sure you have a lot to offer any . . . selections you might . . ."

She gave up.

But Riley waited. And continued to say nothing.

"It's still early, so I guess it can't have been *too*—"

She stopped again.

He allowed a brow to lift as he looked down at her. And deeply enjoyed how red her face was.

"Thank you for helping me with these boxes," she said at last, sounding as if she were choking. "That was very nice of you."

"See?" he drawled, making a meal out of it. "Isn't being friends great?"

"Terrific," she said. "Absolutely the best."

"I couldn't agree more."

And Riley left her there, her cheeks red and flustered and her mouth full of lies, and found himself smiling all the way home.

10

"Absolutely not," Rae declared. "You have to find some-one else."

It was late that Friday night, and she was sitting at a table near the dance floor at the Broken Wheel, vetoing Riley's selections for potential dates.

Happily.

If anyone had ever suggested that this was something that could happen, under any circumstances—ever—she wouldn't have believed it. She wouldn't even have laughed it off, she simply wouldn't have been able to take in the visual. Even a week ago, this would have seemed impossible.

But here they were. She and Riley. *Friends,* apparently.

And currently, friendship involved saving Riley from himself. "You may not remember Alyssa Bond from school, but I do." Rae started ticking off points on her fingers as they both watched the woman in question as she and a couple of her friends giggled and whispered to each other on the far side of the dance floor. "In a nutshell, she plays the victim like a violin. She talks endlessly about herself while pretending she's too shy and introverted to stand upright. And given the slightest opportunity to stab you in the back, she will go at you with a machete."

Riley eyed Alyssa, who, in fairness, looked angelic tonight. Then he turned that lazy gaze of his on Rae. "She's cute."

"It's your funeral, I guess. You're welcome to choose whatever pallbearer you like."

Riley laughed, took another swig of his beer, and stayed seated.

And Rae told herself the little glow of contentment she felt about that had to do with saving him from his own bad choices. *Alyssa Bond,* of all people. When Rae and her friends talked about the dark days of middle school, Alyssa was always the villain.

Some part of her thought Riley probably remembered that too, or at least Rae talking about it over the years. And was only pretending to consider Alyssa as a potential date—but Rae didn't really want to let herself think about the reasons he might do that.

"How's life as an honorary Mortimer sister?" Riley asked then, and it was a measure of how far they'd come that Rae didn't bristle at that. She didn't glare at him suspiciously, trying to figure out what he meant by the question.

It was Friday night, and they were friends. That was new, obviously. And like any new garment, it fit a bit awkwardly at first. But Rae thought she was getting the hang of it now.

"You know Charity works at the church, right?" She waited for Riley's nod. "Well, her passion project is the choir. She sings. A lot."

And her family might have a lot of opinions about her grumpiness in the morning, but nobody knew it better than Riley. The way his eyes lit up with an unholy amusement made her own grin widen.

"Yes," Rae confirmed. "At all hours, but *especially* in the morning."

"At least she has a good voice. That's something."

"There is that. They're all still treating me like a guest. When that fades, we'll see what it's really like. But so far, so good."

There were other things she could have said. Like that living in town was both everything she'd always imagined it was, and nothing like it. It was so *noisy,* for one thing. She could lie in her bed up under the eaves in the graceful old house, and hear . . . *sounds.* Not only the creaks and settling that was a hallmark of any old house, but people. Out in the streets, having conversations, laughing at things she felt could not possibly be so funny in the middle of the night when the bars were closed. She could hear it every time someone fired up an engine, drove away too fast, or took a corner with wheels squealing and music pumping. Rae could theoretically sleep in a bit now that she could walk to work, but she didn't feel better rested when she was up half the night listening to all those unfamiliar sounds in the dark.

But she opted not to mention that, because it seemed . . . disloyal, maybe, because she should love every aspect of this brand-new life of hers. She'd chosen it, after all. She shouldn't feel a strange sense of homesickness now that the choice was made. Not for her parents' house, necessarily. Not for Riley's house, either. Not really.

She'd started wondering if she was more of a country girl than she'd always imagined, down deep in her bones. Maybe she needed the wide-open spaces, the wind and the mountains, to really feel at peace—and she didn't want that to be true. She'd always secretly assumed that *if she wanted,* she could pick up and move to a huge city on a moment's notice and *thrive.*

That was unlikely to be true if she found Main Street in Cold River too busy for her tastes.

"What about you?" Rae asked Riley, because that was far more interesting than realizations she didn't want to have. "Are you doing any more clinics this year?"

"I'm raffling off riding lessons at the Harvest Gala, against my better judgment," he replied. Reminding Rae that she still hadn't gotten official confirmation on her centerpieces. "But no. No more clinics until the new year. I'm only taking on individual clients at the moment, and only if they make me offers I can't refuse."

"I think it's smart not to run yourself ragged at this time of year. You always regret it when you do."

"I do."

When the silence that fell between them seemed almost companionable, Rae found herself working at the label on her beer, wondering how that was possible. How it was that after all this time, she and Riley could . . . talk? Just *talk,* like normal people. Take out the sex and the fighting and the years of hard feelings and he was a man she'd known since birth who she also knew pretty much inside and out by now.

Like the fact that his family boarded so many horses over the holiday season because a lot of wannabe ranchers liked swaggering around their ranchettes in their pristine Luccheses—but not when they could be skiing at Vail. They liked to have someone else take care of the unpleasant necessities of their home-on-the-range fantasies for a spell when there were slopes to shred. In years past, Riley had kept taking on both private clients in the group clinics he offered during this time, but he'd always about worn himself thin.

It was more evidence that they were growing up that

she could simply know that without trying to hurt him with it. Without bracing herself for a cutting thing he might say in return if she carelessly said something that referenced their long, complicated relationship.

This was all good, she told herself, looking around at what she assumed was set to become her typical Friday night these days. This time without furtive looks across the bar to see what Riley was doing while pretending she didn't know he was there. Tonight, she didn't have to pretend anything. She could sit right next to him and they could talk about the people they might move on with in a way that she was sure was healthy, because wasn't that what mature people did? Keep everything amicable no matter what? And meanwhile, their friends could mingle again instead of feeling they had to choose sides.

Really, Rae couldn't understand why they hadn't gotten to this point years ago.

"Check it out," Riley said.

That made her look at him again. Which was, she could admit, more challenging than simply sitting next to him while carefully looking elsewhere. When they were sitting next to each other, it was easy to think about *friendship.* All their years together funneling into that friendship and making it bloom. When she looked at him directly, he was just . . . Riley.

And Riley was still Riley. A whole lot, in other words.

Because she might have made some long-overdue decisions about their life, but her body wanted what it wanted. Still and always, and it didn't particularly care that he was bad for her. Not when he looked the way he did.

Tonight, he was casually mouthwatering, a Riley Kittredge specialty. He was lounging there in the seat beside her with one arm stretched out over the back of the chair on his other side. He wore jeans and a Henley the way he always did, but no one managed to make two otherwise forgettable garments look as delicious as Riley did. All those muscles, lean and hard, showcased to perfection.

And she could pretend all she liked, but she hadn't forgotten how it felt to touch him.

"You okay there?" he asked, laughter in his voice.

She saw a gleam in his dark gaze that made her wonder how seriously he was taking this brand-new friends thing—but Rae shook that off. She was choosing to take it at face value, because it was better that way. Everything was better now, and better was what they both needed.

"I thought you wanted me to check something out?"

The gleam in his eyes intensified, but he nodded over across the crowded room. "You should get your dance on, Rae. That's the whole point, isn't it?"

Her stomach flipped around a bit at that, but she followed his gaze to see Tate Bishop standing at the bar and looking around as if he, too, was looking to spice up his evening.

Though what Rae felt was anxiety, not spice.

Excitement, she corrected herself. *It's* excitement, *not* anxiety, *and you need to break the seal.*

Because the truth was, as Hope had pointed out to her this very morning, for all Rae's big talk about moving on, all she'd really done so far was hang out in public with Riley.

It almost looks like the two of you are back together, Hope had said mildly when she'd stopped by the Flower Pot for a midmorning coffee break before opening the bookstore. Because while Rae opened at six, Capricorn Books opened at the far more civilized hour of ten or thereabouts, as the spirit moved them. But then, they didn't have as many daily deliveries to offices and care facilities.

Rae had glared at her. *Why would you say something like that?*

Hope shrugged. *You didn't speak to each other in public for years. Now you're cozying up in full view of half the town. How did you think that would be interpreted?*

Admittedly, Rae hadn't thought much about *interpretations*. But here was her opportunity to prove that Hope's was dead wrong.

"Tate Bishop," she said as brightly as possible. "Do you think he's a good dancer?"

Next to her, Riley didn't quite laugh. "I can't say I've ever had reason to inquire."

"He doesn't really seem like a dancer to me."

"Only one way to find out, baby."

"And who will you be dancing with?"

Maybe a little belligerently, she could admit. She told herself it was the use of *baby*. There was no telling what she might do if he called her that again.

"I haven't rightly decided." Riley flashed that grin. "You start. I'll follow."

And Rae knew she wasn't imagining the challenging way he looked at her.

He didn't think she was going to do it. He thought she would come up with some excuse to avoid making an actual move, and he wasn't wrong, because she had several excuses right there on her tongue. The fact that Tate had liked Abby, way back in high school, and surely she should be loyal to her friend who had never noticed his existence because she'd only ever seen Gray. Or the fact that Tate had a checkered past—including claims he'd torched a building before disappearing for years—which maybe ought to be considered in full before she did something reckless, like smile at him too intently.

But she knew they were excuses. Just like she knew Hope had a point. And most of all, she knew that if she backed down from a challenge that Riley was clearly throwing out before her, she would regret it.

Because it would prove that despite everything, she had no intention of moving on at all.

And she did. Of course she did.

She smiled at Riley, then stood. And it was instantly worth it when his expression changed. A whole lot less challenging, suddenly.

"Aren't you supposed to say something?" She tilted her head as she looked down at him. "Isn't there some kind of bro ritual that's supposed to happen now? A wingman code of some kind?"

"Go get 'em, tiger?"

"That's disappointing."

"I can sing the high school fight song if you want. I know all the verses."

"You? Sing? In a public place?"

"It's the enthusiasm that matters, Rae."

"I'm not sure we really want to make this a high school thing," Rae said. As diplomatically as possible. "That doesn't seem like the right vibe for a Friday night . . ."

"Hookup?"

His voice was innocent. His expression blank.

Rae counted that as a triumph.

"We'll see," she singsonged at him. "Wish me luck."

Then she launched herself away from him, letting her momentum carry her across the crowded bar floor before she was tempted to second-guess herself. Or second-guess

herself *more*. She wound her way between groups of
people talking and laughing together, sitting at the tables
and standing in groups. She skirted around the dancers out
on the dance floor, some executing clearly choreographed
moves while others simply swayed around in time to the
music, obviously there for the excuse to get their hands on
each other.

She made it all the way across the bar floor on the
strength of her desire to prove . . . whatever this was.
And her desire that Riley should watch her do it, because
she was sure he didn't think she would.

Then she was actually at the bar itself. And it was
harder with every step to convince herself that what she
was feeling was excitement instead of . . . crushing anxiety liberally laced through with dread.

She knew Tate Bishop, but only the way everybody
knew people around here. Meaning they weren't close,
never had been, and she usually referred to him by his
entire name—even in her own head. She couldn't remember having any particular interactions with him
back in high school, but then, high school had been approximately seven million years ago. In case she was
tempted to forget that, the Tate Bishop who stood before
her, leaning against the bar and surveying the scene before him, was very clearly a grown man. Not the boy
she'd only sort of known back then. Whatever he'd done
with his life, it had left him etched into stone and sinew.

He was intimidating, if she was honest.

Was Rae really planning to . . . wander up to him? And
then what?

She had never approached a man. In a bar. *Ever*. She
had only ever been with one man in her life, and he was
currently sitting across the room, smirking at her. Rae

didn't have to look over her shoulder to see him do it. She could feel it.

He doesn't think you're going to go through with this, she reminded herself.

She was so indignant at the prospect that she ignored what felt like a sudden stomach flu, washing over her like doom, as she drifted closer. Closer to Tate Bishop, a man of many contradictory rumors and much local gossip.

Obviously, she wanted to stop, so she kept going. She *made* herself. Until she was standing directly in front of him and waiting for him to acknowledge her. Which he did, though he took his time.

"Rae Trujillo," he said.

She assumed that was a greeting.

"Hi, Tate," she replied. *Bishop,* she added privately, as always.

So far, she was killing this.

"Can I help you with something?" he asked, nicely enough.

Rae did not have an abundance of experience in sultry bar conversation that was supposed to be flirty, then lead to all kinds of other things, but she felt it probably wasn't supposed to start off quite so . . . antiseptically.

All she wanted to do was abort this mission. *Right now.* She could claim she was trying to get past him to the bar to order something. She could do anything at all, so long as she ended this. Because what on earth was she *doing*? Once again, she hadn't thought things through. She had no business trying to act like any other woman her age when she wasn't like them. Because the last time Rae had thought about dating, she'd been a teenager. And the only boy she'd ever liked had been the only boy she'd dated.

She should have tried to take classes in bar behavior before she branched out on her own.

But the only way out was through, she decided in another flash. Retreating was only going to make it worse.

Not to mention she had now been standing here, staring up at him, for entirely too long.

"Well, I hope you can help me," she said. *You sound like you're about to ask him directions to the bathroom.* She flashed a smile and pretended he was a customer. One of those shamefaced men who turned up, usually right before the store was closing, desperate for the perfect arrangement to get them out of whatever trouble they'd caused. "I love to dance, but I don't have a partner."

Tate's gaze sharpened. For a long moment, she panicked and thought he hadn't heard her. She would have to say it again, in the same bright, easy voice. Except now her heart was kicking up a racket inside her, and she was almost certainly sweating.

How attractive.

"I was under the impression you have a partner," Tate said, and she wasn't prepared for his voice forming words that weren't her name. The boy she remembered had been unremarkable, really. He certainly hadn't sounded like this. Gravelly. Serious. *Masculine.* "The same partner you've always had."

He didn't look behind her, over across the bar. But then, he didn't have to.

"Do you mean Riley?" She made herself laugh. "We've been broken up for years."

"If you say so."

Yet he made no move. And as she stood there, it dawned on Rae that she might have to *do* something. When she'd never had to do anything. And wasn't that a kick in the teeth. So much for her mission of empowerment or whatever she was doing. Had she really spent her entire life just . . . sitting back waiting to see what Riley might do?

But she already knew the answer.

Rae heard familiar voices all around her, but she refused to look and see who it was. She refused to let herself get caught up in who was paying attention or how much the center of the town's gossip machine she could expect to be by morning.

But still, something in her quailed. A large part of her wanted to curl up into a ball and die right there.

She thought of that look in Riley's eyes. The smirk that she had every intention of wiping off his face.

Rae didn't know what she was supposed to do in a situation like this, but Tate was still looking at her. Waiting, she figured. So she ran with it. She stretched out her hand and took his.

It was a perfectly nice hand. Male, strong, and surprisingly calloused for a man who, so far as she knew, didn't work out in the fields.

But it was the wrong hand.

Rae ignored that, smiled wider, and even fluttered her eyelashes a little bit as she looked up at him. For the full effect. That she'd seen on television, because she certainly hadn't tried such a thing before.

"Just one dance?" she asked.

Tate studied her for another moment, and only then lifted his gaze to focus on a spot behind her. She knew which spot.

When his gaze returned to hers, he looked . . . entertained.

"If you insist," he said.

Rae wanted to say that she certainly did not *insist,* but

he didn't give her a chance. He left his beer on the bar. He kept hold of her hand. Then he tugged her with him into the crowd and out onto the dance floor.

Rae had danced with a number of men in her lifetime, but they had all been either family, polite gestures by men whose wives were her friends, or Riley.

She had never been pulled into the arms of a single man who she could, if she wanted, do anything she liked with.

Nothing she liked sprang to mind, however, because she was too overwhelmed by an arm around her back and another holding her hand. And the way Tate tucked her into him, so she was almost pressed against his chest.

Rae couldn't breathe, because she felt something like suffocation, even though he wasn't holding her all that tightly.

And then they were moving.

She told herself she was having a delightful time. This was fun. She was dancing. Actually *dancing* with a man who was basically a stranger. Tate spun her around and around.

And every time he did, she caught a glimpse of Riley, still lounging there in that chair.

As she'd suspected, he was smirking.

Rae decided that while she might be suffocating to death, she would do it with a freaking smile all over her face.

She tipped her head back, letting her hair bounce where it pleased. She didn't think that would be too much bouncing, given the amount of hairspray she'd put in it to maintain the curls she'd decided she should wear tonight. Simply because she could. Because it was her hair, not Riley's, and the fact he liked the way it fell naturally shouldn't matter to her. She smiled up at her brand-new dance partner, and she held on—until Tate grinned down at her.

Then spun her around even faster.

And when she stopped worrying about whether or not to breathe, or why it felt so strange and *not right* to be held like this at all, it was easier. And the faster they moved, the more ridiculous the entire thing felt to her.

At some point, she began to laugh.

Because Tate was attractive, he was a surprisingly good dancer, and he seemed to be enjoying himself. So she ought to be enjoying herself too, shouldn't she? And it wasn't his fault that he wasn't shaped right. That he didn't smell right. That his shoulders weren't precisely the right width and that his jawline might be stellar, but it wasn't angled the right way.

None of those things were his *fault,* she thought. Kindly.

For some reason, that made her laugh even more.

Around and around and around they went. And when the song ended, Tate stopped and held her there, a different sort of gleam in his gaze. "Happy to be of service. Can I buy you a drink?"

Rae did not want a drink. She did not want him buying her a drink, because she might not know much, but she was pretty sure drinks always came with strings attached. And she didn't want *strings.* She wanted to call it a night because she'd done it. She'd walked up to this man, asked him to dance, and danced with him. Surely, that was all that mattered.

But she couldn't help glancing over her shoulder. She found Riley's gaze instantly, and this time, she was the one wearing a challenge all over her face.

Rae could feel the way he looked back at her all through her, punching into the parts of her only he had ever touched. She felt *alight*. As if looking at him was plugging herself into an electrical outlet and turning it up all the way.

Riley was still smirking. Then he upped the game by lifting his beer in a little toast.

She wanted to go over and punch him, but that would be showing him far too much. That would be giving in. She refused.

So instead, Rae looked back to Tate and smiled even more brightly.

"I would *love* a drink," she told him.

And laughed uproariously, just to seal the deal.

11

Rae woke up the following morning in her cute little room beneath the eaves in the Mortimer house, done up in soothing blues and her own bright and cozy comforter, not sure whether she had a hangover or not.

And not from alcohol.

Either way, her eyes were a little gritty, and she couldn't stop going over—and over—everything that had happened last night. Tate Bishop. *Dancing.* The dark way Riley had watched her have a drink at the bar with Tate, though with that smirk of his in place.

Maybe she was the only one who'd seen the darkness beneath it. And maybe she was also the only one who found it a little more thrilling than she should have.

She took her usual morning shower in the tiny bathroom that was all hers on the third floor, complete with an antique, claw-foot tub and a view out over a sleepy Cold River, dark and sparkling. And when she dressed and went downstairs, she had the kitchen to herself. Because it was a Saturday morning, and Rae was the only one up early. That meant no sounds of the old pipes to warn her that Charity was about to start her morning shower songs until Monday.

Rae drank down her first two prescription-strength mugs of coffee while settled against the counter in the comfortable kitchen, letting last night entertain her. Because the more she replayed that dance, the better it got. All that spinning around and around, and Riley's dark gaze in the middle of it all, always. Watching her.

Waiting, something in her whispered.

Her breath got a little choppy at that.

"Stop that right now," she ordered herself.

She washed out her mug and set it on the drying rack beside the sink, then marched herself over to the mudroom to stamp her feet into her boots and shrug into her coat, winding her scarf tightly around her neck before she zipped up. Then she let herself out the side door and into the little alleyway that was still dark. Enough to make her imagine she saw Riley there again, like her own, personal ghost.

"And you can stop that too," she muttered out loud, her grumpy voice making clouds in the air as she walked.

It was a cold, crisp morning, with the threat of snowfall later. She could smell it in the air and in the gusts of wind that made her cheeks redden. Rae shoved her hands in her pockets and made her way out to Main Street, welcoming despite the early-morning dark with all its pretty streetlights shining brightly. She set off toward the flower shop, listing the things she was grateful for in this new life of hers as she walked through the cold.

That she and Riley were friends. That however strange that friendship might feel, at times, they were both clearly dedicated to it. That she was living in Hope's house here in town, which meant she didn't have to dress in quite as many layers as she did when she woke up out in the country—because she didn't have to worry about her truck breaking down in the middle of nowhere and her with the wrong thing on.

Every morning during this walk, she saw the same

shopkeepers. The few that were open—or about to open—at this hour. She smiled at Katrina, who worked behind the desk of the little inn, and was always out first thing in the morning, sweeping off the step. Or in this kind of cold, getting rid of any ice.

"Good morning," Rae said as she drew close. The way she always did.

But instead of replying in kind, the way *she* normally did, or saying something about the weather, Katrina glanced up with a speculative look on her face.

Everything in Rae stilled. Because she knew that look. She'd been the subject of it before. Her marriage had been a topic of conversation for years, complete with sniffs from some and snubs from others, but looks like *that* had been reserved for big events. Like when she'd moved back into her parents' house, scandalizing far more people than she'd imagined.

She would have said no one paid her that much attention, but she'd been wrong. Repeatedly.

And she was so surprised to see a look like that again that she actually stopped walking, there beneath the inn's front light. "Is something the matter?"

Katrina blinked, and possibly reddened, though it was so cold out here it could have been that instead. "Oh no. Not at all."

Rae didn't believe her for a second, but what was she going to do? Stand here in the dark on the cold street and interrogate Katrina? Who also happened to be her former sister-in-law's best friend?

She wanted to, so she didn't. Instead, she smiled and walked on.

By the time she made it to the Flower Pot, she'd convinced herself that whatever had been going on with Katrina was Katrina's business, not hers.

Why on earth would you think that every stray expression on another person's face has something to do with you? she asked herself.

Then she let herself in to the shop, took that first, beautiful, deep breath, and got to work.

It was when Matias showed up to handle the day's deliveries that Rae realized Katrina hadn't been an isolated case. Because her older brother was looking at her in much the same way Katrina had.

Except with Matias, everything came with a heaping side helping of older-brother judgment he did nothing to hide.

"Why are you staring at me like that?" she asked when he'd finished loading up the van they used for deliveries and stood there on the other side of the desk, waiting for her to finish the paperwork.

"Am I?"

"You know you are."

He let out a faint sigh. "What are you doing, Rae?"

She kept her expression bland. "You say that as if you haven't seen me prepare our delivery paperwork approximately ninety-five thousand times in the past year alone."

"Not what I mean."

Rae very serenely returned her attention to the clipboard before her. "Then you've lost me."

"Let me remind you. Tate Bishop?"

There was that just-this-side-of-scathing note in Matias's voice, on the off chance she hadn't already discerned that he did not approve. And the minute the name was out there, dancing around between them on the counter in much the same way Rae and Tate had spun around last night, Rae understood that she should have been prepared for this. She should have formulated a plan this morning, instead of mooning around about Riley's *smirk*.

Katrina had been a clue, but she'd missed it.

Because, of course, everyone and their mother and her own older brother would have an opinion on Rae's behavior. Having opinions on other folks' behavior was part of the entertainment around here, particularly as the weather got cold. There was usually no malice in it. It was all part of the same story they all told as they lived it, weaving their various tales together until they became nothing more and nothing less than Cold River itself.

It was nothing new. But somehow, Rae had once again convinced herself that no one would pay too much attention to her. Not now.

It had only been a dance, after all.

"He's a very good dancer," she said now. "Which is a surprise, I guess. Only because I knew him in high school and I would not have said 'good dancer' was going to be something he could add to his résumé down the line."

"You can do whatever you want with your life," Matias told her.

"Wow, Matias. Thanks for that. And here I was under the impression that I had to run it past you first."

"But it's only you and me here. I'll ask again. What are you doing?"

"Whatever I want. As advertised."

"For a minute there, it almost looked like you were cleaning up your mess," her older brother said in that stark, hard-hitting Trujillo way she liked to think was charming when it came from her. Even though she had Matias here to make it clear that there was nothing charming about it when you were on the receiving end of it.

"My mess," she repeated. "Let me guess. You're talking about my marriage."

"Why aren't you?" Matias looked exasperated. "Why are you throwing him a bone and then dancing in his face with *Tate Bishop,* of all people?"

"Riley and I are friends."

Matias laughed insultingly. "Sure you are."

"We are!" She felt stung and really didn't want him to see that, because surely if she had confidence in what she was saying, it wouldn't matter if he believed her or not. "And even if we decided we were bitter enemies, what business is it of yours?"

"It's not like your ex is some random guy," her brother said as if he were explaining something very basic to her. The jerk. "Everybody knows him. They've known him longer than they've known you, as a matter of fact."

"I've known you my entire life, and right now, I can't say I consider that a *good* thing, Matias."

He shook his head. "The problem with everybody knowing Riley is that it's clear he's not evil. He didn't suddenly take to the bottle or worse. If he were stepping out on you, it seems likely that whoever he was stepping out with would have come out of hiding after all these years. He's never met a horse he couldn't tame, which is as good a way as any to tell he's not a bully. And he never shows up in any of the places people go around here when they've decided it's time to walk on the wild side."

"He sounds amazing, Matias. Maybe you should marry him."

Her older brother studied her for far too long. Only her determination that she wouldn't give him the satisfaction of looking away kept her from it. "Whatever he did that made you leave him, how can it be that bad?"

"I don't remember you offering me the opportunity

to weigh in on any relationship you've ever had. Is that something we're doing now? I would have brought my notes on your private life if I'd known."

"What I'm saying, Rae, if you would get your head out of your—"

"I also don't recall asking you for advice. On any topic at all."

Matias stared at her a moment. That wasn't better.

"It looks like you're playing with him," he said quietly. "After years of acting like he doesn't exist, suddenly you're cozying up with him in public. And then the next thing you know, you're dancing with another man, right in his face."

"Riley and I are *friends*," Rae said again, aware that she sounded significantly less at peace with her decisions. But there was no helping that. "Not that it's any of your business, but he's the one who suggested I ask Tate to dance in the first place."

"Maybe you've forgotten how it works around here. Maybe that's true and maybe it isn't, but it doesn't matter what actually happened if everyone around you has a different impression, does it?"

She blinked. "Are you . . . *concerned* about my reputation?"

"You've always been prickly," he replied, which she thought was deeply unjust. Especially coming from *him*. "You've always done exactly what you wanted and never paid any attention to the fallout."

"I know you're not lecturing me. You of all people, who takes pride in storming around this valley like a hurricane, except less approachable."

His mouth twitched as if he liked that description. Or wanted to laugh. It only made her more irritated.

"You've never actually had the pleasure of being

single in Cold River," Matias told her, and if he'd been
close to laughter, there was no trace of it in his voice.
"There are different rules for single people than there
are for childhood sweethearts who are mysteriously es-
tranged. You don't have to take my word for it. Keep it
up. See what happens."

"I'm dating. People date. With or without your permission."

Matias sighed again. "I'm not telling you to stop doing
what you want to do, I'm telling you that people talk
about it differently. But you know what? Forget it. You're
like talking to a wall."

He didn't wait around for her to cobble together a response to that outrage, coming from him, a man of stone
and silence when it suited him. In typical older-brother
style, he tugged the clipboard out of her grasp and left
her standing there with her mouth open while he loped
off out the back, seemingly without a care in the world.

Leaving Rae to fume until the shop door opened and
three women walked in. Rae knew them all. Two were
teachers, and the other was a nurse. They often ate their
lunch together, then bought themselves flowers to take
home. And sure enough, instead of chattering brightly
the way they normally did, they . . . whispered. Or talked
to each other in very low voices, and even though Rae
pretended she wasn't watching them, she could see every
time they glanced in her direction.

When they came to make their purchases, they all
eyed her in that same speculative manner.

And she hated it.

But it was a pattern that repeated itself throughout the
day until she found herself wishing no more locals would
come in.

"Why is it that you can date or not date as your heart

desires?" Rae demanded of Hope later that afternoon, bursting into the bookstore with—she could admit it—a touch of theater. "But I have one dance and I'm the Whore of Babylon?"

Hope gave her a mild glance from behind the counter but returned her attention to the book she was reading. "That sounds like a question only you can answer, Rae. Exactly how do you dance?"

Rae rounded the counter and threw herself onto the arm of the comfy old chair. "I'm serious."

Hope smiled. "So was I."

"My entire day has been spent contending with all these *looks*," Rae complained. She summarized Matias's unsolicited advice. "I assumed that he was just being a little crazy, but then there was a whole day of people looking at me like I grew a new head last night."

"We live in a place that hasn't changed a whole lot for more than a century. Of course any hint of change is suspect."

Rae frowned at her. "Have people been treating you this way all this time and I didn't know it?"

Hope smiled, almost sadly. "No. Because I stare them straight in the eye and remind them of the Mortimer family curse."

That statement, obviously, derailed the entire conversation.

And Rae quickly discovered that a major disadvantage to living in town—with Hope, no less—was that it severely limited her ability to put distance between the two of them when Hope was being impossible.

Instead of heading back to the Mortimer house, seat of the supposed curse, she took a detour to Cold River Coffee instead. She found it fairly empty at this hour on a Saturday evening, thirty minutes before the coffee shop closed for the day. She loved the place, from its battered wooden floors to its distressed brick walls. The fireplace in one corner, the comfortable sofa, the overstuffed bookshelves. Perfect for a sulk and a huge mug of hot chocolate.

Rae was asking herself why she didn't come and hang out here more often when the answer presented itself.

In the form of Amanda Kittredge coming out from the back.

She was Amanda Everett these days, Rae corrected herself. Who had spent years working here, but had given up her job as a coffee slinger to open up her adorable little barn filled with local goods down by the river. Or anyway, Rae had heard it was adorable, because she certainly hadn't gone in and looked herself. She and Amanda had an unspoken agreement to avoid each other whenever possible.

But here they were. Face-to-face.

Rae smiled. Amanda . . . did not.

And Rae was forced to consider the possibility that the reason no one from the fast-approaching Harvest Gala had returned her calls was standing right in front of her.

"I'm surprised to see you here," Rae said, choosing to act as if Amanda was being perfectly polite. And as if the notion Amanda was deliberately excluding Rae—and therefore her family—from the gala didn't make her stomach hurt. "I thought you were busy with your new place."

Amanda smiled then, which wasn't much of an improvement, because it wasn't a particularly nice smile. But the minute she thought that, Rae cautioned herself against it. She barely knew Amanda any longer. She shouldn't be categorizing her smiles, for God's sake.

"I had every intention of extending an olive branch," Amanda told her.

"I wasn't aware we needed an olive branch."

"I meant to. I really did. But that was before you decided to party with some other guy right in Riley's face."

Rae would have preferred to discuss the Mortimer family curse for another twenty hours, conclude that it existed and was the reason all the Mortimer women were single, and then apologize to Hope for doubting her. That would have been much better than this.

"I actually came in here for a hot drink," she said as steadily as she could. "Not for an attack."

"I'm not attacking you. I'm telling you."

"That you decided to stop being mean to me after all these years, but thought better of it? You could have just continued to be mean, Amanda. I wouldn't have noticed the difference."

"I've never been mean to you," Amanda protested. "The same thing can't be said for how you've treated my brother, however."

That was so unfair it made Rae feel scraped raw. Like she'd had a marriage on her own—but this was Riley's younger sister. As much as she might want to, Rae couldn't unload on her. It wouldn't be right, and she knew it.

But it was a close call.

"I'm not having this conversation with you," she managed to say.

Rae turned to head back out again, but stopped, shocked, when Amanda grabbed her arm.

"You have to know how Riley feels about you, don't you?" Amanda looked at her as if she were searching Rae's face for clues. "I've spent all this time assuming that you know, but maybe you don't. Maybe you're not deliberately being cruel. He's been head over heels in love with you forever, Rae. Whether you were together, not together, or whatever in-between state there might have been, that's never changed."

"Riley and I are friends," Rae gritted out, though she was getting tired of saying it, and it was starting to make her mouth hurt. "I don't understand why that's so hard for people to get their heads around, but it's true. And I don't think this is anybody's business but ours, but nothing happened last night that your brother didn't heartily approve of. If not cheer on."

"Oh, come on, Rae." Instead of looking angry or spiteful, Amanda looked almost . . . sad. "You don't really believe that, do you?"

And that was how Rae found herself in her truck, making the drive she'd told herself she would never make again. Out of Cold River, over the hill, and way out into the far reaches of the Longhorn Valley. Skirting the roads that led to Cold River Ranch or the Bar K and taking the unmarked dirt roads that led toward the foothills instead. She followed the road she knew best by heart, into the woods and then up and around that long drive. She knew the way here better than she knew the way home.

It was like déjà vu.

She pulled into the yard and sat there a moment, questioning herself.

This time was different, she was sure of that, but still. She sat where she was, staring up at the house. Try as she might, she could never convince herself that there was a prettier house around. Probably because Riley had built it. And she'd helped. And every last board, nail, window, and porch had been crafted for a future they'd believed in deeply, once.

"Things change," she muttered.

She slid out of the truck, slamming the door loudly behind her. Usually, that brought Riley out, but there was no sign of him. *One of these nights you're going to show up here and I'm not going to open the door,* he'd said a lifetime ago. But she told herself that couldn't be happening tonight.

They. Were. Friends.

Rae stood there a moment, rethinking her decision to come out here—but no. She was here already. Creeping off back into town wasn't going to make her feel any better about things.

There were lights on inside the house, but she made her way toward the barn instead, because if he were in the house, she knew he would have made that clear.

The night and the weather were conspiring against her, she thought as she walked across the yard. The snow had held off, but the air still felt swollen with the promise of it—especially farther up and closer to the mountains. There was that sweet, sharp scent in the wind and a kind of agitation inside her that made her belly tremble in on itself.

Her boots seemed loud against the cold earth beneath them, but then again, her heartbeat was so loud it was drowning everything else out.

Calm down, she ordered herself. *You didn't come here for* that.

For one thing, if she'd been here for the usual reasons, she wouldn't be here so early in the evening. That had always been a late-night mistake. One she'd repeated entirely too often.

She wasn't here tonight to make any mistakes.

Rae slipped into the barn and stood there a moment, another wave of déjà vu and sweet familiarity sweeping over her. While her flower shop smelled like hope, this barn smelled like a whole selection of dreams that had belonged to her at a different point in time. She liked to think of those dreams as lost, but here—where it smelled of hay and horses, rich and comforting and warm—she thought maybe they weren't lost, after all. Maybe they were here and always had been, waiting all the while.

They're not waiting for you, she reminded herself starkly, the sharp edge inside her reminding her it was there. That it could draw blood. *None of this is yours any longer. You chose that yourself.*

She was still feeling buffeted by that when a figure detached itself from the nearest stall, materialized into Riley, and was suddenly . . . right there. Much too close.

Much too . . . *him.*

All she saw was that face of his. That mouth. That gleam in his dark eyes that was wired straight into the deepest parts of her but particularly between her legs.

And worse, her heart.

"Riley . . . ," she tried to say.

"Friends with benefits?" he asked, something too hot to be amusement in that low drawl of his. "Works for me."

Then he slid a hard, possessive hand around the back of her neck, held her where he wanted her, and kissed her.

12

Riley kept telling himself he wasn't pissed.

Rae had danced with Tate Bishop. She'd had a drink with him. Riley had been right there, witness to the entire thing, and had even done Rae the considerable favor of grinning like a fool the whole time so no one could claim he'd had any problem with the scene she was making. The scene he'd encouraged her to make.

Why would he be *pissed* about that?

If he'd happened to pay extra close attention to who left when and where they went, all that meant was that he'd been concerned for Rae. He'd wanted to make sure no harm came to her. He would have done the same for anyone.

Bonus was, he knew that Tate and Rae hadn't gone anywhere together.

One dance and one drink. It was exactly what he'd wanted her to do.

Because she'd been lying to herself for a very long time and hadn't exactly welcomed his attempts to point that out. He figured that meant she was the one who had to work her own way back to the truth.

Riley just hadn't expected it to get to him the way it had. The way it did.

Reason had nothing to do with it. Rational thought? Forget it.

Once he'd made sure that Rae had walked herself to the Mortimer house safely, which he told himself he would have done for any woman wandering around the streets, he'd fumed all the way home. Nor was his mood particularly improved by morning, when he had to listen to entirely too much commentary from Jensen, as usual, and this time with Connor there to get in a few licks himself.

It had taken his new client's treacherous filly to nip at him a little, obviously annoyed that she wasn't the focus of his full attention, for Riley to get it.

He was insanely jealous.

Something he thought he'd wrestled under control until he heard her truck in his yard.

He'd thought he was hallucinating it. But no. There was only one death trap that sounded like that and still only one person who would drive up here in it.

And he hadn't meant to kiss her. Really, he hadn't.

But he also didn't do a single thing to stop himself.

Because Rae didn't taste like a friend. She tasted like his. The way she always had.

All that heat and longing. The grip of their history, the kick of new desire that he was always sure wouldn't turn up again. Not this time. Until it did.

And it had been too long. Weeks without her. It was like torture.

It wasn't only him. Rae made a low, almost pained sound, then melted against him. Her arms snuck around his waist, under his coat, the way she always liked to hold him. And she kissed him back, ferocious and something like feral, and nothing at all like friends.

Not even friends with benefits, to his mind. But he was too busy intoxicating himself with her to point that out.

She shrugged out of her coat. He got rid of his.

All the while, he kissed her again and again, hardly aware of it when she knocked his hat off. But loving it when she launched herself at him, knowing that he would catch her. And he did, hauling her up against him so she could wrap her legs around his waist and he could remind himself that she was in possession of the finest butt in Colorado. And possibly the whole freaking world.

Better still, it meant that all their best parts were pressed tight against each other.

She was little and he was big, and Riley had always enjoyed things they could do with that. He carried her over to the nearest wall, easily, and then wedged her there the way he'd been doing since they were teenagers.

Because he liked to take his time. He liked to kiss his way down her neck until she shivered against him and her skin broke out in goose bumps. He liked to move his hips against hers, a little roll that made her breath catch. He tugged her shirt off and got his hands in all that thick hair of hers, then tortured them both with the way he kissed her. When the only thing separating her from being naked up top was one of those outrageously lacy, feminine bras she wore.

And when she was shaking, and he was half-crazy with it, he took that off too.

Because her breasts were a wonder.

He had thought so years ago, and the wonder hadn't dimmed in the slightest in all the years between. He bent and took one straining peak in his mouth, because she was velvet and she was sweet and, best of all, she was sensitive. When he sucked, she jolted—and that was even better.

She was as greedy as he was. Her hands were beneath his shirt, tracking up his spine like flames. Her nails dug into his back, and that was like throwing gas into the situation.

Riley welcomed the rush of the ignition.

He lifted her away from the wall, one hand on the back of her head and the other around her hips. Their mouths crashed together. They each plundered and explored, tasted and teased, because this fire had always been uncontrollable. It had always burned too hot, too bright, too wild.

He liked carrying her. All those curves pressed against him, his arms full of her and the way she liked to ride him with her ankles crossed around his back.

But he wanted her too much. He always had.

Riley carried her over to the nearest stall, filled with sweet-smelling hay and empty of any occupant at the moment, and set her down. But only long enough to strip off his shirt, throwing it over the hay like a blanket.

Then she was in his arms again. And they were fighting the way they always did, but this fight was the one he liked. This was a fight of clever hands and hot mouths. This was a fight to tear off each other's clothes, and once they did, they fell down together into the bed he'd made.

And it had been so long. They always burned hot, but this seemed brighter.

His hands moved over her skin, reveling how soft she was, how warm. How perfectly she fit him, wherever he put his palms.

Rae was throwing a leg over him, straddling him as he fell back into the embrace of the hay. And he was helping her, or she was doing it. It didn't matter which.

It was the fight of it, the battle, his favorite thing in all the world, and then—

She reached between them and took hold of him where he was the hardest. Her breath came in desperate pants as she guided him between her legs.

He felt her heat. Her need. He felt his own like a pulse. Then he slid himself home.

And Rae exploded.

He gripped her hips as she arched backward, surrendering herself completely. It was the hottest thing he'd ever seen. It always was. She gave herself fully, and watching her come apart was raw and beautiful. It made him so hard he had to fight to maintain his control.

She shook and she shook. And before she was done, he began to move her. He lifted her up, then slammed her back down, and laughed at the sheer joy of it.

Of this.

Of finding himself deep inside her again. That seamless, perfect fit that she would say was the ruin of them when he thought it was their glory.

And it didn't matter which one of them was right, or if they both were, because there was only the thrust, the retreat.

The way she said his name and the way she slumped forward, so that her hair fell between them and around them. The way he lifted up so he could get his mouth on one of her nipples again.

This dance that never ended.

Riley didn't see how he would ever have enough of it. Of her.

He felt her begin to tighten again. And still he kept going, that fierce, hard, demanding rhythm he knew she loved as much as he did.

And soon enough, she began to quiver, then shake. He watched her do it, marveling in all that raw beauty that was only for him, only and ever for him—

Rae cried out his name. And as she shattered and soared, Riley went with her.

And for a long time afterward, there was only the weight of her against his chest. The way her breath and his sawed in and out of their lungs, tangled together. He was still inside her. His hands were still tangled in her hair, he could feel her heart hammering in her chest and his own too.

At moments like this, Riley sometimes forgot there was any tension between them or ever had been.

Because how could there be? When they had this?

But that wasn't a question that he was likely to ever know the answer to. He was better off lying there and enjoying what he had. Because soon enough, she would stir. And when she did, she would come to her senses the way she always did. And then take off, the way she always did.

Riley knew that if he wanted anything to change, he had to change first. And maybe do something neither one of them *always* did.

When she finally did move again, pushing herself away from him, he didn't do what *he* always did. He didn't ask a rough question designed to scrape at her. He didn't act like he didn't know exactly what she was doing. He didn't start up their endless fight again.

Riley was amazed how difficult it was not to poke and prod at her with all the same old weapons. Suggesting that he was not, in fact, the saint in this he sometimes liked to pretend he was.

Especially when her face fell and she looked at him as if she despaired of them both. That he was familiar with that expression didn't make him like it any. He knew this was usually when he started in on her with the same old questions she never answered.

You're about as far from a saint as it's possible to get, he told himself then. *Who are you kidding?*

But he was being friendly tonight. If it killed him.

"Hey," he said, in his best approximation of the kind of genial, amiable person who engaged in these scenarios with *friends*. "We're friends with benefits, that's all. And you have to admit, Rae. It's a pretty great benefit."

She rolled away from him, shoving her hair away from her face and not meeting his gaze. "I promised myself this was never, ever going to happen again."

"What you're talking about didn't happen," Riley said, practically hurting himself in his attempt to sound completely casual. And so freaking *friendly* it made his throat ache. "This was something else."

He jackknifed to his feet and tugged his jeans and boots back on. Then he moved around the stall, gathering the rest of their clothes. He handed her what was hers, pretending he didn't notice the way she kept her eyes downcast. Unfriendly Riley would have been all over that, but *Friends with Benefits* Riley left her to it. By the time she finished pulling her pants back on, he was already dressed and coming back into the stall to give her the shirt he only vaguely recalled stripping off her.

Riley restrained the urge to help her dress, suspecting she would not take to it kindly. Instead, he waited, trying to exude friendliness without any strings attached. Not an easy thing to do when he thought sometimes that he was made of strings. Woven together, gnarled and matted, and her name imprinted on each and every one.

"Come on," he said, urging her along the way he might if she were one of his clients.

And she knew it, was the thing, because her dark gaze flicked to him as she smoothed her shirt down into place. "Are you talking to me as if I'm a horse?"

"All mammals get fractious when they're not properly fed," Riley said, somehow keeping himself from laughing. "Particularly wives."

He chose not to ask himself why he was amused in the first place when normally, he was the opposite.

And he didn't wait for her to come up with a thousand more arguments. He ushered her out of the barn, picking out little bits of hay that were stuck in her hair as they went. And it was saying something about how off-balance she was, visibly, that she didn't swat his hands away.

When she veered toward her truck, he held her by the arm and marched her into the house instead.

"This isn't a good idea," she muttered as the door shut behind her.

Riley ignored her, kicking off his boots and tossing his hat and coat, then heading for the kitchen. Trying to give the appearance of casual, friendly carelessness. But he didn't actually relax until he heard her kick her shoes off too.

He glanced back over his shoulder as he went to the sink to wash up and found her drifting closer, hugging herself around her middle as she followed him into the kitchen. When he was done washing his hands, she took his place at the sink while he moved over to the refrigerator.

It was a little too tempting to let himself think that things were finally back to normal. The two of them quietly moving around the kitchen together, a kind of choreographed dance they both knew by heart.

When he knew better.

Friends, he reminded himself.

"I'm starving," he said, pulling ingredients out of the fridge.

"I'm not hungry."

"Okay."

He set about making an omelet. He cracked eggs into his big cast-iron pan, then threw in cheese and vegetables and whatever else caught his fancy, fully aware that what happened to catch his fancy tonight were ingredients he knew Rae liked best.

When the omelet was cooked and flipped and perfect, he cut it in half, then slid each portion onto its own plate. He set her plate down next to her where she stood with her back to the counter, slid a fork on the plate, then retreated to the other side of the kitchen to hold his own plate in one hand and eat.

He managed not to grin too widely when Rae hopped up onto the counter, picked up her plate, and started eating hers too.

And *friends* probably didn't stand around eating in potentially awkward silences, he told himself. So he needed to get on that.

"What made you want to start dating?" he asked, picking a topic at random. And regretted it when she frowned at him. He kept eating as if he didn't notice the frown. "You know what I mean. We were going along the way we always do, then you wanted to change things. It seemed out of the blue to me, but I figure you have your reasons."

"Not at all." She poked at the fluffy omelet on her plate, and he thought she sighed a little as she used the side of her fork to separate a bite. Surrender, maybe. "It was a completely random decision, brought on by nothing more than the urge to cause as much pain as possible."

"Or that."

He, personally, would have pushed. So the friendly version of himself didn't. He waited.

After Rae had a few bites and the frown smoothed

from her brow, she kept going. "We're not getting any younger. I don't want to . . . waste any more time."

Riley could feel her gaze on him, so he didn't look up.

"Agreed," he said. Almost merrily.

"Well. I guess . . . I'm glad you agree."

"I saw your mom in town the other day," Riley said. Very casually. The way friendly people who weren't pretending not to be married would, by his estimation. "She was in Cold River Coffee. With two women with Southern accents."

"Hannah Everett's mother and aunt." Rae made a face. "My mom wants to recruit them into one of her charities, but they're both really, really good at being Southern. She keeps thinking they agreed to it, but then somehow they didn't. Masterful, really."

"It's that peaches-and-cream drawl," Riley agreed. "It's easy to get lost in. Besides, I think Ty and Hannah like having all that babysitting on tap whenever they want it."

"I know this is ancient history, but I still can't get my head around the whole Ty-and-Hannah thing. Secret marriages, rodeo shenanigans, and somehow they ended up happy, anyway? It's crazy."

Riley did not make a crack about the things love could do to a person if given the chance, but it hurt. A lot.

He made himself grin. "That's Ty. He's always been a little more bright and shiny than the rest of us."

"Sometimes I catch myself feeling almost sorry for Abby," Rae said, and she sounded different from how he'd heard her sound in this house in a long while. This wasn't about them. This wasn't a fight. This was Rae talking to him the way she'd used to, easy and offhanded. Kind of the way they'd been interacting out there in the Broken Wheel, except better. Less . . . fraught with dating nonsense and games. "I know she's as happy as can be, but those Everetts seem like a lot of hard work."

"I'm going to take that as a compliment," Riley said, and laughed, surprised that it wasn't entirely forced, either. "I guess the Kittredge family nonsense isn't up there with mean old Amos Everett swaggering around, ruining lives."

"You Kittredges always seem relatively well adjusted."

"Sure. We get that a lot. Zack is a control freak with a badge. Jensen clearly has a death wish, jumping into all those fires. Connor is a clown. I'm . . ." For once, he didn't feel a rush of that too-familiar darkness take him over. He shrugged, grinning. "Well, at least Amanda's okay."

"That's a little harsh." Rae bit back a smile. "Connor is a *really good* clown."

"My mother is an ice sculpture. My father is a brick wall. Well adjusted all around."

"At least no one's flipping tables," Rae said, grinning back at him. "Or chopping them up into firewood."

Riley wished he'd seen Brady go ahead and take apart his family's kitchen table. As it was, that he'd done it was already legendary. But he and Rae were having a perfectly nice and friendly conversation about their lives. Not legends.

"How's the war going between your mother and grandmother?" he asked.

"It's incessant, of course." Rae laughed again, then returned her attention to her plate. "It's one of the reasons I moved out. At least they're not violent. Just relentless."

"I think they like it." She looked up at him as if what he said didn't make sense. "I'm serious. Your mom only feels good when she's forcing charity on someone. You know it's true."

"I . . . can't argue with that."

"We know that she likes doing it, because that's all she does. But what's the other thing she does? Constantly?"

"I see your point," Rae said, sounding almost . . . rueful. "But my grandmother is a whole different kettle of fish."

"Always has been."

Riley remembered Rae's forbidding grandmother all too well. She'd spent years pretending he didn't exist when he was sitting at the same table. She'd never been all that loving to her own granddaughter. He couldn't remember her taking any notice of Rae until a couple of years after they'd gotten married.

"Maybe your mom doesn't like kettles. Or fish. Or your grandmother." Riley considered. "Or maybe the pair of them get a kick out of fighting for the sake of it. Could be it's a family trait."

Rae's head was bent toward her plate, but he heard her laugh. When she looked up, his ribs got tight because her eyes were sparkling. And she was smiling. For a moment, he was almost light-headed, because this was the way it was supposed to be between them.

Though it hadn't been for a long time. Even before she'd left.

But tonight, he was her best friend, not the man she claimed she was divorcing. He knew that if he let ghosts in, he would ruin it.

"Not that I'm suggesting *you* like fighting just for the sake of it," he said.

She rolled her eyes. "Not like the entire Kittredge family is known for bullheadedness or anything."

"My current theory on my father is that he could, at any point, open his mouth, offer his opinion, and drown us all out with the endless talking. But won't because he knows we want him to." He could hear his mother's voice suddenly. *You might ask yourselves where all your stubbornness comes from sometime, Riley. It isn't me.* He shoved that aside and kept his grin in place. "On some level, I almost admire it."

"Maybe he doesn't know what to say," Rae offered softly. "Maybe he meant to say something a long time ago but could never figure out how. And the words wouldn't come, year after year, until it was easier to stop trying."

That ache in Riley's chest got deeper and a whole lot darker.

"Maybe," he agreed, because he couldn't let himself chase that down. Not when this was supposed to be a friendly thing. Instead of a way for Rae to obliquely tell him things that, it turned out, after all these years, he wasn't sure he wanted to know. "I prefer to think of it as an elaborate revenge strategy."

Rae swallowed, then visibly rallied. "If I were going to pick between your parents as to who was more likely to be plotting revenge, it would not be your father."

Riley nodded. "That's fair."

"I always wanted to be like her," Rae said, surprising him. Just like that wistful note in her voice did. "All the women in my house do is snipe at each other. But your mom is always cool, elegant. Quiet. And perfectly capable of handling horses, people, and anything else that pops up with the same ease."

She seemed to remember herself then, and that was a shame. Riley had to fight to stay where he was. Not to go put his hands on her again, the way he suspected he could in that moment.

Because if he did, he could pick her up and have her again, the way he wanted her.

He had to remind himself that wasn't the only way he wanted her.

But it was harder than it should have been when she looked at him, too much turmoil in that gaze of hers.

"Riley . . . ," she began.

"I knew you were hungry," he said, ignoring the way she'd said his name. He crossed to her then, but only to swipe up the plate. He took both and dropped them in the sink, congratulating himself on his restraint.

"I saw your sister earlier." He didn't turn back around when she spoke, and Rae sighed a little. "She had some opinions she wanted to share with me."

"Amanda is full of opinions. It's part of her charm."

Riley took his time turning around again, so he could lean back against the lip of the sink, cross his arms, and look casually unbothered.

He figured he hit his mark when Rae blinked.

"I really didn't come here for . . . Because I get that it's . . . a pretty intense mixed message."

"I don't see any reason for us to tie ourselves up in knots on this." Again, Riley kept his voice low, the way he would if he and a horse were coming to terms. "And I don't see why, until one of us really does move on, we should ignore the benefit side of our friendship."

"Are you really suggesting we carry on exactly as we always have, but we . . . call it something different?"

"Modern dating can be overwhelming, I hear. Why not make sure that you relax when you can?" He grinned when she shot him a look. "What? I'm trying to help you."

"Right. That's what this is. *Help*."

Riley wanted nothing more than to jump on that. But she was laughing again, and he wanted to bask in that as long as he could. And the more she laughed, the more they veered away from the intensity. He knew that he had to let that happen.

Because there would be time enough for intensity when she came back to him.

Riley grinned. He kept his hands to himself and his body across the room like a man who didn't particularly care if she came or went.

Like a *friend*.

"That's exactly what this is," he told her, easy and care-free and so friendly he thought he might have dislocated something. "What are friends for?"

13

"I'm considering dating Tate Bishop," Rae announced one evening further into November as Hope moved around the kitchen, busy preparing dinner for the house because it was her designated night to cook.

The Mortimer sisters might like to give every appearance of being completely disorganized at the shop, but that was not how they ran their home. There was a giant chore wheel that hung on the wall the kitchen, breaking down daily and weekly chores between the three of them, including the preparation of dinners every night except Sunday.

When Rae tried to pitch in, determined to do her part, the sisters didn't like it. And refused her help.

Of course you can't help, Hope had said with a laugh when Rae had pointed this out to her. *How would we compete to be the greatest Mortimer saint of all time if you're here, lightening the load?*

She was the only one who allowed Rae to help her out, but only when it was one of her nights to cook. And tonight, she straightened from the pot she was stirring on the stove and turned around to give Rae a long look.

"What?"

The look intensified. "You know what, Rae."

"If I knew, I wouldn't ask you to clarify."

"Why are you picking anyone?" Hope demanded.

"I didn't say I was *picking* him. I said I thought maybe I should try *dating* him."

"Right, except I know you. You're going to settle on him, literally become blind to the existence of anybody else, and then what? Replay your entire relationship with Riley Kittredge?"

Rae jolted at that, though she tried to conceal it. "Unlikely. Since I'm not a teenager. And as far as I can tell, neither is Tate."

Hope shook her head, and the way she turned back to her pot somehow made it worse. As if she *despaired* of Rae. "I get that you have a plan. That you want to date with purpose. But you haven't actually dated anyone yet, Rae."

"I'm a dating machine," Rae argued. "There was dancing with Tate Bishop. And a drink. And I had coffee with Noah Connelly."

Hope made a derisive noise. "You had coffee in the coffeehouse Noah Connelly owns. And he spoke to you, yes, but that doesn't qualify as a date."

That was technically true. "And then that night he came to the Broken Wheel, where I'm becoming a barfly."

"He always comes to the Broken Wheel on Wednesday nights. You don't know that because you're not actually a barfly."

"I have dressed up. I have flung my hair around. I have *had a drink* with whoever asks me."

"So the one time, then."

"I have *scoped out the local talent,* which I thought was the entire point of wearing deeply impractical shoes on the cold, frozen streets of town. Night after night."

"Do you like Tate Bishop, Rae?" Hope looked back over her shoulder. "Do you think he likes you?"

"What I think," Rae said, trying to keep her voice as steady as possible when she didn't know why it wasn't already, "is that I'm running out of time."

Hope studied her for a moment that seemed to go on for far too long. "Have you found a lawyer?"

"What?"

"A lawyer, Rae." Hope's brows rose. "They're generally recommended for things like divorces."

Rae hadn't given a single stray thought to finding a divorce lawyer. Or to the mechanics of a divorce, for that matter. Deep inside, she felt that sharp blade prick at her. "I'm weighing my options."

"Have you filed?" Hope's gaze was far too steady. "You know you can download the forms from the internet, right?"

"I'm on it," Rae assured her, smiling as Hope turned back to the stove.

She was not, in fact, on it. When she should have been. For a hundred reasons, but mostly because the game she and Riley were playing now was, in many ways, more dangerous than the one they'd been playing all these years.

Unlike Hope, he seemed to take a particular delight in talking about her dating options.

But she could hardly tell Hope that. Because if she did, she would have to tell Hope when, exactly, these discussions with him took place.

And Rae found she wasn't prepared to announce to her friends all the benefits her friendship with Riley now contained. Benefits in her truck. In his. Benefits in the stockroom of the flower shop in broad daylight, when any customer might walk into the store. Or worse, a family member. Benefits everywhere, if very rarely at night, because Rae had no idea how she would explain sneaking off to her new roommates.

It felt like a before-and-after picture. Before, they'd been stuck in the wreckage of their marriage. Fighting, exploding with it, lighting up the night with that impossible passion that always flared between them. Now there was a lot more laughter. Silliness, even. They talked more than they had in years—though not about all the huge things that had torn them apart. About their lives, not their losses. Their parents. Their siblings. Their opinions about other people's scandals instead of their own. Their shared memories. This valley they'd both been born and bred in and knew inside out.

And all kinds of benefits.

So many benefits it could almost make her head spin, except this was about friendship. Only friendship.

There will be no head spinning, she lectured herself sternly, setting the table in the kitchen where the Mortimer sisters gathered every night for their family dinner. *Friends do not* spin, *no matter what benefits they might enjoy.*

"That smells like Aunt Helen's stew," Charity declared as she came in through the side door, bringing a rush of snow with her. She stepped out of her boots and pulled off her knit hat, shaking the remaining snowflakes out of her dark curls. "I must have died and gone to heaven."

"It will be a pale imitation," Hope replied from the stove, though she was smiling. "You might not want to get too excited."

"It will be *amazing*," Charity said fervently.

She smiled at Rae, then disappeared into the house, singing all the way. Only to reappear a few moments later, having changed into cozy flannel pajamas and what she called her *house boots,* fuzzy slippers with rubber soles.

Charity dropped down into a chair at the table.

"How was church today?" Hope asked. "Ripe with all the usual whispers and gossip?"

Charity rolled her eyes. "Theresa Galace accused me, not in so many words, of having *designs* on Pastor Jim."

"Pastor Jim is old enough to be your father!" Rae protested, though she shouldn't have been shocked. Charity was the church secretary, a position a great many members of the congregation felt she did not deserve, given her youth.

Something they made clear in all kinds of ways.

"Theresa Galace is obviously projecting," Hope said from the stove. "And *she* could be his mother."

"Pastor Jim is a hot commodity." Charity shrugged at Rae's expression. "His poor wife has been dead over a year now. The ladies line up to see him every day. Luckily, they no longer come bearing casseroles, but you may be surprised to learn that for certain segments of the Longhorn Valley female population, this fall is a time of great spiritual upheaval that only the pastor can help them navigate."

They were all laughing about that when Faith swept in, tall and regal with a cloak swirling around her as if the snow dared not fall upon her head on her quick walk from the store to the house. Rae had always found the oldest Mortimer sister particularly intimidating. Living under the same roof with her hadn't changed that. There was something about Faith that always made Rae feel as if she ought to apologize.

But she'd discovered long ago that it only made things worse—or more awkward, anyway—if she did.

Maybe the lesson was, no family was perfect. Or even comfortable all the time.

"That almost smells like Aunt Helen's stew," Faith said when she came back into the kitchen after she, too, went off to her bedroom to change her clothes. Though her version of loungewear looked like an upgrade. She inhaled as she paused at the stove. "But without the rosemary?"

Hope rolled her eyes as Faith glided to the refrigerator to pour herself a glass of wine. "I appreciate you being disappointed in advance."

Then she made a small production out of dishing out the savory-smelling stew into bowls.

Rae knew better than to catch anyone's eye in the middle of these sisterly exchanges. She concentrated on the fresh bread she'd baked earlier—the contribution she'd been grudgingly allowed to make. She grabbed the basket she'd put it in and carried it over to the table. Then she accepted the glass of wine that Charity handed her, having liberated the wine bottle from Faith.

"I don't think I expressed disappointment," Faith was saying. "I said that there's not the same amount of rosemary that Aunt Helen puts into her version. It wasn't a personal attack, Hope."

"It's your turn to cook tomorrow night," Hope pointed out as she started shuttling the heavy bowls of stew to the table. "You can do it correctly and wow us all. I can't wait."

"*Well,*" Rae said brightly once Hope set down a bowl of stew at every place and sat down herself. "I don't know what this is supposed to smell like, but it looks delicious to me."

Across from her, Charity shook her head slightly over the rim of her wineglass.

"Are you leaping to Hope's defense?" Faith asked, giving Rae the full force of her attention. "Honestly. I know Hope is very sensitive, but I wasn't attacking her. I promise."

"This is Faith being *helpful*," Hope explained in an exaggerated tone. "She wants to *help* me."

"Bread?" Charity asked, thrusting the basket at Rae.

Rae took it gratefully. Though she only found herself relaxing again when the arch, barbed conversation subsided and they all started talking about their bookstore, the major unifying force between them. That and their insistence that they were all single forever because they were cursed.

"I didn't realize you knew Jensen Kittredge," Rae said, much later, with her belly full of stew and too many slices of bread slathered with butter. She was sitting back in her chair, contemplating whether or not she wanted to celebrate the choices she'd already made tonight with dessert.

"Everybody knows Jensen Kittredge," Faith replied.

Faith was neither Rae's particular friend nor Rae's sister, so there was no opening for Rae to ask her why, exactly, she had to make every conversation a battleground. She knew Hope had asked her sister that very question on more than one occasion. But there were never any satisfactory answers.

"That's not what I meant." Rae already regretted attempting to have a conversation with Faith. "You know him enough to actually sit and have a conversation." She wanted to stammer under the force of Faith's gaze. She didn't, somehow. "About his brother's ex-wife, even."

"Is that an accusation?" Faith asked coolly.

Rae blinked. "No! No, of course not." She cast around wildly, not sure how this conversation had gone off the rails so quickly. A glance at the other two Mortimer sisters was not helpful. Charity was still shaking her head. Hope looked entertained. "I always think of Jensen as someone who talks around you, loudly. Not someone you would sit and have an actual conversation with."

"I have all manner of conversations, Rae," Faith replied. "Even with the likes of Jensen Kittredge."

"Oh, come on," Hope burst out then. "Will you stop?" She didn't wait for Faith to answer. She refilled her wineglass, then leaned over to fill Rae's as well. "Don't pay her any attention, Rae. She's been in a mood all day."

Charity laughed. "When is she not in a mood?"

"She's having a full-blown panic attack," Hope continued. "A responsibility overload, you might even say. Mom and Aunt Helen were supposed to be coming home for Thanksgiving. They promised."

"Their promises are worthless," Charity said airily. "Why am I the only one who realizes this?"

"I don't care if they come home for the holiday." Faith sounded as if, actually, she minded very much. "Any holiday. The last thing I need is Mom barreling through the house, ordering us all around."

"Faith suffers from oldest-child syndrome," Hope said sweetly. "She doesn't feel alive unless she feels truly forced to be overly responsible for something."

"Thank you for dinner," Faith said primly. She rose from her seat, swept up her glass of wine—and the wine bottle—as she went, and then left the room.

"The question is," Hope said as Faith walked into their family room, "what kind of night is it?"

Charity made a face. "You already know the answer, Hope."

They heard the television go on. The sound of Faith arranging herself in her preferred position on the couch, so she could slam her wineglass and wine bottle down on the side table with abandon. Then the opening notes of the program she'd chosen began to play.

"The *eight-hour Pride and Prejudice*," Charity said in mock astonishment. "And here I was sure it was going to be a Keira Knightley kind of a night."

"Stop talking about me," came Faith's voice from the other room. "I'm not pausing the show, so if you want to watch, you'd better get in here."

Charity did exactly that, while Hope and Rae remained at the table, grinning at each other.

"I only promised you a room," Hope said quietly. "Not domestic bliss."

Rae took another piece of bread, because she could do what she wanted. "Why isn't your mother coming home for Thanksgiving?"

Hope rolled her eyes. "Who knows? I could tell you the excuse she gave, but that's all it is. An excuse. She doesn't *want* to come home."

"Do you want her to?" Rae pulled the thick slice of bread apart with her fingers. "When she's not here, you're the co-owner of a bookstore. If she comes home, you're just an employee again. I'm not sure you'd like that."

"I don't know that I want my mother to come home," Hope said after a moment. Her gaze met Rae's. "But it would be nice if she wanted to, you know?"

That scraped at Rae, though she looked away, so her friend couldn't see.

"I've got the dishes," she said. And the Thanksgiving thing must have been bothering Hope more than she wanted to admit, because she let Rae do it.

Rae was just finishing wiping off the table when Hope sailed back in from the other room, where she'd left her sisters laughing.

Hope leaned back against the counter. "Are you going out tonight?"

"Not after you told me I was dating incorrectly, no."

"I think that maybe, just maybe, I suggested that you actually date people awhile before you settle on one. As that's the actual purpose of dating."

"Says the woman who refuses to date anyone."

"If I wanted what you say you want, I would," Hope said simply.

Rae felt entirely too . . . naked, suddenly. As if Hope were seeing things in her it had never occurred to her to even look for.

"I don't want to go out tonight," she said with as much dignity as possible. She inclined her head toward the other room, where, on-screen, the Bennet family was very noisily discussing the new arrivals to Meryton. "Should I make popcorn?"

There was only one answer to that. Once Rae had made a few heaping bowls, she brought out the various toppings that the sisters preferred. Then she settled down in her own seat in the armchair next the couch where the Mortimers piled together, all the dinner table squabbling forgotten. She pulled her feet up beneath her, gazed at the screen, and found herself completely unable to pay attention to the show she'd seen a thousand times before.

Was Hope right? Had she decided to pick someone simply so she wouldn't have to spend any time choosing? That hardly made sense.

Just like the fact that she hadn't started her divorce proceedings didn't make sense.

But the real truth was, when she closed her eyes and tried to daydream about divorcing Riley and dating Tate Bishop, she just . . . found herself thinking about Riley.

Who she'd seen this morning, in the dark, when he'd

picked her up while she was walking to work and presented her with her coffee done just right. And had then taught her a few things about herself right there, in the dark, with his hands all over her.

Benefits, baby, he'd said with a grin before he'd driven away.

And despite *Pride and Prejudice* and this cozy house she got to live in with friends, she found herself daydreaming about that until she went to bed.

Then dreaming about it all night.

When she got to the shop the next morning, she opened it up and settled into a new day that might or might not offer her further *benefits*. It was a slow morning. When the bell jangled over the door while she was fussing over an anniversary arrangement for an older couple she knew from church, she looked up quickly, her body already shivering into awareness.

But it wasn't Riley.

It was her grandmother.

"Um, hi, Grandma Inez," Rae said, standing straighter. And trying not to sound alarmed. "I didn't know you were coming into town."

Inez cast an eye over the shop, looking for flaws. And, if the way her lips curved down was any indication, found many.

But then, all Inez looked for was flaws. Therefore, flaws were all she found.

Rae knew that and still, when Inez turned that same look on her, found herself standing straighter as if *this time* she might actually impress the woman who couldn't be impressed.

Someday, she thought, she would grow out of this.

Someday, she wouldn't care anymore whether or not

her grandmother loved her. Or was even vaguely supportive of her.

But today was apparently not that day.

"I had lunch with Marisol Dewitt," her grandmother replied, and paused as if she expected Rae to . . . genuflect, or something, at the name of one of the old ladies her grandmother played bridge with while plotting the downfall of their many enemies. "Can you explain to me why our family is not providing the floral arrangements for the Harvest Gala this year? For the first and only time in *decades*?"

Rae blinked. She glanced down at her calendar, but that was more of a reflex. Because she already knew that there was a Harvest Gala issue. She had her designs tested and ready, but no confirmation. Something she'd meant to call about, but she'd been distracted.

By her *benefits*.

She felt certain her grandmother would use a different word. Like *selfishness*.

And she also knew the answer. She'd meant to follow up on it before she'd gone racing off to Riley's place after the confrontation in Cold River Coffee that had led to all these supposed benefits in the first place. *Amanda*.

"I don't think we're *not* doing the arrangements," she said to her grandmother as soothingly as possible.

Not that it appeared to help.

Or did anything for the rising tide of guilt inside her that she'd completely dropped the ball on this.

Why *hadn't* she even looked up how to start the process of divorcing? Why was she letting Riley distract her when she was supposed to be moving on? Why was she pretending she wanted to date other people when she very clearly didn't?

What was she *doing*?

"How can you not *know*?" Inez asked, aghast. "You're supposed to be in complete control of the Flower Pot. You're supposed to have a handle on all events, not just those little weddings you like to do. Do you need more oversight?"

What Rae needed, she thought darkly, was to get her head on straight.

A few rounds with Inez and the sheer injustice of having her ability to run the shop no one else in the family cared about—until they did—called into question might just do the trick.

"I haven't been able to get the committee chair on the phone," she said quietly, still standing too straight. Still too aware that she was a failure in her grandmother's eyes no matter what she did. And still too affected by the judgment she could see in Inez's gaze—especially when she was judging herself so harshly at the same time. "But I'll be sure to chase her down and fix this, Grandma. I promise."

14

Riley spent the better part of each day convincing an uppity horse or two to settle down. Some days, the horses won. And knew it, more often than not. But today, he left them feeling that he had the upper hand, for once.

When he finally left the stables, there was still some daylight left. His boots crunched into the cold earth as he walked across the yard, his eyes not on the light spilling out from the ranch house where he'd grown up, witness to his parents' various wars—cold and hot alike—but across the frozen pasture to where his grandparents' house stood. There was smoke coming out of the chimney, and Riley knew that if he headed over, his grandparents would be puttering around the way they always were. Easing into their evening with their time-honored rituals and habits that Riley had always found more comforting than he liked to admit.

He could smell the wood smoke in the air, fighting with the fresh, cold scent of the coming winter, and that, too, was a comfort. It reminded him of being much smaller, sneaking out of the ranch house while his mother shouted and his father growled out his patented nonresponses. He and his brothers would run as fast as they could across that pasture no matter if the snow was nearly over their heads. Riley could remember the cold like a tight fist around his chest, his breath coming in short, hard scrapes. The exhilaration and terror of being out in the night, as if he had to be careful or he'd slide straight off the world and into the heavy, dark sky.

He couldn't tell if he missed that feeling or longed for it.

It made him think of Rae.

Everything makes you think of Rae, he growled at himself.

Riley swung into his truck and headed down the drive, thinking he would take the dirt road over to his grandparents' house even though it was the long way around. The road was currently nothing but two deep, parallel grooves in the few feet of snow remaining from the last storm, but this time of year, a ten-minute drive was better than staggering across that pasture in the snowdrifts.

Or maybe you still think the sky is going to get you.

He was smirking at that as he bumped his way down the drive. But when he got down to the fork that headed out to the county road, eventually, or back over to his grandparents' house, there was another truck in the way.

Zack.

Riley maneuvered his truck out of the set tracks while Zack did the same, so they could come up alongside each other, driver's window to driver's window.

His grandfather liked to cackle and call this kind of communication *old-school email.*

Zack wasn't in uniform. He rarely was. Even when he was on duty, he preferred the emblazoned SHERIFF on the side of his truck and the badge he wore pinned to the front of his coat to make his announcements for him.

And Riley could have worked up an objection to the way his oldest brother looked at him then, all cool-eyed and assessing, but that wasn't a sheriff thing. It was just Zack. Becoming a cop and then winning the sheriff's position had only made his natural inclinations worse.

"I was heading over to check on Grandma and Grandpa," Riley said, grinning genially and drawling more than necessary because he knew it irritated his brother. And as such was his calling. "What are you doing out here? Not enough to do in Mayberry?"

Zack eyed him. "Just as funny as when I was a deputy."

"Glad you're in your usual sparkling good mood," Riley said. He thumbed his hat because acting like a cowpoke of the first order always got on Zack's nerves. "Don't let me keep you from sharing it with someone else. It looked like Mom and Dad were home if you're looking for worthy recipients."

Because most of the Kittredge brothers liked to avoid their parents, but not Zack. He brought new meaning to the term *confrontational*.

"Actually, I was looking for you," Zack said.

"Was I robbing banks again? I hate when that happens."

"Not robbing banks. But I'm betting that if I'd actually investigated what was going on in your truck outside the Flower Pot after I saw Rae Trujillo climb inside yesterday, I could probably arrest both of you for indecent exposure."

That was . . . unexpected.

Riley tried to maintain his poker face. "You'd lose that bet."

That was the truth. There had been no actual, technical *exposure*. Not that he intended to argue the point. Or discuss where, precisely, his hands might have been.

He watched a muscle tense in his brother's lean jaw. "I don't know where to start," Zack said gruffly.

"Then don't. Problem solved."

"How about the fact that the two of you are grown, supposedly. Yet you're running around like teenagers. Sooner or later, it's not going to be me who sees you. And then what?"

"Like you said, we're all grown up. It doesn't actually matter if people see us."

Zack glared. "That kind of depends on what you're doing. Because I highly doubt it's a Bible study, which as I recall is the excuse you tried to float when the two of you were in high school."

Riley stared back at him. "I had no idea you were paying such close attention to my teenage years. I'm touched."

Zack's elbow was resting on his open window, pretending to be casual. Too bad Riley could see his face. "Not to mention all the carrying on in the Broken Wheel. With that Tate Bishop character, even. What's *that*? Or did you suddenly decide to be kinkier that I thought you were and start sharing—"

"Not big on sharing," Riley clipped out. "Comes from having too many brothers, I'm guessing."

"Meanwhile, you're telling everybody that you're 'friends.'" Zack shook his head. "Is this her influence?"

Riley laughed at that. "Her *influence*? I don't even know what that means."

"As far as I know, you've been straight with Rae since the day you started dating her," Zack said. Intensely.

So intensely that it made Riley blink and recall his own overinvestment in Amanda and Brady's relationship initially. If this was what that felt like, no wonder Amanda had told off half the world and him in particular. He wanted to take a swing at Zack—or, alternatively, laugh in his face.

He was retroactively embarrassed for himself. And definitely wanted to knock his brother's head off.

Especially because Zack was still pushing. "You built her a house. You married her. And she left you, Riley. She keeps leaving you. Now she's living in town, making her way through the single population. And you're still in that house. Still picking her up in your truck. Still acting like a whipped little puppy."

Ouch.

He tried a grin but was pretty sure he missed the mark. "You're pretty lucky you're saying that to me with the frames of two trucks between us."

"Every day, I wake up thankful that you didn't have any kids with her," Zack told him, his usually calm voice hot enough to suggest he really meant it. "Because it's bad enough when she does these things to you. Can you imagine if there were kids involved?"

Riley was taken aback. Not sure how he was supposed to feel about his brother showing all this . . . fervor. It was true that Riley had no interest in kids. He and Rae had agreed on that, at least. But he couldn't say he liked having Zack jump in with commentary on the subject.

And most of all, he didn't like Zack talking about Rae.

"You're being a little harsh on Rae, don't you think?" Zack stared back at him. "No."

"Guess what? I do. And it's my opinion that matters, not yours, because I'm the one in it."

But Zack stared back at him, unmoved.

"No, I wasn't stupid enough to have children," Riley continued, aware his voice was harsh. It was better than trying to slug the sheriff. He had no doubt Zack would take pleasure in locking him up. "I notice you're not exactly racing to expand the family tree yourself. I spent half my life watching Brady's drunk father rip that family apart and the rest of my time watching Mom and Dad prove that no one needs to be drunk to have a terrible marriage."

And he couldn't say he liked the way his own words settled in him. Because he and Rae hadn't been drunk and disorderly, either. They'd never had that excuse.

He shoved that aside. "Why would I ever put a kid through that? Why would anyone?"

"Funny how when it comes to kids that don't exist, you can see sense. But when it comes to you? You're a glutton for punishment."

"I didn't ask for your take on my life, but thanks."

"I don't get it," Zack retorted. "Sure, she's pretty, Riley. But the two of you are poison. And I think you deserve better than whatever scraps she throws your way when she's not cuddling up to other guys in public."

"You need to stop. Now."

But Zack shook his head in that cold, authoritative way of his. "Don't defend her to me. I'm not Amanda. I'm not going to get in Rae's face. It's not her fault that my little brother can't seem to see straight where she's concerned. But it's time to wake up, buddy. She's never coming back."

Riley would have preferred it if Zack punched him. Right in the face. "You don't understand the situation."

Zack's gaze was entirely too direct. "I think you'll find I do understand it. I know exactly how broken up you haven't been. But her moving into Hope's house is a sign, Riley. Make a clean break. Be done."

"Thank you for the advice," Riley gritted out, so tense he was surprised he could form words. "It's particularly meaningful coming from you, a control freak who's had exactly zero meaningful relationships in his entire life."

"Yeah, I have issues. Big deal. My issues haven't been

playing cat-and-mouse games with me since I was a teenager. My issues don't treat me like crap while I'm waiting out in a house I built for them like it's a vigil."

"Enough," Riley growled. "I heard you."

"I hope so," Zack retorted. "Because if I see the two of you acting like teenagers again, I'll treat you like teenagers. And you're not going to like it."

"I don't know which is worse," Riley threw back at him. "The threats or the advice. Maybe pick a stream, Zack, because you suck at both."

Before his brother could get even more sheriff-y—or worse, big-brother-y—Riley threw his truck into drive. He made his way around Zack until he was back in the deep grooves of snow and, because maybe he really was a saint, did not reverse to give Zack a little bump in place of a fist or two.

And then, because he refused to let his brother change his plans no matter how the things Zack had said sat on him, he continued on to his grandparents' house.

Inside, his grandmother fussed and insisted on feeding him. Riley sat in the front room that smelled the way it always did, tart and sweet, and let her. His grandfather had the game on, and neither one of them asked him about Rae. Only his horses, whether he wanted another serving of his grandma's potato salad, and what his father was planning to do with the north pasture.

By the time he made it home, Riley couldn't decide if he was relaxed or agitated. Some strange combination of both, but either way, when he finished tending to his own home and stable—*his* home and stable, no matter what Zack seem to think—he washed up and headed into town.

Even though he knew that what he really ought to do was stay home, if only to prove he had no particular *need* to go out. Nothing drawing on him, making it impossible to sit still in his own house.

He decided he was pissed at Rae and Zack equally.

But he still went.

By the time he made the drive into town, over the icy hill that could turn treacherous in a moment, the usual Saturday-night shenanigans were in full swing. Down by the river, the Coyote was doing its usual brisk business. More restaurants seemed to be full this time of year than in years past, which, as a local businessman and landowner, he liked to see. Even if he would personally rather beat his head against a wall than eat out at, say, the Sensitive Spoon, with such offerings as *quinoa cutlets*. Whatever those were.

Inside the Broken Wheel, there was a band playing, and the place was more packed than usual. But that was a good thing. Because Riley didn't like the fact that Zack had seen right through him—and apparently had been seeing right through him for some time. And since he was nursing that particular body blow, he was happy to do without the entire town staring at him the way they always did when it was only locals and gossip.

He nodded at the folks he recognized as he made his way to the bar and got himself a drink. He chatted a little with Tessa behind the bar, exchanged a few words here and there with folks who happened by, and spent a lot of time assuring himself that just because *Zack* seemed to know things he shouldn't, that didn't mean anyone else was sitting around taking notes on Riley's life.

But it rang hollow.

And he wasn't even looking for Rae, but he found her. Out there in the middle of the dance floor with two of the three Mortimer sisters. She had her head tilted back and her arms up as she danced, and it was like another punch.

This one to the gut.

And a whole lot harder.

He hadn't wanted any clarity when it was Zack trying to deliver it, but here it was anyway. In an unavoidable rush.

Riley was in love with her. He had never stopped being in love with her. And he might spend a lot of time telling himself that she was in love with him, too, no matter what she did or said. That might even be true. He thought it was.

He knew it was.

But the facts were pretty clear. She'd left him a long time ago, and she hadn't come back.

Not to stay.

And like Zack had pointed out, little as Riley wanted to hear it, when she'd moved again, it had been farther away from him.

All of this, all these years and all the games they'd played before and after she'd told him she wanted a divorce—another sign he'd chosen not to heed—was an extended exercise in futility. A desperate attempt to hold on to something that he probably should have let go of a long, long time ago.

Riley kept thinking that if he hit on the right argument, or played the right game, Rae would remember that back in high school she'd loved him so much and so deeply that she'd cried sometimes when they'd gone to sleep in their different houses. She'd insisted that they go to sleep still on their phones, so they could hear each other breathe.

He couldn't accept that they'd lost that. That it was irretrievable. Maybe he never would.

But he also couldn't accept this.

Maybe he was right. Maybe she was going to go out there and date around and realize she was making a terrible mistake. But he didn't have to help her do that.

They weren't friends. They'd never been friends. She was the love of his life. She'd been, for a while, his wife. She was the only one he'd ever wanted to share his life with.

But if she didn't want that, he shouldn't want her.

Riley didn't know how to stop wanting Rae. But he figured it probably had to start here. With him.

Even if he had no idea how to go about changing himself from the inside out.

The song ended, and Rae staggered off the dance floor, her arm around Hope as they laughed and shouted things into each other's ears. She was wearing another dress that made his heart threaten his rib cage. She was glowing from the exertion out there, and her hair was messy enough to make him remember all the times it looked that way thanks to his hands.

But it wasn't that she was pretty, though she was. God knew she was. It was that she was his.

You need to let go of this, he ordered himself.

Rae didn't make it any easier. She looked up and saw him, and Riley watched her whole face light up. The way it had years ago, before they'd spent all that time pretending not to see each other in public.

She cut through the crowd, once again wearing ridiculously high shoes that made her taller, but still nothing approaching *tall*. She barely came up to his shoulder when she stopped in front of him, and she was always beautiful. She was Rae.

But tonight, she seemed radiant to him. She was piling that silky, wavy hair of hers on top of her head as she smiled up at him.

"I didn't think you were coming," she said. "I guess our current benefit package doesn't include texts."

"I think that qualifies as bells and whistles," he said, and reasoned that he didn't jump right into it because that would be rude. Too abrupt.

Unlike when she left you the first time. Or all those other times. Or when she showed up on your front porch last month and announced that you needed to divorce.

He shoved that voice away because it sounded far too much like Zack's.

"I'm surprised you're out at all," he said, and the fact he knew her life intimately seemed like another punch to the gut. How could they share everything, one way or another, and still not work? And how was he going to find a way to be okay with never knowing the answer to that? "The Harvest Gala's next week. Shouldn't you be hard at work on all those centerpieces?"

Her smile faltered. "I am hard at work. So hard at work that I thought it might be time to come out and shake it off. You know me. I love the Harvest Gala. I haven't missed one in years."

Neither had he, of course. They usually pretended not to glare at each other as usual there, only in nicer clothes.

Everything his brother had said to him seemed to crowd in on him, as if Zack were standing right there before him, watching him sternly. Riley did not enjoy the sensation. But that didn't make the things Zack had said any less true.

It didn't change the things he actually felt.

No time like the present, he thought.

"Who are you bringing as your date?" he asked.

He watched her freeze, then blink in confusion. Her gaze moved over his face as if she hadn't understood what he'd said.

"My date?"

"It's one of the fanciest events of the year," Riley pointed out, in case she might have missed that every other year she'd attended. "Most people go with a date."

"Yes," she said, sounding flustered. "But I don't. You don't. We've both been going on our own for years."

"It's not so surprising that the whole town thinks we've been together all this time. Or anyway, involved in some other complicated drama that kept us from taking a date like any normal person would have. It's kind of funny that never occurred to us, isn't it?"

"I'm not sure I'd call it funny."

Riley could see something flicker on her face then . . . but he told himself it couldn't be helped. Maybe Zack was right. That they really were poison.

Because surely, if they loved each other as much as he'd always thought they did, no matter what, there wouldn't be all this hurt.

"Are you really . . . ?" Rae began.

But she faltered.

Riley waited. He wanted her to ask the question. Because if it were up to him, he wasn't sure he'd do it. Or he'd default to that temper he'd been keeping locked up since that night she'd come to drop her divorce bomb on him.

No good could come of him letting his temper loose. No good ever had, as far as he could see. But it was high time he reminded her that they were supposed to be friends. And they might have been indulging in some benefits lately, but they were never supposed to be acting like they were *together*.

It was high time he reminded himself of the same thing.

Rae only stared at him, almost as if she knew they were standing at the end of a huge cliff. Steep and unforgiving.

Possibly final, Riley admitted privately. He had to be ready for that.

"I hope you're bringing a date this year, Rae," he said at last.

And he grinned at her, as friendly as he could, to underscore the point that this was supposed to be casual. Easy. Not one more version of the same old song he was so sick of, it hurt.

Ready or not, he told himself. "Because I am."

15

Riley was bringing a date to the Harvest Gala.

Rae couldn't seem to get that out of her head. It throbbed there at her temples like a migraine.

She spent the next day brooding about it, and a trip out to her parents' house for Sunday dinner didn't make it any better. Especially not with her grandmother there, haranguing her about her failures to confirm the center-pieces until Rae's mother—unable to engage Inez in one of their usual battles—joined in.

"There must be some mistake," Kathy said, frowning at Rae. "The Trujillo family has always contributed to the gala. Has something changed? I thought you were handling all the retail accounts and charity events."

"I am." Rae tried to smile. But it was a stretch when she had not, in fact, handled it. Because *handling it* meant dealing with Amanda again, and to her great shame, she was avoiding it. She had been avoiding Amanda for years now. For good reason, as their last run-in at the coffee shop had proved. "I'm taking care of it."

But no matter how many times Rae tried to assure the two of them that she was on it, they kept circling back. Almost as if they knew she wasn't telling them the complete truth. She was forced to acknowledge that maybe it was better when they focused their spite and ire on each other.

"Who knew you two made such a great team?" she asked on round fifty or so of the interrogation.

"What matters is the Trujillo family name," Inez said severely.

"Or that's what ought to matter, Rae," Kathy said, still frowning. "I would have thought you knew that, as the primary contact point for the family in the Flower Pot. I hope we don't have to revisit our roles."

"Like how?" Matias asked. He'd spent the bulk of the interrogation talking quietly with their father, the two of them pretending not to notice what was happening.

Too little, too late, jerk, Rae thought, glaring at him.

He ignored her glare. "I don't think we want me making flower arrangements. That won't end well. And we all know Grandma's arthritis means she can't keep up with demand the way she used to."

"That's not the point," Kathy argued.

"I get it. You want to make Rae feel bad." Matias's mouth curved a little as he gazed back at their mother and grandmother. "Mission accomplished."

Neither Inez nor Kathy liked to admit they could ever be in the wrong. Instead, they simply slid into one of their other long-standing sniping matches, this one concerning the long-disputed Blue Chair Incident. Who had torn the upholstery of the blue chair in the living room? Who had replaced it the first time? The second? And most crucially, which one of them had better taste in decorating?

None of these questions were ever answered to anyone's satisfaction.

Rae made her escape as soon as she could, following Matias out into the sharp punch of the cold, sharp enough to take her breath away for a moment.

"Are you going to the gala?" she asked her brother as they walked toward the same old trucks they'd both been driving forever, parked out by the fence. Matias's looked sleek and well cared for, and purred when it moved. Rae's looked like the vintage vehicle it was, and purred about as much as she did.

Meaning it did not.

"Trujillos always contribute to the gala, Rae," Matias replied, grinning at her. "You know that. Or did you not hear it mentioned nine hundred times tonight?"

"Never fear. I'll do my best to uphold the family honor through flowers."

Matias stopped before he rounded the back of his truck, looking at her a little more closely. "You need me to go beat someone up?"

It was such an offhanded offer. So matter-of-fact that she actually believed that if she told him she needed him to do just that, he would execute said older-brother beatdown in the same almost detached manner. Just a service he offered, like the morning deliveries from the greenhouses.

Absurdly, it made her want to giggle. "Do I look like I need someone beaten up?"

Matias shrugged. "You look like something."

Rae meant to smile, but she couldn't quite get her mouth to work. "Nothing I can't handle."

Because she couldn't say, *My ex-husband is bringing a date to the gala, he told me to bring a date, and I want to die.* Just like she couldn't say, *Said ex-husband's younger sister is running the gala, and she refuses to return my phone calls about the centerpieces.*

Matias might condemn Rae in this scenario, the way so many others did. He had never *said* he was on Team Riley. But he also hadn't signed up for her team, either. And there was always a lot of glowering . . .

She really wasn't sure she could handle it if she pushed him and he revealed that he didn't support her at all. She would rather hold on to this moment instead, where he was just her big brother. Without *opinions* about her life.

"That doesn't sound convincing," he said, studying her face.

"Thank you for offering to have my back, Matias. I would hug you, but I figure that would break your Marine code."

"No, but it would be gross." Matias grinned. "Cooties, you know. But, Rae."

She had been turning to open her door, but stopped.

"If you need reinforcements, you know where to find me," Matias said gruffly. Then slammed into his truck before she could do anything crazy, like force that hug on him. Something he only tolerated in small doses.

The next morning, when one of the hourly employees appeared for her shift, Rae told her to take over. She marched out, got into her truck, and drove herself to the Lavender Llama before she could talk herself out of it.

She parked out in front of the renovated barn and took her time getting out of her truck. And she wasn't *actually* dragging her feet, but she felt as if she were filled with lead as she walked across the little parking area and let herself in.

It was adorable, just as she'd heard. From literally everyone. More than adorable, it was the perfect mix of all the things that made Cold River the perfect mountain town, in Rae's opinion. Every surface in the barn was piled high with beautiful things that people Rae knew had created, grown, crafted, or prepared. Artisan jams. Local honey and cheeses. Freezers of Everett beef. Yarn and sculptures and pottery. It was a permanent local craft and growers' market.

A love letter to this valley and all the people in it. She

sighed a little, taking it in while her heart grew a few sizes.

When she heard movement behind her, she turned. And found Amanda standing there in the door to what she assumed was an office.

"This place is absolutely magical," Rae told her. She meant it. "It's like you made the entire Longhorn Valley come alive in one big room. I love it."

The Amanda that Rae had known when they were both younger could never have stared back with a face like stone, but this Amanda did it with seeming ease. It seemed like an uptick in hostility from their last run in. It made Rae's stomach hurt.

"I'm glad you like it," Amanda said evenly. "What are you doing here?"

Not unkindly. But not all that friendly, either.

Okay, then. Rae told herself to get right to it.

"The Trujillo family has provided centerpieces for the Harvest Gala since its inception," Rae said, choosing not to focus on the stone face before her. Or all the things she'd lost that always seemed to outweigh whatever new thing she was trying to do. This wasn't the place to dwell on . . . any of that. "I'm sure you know that."

"I'm aware of your family's contributions in past years, yes."

Rae smiled the way she did in the shop. At her most difficult customers. "It's hard not to take the new chairperson's disinterest in continuing that tradition personally. If I'm honest, it feels a lot like a vendetta."

"We're talking about flowers, Rae. Not pistols at dawn."

"No, we're talking about you deliberately messing with a beloved tradition because you're mad at me." Rae waved a hand at all the Longhorn Valley's finest goods, arrayed behind her. "Kind of like you've managed to track down every artist in the entire Longhorn Valley, but somehow never stopped by to ask if the Flower Pot, a Cold River institution, would like to be involved."

"I'm not required to include you in anything," Amanda said softly, though her gaze flickered. "Just like you're not required to stay married to my brother. These things happen, and we make the best of them."

And all the times in the past that Rae had run into Amanda, she'd been too busy drowning in her own guilt and loss and confusion to do more than shuffle off, miserably, and poke at her own wounds. The sharpest one first.

She'd never given an explanation. She'd waited for Amanda—and everyone else—to do what they would and had reacted accordingly. Rae had told herself it was a noble thing to refuse to defend herself, and maybe that was true when it came to gossipy old dragons like Lucinda Early.

But Amanda had once looked up to her. Rae had loved that.

Rae had loved *her*.

"Riley doesn't hate me, Amanda," she said softly. "Why do you?"

"He loves you," Amanda threw at her. "But I love *him*. I don't think you ever did."

That tore through Rae, and it shouldn't have. She blew out a breath, not entirely sure she was going to be able to remain on her own two feet. She felt dizzy and sick, and *incandescent* with the need to defend herself. To explain.

Just this once.

Instead, all she did was gaze back at this girl she still considered a younger sister. All the years and fighting and benefits in the world couldn't change that. She accepted that Amanda no longer felt that bond, truly she did. She even supported it, because she'd likely feel the same way if Matias were ever messed up about a woman.

But that didn't make Rae ache any less.

"I understand what you're doing," she said when she was sure she could speak without showing any of her inner turmoil. It was hers. She held it tightly, blade always facing her, and she felt it cut at her now. "But this is a small town, Amanda. You know that as well as anyone."

"What does that mean?"

Rae shrugged. "I don't think you're going to find you can throw a stone without hitting *someone* who has hurt feelings about some or other member of your family. All your brothers have exes right here in town. Are you going to bar them all from the Harvest Gala? It would be empty."

Amanda shifted where she stood. Rae took that as a minor triumph.

But her chin lifted, because she was as stubborn as any of her brothers. "I'm surprised you're even aware of the Harvest Gala this year. What do you care about a stuffy event from your old life when there's the Cold River social scene to throw yourself into?"

That was obviously intended to sting.

Rae decided she would die before showing that it did.

"My grandmother cares. A lot." She smiled at Amanda even though she didn't feel much like smiling. "Do you think maybe I should go talk to your grandmother? If memory serves, there's not a whole lot Janet Kittredge likes more than a Longhorn Valley tradition."

Amanda sighed. Then inclined her head slightly. "You make an excellent point."

Rae pushed her advantage. "I'm glad that we get to live in a place where our grandmothers' feelings matter.

It would be great if this were also a place we didn't have to hate each other because of a relationship that started when your brother and I were practically babies."

"I'm practically a baby," Amanda replied lightly, though her gaze was dark. "Ask anyone. They'll line up to tell you all about how I'm practically still in diapers. And yet I've managed not to treat anyone in my life the way you've treated Riley."

"I'm not going to debate you."

"Maybe you should!" Amanda threw at her, emotion all over her face. "Maybe you should *feel something,* Rae!"

Rae remembered this Amanda. The cute little girl with four overbearing older brothers, who had clung to Rae as if Rae were the only thing that might save her. When Rae's actual younger sister, Tory, had spent half her time annoying Rae and the other half acting like she wished Rae didn't exist.

Amanda had been intense and offbeat and *invested.*

She still was, clearly. "Maybe you should stop walking around letting everybody think the worst of you. It's like you *want* all the judgment and commentary and gossip. Is that it? *Do* you?"

Rae laughed, though it came out a little rough when her heart was kicking at her and her throat felt tight. "But everyone takes such pleasure in thinking the worst of me. I'd hate to deprive them."

Amanda didn't look made of stone now. She looked as if she ached as much as Rae did—and that made Rae shake deep inside.

"I don't understand how you could be so happy," Amanda said, her voice rougher. Quieter. "And then so miserable. I don't understand how it's possible."

"Not everything works out," Rae managed to say, her

eyes wet. "I know you're still a newlywed, but you know that. More marriages don't work out than do."

"But not yours," Amanda whispered. She lifted her hands, but then dropped them again as if she didn't know what to hold on to. Or how. "You two were supposed to last forever."

Rae understood that this was why she'd been avoiding Amanda all this time. Guilt and shame and hurt feelings were ways to hide. She could wallow in them, then quickly turn to self-righteousness. How *dare* people blame her, she *had* to leave, and so on. It fired her up and made her feel better about her choices.

Strip all that away and there was only this.

There was only grief.

Love turned upside down and emptied out.

"It's like flowers," Rae managed to get out, wishing she hadn't come here. Wishing she'd never started this conversation, no matter what her grandmother thought about the Harvest Gala. No matter what dinner table attacks she had to withstand. "They're beautiful. They make people happy. A little water and they can brighten up whole rooms. But they don't last, Amanda." Her voice was tellingly, horrifyingly thick. "They were never, ever supposed to last."

And she didn't wait for Amanda to reply to that. She couldn't. She wheeled around and bolted, pushing her way out into the glare of the too-cold morning, telling herself that the water on her face was from the frigid slap of the wind.

She wiped at her cheeks when she got in her truck, but her heart was pounding in a sickening sort of way that meant she could do nothing but sit there and *let* it. That Riley-shaped headache at her temples was blooming, punching in deep, and she could barely manage to get a breath in.

And all the while, deep inside, that sharp blade cut and cut and cut and warned her to keep her secrets to herself.

Sometimes she thought secrets were all she had.

"You're doing the right thing," she muttered at herself. Over and over again. "You *are*."

But instead of pointing her truck toward the Flower Pot and getting back to work the way she knew she should, she went to find Abby instead. Her friend wasn't working at Cold River Coffee today, a bored teenager with confusing hair informed her.

"She has reduced hours," the teenager said. Then, as if she expected this to be news to Rae, "She has a little kid. So."

Somehow, Rae did not take the teenager's head off. Or shout that she had held tiny little Bart Everett within a day of his birth, thank you very much.

Rae drove out of town, heading out into the sweeping, spectacular part of the valley that waited on the other side of the hill. She tried Cold River Ranch first, driving up the long dirt road to the sprawling Everett family ranch house that was a happier place these days entirely because of Abby.

And, okay, the other Everett additions too, she amended when Ty's wife, Hannah, appeared at the ranch house's kitchen door in all her rodeo queen glory, her mascara perfect and her blond hair missing only a tiara.

But then, with Hannah Everett, the tiara was always implied. Even when Abby could hear the overly eager sounds of a children's program playing from somewhere behind her, and excited cries from her little boy, Jack.

"Abby's next door, sugar," Hannah told her. "She and her grandma are getting ahead of the Thanksgiving baking, bless them."

And that was how Rae found herself five miles back in the other direction, pulling up outside the old Douglas farmhouse the way she had so many times before she could almost let the truck coast her into her usual parking spot on autopilot.

She shivered when she got out, sinking deeper into her coat. She hurried across the yard toward the farmhouse's kitchen door. Out back, the orchards where she and Abby and Hope had played as girls stood there, gnarled and empty this time of year and ominous against the cold gray sky.

They're not ominous, she corrected herself. *They're apples. Get a grip.*

Her heart had stopped beating quite so hard and heavy. Her throat wasn't quite so tight. But that grief was still there, wrapped around her, a grip she couldn't shake.

Still cutting at her way down deep.

Rae didn't knock on the farmhouse door. She threw it open and let herself in, almost tripping her way inside in her haste.

And instantly found herself wrapped up tightly in nostalgia and pie.

Abby and her grandmother were sitting at the sturdy kitchen table dusted with flour, cutting up fruit, making fillings in old glass bowls, and rolling out dough. Behind them, arrayed along the counter, the pies they'd already baked sat cooling.

Rae felt her eyes prickling with tears.

"I thought you were working today," Abby said mildly.

Martha Douglas eyed Rae over the heap of fruit before her, her hands almost as gnarled as the orchard's bare branches outside. But there was nothing ominous about the way she wielded her paring knife. Her hands were nimble and quick and infinitely comforting.

"I've never turned down an extra pair of hands," she said in her usual matter-of-fact way.

Rae felt as if something inside her was quivering. Like someone had hit a tuning fork and it was vibrating so loudly that it should have been shaking the walls of the house. The whole way out here, she'd been desperate to get to Abby, sure that her friend was the only one who could settle her. Make sense of her. Make this mess she'd been in for years seem reasonable and rational, because that was what Abby did.

Because try as she might, Rae couldn't seem to dislodge the conversation she'd had with Amanda. It was pressing down on her like stone. Every now and again, it took her breath.

I don't think you ever loved him, Amanda had said.

But here in this kitchen, she couldn't muster up the argument she'd used at the Lavender Llama. Because the Douglas farmhouse was the opposite of temporary. It was exactly the same as Rae remembered it, always, stretching back all the way to her earliest memories. And Martha Douglas was the same. Quietly competent, profoundly no-nonsense, and as likely to dispense a brisk attitude readjustment as she was a piece of pie in place of a hug.

No pointless, perishable flowers here. The Douglas family had always been about the land. Seasons came and went, but the land remained.

Rae wanted to spill it all out. Everything inside her. Throw it on the table with all the baking supplies, rolling pins and sugar and baking soda. Because between them, Abby and her grandmother could solve any problem, surely. Even hers.

But instead, she shrugged out of her coat, found a seat, and pitched in.

"How's your project going?" Abby asked her sometime later.

"My project?"

Abby smiled at her grandmother. "I told you Rae moved into Hope's house in town. She's striking out on a brand-new path."

Rae braced herself for Martha's disapproval, but the older woman merely gazed at her a moment, then returned her attention to the crust she was rolling out with a quick, deft hand.

"It's going *great*," Rae said, maybe a little too intensely. She cleared her throat. "It's fun living with Hope and her sisters. To be honest, it makes me wish that Tory and I were closer."

Geographically and emotionally, she thought. Then bit back a smile, because her brother and sister and she had always adhered to yet another unspoken Trujillo family rule. Sometimes they had tense interactions, but only between themselves. No public theatrics—that was better left to Inez and Kathy. They mostly got along.

Though as she thought that, it occurred to Rae that if they'd been close the way Hope and her sisters were, maybe they would have worried less about theatrics and been more about the unwavering support whether they agreed with each other or not.

Something she'd never really noticed about her brother and sister because she'd always had Riley.

Ouch.

"I always wanted a sister," Abby was saying. She smiled at Rae. "But then, I had you and Hope, so who needs sisters? And now you get to live in town. That must be fun."

"I can walk to work." Rae paused, a knife in one hand and an apple in the other. And decided this was as good a time as any to count her blessings. "It makes me feel more connected to things. Cold River itself, I mean. All the people who live and work there. And things are so *convenient.* If we run out of something while cooking, for example, I can just run down to that little market by the courthouse. You can't do that when you live in the country."

"You better hope you can milk it or pick it," Martha agreed. "Or you'll have to do without."

Abby's smile widened. "I'm really glad that you did this. I think it's really good for you. And . . . I'm glad that something changed with you and Riley, because I don't think it's the healthiest thing in the world to live in a small town and pretend someone you have so much history with doesn't exist." She said all that in a burst and then looked apologetic. "I hope it's okay to say that."

"It's more than okay," Rae assured her. She did not think about the Harvest Gala. She certainly did not think about Riley with *a date.* She tried not to squirm in her chair, even though she was desperate to dislodge that heavy stone that still sat on her, and the other, sharper one sunk deep inside. Maybe that was why her voice went up a couple of octaves. "Riley and I are friends now. It's fine. More than fine, it's great. Fantastic, even."

She pulled in a breath at the end of that little display and pretended she didn't feel the weight of two sets of Douglas eyes on her. Rae focused on her apples instead.

For a while, there was nothing but the sound of the radio tuned to the oldies station Martha preferred. The older woman even hummed along when she really liked a song. And it was like a lullaby, though Rae didn't feel sleepy. A lullaby for her heart, maybe.

She was breathing easier when it was her turn to roll out some dough. It was therapeutic, she could admit to herself. The kneading, the rolling pin. Making flour and water do her bidding.

"I remember when it occurred to me that my marriage could only be as good as I let it be," Abby said conversationally. "I mean, when it dawned on me that if I couldn't sit down and have a conversation about my marriage with the person I was actually married to, it wasn't really a marriage."

Rae rolled her eyes. "Subtle."

Abby grinned. "I didn't actually mean to aim that right at you. Not really. I was thinking about you and Riley figuring out a way to be friends after all this time. That's what it's about, isn't it? One way or another, figuring out a way to communicate. That's any relationship."

"I wouldn't say Riley and I have a relationship. We have . . ."

She couldn't say *benefits* in front of Martha. She was sick and tired of the word *friendship*. He was just . . . Riley. His sister thought she'd never loved him when she'd never loved anyone else. And all this time, she'd managed to avoid thinking *too* hard about all the ways she'd hurt a great many more people than simply Riley himself. She'd been focused on the fires between them they couldn't put out, and on the way some people liked to judge her for the things they couldn't understand. She'd felt downright pious about her refusal to defend herself, to let everybody think what they wanted.

Self-righteous but never grieving.

"History," she managed to say, when she realized her words were hanging over the table, unfinished. "That's what Riley and I have. A whole lot of history."

"The point of history is to learn something, Rae," Martha said sedately. "Otherwise, it's a collection of things that happened, as easily forgotten as remembered."

Rae told herself she had absolutely no idea why she felt like sobbing into her pie.

The baby monitor on the counter crackled to life. Abby cocked her head to one side, smiling faintly as the staticky sounds became a wordless song that filled the kitchen.

And Rae's heart . . . *ached*.

"He *should* go back to sleep." Abby grinned conspiratorially at Rae. "Sometimes he does this. He wakes up in the middle of his nap, sings himself a lullaby, then sleeps a bit more." She laughed. "Mind you, other times he wakes up with a mood on and is utterly inconsolable."

She pushed back from the table, wiping off her hands on the apron she wore tied around her waist. "I'll just go check."

Abby hurried out of the room. Rae stayed where she was, listening as the singing carried on, imprinting its off-key melody into all the places she ached.

"I love that you bake all these pies," Rae told Martha after a moment. Because her heart felt swollen and song-heavy, but the kitchen smelled happy and good. And Bart singing himself lullabies was a joyful thing, no matter how complicated it made her feel. And she'd been so committed to moving on, to starting something new, that she'd forgotten that there was so much love tangled up in the roots of things too. How had she let herself forget? "I love that you bake. My grandmother can barely heat a pot of water. And my mother always says that *her* mother baked a lot, but she didn't pick up the gene."

Martha snorted. "Inez Trujillo has always been more

interested in cooking up a controversy than a casserole. We all have our gifts."

Rae almost forgot what year it was. Because it could have been any afternoon from her childhood or adolescence, sitting at this table and pretending Martha was hers instead of Abby's.

"I think the best gift my grandmother could give anyone would be to stop fighting with my mother," Rae said. "But then, if she did, who would my mother have to fight with? I guess some people are really comfortable with their own misery."

Her words landed on the table before her, hard. Setting off that tuning fork inside her yet again, until she thought her bones might shake apart.

Was she talking about her mother and grandmother? Or was she talking about herself—and all these years with Riley, chasing their own tails around and around and around?

Amanda's voice echoed in her head. *I don't think you ever loved him.*

She held her breath, wondering if there was time to run out the door before Martha's frank gaze shredded her. But the older woman merely carried on preparing her fillings, her hands far quicker and more agile than Rae's and her eyes on what she was doing.

"I guess I really shouldn't comment on other people's happiness," Rae said after a moment. She cleared her throat. "It's not like I'm any good at it myself."

Martha let out a hoot. "Nobody's good at happiness, child. It's not a merit badge. It requires choosing. Day after day, hour after hour. It's not where you end up that matters, it's how you get there."

"So far," Rae said to her pie crust, "my journey has mostly been upsetting."

"That's a choice," Martha said. Placidly. "And that's the good news. Because if you don't like what you have, you can choose something else."

Rae told herself her throat hurt because it was November. If she didn't have a cold yet, she would soon. Maybe a full-on flu. There could be no other reason at all.

"Some choices you make," she said when her throat ached a little less and Bart wasn't singing any longer over the intercom. "Others are made for you."

Martha looked up then, putting down her utensils and fixing that gaze of hers on Rae. Direct and occasionally relentless, though never unkind. Rae couldn't look away.

"I've known your grandmother for a long time," Martha told her. "Your mother too. They never cared for each other back when your parents were dating, and I can't imagine anything's changed since. Like chalk and cheese, the two of them."

Rae tried to smile. "That's one way of putting it."

"But I'll tell you this. They both love your father. And you too, whether it feels that way to you or not." Martha's gaze seemed to bore deep into her, digging down into all those tangled roots Rae had been pretending weren't there. For far too long. "Love is still love, even if it looks different than you think it should."

Abby came back into the room, smiling widely and not carrying Bart. "He went back down. That means we should get another hour before—"

She stopped halfway into the kitchen and looked back and forth between Rae and her grandmother. "Everything all right?"

"Everything's *great*," Rae gritted out before Martha could make her cry. Openly. "I keep telling you."

"So you do," Abby agreed. She took her seat again. "Maybe one of these days, I'll believe it."

Rae ignored her, because it was that or curl up into the fetal position in the middle of the kitchen floor. Martha Douglas would disapprove of that sort of display, she knew.

Instead, she lost herself in fruit and dough and the seductive notion that if she assembled all the pieces of what she wanted in just the right way, just like a pie, she could put it all together and come up with something sweet.

No matter who judged her for it, she told herself boldly.

Even if the person she feared might judge her the most was herself.

16

"That dress is entirely too pretty to mope in," Hope announced the night of the Harvest Gala. It was always held on the night before Thanksgiving—before folks started fattening themselves up for winter, as the head of the Heritage Society liked to say. In every speech, every year. "You have to stop."

She was shaking her head at Rae as if Rae had tripped and ended up face-first in one of the centerpieces she'd only then finished arranging *just so* on all the tables in the ballroom of the Grand Hotel.

Hope's version of helping had been to lounge at a seat at her duly reserved table, looking like a deeply bored angel in a sparkly gown that hugged her willowy body, somehow showing everything without showing a thing. A work of art, really.

Rae, meanwhile, had allowed Hope and her sisters to talk her into a fire-engine-red dress she already regretted. It was too bright. It swished and swayed while she walked, calling attention to her legs.

It felt like it ought to be worn by someone far more sophisticated and *together* than Rae. To say she regretted it was an understatement. Why had she imagined—for a brief, giddy moment while surrounded by the Mortimer sisters, with even Faith looking on admiringly—that she might actually *want* extra attention? She'd caught Douglas Fowler, the owner of the hotel, who was older than her father, *looking* at her when she'd walked in, to her horror.

But it was too late now. She was stuck. The lobby and graceful Old West reception areas were already filled with people, and the ballroom doors had just opened. She was a screaming red beacon to one and all, like it or not.

"The dress is the least of my concerns," Rae told Hope loftily. And almost entirely truthfully, because she was looking around the ballroom, trying to make sure she saw any possible mistakes on any of the tables.

Because her grandmother certainly would.

"Then you need to get your priorities in order," Hope said sternly. "Because that dress is beautiful. *You* are beautiful. You should take five seconds out of your life to appreciate that, and where better than the grand ballroom of the Grand Hotel?"

Rae looked around again, this time to see if any of the other volunteers or charity donors were within earshot. "None of this was necessary. I don't know why you wouldn't listen to me. The dresses I have—"

Hope waved a hand. "Every dress you have is fine, sure. Perfectly suitable if you happen to be, say, staff at someone else's wedding. But this is a gala. The entire point of which is to make like Cinderella, dance until a shoe falls off, and sparkle while you do it." She smiled. "Feel free to put that on a T-shirt."

Rae sighed, though it was mostly for show. Hope was, after all, the person who—when Rae had asked her who she planned to take as her date to the gala—had stared straight back at her and said, *my magnificent self.*

That Hope was likely to have a Cinderella-worthy

evening was certain. She would see to it personally. Rae, however, did not feel like Cinderella. Not Cinderella at the ball, anyway. She'd spent years coming to the Harvest Gala without a date, so there was no reason it should feel so *agitating* tonight. She was sitting at a table with Hope and her sisters and some other, younger shop owners, because that was their tradition—adopted right around the time Rae had stopped bringing her usual date, if she recalled correctly. The past couple of years, Matias had been here too, and as annoying as he could be and often was, he managed to pull it together in a nice suit.

Rae was all too aware that she wouldn't have thought about a date for even a second if Riley hadn't said he was bringing one. In years past, he'd sat at a table with his brothers and the rest of his family, brooding darkly while she pretended she didn't see him, and life had carried right on as normal.

"Personally," Hope said then, "I'm looking forward to see who appears on Riley's arm."

His name out loud was like a punch. It was why she'd banned it for so long.

Rae ordered herself to calm down. And did not, in any way, calm down. "That makes one of us."

"I want to see who's brazen enough to do it." Hope rose from her seat in a sparkling, shimmering rush. "It's big fun when you're playing your little barroom games. Have a little dance, maybe a drink, with Riley right there looking on. Spicy. But who in Cold River is idiotic enough to actually turn up at an event like this with your husband?"

"My ex-husband," Rae corrected automatically. Then scowled at her friend. "And it's not a game, Hope. It's not—"

"Don't mind me," Hope said, but she was smirking. "The champagne must have gone straight to my head."

"You haven't had any champagne."

"Yet."

The room started filling. For Rae, it was kind of like Halloween in reverse. She'd liked Halloween as a kid, in theory, but it was less fun out in the country than it was in town. Some years, her parents would drive the three of them in so they could march around the few neighborhoods in town with houses close enough together to lend themselves to trick-or-treating before being packed back into the car for a sugary trip home, but some years the weather was too foul to allow for that kind of thing. The gala, on the other hand, was a different kind of dress-up party. The Heritage Society liked to pack the room, and they did. People came from all over the Longhorn Valley to drink, eat dinner, and dance the night away while contributing to a cause that benefited all of them.

And they did it wearing fancy clothes that otherwise only turned up at the odd wedding. Or funeral, depending.

Rae's grandmother swept in, looking as ferocious and unimpressed as she did regal. This was more or less the Inez Trujillo brand, really. She saw Rae across the room and bore down upon her, making no secret of the fact she was inspecting the centerpieces as she went.

Inspecting them and not looking pleased. Rae had the urge to hide. Maybe crawl beneath one of the tables and stay there. But instead, she remembered what Martha Douglas had said about love not looking as expected, at least not from the outside, and smiled when Inez marched up to stand beside her.

Dressed head to toe in black, as was her preference at such events.

Imagine, Rae thought, your sense of self being so

precarious that you have to dress for a funeral when you knew it was a party, the better to stand out. Or punish a child for daring to repeat things you said.

The world looked a bit different, suddenly.

"You look terrific, Grandma," Rae said.

Inez sniffed. "Parking is a disaster this year. I don't know what they were thinking. That lobby can't handle such a crush of people. I expected my sciatica to hobble me before I could make it through the door."

"But you made it, anyway." Rae did her best to sound encouraging.

Her grandmother peered down her nose, which might have been more effective if she were taller than Rae. She was not.

"Don't patronize me, please." Inez shifted her gaze to the table beside them and sniffed again. "Let me take a look at these arrangements."

Rae was still standing there—waiting for Inez to finish her forensic examination of compositions Rae had stayed up for several nights in a row making come alive, then render her judgment—when her parents walked up. Her father looked the way he always did, calm and kind. Her mother, by contrast, was already showing signs of wear.

They must have carpooled into town.

"Absolutely beautiful flowers, sweetheart," Kathy said, kissing Rae on the cheek. "People will love them and bid accordingly."

"I'm waiting for Grandma to grade them," Rae replied. Not in as much of an undertone as she should have used, maybe.

She could tell exactly how long the ride into town had been when her mother sighed. And made no attempt to hide it.

"I love the rustic boxes," her father said, eyeing the wooden rectangles critically. Then smiling at her. "You have your grandmother's eye."

That was a compliment. And Rae might find her grandmother a lot to take, but there was no arguing with the fact that Inez was responsible for building the Trujillo reputation—mostly through her glorious arrangements. Glossy pictures of her best compositions hung all over the business office out near the greenhouses.

"Thanks, Dad," Rae said, permitting herself to get a little emotional. Just a little.

"You young people and your floral theatrics," Inez said then, turning back to face the rest of them. "Why not go with a classic, circular shape for a traditional audience? Why a distressed rectangle, of all things? It looks like a trough."

But Rae knew that was a compliment too, almost. Any real complaint would have been about the flowers, not the base they sat in.

Love looked the way it looked, not the way you wanted it to look.

"It's lively and fun, Inez," Kathy was saying. "And perfectly suited to a historic Western town, I think."

"You need to learn your audience," Rae's grandmother said, though it was unclear who she was talking to. She threaded her arm through Rae's father's and pulled herself up high as if she'd won something. "Now I would like a drink."

Rae and her mother stood there, fixed smiles in place, as Grandma Inez led him away. Or more precisely, he let her.

"Why do you put up with her?" Rae asked her mother when Grandma Inez and her father were out of earshot. "All these years of her poking and poking. And it's not like she's declined since Grandpa died. She was always like this."

"She's getting worse," Rae's mother agreed. "No doubt about it."

"But you stay," Rae said.

Out of the corner of her eye, she saw Hope on the far side of the table, laughing as she spoke with some of their neighbors and fellow shopkeepers, all of them looking slick and shiny. Over by the ballroom doors, she heard an even bigger laugh and knew before she turned her head that it was Jensen.

And where there was one Kittredge, there was bound to be more.

Her stomach tied itself into a knot. She thought maybe she started to sweat.

"Where would I go?" Rae's mother asked with a laugh. "I suppose I could go on an extended vacation to Santa Fe, like Stella Mortimer, but I think your father would have something to say about that."

Rae's eyes were glued to the door now. Connor Kittredge came in after Jensen, looking as cocky as he always did as the youngest of the Kittredge boys. Donovan and Ellie were behind him. Donovan looked as stiff and remote as always, while Ellie radiated that cool Western elegance that was her trademark.

She didn't expect to see Zack with the rest of them, and sure enough, a quick glance around showed her that the sheriff must have come in on his own. He was currently fending off the red-faced concerns of garrulous old Charlie Dunn and one of his old cronies, Victor Mansell. And to his credit, Zack looked fully engaged in the conversation when both old men were known for their extreme talent in talking the ear off anyone who ventured near.

Rae tried to concentrate on her mother and the conversation she was having, not assorted Kittredges.

"You don't have to let Grandma live with you, Mom," she said, even though it was something she'd held back from saying for years. Because maybe someone needed to say it to her. "You could have put your foot down years ago. Fix her up a little in-law pad and be done with it."

"Rae Lynn Maria Trujillo." Her mother sounded legitimately shocked. "What's gotten into you?"

And as if on cue, Riley appeared in the door to the lobby. Rae could see him perfectly despite the crowd, and that wasn't exactly a good thing.

Because Riley was a cowboy, through and through. His jeans and his boots were as much a part of him as his dark gaze and his impossibly clever hands. Many a cowboy in this room wore the same uniform, and made the transition to a suit . . . reluctantly.

All around him, there were examples of men who preferred to live and die in their work clothes, uncomfortably packaged into suits they clearly hated.

Not Riley.

He looked like dessert.

Rae understood in that moment that there was no chance whatsoever that she was going to react well to whatever date he planned to parade around in front of her tonight. That it was going to kill her.

It made her wonder what on earth he'd been doing, encouraging her to dance with Tate Bishop. Who she'd also seen here tonight and had already forgotten. Was it possible that despite all her big talk and attempts at action, *Riley* was the one who'd actually moved on?

Something ripped open inside her, a black, wide pit.

The crowd shifted as he looked down at whoever was clinging to his arm with an indulgent and affectionate sort of smile that made that pit in Rae roar even wider. Even darker.

Even worse.

God, she'd been a fool. Rae was pretty sure that this was the textbook definition of cutting off her nose to spite her face, and now all she had was a noseless face and enough spite to set the world on fire.

But what she didn't have was Riley.

She didn't think she was breathing. And then the crowd shifted again, and she saw Riley's date.

It was seventeen-year-old Becca Everett. Gray Everett's teenage daughter from his first marriage, Abby's step-daughter, and for all intents and purposes, Riley's niece. That was how close he and Brady had always been.

He hadn't brought a real date, after all.

The first thing Rae felt was relief. A wave of it, so intense she thought she might topple over. And on the other side of it, she felt . . . weak with panic.

And worse, a terrible realization.

"I hope you never let your father hear you talk about bundling his mother into an outbuilding," Rae's mother was saying.

Because, of course, Kathy didn't understand that Rae's world had ended, then begun again in a new form Rae didn't quite know how to accept. She couldn't hear her daughter's heart clattering around.

Over by the door, Riley looked up again and unerringly found Rae. His gaze was dark, as always. But this time, she didn't fight that electric surge between them. That intense connection that had always been there, like it or not.

Once upon a time, she'd called it fate. Later on, she'd called it her due as his love and his wife.

Tonight, she didn't know what to call it.

"Mom," Rae managed to say, so much noise in her head that she didn't have the slightest idea whether she sounded normal or not. But her heart was still beating so hard she couldn't bring herself to care, and the press of that sharp-edged thing inside her almost felt like relief. "Nothing's gotten into me. All you and Grandma do is fight." She wrenched her gaze away from Riley's. Even though that felt like more of that same grief that had been swamping her ever since she'd talked to Amanda. A hard, merciless stone no matter what she pretended. "Don't you ever want peace?"

For a moment, Kathy looked shocked. Then, far more surprising to Rae, she laughed.

"I wouldn't know what to do with myself without your grandmother around. Your father spends most of his time talking to his plants, like his father before him. I would be bored silly if your grandmother weren't there in all her glory." Her laughter faded as she regarded her daughter. "It wasn't your father who insisted she move in with us, Rae. It was me. Just as I'm the one who begs her to stay every time she announces she's leaving. At least two or three times a month."

Rae thought her mouth might actually be hanging open. "I can't process anything you're saying right now, Mom."

"Honey." Her mother looked at her as if she were both precious and silly, when Rae had felt neither for . . . eight years. "Life is supposed to be sour as well as sweet, or how would you ever tell the difference?"

Rae couldn't seem to do anything but stand there, dumbstruck, convinced that if she looked down she would find that the world had been snatched out from beneath her feet. Her father returned, dispensing glasses of wine, and she clutched hers close, wishing that it were a lifeline. Doing her best to keep all heavy stones, knife-sharp edges, and ripped-open abysses inside her, because what would happen if she let it all out?

She didn't realize how bad it was until there were fingers snapping in front of her face.

"It's not a good sign if you're *starting* the evening in a fugue state," Matias rumbled at her.

He, too, should have looked ridiculous in a suit, but didn't. It was one of the few times a year that Rae was forced to accept the fact that her brother was handsome. Something she could see with her own eyes, but if not, it would have been made crystal clear to her by the fluttering women who were gazing at him from all sides.

"I'm not in a fugue state," she told him, ordering herself to make that true. Or at least act like it were true. "My whole world is askew. Did you know that Mom and Grandma *like* fighting with each other? That Mom *insists* that Grandma stay and continue the daily wars?"

Matias looked at her pityingly. "The inmates run that asylum, Rae. Pay better attention."

Rae wasn't sure attention was required. What she felt was thrown.

A sensation that didn't go away even after the long dinner and all the speeches that Hope made hilarious with her under-the-breath commentary.

"We are going to have to have a talk with Abby," she said at one point. "I get that she and Gray Everett, the enemy of fun, don't come to things like a gala."

"The Everetts never come to the gala," Rae pointed out. "I'm sure that's why Amanda isn't here with all her brothers. She's an Everett now."

Hope nodded. "But you'd think Abby might have sent a text to let us know who Becca was attending with."

"You'd think," Rae agreed. She made a face. "She probably thought I already knew. Or wouldn't care."

Hope gave her an arch look. "She knows you care, Rae. Believe me. I'm betting they put the baby down early and got . . . preoccupied."

That was a far more likely scenario. The only thing more intense than the way Abby had always loved Gray was the way he loved her back.

The dancing started, and Rae arranged her features into the appropriate stab at composed serenity, because her experience was that no one was going to ask her to dance. Not with Riley there.

It's big fun when you're playing your little barroom games, Hope had said earlier. *Have a little dance, maybe a drink, with Riley right there looking on. Spicy.*

But that was a bar. This was a ballroom. People's grandparents were here.

She was so busy concentrating on her serenity and composure that she jolted when a man appeared before her. But it was only Matias again.

"Come on," he growled at her in a tone that could in no universe be considered inviting. "I can't stand you sitting here, looking pathetic."

He didn't wait for her to extend her hand. He tugged her up onto her feet using her elbow, and she decided to walk along with him as he pulled her onto the dance floor because if she didn't, he would probably just drag her.

Which would not exactly be *serene.*

"Do I look pathetic?" she asked dryly as they started dancing. "Or are you trying to keep the hordes of your admirers at bay now that they've had entirely too much wine?"

Her older brother smirked at her. "Six of one, half dozen of another. You're welcome."

The band, a collection of locals who came together only on occasions like this one and enjoyed themselves almost more than the crowd enjoyed them, was as good as ever. She and Matias danced, and Rae found herself acting a little goofy, the way she had when they'd been younger and her older brother hadn't taken himself quite so seriously.

Maybe Matias challenged her about her life not because he didn't support her or love her but because he did. In his very own, ornery older-brother way.

Complete, tonight, with dips that made Rae clutch at him in case he dropped her on her butt.

She was still laughing from the latest dip when he traded partners with Jensen, who had been dancing with Becca.

Rae and Jensen stared at each other. She felt her smile fade.

"Jensen," she said.

"Rae," he rumbled at her, no sign of that big laugh of his that he shared with literally everyone else.

Maybe someday things like this would stop hurting, but she doubted it.

And then the next moment, she was traded yet again.

But this time, it was Riley.

17

The dress Rae was wearing pretty much sucker punched all of Riley's good intentions into oblivion.

It was red. It flowed. And clung. It made her look even more beautiful than usual, which shouldn't have been possible.

He knew he should say hello. Act like a functioning adult. A grown man, perfectly capable of controlling himself, handling challenging situations of any stripe, and—

But she slid into his arms the way she always had. Like a dream come true.

He liked when she wore heels like the ones she had on tonight, because it brought her face that much nearer to his. And it meant when he pulled her close, he could feel her breasts higher against his chest.

And for somebody who was supposed to be over playing these games, the only thing he could seem to think about was playing. Hard.

"Becca must be thrilled," Rae said when the silence between them had long since turned into tension, and the tension had rocketed straight into *want*.

He couldn't read the look in her eyes. Too dark and too mysterious, but he felt her voice kick around inside him all the same. It didn't make the *want* any better. Nothing did.

"Brady said she wanted to wear a real dress to a real dance, and not with some kid from high school. How could I resist?"

Rae smiled, and it lodged in his chest, and he didn't understand how he was supposed to go about the necessary work of handling himself when she could do that. Just cast a spell offhandedly, in the middle of a crowded dance floor.

"No one could resist," she agreed.

And they danced, her head tipped back so she could look him full in the face. He had her hand in his, and another in the small of her back, and there was a point where he couldn't tell the difference between them.

There was Rae and there was him, and he was fully aware of each and every point of contact, but he was also conscious of something bigger.

Them. Together.

And that was the trouble. He still didn't know how to be something other than *them*. No matter what that looked like.

"Did you bring a date?" he asked her roughly.

Though he already knew the answer.

"I consider myself my own date. All of the fun, none of the hassle."

"Is somebody hassling you?" Riley asked, and only realized after he'd thrown out the question that he sounded . . . gravelly.

And was, maybe not subtly, looking around the room for Tate freaking Bishop.

"I find the notion of dating a hassle." She did something with her chin, lifting it up in a way that normally meant she was preparing to fight. But all they were doing was dancing. "This is the holiday season. Thanksgiving is tomorrow, and all I want to think about is turkey, my dad's gravy, and more sweet potatoes than one body can bear."

Riley searched her face, trying to see what it was that made her sound so . . . determined. "Why are you telling me that like you expect me to keep you from Thanksgiving dinner?"

"Full disclosure, Riley," she said, that smile creeping back into her voice, if not quite making it onto her face. "I shamelessly stole your grandmother's carrot soufflé recipe and have been passing it off as my own for years. There. Now you know the depths of my deceit."

He gazed down at her in mock astonishment. "That carrot soufflé recipe has been in my grandmother's family for generations, or so she claims."

Rae nodded soberly. "I can offer no excuse for my actions. Except it's delicious."

Riley laughed. Big and loud. So big and so loud that he saw heads turn.

He didn't care if people stared at them, but Rae stiffened in his arms. He looked down and saw her glancing around, that little frown appearing between her brows.

"What's the matter? Confessions are supposed to be good for the soul. You should feel all light and airy now that you've told me you're a Thanksgiving thief."

"Nothing's the matter." Rae scanned the ballroom, and when she looked back at him, there was more distance on her face than he liked. Almost as if she were bracing herself. "I'm starting the countdown, that's all."

"Countdown? That's the wrong holiday, baby. It's Thanksgiving tomorrow, not New Year's Eve."

"Not that kind of countdown." She didn't object to

him calling her *baby*. That probably wasn't a good sign. "I mean the countdown before someone—usually a member of your family, but not always—will take me to task for my treatment of you."

He laughed again. "How are you treating me?"

"Badly, Riley. That's the consensus." Her chin jutted out even more.

He spun her around, maybe a little too fast. But whatever else she might have said was lost in the swirl of it. In the grip of their hands, her face upturned and open, and the way her dress flowed around him. And for a while, there was only that. Riley thought he could feel her heart beating, low and hard.

Then he realized it was his.

"They're not my minions, Rae." And maybe he pulled her closer too. "I don't send them out to do my bidding. They have their own opinions. I don't necessarily agree with them, and you certainly don't have to listen to them, but I can't keep them from feeling what they feel."

"Of course you can't," she said, something he didn't understand glittering there in her eyes. "But that doesn't change the countdown or the consensus, does it?"

The song ended then. All the people around them were letting go of their dance partners, folks were clapping for the band, and the last thing in the world Riley wanted to do was let go of her. But he had no choice.

Just like he felt he had no choice but to follow her when she turned and dove through the crowd as if she couldn't get away from him fast enough.

Did he ever have a choice when it came to Rae?

She didn't go to her table the way he'd expected she would. Instead, she headed toward the large double doors that led into the reception area right outside the ballroom.

The bar was out there in the middle of a happy throng, but she headed in the opposite direction.

Riley caught up to her in the lobby, filled with polished dark woods and gleaming chandeliers, none of which he cared about at that moment.

There was only Rae.

Nothing new there.

"What are you doing?" he asked, and only when his voice echoed back at him did it occur to him to look around, because this was a lobby. Not his house. Not anywhere private.

But they had the lobby to themselves, more or less. Almost everyone else who was here tonight was inside the ballroom—or, more likely, at the bar. Riley wished he'd had the foresight to grab himself a whiskey before trailing after his runaway bride for the millionth time. Maybe that would make the mess in him settle.

Not that whiskey had ever done him much good on that score.

"What does it matter?" Rae asked, sounding . . . weary.

It made everything in him go ominously still.

Because her tone reminded him entirely too much of that night on his front porch.

Good, he growled at himself. *Maybe this time, don't come out of it thinking something as stupid as the two of you trying to be friends.*

"I'm sorry that you don't like it that people have opinions about us," he said to her back, and thought it came out remarkably calm, considering. Though the way she stiffened suggested maybe not. "I don't know what you want me to do about that. The fact is, we can dance around this for another ten years, but it's not going to change. You left me. You won't come back. That's the whole story right there."

She turned slowly. Too slowly. And her dark eyes blazed when she finally faced him, but that was better than *weariness*.

"That's nothing close to the whole story."

"So you've hinted. A thousand times. But it might as well be the full story because it's the only one you've ever given me."

She pressed her lips together into a straight line that had never led him anywhere good.

"Let me point some things out to you, Rae," he said, and sure, that didn't sound as friendly in his mouth as it had in his head.

"I would rather you didn't."

"Tough." He moved toward her until they were almost as close as they'd been on the dance floor. And after all these weeks of keeping his temper under control, he found he had a much lighter grasp on it tonight. It was that red dress. It was the feel of her in his arms, like she'd never left. It was the past eight years. He could feel temper pouring out of him, as if a dam had broken, and he knew that *temper* was only the start of it. "You can't stay away from me, Rae. You don't even try to stay away from me very well. Whatever we call ourselves, wherever you actually live, we're still us. It hasn't changed since we were in high school. When are you going to wake up and accept that it's not going to change?"

"I'm trying," she whispered.

"No, baby. You're not. You can't even stomach the idea of dating someone else. You barely tried. The moment it looked like maybe we we're finally going to make a clean break, what happened? Friends. Then friends with benefits."

"I didn't mean for that to happen!"

"But it always does." And again, his voice came back

at him, suggesting he was much too loud—but Riley didn't really care if the entire Longhorn Valley were standing there listening. Watching. Judging them the way Rae seemed to think they did when maybe they were just invested. "You're good at a lot of things, Rae, but leaving me isn't one of them. Can we just stop?"

Her chest was lifting and falling as if she were running. Sobbing. Breathing way too hard. Her hands were in fists and her eyes were so wide, so slicked with misery, that he couldn't help himself. He reached over and gripped her upper arms, holding her still. Connecting them again, in case she needed the reminder.

Maybe he did.

"Can we be done with all the leaving?" he asked her, his voice low. "At last?"

Rae's eyes filled with tears. He expected her to pull away, but she didn't, and somehow that made it worse.

"You're right that I'm no good at staying away from you." There was something much too raw in her voice. He hated it. "I need to figure it out. Because I want things you can't give me, Riley."

Of all the things she'd said to him over time, that had to be the worst. He felt an icy hand squeeze tightly around his heart.

Especially because she didn't sound angry. She didn't sound like she was trying to score points. If anything, she sounded defeated.

"Name it." He belted that out at her, his hands tightening slightly around her shoulders as if she were already pulling away from him again. "Name one thing I can't give you."

"It's not a question of *can't*. You won't."

"Name it, then."

It seemed to take her a lot, then, to get in a breath.

Then she exhaled, harder, clearly trying to steady herself. She met his gaze, and while hers was direct, it was also . . . defiant? Sad? He tensed.

"A baby," Rae said quietly. "I want a baby, Riley."

He was stunned by that. He frowned, but she didn't change the way she was looking at him. Like she expected him to punch his fist through the nearest wall.

She nodded as if he had. "I told you. You won't."

He could feel his frown deepen. "You spent years saying you wanted nothing to do with kids," he reminded her. "I'm not real clear on why you're holding something you said against me."

She flushed. "I said I didn't want kids when I was a kid. You're the one who was always so *sure,* Riley. But then Abby had Bart, and everything shifted for me. And I can't seem to shift it back."

She stepped away from him then, giving him no choice but to drop his hands. That usually meant she was about to run off, and he braced himself for that, but she didn't. She stayed there in front of him, still looking at him in that way he liked less by the moment.

"I'm older now. And everything with us was . . ."

Rae looked as if she were casting around for the right word. Riley didn't supply one, because what did he know? There were a lot of words to describe the two of them.

Quite a few he knew she didn't want to hear.

"From the very beginning, we were either fighting or making up." There was a different note in her voice now. It thudded through him. *Resolve,* he thought. "In high school. When we were first married. All these years since. That's all we do. It's always easy to start a fight, because we both know where that leads. But do we ever talk to each other? Comfort each other? We've only ever been intimate in one way, and it's not enough."

"Not enough," he repeated, because the words didn't make sense.

"No." She stood a little straighter. "I want everything."

"First of all," Riley gritted out, trying not to show her that he was reeling when the truth was, he was amazed he hadn't staggered back already. "We have all those things."

"When's the last time we talked, Riley? Just talked, no expectation of anything else, no playing games?"

"This entire past month."

Well. That wasn't entirely true. But he wasn't sure he'd categorize what he'd been doing as *playing games*. Not really.

Not when it was their life he'd been trying to save.

"Right. This past month. When we were pretending to be something we're not."

"Rae. For God's sake."

"I don't want to argue with you," she said quietly. "This is not another one of the fights we always have. But, Riley. You must know you comfort your horses more than you comfort me. You always have."

She might as well have punched her hand into his chest, ripped out his heart, and thrown it against one of the old brick walls.

"That's a messed-up thing to say," he managed to get out. "Even for you."

He expected her to come at him. To hurl more accusations at him. To launch herself physically closer, eyes snapping and fingers pointing.

All the usual weapons that led them to the same place.

But instead, she wrapped her arms around her middle. And looked small.

Compared to all the other ammunition she'd used on him in the past, this one was the nuclear option. Because all he wanted to do was help her. Save her.

Even if he hurt himself in the process.

Rae shook her head, almost as if she were reading his mind. "I shouldn't have said that. It's not fair. We can't be together, and now you know why. That's the point. That's why we need to divorce and stop pretending we can be friends." She clasped her hands together. "Apparently, I'm so much of an addict when it comes to you that I can't go cold turkey, but I have to, Riley. I hope you understand that. I hope you'll help."

"I can help."

Riley hardly heard himself. Because all he could see was his Rae looking broken and earnest at the same time. And he couldn't have that. He couldn't allow it.

Not when it was in his power to change it.

"None of this has to be so hard," he told her. "You want a baby? Great. Let's have one. Problem solved."

Then watched as her pretty face crumpled.

And his tough, stubborn, fiery Rae . . . burst into tears.

18

Rae couldn't believe she was sobbing. Full-on sobbing, in a public place.

But she also didn't have it in her to hold back any longer.

The weight of all the decisions she'd made, each one stacked on the one before like a precarious set of awful dominoes that had gotten higher and higher over time— it all crumbled. They all came crashing down.

That vicious knife in her belly cut her, deep.

And while some part of her was only too aware that they were standing in the lobby of the Grand Hotel, dressed like people they weren't and in view of the whole town if anyone cared to look, she accepted that she'd run away from this for as long as she could.

She had to face it.

She *finally* had to face it.

"You want to have a baby," she managed to get out. She wiped furiously at her eyes, not caring if her hands came away covered in mascara. She didn't even look. "You, Riley Kittredge, want to have a baby."

He looked back at her, his expression almost frozen, clearly aware that there was no right answer to that question.

"You used to go on and on about how little you wanted

children. Even when we were in high school. You talked about it all the time. As long as I've known you, you've been outspoken about how little you want anything to do with babies, raising kids, all of it."

"I don't deny that." Riley looked baffled. "I had to babysit my sister from the moment she was born. My parents were never very good at parenting in the first place, then they had a magical baby to hold us all together. But guess what? They had to work. Who do you think took care of her?"

"I know," Rae threw back at him. "I know all of this. This is what I'm trying to say to you. When we got married, everyone thought it was a shotgun wedding. But it wasn't. And each and every time people asked us when we were going to start a family, what did you say?"

His dark eyes looked hooded. "I don't remember."

"You do remember. You said, every time, *Not in this lifetime.*"

"I don't understand how this is turning into a trial," Riley shot back at her. "I don't remember you feeling any differently. Are you telling me you did? And didn't mention it all this time? That sounds like another you thing, Rae."

And this was the moment.

A moment that Rae had been avoiding for so long now that it was second nature to do it again. She almost started. She almost threw up her hands, told him it wasn't worth it, and walked away.

She almost curled herself around that ugly little secret inside of her, again, to shove it back down.

But she knew that if she did it again, it would be all she did. Because it was all she'd done. She would keep doing it, over and over again. And this holding pattern they were in would never end. They would keep right on circling the same drain until it ruined them both.

Or until they were so old and withered that they would have nothing left to do but carry right on hurting each other to death.

She didn't have it in her any longer.

So she reached down and took hold of that sharp, terrible thing, then dragged it into the light.

"I got pregnant," she told him.

It was such a simple sentence, in the end. Three words. That was all.

And Rae wanted to die. She wanted to wail, hit him, crumple to the floor. But she'd already done all that.

So instead, all she did was say the words.

Riley's face went blank. She'd never seen that particular look on him before, and it felt like another blow.

It turned out there were still new ways to hurt each other. Even after all this time.

"What?"

He got that word out, but just as he didn't look like himself, he hardly sounded like himself, either.

"I got pregnant," she said again, and it was both harder and easier the second time. She nodded at him. "You know when."

"I have no—" But he stopped. Blew out a breath. "That summer."

"That summer," she agreed.

Someone opened the front door to the hotel, and the blast of frigid air from outside washed over them. They both moved at the same time, until they were behind one of the pillars in the old lobby, about as hidden as it was possible to be while still standing in a public area. Rae told herself she was grateful for the slap of cold. For the reminder.

That there was a whole world outside this little circle of pain. All she had to do was step away from it.

She wiped at her eyes again, cleared her throat, and made herself look at him. Because that was only fair. All these years later, it was the least she owed him.

"I felt weird, and I didn't know why," she told him, trying to focus on him. On now. On Riley in a suit in the lobby of the Grand Hotel, not that lonely summer long ago. "We were so careful. I never missed a pill. I took it at the same time every single day, religiously. So religiously you used to tease me about it."

His dark eyes glittered. "I remember."

"I thought I had a summer flu or something that I couldn't kick. Then one day, when you were over at the stables, I woke up late and got sick for no reason. And I figured I should take a test. Just to rule it out, because it was impossible."

She'd never seen that look on his face before. And she could see the tension in him, making his entire body look like granite. That both broke her heart and spurred her on.

"You really haven't lived until you've driven across the Rocky Mountains, halfway to Aspen, to buy a pregnancy test at a dollar store where no one would recognize you." Did she think he would laugh at that when she didn't think it was very funny herself? He didn't. She swallowed, then hurried on before she thought better of this. "The first one was positive, so I went back and bought about ten more. But they all said the same thing."

Rae stopped then. To breathe, maybe. To grieve.

It seemed to take Riley a long while to unlock his jaw. "Why didn't you tell me?"

"How could I?" And it was worse then, because she wasn't hiding behind anything now. Not even that self-righteous sense of injury that had carried her for so long. "Every time someone we knew from high school had another baby, there was another rant from you. I was terrified. I didn't know what to do."

"I can't believe that none of your friends told you that the best thing you could have done was *tell me,*" Riley gritted out, his eyes gleaming with a terrible sort of brightness. "Sure, maybe you getting pregnant wasn't the plan, but I would never—"

"I didn't tell anyone else. That didn't seem right. If you didn't know, it seemed like a betrayal to tell other people." She laughed a little, but not with amusement. "Last Sunday, Abby was telling me how a big turning point for her was when she realized she needed to talk to Gray about the stuff that affected them both. She needed to be in her marriage, not off talking about it."

"But you never told me. You were never in the marriage after that, were you?" She could see him swallow, hard. She saw something stark move over his face. "What did you do, Rae?"

That wasn't exactly an accusation. But it wasn't not an accusation, either.

Rae laughed again, and this time, it was such a bitter sound that she was half-afraid it stained her lips. "You and Jensen were taking horses up to Montana. I planned to tell you everything. When you got back, I was going to sit you down. I was going to break the news. I was so nervous about it that I was practicing speeches in the mirror, Riley."

"What . . ." He shook his head as if the words themselves didn't make sense. "What did you think I was going to do?"

"I didn't know what you were going to do."

Her heart was beating so hard she thought it was going to explode. There was nothing but a bruise where that sharp thing had lodged inside her for so long. And Rae

wanted nothing more than to run away from this conversation, the way she'd always done. It would be easy
enough. She could run out into the street or back into the
crowd. She didn't have to do this.

But she did. She knew she did.

"You've always been so definite about who you are
and what you want," she said then. "I remember, you
couldn't have been more than ten years old and Lucinda
Early asked you what you were going to be when you
grew up. You told her you were going to train horses better than your daddy did. You were matter-of-fact about
it. So matter-of-fact I remember it, and I was only eight."

"What does this have to do with you thinking that I
would . . ." He couldn't finish. "Is this what you really
think of me? You really believe that I would—what? Lift
my hand to you? Throw you out?"

"That's what I'm trying to tell you, Riley," Rae said
urgently. "I'm not going to pretend that I've done a good
job of it, but this is what I've been trying to tell you for
years. You're so sure of everything that it leaves no room
for anyone else to be uncertain. Or scared. Or worried.
It's not a simple as your way or the highway. There is no
highway. There is only your way, because you don't allow for anything else."

He let out a sound then that she couldn't possibly consider a laugh.

Especially when that dark gaze of his slammed right
through her.

"I've spent eight years paying for a crime you never
bothered to tell me I'd committed," Riley hurled at her,
his voice not particularly loud. But lethal all the same.
"It's not my way or the highway, or anything to do with
me. It's your way. It's always been your way. You're the
only one who's ever known what happened between us.

How can you look me straight in the face and tell me that's my fault?"

She knew he was right. But that didn't change anything.

"I'm not saying it's your fault. I'm telling you it was a factor." She threw up her hand when he started to come back at her. "Riley."

And he stopped when she said his name like that. Because that was who he was.

Why did she know that beyond any doubt and yet had still been too afraid to tell him any of this while it happened? Why had she kept all of this bottled up?

But she had to tell him everything, because she didn't think she could bear to do this again. And she doubted he'd want to.

She tried to calm herself. "The cramps started while you were away. The night you left."

"The cramps."

She saw when he got it. He paled. "It happened fast, I guess. Though it didn't feel fast at the time."

He only shook his head, like he couldn't speak.

"I spent the night on the bathroom floor. It hurt. God, did it hurt. But then it was done. The . . . the worst part was over. And I was the only one who knew."

Riley looked sick.

"How could you keep something like this to yourself?" He ran a hand over his mouth. "*Why* would you?"

And that was the question, wasn't it?

Rae sighed. Or maybe it was a quieter sort of sob. She couldn't tell the difference tonight. "I hadn't told you I was pregnant in the first place. How could I tell you that I'd lost the baby? It seemed . . . kinder not to tell you."

"Kinder."

"In retrospect, maybe I wasn't thinking clearly."

Maybe she hadn't been. But she could remember those days almost too clearly. She'd tried so hard to act like herself. She'd tried to sink back into her life. She'd tried to forget any of it had ever happened.

But the more she tried, the harder and harder it became to even remember what she'd been like before. It began to feel like her skin didn't fit. Soon enough, that began to hurt.

She didn't know how to tell him that part, but she tried. "And then, as time passed, I didn't want to tell you. I started to resent you instead."

He broke away then, turning his back on her. That wide, strong back that she'd used to press her cheek against to feel his strength and the rumble of his voice when he spoke. She'd believed he could save her from anything and he hadn't. She'd been drowning right in front of him and he hadn't seen it.

It wasn't fair. She knew that.

But what she felt and what was fair weren't the same things.

"Those last two years." Riley sounded like a dark, forbidding stranger. "The coming and the going."

"I was confused. Most of the time, I think I was lashing out. Then I decided there was no point staying with you when it was nothing but bad, all the time."

"That's not how I remember it."

"Because you remember the sex." Her voice was shaky, and she didn't know what to do about it. "Fight, then make up. Fight, then make up, then fight again. But every fight seemed to hurt worse. And the making up was fake, because you didn't *know*. I thought that if I left, it would be better. I truly believed that."

"Did you?" Riley sounded even darker, and Rae was happy she couldn't see the expression on his face. "I

went down to Denver. Tried to get my head on straight."
He wheeled around again, his gaze like a punch. It made
her wheeze a little. "And there you were on my doorstep
when I got back."

"I wanted to see if you were okay."

"I bet. And you checked in on me almost every night
after that, out of the goodness of your heart, I'm sure.
For six years."

It would be easy to let her temper take over. Familiar.
She could lean in, let her mouth take her away, and see
what happened.

And nothing would change. Everything would stay
exactly the same. They would be standing just like this
ten years from now, nothing left of either of them but a
collection of the scars they'd left on each other.

Rae knew she couldn't let that happen. "And every
time, I would vow that I was done. Because all we did was
get further apart."

"Once again, Rae, you're not remembering this the
way I do."

"We're good at fighting. We're even better at making
up. But when it comes to actually being *married* to each
other? Riley, come on." She leaned forward a little to underscore her point. "We suck."

"How would you know?" His voice was like a blade,
a low, gleaming, terrible thing that cut straight through
her. "You never gave me the opportunity to figure out
how to weather this crisis with you. It never occurred to
you in all this time to clue me in on any of this."

"*I couldn't.*"

Riley blinked as if her voice, so raw it felt torn from
her, hurt him too.

He kept going. "I don't believe for one second that you

thought that I was going to react badly enough that I deserved . . . all this." As blades went, his voice was bad enough. But the way he looked at her cut her to pieces. "When have I ever been violent with you?"

Rae wished, deeply and wildly, that she hadn't started this. That she'd let things stay the way they were. Anything was better than *this*.

"I didn't think you were going to hit me, Riley," she made herself say. And now that it had gotten to this part, she still sounded raw, but she was quieter. Much, much quieter, when she would so much prefer to yell. "I thought you weren't going to love me anymore."

His head jerked back at that, as if she really had hauled off and hit him. Hard, the way his brothers did when they were pretending their roughhousing was casual. Harder, even.

But she knew, didn't she? She knew that love might look different than expected, but it was conditional. It could be rescinded at any time.

All you had to do was make the wrong mistake, and people disappeared.

"And after all this," she managed to say then, though her voice started to shake. And tears started pouring down her cheeks. "After all the times you would tell me how you wanted to be free, not tied down like every other parent you knew, you just . . . Say we could have a baby together. Just like that."

Riley let out a low, awful noise that could only be pain. "Maybe I would have said that then. You don't know. You'll never know."

"I do know," she whispered. "And so do you."

She thought he might argue with that, but he didn't. And that was worse. Why hadn't she stopped to wonder who they were when they stripped away all the temper and fire? Why hadn't she been more worried about what was underneath?

Then again, maybe she had been.

He stood there, a few feet away from her, and it might as well have been an ocean between them. Several oceans, here in Cold River, high up in the Rockies, nowhere near any oceans at all. She could taste the salt in her mouth when she'd never even seen an ocean in person.

She wiped at her eyes. She stood where she was, close to him but apart from him. It seemed fitting.

Rae could see Riley sifting through the wreckage of this near decade of theirs. Looking for clues, turning this year and that night over and over in his head. Because she'd given him the code to what happened in their marriage, finally. Everything must look different.

She regretted that too. She regretted everything.

"How long were you . . ." He stopped. He cleared his throat. "Were you hurt? Then or . . . permanently?"

"These things happen," Rae said, and she felt . . . small. Forlorn and alone, in a way she never had. Not quite. Because there was always him. She'd always had him, one way or another. How had she waited until tonight, when she was letting go of him, to realize that? "They happen a lot, it turns out. I bet if I asked in the ballroom, most of the women there would have their own similar experiences."

"That doesn't sound like a good thing."

"They say it helps to talk. But I didn't." Rae tried to summon up a smile, but it dissolved, and there was salt in her mouth again. "The only person I wanted to talk about it with was you. And at the same time, you were the last person I wanted to talk about it with."

He looked at her for a long, long time.

"Maybe," Riley said, "you weren't really worried that I might stop loving you. Maybe you were worried that if you actually told me what was going on, we'd both have to face the fact that you never loved me that much to begin with. Because I have to think that if you did, none of this would have happened."

Rae felt dizzy. Amanda's words mixed with his and sloshed around inside her until she thought they might make her ill. She managed to swallow it back. Barely. "You know that's not true."

Riley ran his hand over his jaw again, and he wasn't normally a fidgety man. Watching him not know what to do with all that leashed power inside him made Rae . . . empty. "I hate that you were scared. I hate that you went through something like that by yourself. Both thinking that you couldn't tell me you were carrying my baby. Then losing it. There in our house where I've been living for years, thinking I knew all the ghosts by name."

She flinched at that and almost wished he really would hit her. Some part of her thought that had to be better. Quicker.

But she couldn't even seem to speak anymore. Not when he looked at her, not like he'd lost her but like he'd never known her at all.

"I hate all of that, Rae." He sounded like gravel, and she was still tasting oceans. Or maybe that was just regret. "But what I hate the most is that you never trusted me. You didn't trust me enough to tell me then. Or in all the years since. If you'd never decided your biological clock was ticking, would you ever have told me?"

"You have no idea how many times I've tried to tell you."

"You're right. I don't. I just know you didn't."

"Now you know."

She wanted to tell him so many things. How many times she'd wished she could go back, do it over, do it better. How she'd second-guessed herself, then and now.

How regret tasted like rain and the sea, and she was drowning, and had only herself to blame.

"Maybe I never should have told you," she said shakily. "Maybe, since I didn't tell you then, it's selfish to tell you at all. You can't do anything about it. You can't change it."

"No. I can't."

He sounded so final.

Rae heard a faint, whimpering sort of noise, and only distantly realized it was her.

And Riley looked at her with nothing but anguish on his beautiful face. He moved as if he were stuck in someone else's body, as if he didn't quite know what his limbs might do. But he moved toward her, not away. And very carefully, as if he thought at least one of them was breakable, he fit his palm to her cheek.

"Riley . . . ," she began.

"I want to comfort you, Rae," he told her. The look on his face was devastating. She couldn't breathe. "I always want to comfort you. You're my wife. But you wouldn't let me when it mattered. And I can't do it. This time, I can't."

And this time, he was the one who walked away.

Giving Rae what she'd always said she wanted.

There were no more secrets, she tried to tell herself as she stood there, staring out at the cold street she couldn't see thanks to the bright chandeliers above her.

There were no more secrets, but Rae was very much afraid that there was nothing else.

Just a ghost whose name she knew only too well.

19

Riley had always thought that having the Harvest Gala the night before Thanksgiving was dumb, no matter how many jokes the Heritage Society told about folks fitting into their finery on Wednesday so they could feast on Thursday.

A joke he'd been pretending to laugh at for years.

But he'd never thought it was dumber than he did this year.

Because it was a national holiday, he was forced to both handle himself in the wake of last night's revelations and present himself at his parents' house. Where he could look forward to being under the intense scrutiny of every single member of his nosy family when he had no intention of talking about the things Rae had told him.

Riley didn't particularly want to *think* about the things Rae had told him.

It was more like he couldn't.

Had it been any other Sunday-dinner-type thing, like the ones they usually had throughout the year that people showed up to as their schedules allowed, he would have avoided it. Come up with some excuse to stay away and not really cared what anyone thought.

But there was no way that his family would let him get away with missing Thanksgiving.

Especially not after they'd seen him with Rae last night.

They would show up in a fleet of pickups and drag him over to the ranch house whether he liked it or not, then use the opportunity to interrogate him on his personal life until he actually gave in and told them, just to shut them up. He could envision all of that a little too clearly.

Riley did his usual chores, showered longer than necessary without managing to clear his head, then made his way over to the main house.

It had snowed again in the night, dusting over the fields that stretched across the valley and clinging, wet and heavy, to the branches of the trees in the forest. Riley took his time, not because the roads were treacherous but because he was putting it off. The roads were what dirt roads always were in snow—an opportunity to forget whatever might be pressing in on him because they required a little more of his attention.

That ended when he made it to his parents' drive, where his family members had already created snow tracks for him to follow.

Great.

He bumped his way over the snow and parked out in the yard in his usual spot. Then he took his time climbing out of his truck, wishing he could take even more time on his horses in the stable complex. An excellent way to avoid his family—but Connor had texted earlier to say he'd taken care of all the horses already this morning. In an unprecedented show of self-motivation.

Demands for future repayment in kind were implied, obviously.

Riley faced facts. He had no choice but to suck it up and go inside.

He ducked in the side door, hanging up his hat and coat and kicking off his boots. And instantly wondered if maybe he'd been overestimating how rough this was going to be, because the house he'd grown up in smelled like sugar and gravy. He could hear conversations and laughter, pots and pans clattering in the kitchen, and the sound of the television from the family room.

It all felt like a big old hug, not that he would allow one.

Riley might like to pretend there were no good memories in this house, but that wasn't entirely true. Just because his childhood had felt a lot like a front-row seat to a circus, that didn't mean there hadn't been days like this. Pie and turkey and his grandparents, who had always stood like a stoic wall of much-needed sense between the generations.

Settle down, he told himself. *Give some thanks, eat some stuffing, and go home.*

Because his life hadn't changed last night. Only his understanding of it.

"Nice of you to show up, sunshine," Zack drawled when he walked into the family room.

"Who called the cops?" Riley replied in kind. "Not very festive."

Zack replied with a razor-sharp smile and a hand gesture—but not where their grandparents could see.

Riley didn't relax, exactly, but he did a good impression of it. He and Brady talked about a whole lot of nothing while Connor and Amanda cheerfully insulted each other under the guise of a conversation about tractor parts.

"Are you a farmer now?" Connor asked, kicked back on the couch while Amanda mirrored him from across the room, each one of them trying to outdo the other with the force of their studied disinterest. "Thought you were a farmers' market, monkey."

"And here I thought you mucked out stables, Connor. But apparently, you're also the local authority on tractor repair?" Amanda smiled. "Quite the Renaissance man."

"I'm pretty sure I'm the only person in this room who's an expert on farming equipment," Grandpa offered after a moment, sitting in his favorite armchair in his Sunday best. Almost as if he were musing out loud, possibly to the football game on the television.

But that ended that squabble. Grandpa had never needed to be loud.

As the late morning wore on into afternoon, Ellie continued to refuse all help in the kitchen. The way she always did. But because it was Thanksgiving, when it started to get even later and there were more sounds of crashing from the back of the house, everyone quietly helped, anyway.

The way they all did every year.

Maybe, Riley thought, he and Rae weren't the only people around stuck in cycles that turned for no reason and never seemed to stop.

By the time they all sat down around the table, Riley was almost lulled into a false sense of security.

But he should have known better.

"Will you pass me the sweet potatoes?" Amanda asked. She smiled when Riley obliged. "That was an intense dance with Rae last night, wasn't it?"

Riley stared at Brady like he ought to do something, but his best friend only shrugged, so he redirected his glare toward his sister. "What dance? You weren't there."

"I was there," Jensen announced, reaching over to help himself to the stuffing and getting his grandmother's frown for his trouble. Though, being Jensen, that didn't stop him. He only grinned unrepentantly and—being Jensen—got away with it. "I danced with Rae too. It wasn't intense at all."

"Good thing," Riley muttered. "For you."

And only after he'd said it did he realize what a reflex it was. Especially when Jensen grinned even wider in response.

"I received *multiple* reports," Amanda said, a certain look on her face that Riley recognized all too well. It brought him back a year to last fall, when his little sister had charged out to have her own life no matter what anyone else thought about it.

He hadn't liked it much then, either. He liked it less now.

"I doubt very much that Riley wants to talk about this," his mother said. In her usual chilly way that probably meant *she* didn't want to talk about it. Or anything else that veered too close to an actual feeling.

Riley wanted to cheer. But then, it wasn't as if not talking about it all this time had saved him from having to talk about it, was it? Because here they were.

Just as Rae had predicted last night when she'd told him there was a countdown.

That only pissed him off more.

"By all means," he said, sitting back in his chair. "Let's have a family roundup about my marriage, here and now. I'll start." He glared at Zack. "I'm tired of you all sandbagging me with your opinions." He shifted his glare to Amanda. "Or worse, Rae. Ask me whatever you want at this table, or forever hold your peace. That's the deal." He shared his glare around, from Jensen's too-innocent expression to Connor's frown to his father's usual remote and unreadable look. "Any takers?"

"Do you get to make that kind of deal?" Amanda

asked, and he could see that she was enjoying herself. "I'm trying to think about how it worked when it was my relationship that everybody wanted to talk about." She pretended to think it over while, next to her, Brady sighed. "Oh, that's right, you all threatened Brady with bodily violence. And you, Riley, punched him in the face."

"I deserved that punch," Brady said at once.

"You did," Riley agreed.

"I'm not going to punch Rae in the face," Amanda said sweetly. "If that's what you're worried about."

"I wasn't worried about it." Riley scowled at her. "Should I start worrying? That will give the town something else to talk about, won't it?"

"The town is going to find something to talk about, Riley," Amanda replied. "Even if they have to make it up. Don't you worry about the town. Creative telling of tales is what we *do*."

"Seriously, man." Connor, still frowning, shook his head. "Welcome to Cold River."

"This is a pointless conversation," Zack said in his usual authoritative way that clearly irritated each and every other member of his family. Except possibly their grandparents, who looked as if they either didn't understand what was going on or were deliberately reserving their judgment.

"Because you say so?" Connor asked Zack. "Weird how I'm suddenly convinced there's never been a conversation with more of a point."

Zack ignored him. "Riley likes letting Rae walk all over him. No point talking about it anymore."

Riley should have taken that as a cue to prove that like him, his family had no idea what had gone on between him and Rae. He should have leaped at the opportunity to *do something* about what he'd learned last night. Throw it on the table and let them choke on it, since they wanted to know what had happened so badly.

But it wasn't theirs.

It was his, and it was Rae's. There had been a baby and she couldn't trust him, and he'd thought he knew their history inside and out. He'd thought all kinds of things about why she'd bailed on him, depending on the day or the week or the year. And now his own memories seemed twisted to him. He did too.

God, he thought he was twisted up so bad he might never get himself unknotted again.

"I really think that—" Amanda began.

"You want to talk to me about my marriage?" Riley asked with a deadly calm. "Go right ahead. I'm not going to stop you. But, Amanda. Leave Rae alone."

Amanda flushed. "I never—"

"She doesn't deserve it," Riley growled. "And even if she did, it's not up to you. Is that clear?"

"It's clear to me that all of you need to mind your own business," Grandma tutted, her tone enough to make everyone else sit up a little straighter. Even Riley's father, which might have amused Riley at another time. Janet Lowe Kittredge cast a steely eye around the table. "In my day, we considered that a virtue."

And everyone sat there in a silence broken only by the sound of utensils scraping against plates, until Grandpa brought up football again.

Riley could practically hear the universal sigh of relief.

Later, Riley helped with the dishes. In his mother's house, that meant nudging her aside so he could take over. Not that Ellie then wandered off and put her feet up. Perish the thought.

For once, Riley was grateful that his mother preferred to keep her own counsel as she puttered around, wiping down surfaces and emptying loads of washed dishes as fast as she could. It was a pleasant sort of vacation from the rest of his family without his having to leave, giving them something else to talk about.

And when all the dishes were cleaned and put away, Riley and his mother stood there in the bright, happy kitchen where he remembered her screaming and screaming at his father. Tears pouring down her face, accusations flying, sometimes even lunging at Donovan.

Good times, he thought darkly.

Ellie fixed herself a cup of coffee. She raised a brow at him, then fixed Riley some coffee as well when he nodded.

She brought both mugs over to where he still stood at the sink, looking out the window. And for a moment, he and his mother stood there in a quiet sort of companionship, looking out over Kittredge land, tucked up in its blanket of snow as the shy winter sun made a break for the mountains.

But the longer they stood there, the less companionable it felt.

"Go ahead and say something," Riley muttered when he couldn't take it any longer. "You standing there, not saying anything, is pretty noisy, Mom."

"You made it clear you don't want opinions," Ellie replied coolly.

"Suit yourself."

But Ellie didn't move away. She stayed there, tall and elegant as always, even after spending hours cooking and cleaning. He thought about Rae telling him how much she'd looked up to Ellie over the years, and he didn't know why that seemed to sit in him differently today.

Something about Rae in her red dress, tears pouring down her face. When if things between them had been the way they should, she ought to have been nothing but gorgeous and happy. The way she deserved.

But then again, everything was different today.

For him, he amended. Rae had known all of this all along.

"Did a baby really bring you and Dad together?" he heard himself ask as the sun melted down behind the hills off to the west, leaving a little light behind in the frozen sky as if it didn't quite know what it wanted.

He could relate.

Riley felt his mother's gaze on the side of his face. "Do you mean your sister?"

"Since we're all so interested in sharing opinions today." Riley blew on his coffee even though it likely wasn't hot any longer, then set it aside, anyway. "I guess that's a choice I don't understand."

Ellie appeared to think that over. And when she spoke, her voice was very careful. "Are you being called upon to make that choice?"

"No."

"I could explain to you the inner workings of your parents' marriage, if that's what you'd like, Riley." Riley could hear her amusement, hidden in that cool tone that was always so distancing. Deliberately, he'd always thought, because he could remember when there was no distance at all. And only yelling. "But I'm going to go out on a limb and guess you really wouldn't like that at all."

"I don't need inner workings, Mom. But maybe you can explain . . ." He shook his head, and maybe the kitchen was what got to him. Or the fact that his own history wasn't what he'd thought it was, so maybe nothing was. Even this. "All I remember is the fighting. You fighting, mostly. And Dad just . . . a wall. I don't understand how you switched from that to this. It's like you had Amanda and stopped being who you were."

His mother didn't say anything. It felt like an indictment.

Riley was so sick of indictments.

Because that was why he felt the way he did today, wasn't it? Rae had stared at him, crying, telling him a terrible story that was about *them*. And all he could think about was what she wasn't saying.

That he should have saved her, or helped her, and he hadn't.

That, at the very least, he should have seen that something was wrong and tried to fix it.

His whole relationship with Rae had been based on her flying off the handle and him quieting her. Her thinking the worst and him soothing her.

She was the catastrophe. He was the calm.

When they fought, she was the yeller. He was more about the quiet, lethal responses.

Until she threw herself at him, and neither one of them was quiet.

That was how they'd worked. And he guessed that was why they hadn't worked too.

Inside him, there was this mess—more like a dark, tangled swamp—of what he'd lost that he hadn't even known he had. And underneath that, but in some ways even more dislocating, the loss of who he'd been so sure he was throughout this thing.

He didn't know how to say that to his mother. He wouldn't have said it, anyway.

Instead, he tried to concentrate on the only other marriage he'd ever seen up close and personal. "It's like one day you woke up and magically decided to accept that Dad was never going to change. So you changed instead."

"Riley." Ellie held on to her mug, her gaze focused on the dwindling daylight outside the window, though who knew what she was seeing? She was as much a mystery to him as ever. "What do you want me to say? Yes, that's exactly what happened. And no, that's not at all what happened. You've been married. You know exactly how complicated the simplest things are. And at the same time, how simple some incredibly complicated things become."

That landed on him with a heavy sort of thud, but he didn't want it to.

"Thanks for not answering," he muttered.

He should have known better than to try. He turned, but his mother shifted to catch his gaze, and he saw a kind of fire there in her normally serene gaze. It stopped him in his tracks.

"I did answer you. You don't like the answer. And that's fine; you don't have to." Somehow, her gaze got even more penetrating. "But I actually did see you and Rae last night. It's never been over between you two, has it?"

Riley didn't actually growl. Because this was his mother. "If you wanted to talk about me and Rae, you should have taken the opportunity I gave everybody at the dinner table."

Ellie sighed. "I don't need an opportunity to talk to or about my son, Riley. I'm your mother. I haven't listened to your rules before, and I'm unlikely to start now."

Riley didn't pretend to hide his astonishment at that. "Wait. Is this maternal concern? You can see how that might be confusing. After the last *entire life* I've had with none of that."

He shouldn't have said that. He knew he shouldn't have. But the truth was, he felt as if something inside of him had come undone. And whatever it was, he lacked the tools to put it back together.

Riley had no idea how to put any of this back together. Especially him.

He thought Ellie would do what she normally did. Disengage. Sigh, retreat behind that cool veneer of hers, and walk away, leaving him to deal with his guilt alone.

But instead, she met his gaze head-on. And worse, held it.

"You are so much like your father," she told him, very distinctly. "It's mind-boggling."

That went through Riley like she'd reached over and tossed the contents of her mug in his face. Then lit him on fire.

"I'm nothing like him," he managed to get out, with no control over his voice at all. He was lucky he wasn't shouting. "Why would you say something like that?"

Ellie didn't look away. If anything, her gaze seemed to intensify. "You are deeply unforgiving, Riley."

He thought of all the times Rae had turned up at his door, all the years she'd let him think she'd left him . . . just for fun. "That's not even a little bit true."

"Ask me how I know," she said softly, and his own words came back to him. Words he shouldn't have said about his own mother, his parents' marriage—and none of it particularly kind. It had literally *just happened*.

But she didn't wait for him to face himself.

"You've been lucky enough to always know exactly what you wanted for your life," she said in the same devastatingly quiet way. "Not everybody has the same luck.

Some of us are human, disastrously so. We flail, fall, and don't have the slightest idea how to pick ourselves up again. Or figure out the right direction to head in once we do."

He could hear Rae saying almost the same thing the night before, and it tore around inside him like a terrible storm. Part of him wished it would pick him up and carry him away. Because anything had to be better than feeling like this.

Than feeling all of this.

"Your father was always the same," Ellie told him. "He knew the ranch was going to be his since he was small. He never wanted anything else. He put his head down, worked hard, and never had the slightest doubt that he was heading in the right direction. Sound like anyone you know?"

Riley wanted to tear the cabinets apart with his hands, if only to prove that he was nothing like the walking slab of impenetrable granite that was his father.

"Your father lived on his own the minute he turned eighteen," Ellie said. "Out in the bunkhouses behind the stables, so he had access to the horses 24-7. He was running his own breeding program before he left high school. He and your grandfather used to knock heads all the time. Again, are you hearing anything familiar?"

It wasn't that Riley hadn't known these things. He had. But he hadn't . . . put them all together in a pattern that made sense of a man he'd long ago decided wasn't worth the fight, so had written off—more or less.

A thought that moved in him a little differently today.

Because he sure did make a lot of decisions about people without knowing the full story, didn't he?

"I guess that's convenient," he managed to say to his mother. Who he'd thought had checked out so long ago that having her see right through him tonight was as surprising as it was painful. "It's Dad's fault for being exactly who he was. And my fault for knowing what I wanted. I see how those things make us both into monsters."

The irony wasn't lost on him that somehow he'd ended up not only defending his father but linking him and his father together. It was taking *twisted* to a whole new level.

"I'm not the one who thinks in terms of monsters, Riley," Ellie said softly, her eyes on him.

Through him.

Riley shook his head, wishing the floor felt a little more solid beneath his feet. "That's not how I remember it, Mom. All the yelling. All the screaming. The poking and poking. I couldn't wait to get out of this house."

His mother barely reacted. All she did was tilt her head forward the littlest bit, and it still made Riley feel like dirt.

"I know you did. You put down roots as quick as you could, so you could do it differently. Better."

Riley felt his mouth twist. "You don't have to point it out. It worked out really well for me. I'm aware."

Ellie's mouth curved, though her eyes stayed steady on him. "The thing is, Riley, you aren't doomed to repeat the mistakes of your parents. That's a choice."

He shoved his hand through his hair. "Rae and I have nothing to do with you and Dad."

But even as he said that, he wondered. Until last night, the Rae he'd known had always been fiery. Determined. She flung herself at him. Stuck her finger in his face. Hauled off and hit him sometimes. She had always been the one to push. Poke. He had always been the one to stand stern, to insist they never compromise.

To insist *he* never compromised, and he hadn't. Not ever.

Whatever he wanted to think about what she'd told him last night, Rae had clearly, honestly felt she couldn't tell him about this huge thing she'd gone through. Why? Because according to her, he was so *definitive* he'd given her no room to be anything but.

Where had he seen that play out before?

But he couldn't accept that. He didn't want to accept it. He shook his head at his mother. "For one thing, Rae left. You never did."

"I never did," his mother agreed. "And let me tell you something about that. If you've never heard another thing I've said to you in your life, hear this."

"That sounds ominous."

And he felt chastised when all Ellie did was smile.

"Marriage isn't a charity," she told him. "If you want to fix things, it has to be because you love the person you married. With your whole heart. And for no other reason. Because otherwise, Riley, it won't work. No matter how long it takes you to come to that conclusion, I promise you—it won't."

Then she walked out of the kitchen, leaving Riley to his Thanksgiving vigil over the dark fields and the tangled mess inside of him that seemed to grow bigger with each breath.

20

Rae processed her feelings about the night before with food.

Lots and lots and *lots* of food.

The turkey in the Trujillo family was a joint project most years. Oftentimes, a failed project. But Rae didn't really care if the bird were tender and juicy or dry to the bone. As far as she was concerned, the turkey was nothing more than an appropriately unremarkable conduit for all the good stuff.

And *the good stuff* tasted like all her feelings, none of which she cared to feel when she could eat them instead.

She ate the crispy onions off the top of the green bean casserole—the entire purpose of the existence of green bean casseroles, in her opinion, though she did like eating the bean part with stuffing too. She ate extra marshmallowy sweet potatoes, which she liked to think of as a vegetable even when it was clearly more of a dessert.

Because her mother and grandmother could never agree on anything, they had twice as much food as necessary. Competing stuffings. Competing gravies, in addition to Rae's favorite, which was quietly made by her father. Kathy liked roasted brussels sprouts, while Inez preferred roasted small potatoes. Rae liked them both.

Matias handled the mashed potatoes, always less about potatoes and more about the cream, butter, and salt.

Rae made her stolen carrot soufflé and resented it every time someone else helped themselves to any of it.

The Trujillo Thanksgiving was the one meal of the year where everyone was usually too busy eating themselves into a food coma to engage in the usual skirmishes.

Rae considered it her family duty to eat as much as possible.

After Riley had left her there in the lobby, Rae hadn't really seen the point of going back into the gala. She'd snuck into one of the bathrooms off the lobby and did what she could to wash away the evidence of all that sobbing. She'd found her coat and had snuck outside.

It had been so cold. She'd hunched into her coat and walked as quickly as she could, wondering what on earth had possessed her to wear high-heeled, open-toed shoes on the night before Thanksgiving. But then again, as each step made her toes feel more and more numb, she almost appreciated it.

Maybe all of her could go numb, she'd thought. Maybe, finally, she could stop all this *feeling* that had gotten her absolutely nowhere.

The Mortimer sisters were still at the gala, leaving Rae the run of the house when she finally made it there. But unlike all those mornings where she'd stood in the kitchen and imagined this was her house, tonight it felt . . . empty. Alien, even.

Or she did.

Her temples had pulsed with a sharp sort of pain, and she'd told herself she needed water. She kicked off her shoes, hissing a little as the feeling surged back into her cold feet, there against the kitchen floor. She chugged one glass of water. Then another. And when she turned around to face this dark house where she could only ever be a tenant, that, too, felt distinctly opposite of any numbing.

She'd gone upstairs and showered until her entire body was pruned. Then she'd curled up in her new, narrow bed, prepared to cry her heart out.

The tears hadn't come.

Maybe, she'd thought eventually—curled up there beneath the eaves in a life she hardly recognized because it was built, brick by brick, on terrible secrets—she'd cried all the tears she was going to in the hotel lobby. All the tears she had left.

And today, because she still couldn't seem to find the sobs she'd been sure were lurking around in there, she ate.

Until she was so full she had to breathe in slow gasps. And when she looked around the table, everyone else was doing the same.

It made them all laugh.

"In the spirit of family harmony—or gluttony, as the case may be," her father said, casting a particular glance between his wife and his mother that Rae was certain she wasn't hallucinating, here in the middle of her carb and sugar high, "let's go around the table and say something we're thankful for today."

"Bummer," Matias said darkly. But not as grimly as he usually did, indicating all that butter was doing its good work, even in him. "I forgot to bring my gratitude journal."

Rae couldn't help laughing at the notion of her big, bad brother with any kind of journal, much less one brimming with thankfulness. Then stopped laughing, because she was too full.

"I'm grateful that we can gather as a family," their

father said reprovingly. "I'm more interested in what we'd like to see in the coming year."

Matias brightened. Slightly. "Oh. Business? That's easy."

Their father sighed.

"We're Trujillos," Inez said grandly, clearly drunk on both the Thanksgiving wine and the six helpings she'd managed so far. "We don't do emotions."

"Hear, hear," Rae said, lifting her glass.

And to her astonishment, her whole family toasted. Even Matias.

"I'd like a promotion," Kathy said, her voice serene but her gaze wicked. "I'd like to be president of the Trujillo Corporation."

The current president drew herself up in her chair, an effect that was ruined somewhat when she wobbled. "Over my dead body."

Kathy inclined her head. "If you insist."

Inez refilled her wineglass. "I would like better staff, if we're making wish lists."

Obviously, things got loud from there.

"I guess saying I want to expand our profit margins sounds a little boring," Matias said, leaning back in his chair as if even he, who treated his body like a pristine chapel every other day of the year, were stuffed to the gills. "I didn't realize I could have gone for a power grab."

And while her mother and grandmother bickered—which she was now forced to see with a new set of eyes, after last night's discussion with her mother—Rae had time to take a few more bites she definitely didn't need.

But all those feelings were sloshing around inside of her like too much pie, and not releasing themselves in floods of tears the way she'd expected they would.

She felt almost washed clean, somehow.

Maybe because of that, she was convinced that she could finally see everything clearly in a way she hadn't before.

She'd had one life with Riley, and she'd loved that life. But it had ended on a terrible night eight years ago when she lost a secret she shouldn't have kept in the first place.

And yes, she'd clung to that night. She'd had reasons—good reasons, she thought even now, even if she regretted them—for keeping that night to herself. But because she'd wrapped herself around that secret and hoarded it, it had become a kind of scar tissue.

That sharp-edged blade that had stabbed at her.

Rae had stayed like that ever since.

She hadn't grown. She hadn't changed. Even this latest attempt to break out of the cycle of her life hadn't worked.

She'd thought the problem was her. Or her and Riley together. Friends, not friends, drawn back together to their own doom—however she wanted to think about it, the fact was that until last night, it didn't matter what she did. Because whatever it was, whatever she wanted, some part of it was built on lies.

Lies of omission, but lies all the same.

And now everything was swept clean. Everything was out in the open. When she thought about the future, it was as if she could suddenly *see* it. She might not know what it held, but she believed it existed. She wasn't afraid of it any longer.

Rae had shaken all the dust and scars and lies off the past. That meant the future didn't make her despair any longer.

That was why, when the sniping around the Thanksgiving table died down and everyone was suddenly looking at her, she smiled as if she'd known exactly what she wanted all along.

"I want to completely change the Flower Pot," she announced. "First, enough with the uniforms. We're not a big-box store, and we shouldn't look like one. Cold River is becoming more and more eclectic and funky, and we need to keep pace with that."

"What do uniforms have to do with anything?" her grandmother demanded.

"They're ugly, Grandma," Rae said gently. But firmly. "And if you stop speaking to me for another nine years, they'll still be ugly."

Across the table, Matias smiled.

Everyone else looked stunned. Especially Inez.

Rae smiled. "And the reason that matters is that we want the entire experience when a customer enters the shop to be beautiful. From top to bottom. The shop should celebrate individual expression, from my arrangements right on down to our staff." She cut her gaze to her father. "And while we're arguing about titles, I want one."

"You have a title," her father said, and though his voice gave nothing away, she was sure there was a bit of twinkle in his eyes. "You're an employee of the Trujillo Corporation like everyone else at this table."

"Artistic director and events coordinator," Rae countered. "No uniforms. And it's time to promote the hourly staff to do those cold openings instead of Matias and me. That's what I want."

"Everybody hates the uniforms, Grandma," Matias added, staring down the table toward Inez. "Literally everyone. Silent treatment or not."

"I've always liked the uniforms," Inez protested. "Who doesn't like a neat, orderly appearance?"

"You don't have to wear it," Matias retorted.

Inez sniffed. "Very well, then. And don't be childish, either of you. *The silent treatment.* As if."

Kathy laughed at that. Matias and Rae stared at each other in disbelief.

But their father smiled. "I like all of it. And why wait for next year? You can start tomorrow. Wear whatever you like, Ms. Creative Director."

Rae helped with cleanup, then zoned out on the couch in the living room with everyone else until her food coma lifted its grip a little. Then she staggered into the kitchen to fill up the Tupperware she'd brought with leftovers, feeling surprisingly . . . buoyant.

Especially for someone who hadn't been able to resist an extra helping of pie the moment she hadn't felt actively uncomfortable.

She left her father and brother debating the merits and uses of the often overlooked carnation. Her mother and grandmother were still arguing about the best corporate titles, and more importantly, which of them deserved an upgrade. The football game was on the television, a happy little background noise.

Rae let herself out the back door and walked out into the dark.

It was cold. The kind of bitter Colorado cold that punched out a space between her ribs and settled in, no matter how many layers she was wearing or how much she'd fattened herself up today. Her boots crunched against the frozen ground as she walked over to her truck, and it sounded like more of that happy noise. She slung her leftovers into the passenger seat, then walked around the back of her truck, the night around her so deeply quiet it almost felt like its own kind of song.

And before she got in, she tipped her head back and let the stars make her dizzy.

The good kind of dizzy, until she felt as if she were dancing.

She meant to head straight back to town once she pulled out of her parents' drive. But instead, out there on the county road where there was nothing around for company but the slumbering fields and the crowded night sky, she found herself rolling to a stop instead.

There at the crossroads where she could turn toward town or turn deeper into the valley instead.

Rae switched off her headlights. She folded her arms on the steering wheel and gazed out through her windshield.

There were so many stars tonight that they crowded into her, filling her up, shoving aside all the helpings of Thanksgiving dinner she'd eaten, and making her feel . . .

Hope.

The minute she thought the word, it seemed to burn even brighter than the Thanksgiving night sky. Brighter and deeper and wilder, until that was what filled her, and burst out of her, as if that were what she'd been waiting for.

Rae finally cried then. Oh, how she cried. But she was laughing at the same time. Laughing and crying, both at once, and all of it was a part of that same brightness outside and in her too.

Because she wasn't afraid any longer.

She wasn't *afraid.*

There were no more secrets, and that meant the past was finally past. The future was as unknowable as the sky.

But that didn't make it any less bright.

All she had was tonight. The stars, the quiet song in the dark, the Colorado cold.

All she had was *her*.

And hope.

So much hope, at last, long after she'd given up on it. Long after she'd resigned herself to a life without it, filled with necessity instead of wonder, because those were the choices she'd made a long, long time ago when she'd been scared.

She wasn't scared any longer. And she was only as scarred as she chose to be.

So Rae did the only thing she could.

She headed home.

21

Riley's mood had not improved by the time he made it to his own, private road. He bumped along the track he'd made earlier, but all he could think about was that talk he'd had with his mother.

He wasn't like his father.

That was a ridiculous thing for her to say.

"Ridiculous," he muttered out loud as punctuation.

It didn't matter how many times he thought it or said it. His words felt hollow inside and outside of his own head. Luckily, he had a remedy for that. In the form of a bottle of Maker's Mark waiting for him in his house.

But when he finally made it up the drive to his own yard, he slammed his foot on the brake, fishtailing a little until the truck stopped dead.

Because Rae's ancient truck was parked in her usual spot out front. And all the lights were on inside the house when he knew he'd left only the porch light on.

Riley didn't bother thinking or talking himself down.

He reacted.

He was out of the truck and up on the front porch in a single beat of his heart. Maybe less. He threw open the door, expecting to find Rae simmering with the usual temper or fury on the couch, but the living room was empty.

He didn't bother to strip off his layers, because his heart was like a jackhammer in his chest. And all those feelings he had absolutely no desire to share with his family—or himself—pounded at him. Through him.

Until he couldn't really tell if this was some kind of late-in-the-day hangover, if he'd eaten too much, or if he was simply so angry he thought tonight might be the night he tore down this house he'd built. Then burned it to ash.

Because that would be better than these *things* in him that were making him crazy, making him feel as if he were running when he was standing still, making him *feel*—

He heard a faint noise, and then she appeared, drifting out from his bedroom to stand there at the other end of the hall.

Wearing—

But his mind refused to take it in.

Or maybe he actually blacked out for a moment there.

When Riley was in control of himself again, Rae was still there. Still standing there at the end of the hallway—and the fact he was surprised about that told him that some distinct part of him had really thought that maybe she was a ghost.

Because Rae was in bare feet. Her dark hair was down, flowing around her shoulders in glossy waves, the way he liked it best.

And otherwise, she was wearing a tiny, silky thing that he'd last seen—

But again, his mind couldn't quite process that.

"I can't believe you didn't get rid of this," she said softly. She ran a hand down the front of it, and it wasn't any kind of seductive gesture. That made it worse, some-how.

Why was she so *comfortable* when he was coming out of his own skin?

Riley was standing so still, every single bone and muscle in his body so tight he was amazed his jaw hadn't cracked in half.

Or *he* hadn't cracked in half.

"What are you doing here?" he managed to get out over the pounding in his head and the racket in his heart. "Are you trying to torture me?"

She dropped her hand. Then she started toward him, and Riley couldn't decide if he hated that or wanted it. Both, maybe. Because this was Rae.

This was still Rae.

But he didn't understand how he was supposed to let go of the things she'd told him only last night.

"This isn't going to work," he gritted out, though his words didn't stop her. "You can't drop the kinds of things you dropped on me last night and then show up here like this. You don't really think that's going to work, do you? Even if you are wearing that thing you wore on our honeymoon."

He expected her to stop dead. She didn't.

And there was something different about her. He couldn't put his finger on it. Rae glided down the hallway, moving closer to him with a smile he didn't understand curving her lips.

Maybe she really had come here to kill him. To finish the job.

Riley figured it wouldn't take much.

"Remember our honeymoon?" And now she was too close. Because she was right in front of him, tipping her head back to aim that smile at him. The scent of her filled his head, he could almost feel the warmth of her soft skin, and she made him feel liked he'd drained that bottle of Maker's Mark. "You told me we were going camping. Then you took me up to that cabin instead."

"That cabin's about as far off the grid as it's possible to get," Riley said. Against his will. "It was camping."

"It's not camping if there's a bed and a roof. That's the law."

Riley shook his head, off-balance and filled with too much darkness.

And her. Always her.

"This isn't going to work, Rae. You can't show up at my house and start talking about our honeymoon. And beds. And think that's somehow going to make me forget what you told me last night."

Her gaze softened, and that hit him like a punch.

Then she shook him even more, because she reached over and took his hands in hers and he . . . stopped breathing, maybe.

Rae held his hands between her much smaller ones as best she could. When she looked up at him again, he was reminded how tiny she was. There in her bare feet, without those crazy heels she'd been wearing lately. Tiny and delicate and still the toughest woman he knew.

He told himself he hated this power she'd always had over him. That she was one-third his size and made him feel small, just by looking at him like this.

"I don't want to forget it," she told him, her voice soft but her words distinct. "I didn't come here to make you feel bad, Riley."

"Oh, okay. I guess that's just a happy bonus to you showing up here, then. Great."

But he didn't pull his hands away. And she didn't let go.

And time seemed to flatten out between them. Or maybe that was his heart again, doing strange things to his chest.

"I should have told you the moment I got pregnant," Rae said quietly. "I regret that I didn't. I regret it more than you'll ever know."

He wanted to jump on that. He wanted to howl out all the things that were still pounding around and around inside him, making it difficult to breathe. And stand. And do anything at all but look back at her. But somehow, he couldn't seem to find the words.

"I told you all the reasons why I felt I couldn't last night," she said, and he could feel her grip tighten. "And those reasons kept me from telling you all this time. But I want you to know that if I had it to do over again, I wouldn't wait eight years to face all those fears. I wouldn't try to do it alone and hurt both of us even more in the process."

"I don't know what you want from me." The words were torn out of him. Again. He hardly recognized his own voice. "After all this time, even after last night, I don't know what you *want,* Rae."

She took a breath, and he could hear the shudder in it. "How could you? I didn't know myself. For years."

Riley pulled away then. He had to get some distance. He had to *do* something.

He turned away from her, retracing his tracks into the living room and shrugging out of his outdoor gear before he spontaneously combusted. He kicked off his boots and tossed off his hat in the general direction of the hook where it belonged.

And he didn't pretend that he wasn't collecting himself as best he could. Just like he couldn't pretend that he wasn't hyperaware of everything she was doing. Following him into the living room and then sitting there on one arm of the couch, watching him.

As far as he was concerned, it might as well have been a declaration of war.

"Here's what I can't get past," he gritted out at her when he finally faced her again, feeling like some kind of world champion that he didn't get something to blunt the edges of . . . whatever this was. "You wanted to divorce me. Just like tonight, you showed up here, told me you were done, and said divorce was the only option. In case I thought you were kidding, you moved back out of your parents' house, into town, and announced you wanted to start dating other people."

She nodded, there on the couch. "And yet oddly enough, I never even looked up how to go about filing for divorce. And only ended up dating you."

And Riley wasn't calm. He wasn't *soothing*. He was coming apart. "You had no intention of ever telling me. You would have divorced me, moved on, and never seen fit to tell me about something that happened to *both of us,* Rae. It happened to *me,* and I didn't even know it."

She was holding herself very still, her arms locked around her middle. And she gazed back at him with whole worlds in those dark eyes of hers, but she didn't say a word.

It made him feel even more off-balance. "You can't even defend yourself, can you?"

She swallowed hard. "I've already told you why. Whether that's a defense or not, I don't know."

As far as Riley was concerned, she might as well have hauled off and thrown a grenade at his head. "What did you say?"

Where was the fight? Where were all her usual weapons, specifically and perfectly honed to slam right into him and jump-start his temper? He was a brick wall until she knocked a hole straight through him. He wanted that rush, that oblivion. He wanted the familiarity of it.

He wanted something to make sense again.

"I don't blame you." Her voice was upsettingly quiet again. With that same soft look in her eyes that made him want to kick out his own wall. "I don't blame you for anything, Riley. That wasn't clear these past years, I know."

"I asked you a thousand times to tell me what happened. I begged you. And you must have wanted me to, because you came back, Rae. Over and over and over again."

"I couldn't stay away."

He rubbed his hands over his face. "Did you think that sooner or later I would . . . guess?"

It took her a moment or so to consider that. "I think I must have."

"All these years. All these wasted, pointless years when we could have . . ." But he broke off. Because it was too much, he hated it, and the loss of it all weighed on him so heavily Riley didn't understand how he was still upright.

"When we could have . . . what?" Rae asked, that half smile reappearing, and he was pretty sure it was going to be the death of him. And soon. "The police haven't had to get involved. There are no restraining orders, no cheating scandals acted out in bars, no gambling debts or drug addictions here. Compared to a lot of the other couples we know who got married right out of high school, we're not doing so badly."

"We broke up eight years ago," Riley bit out. "All of this has just been you trying to make yourself feel better about keeping your secrets. It's been your guilt, plain and simple. All this time, I thought that if I weathered the storm, it would change. But it was never going to change." He shook his head then like he was shaking sense into himself. "I thought I was waiting you out. You were waiting to come up with a good reason to divorce me."

Rae didn't deny any of that. Making it all that much worse, to his mind.

"Despite all that, you still came back here tonight," he said, his words like bullets. And he was aiming straight at her; there was no pretending otherwise. "This time you want to talk about our honeymoon, for God's sake. One of these nights, I wish you would show up with a gun, shoot me in the head, and be done with this, Rae. I want to be *done* with this."

That was exactly the sort of statement that would normally make her scream her head off at him. Charge him. *Do something.*

But she only stayed where she was. So still. So unlike the Rae he knew.

And while he watched, her eyes filled with tears.

For him.

He knew that without question.

Riley could feel it coming at him then. A freight train barreling down a questionable track, but aimed straight for him.

He felt the walls closing in on him. Or maybe that was his chest, shutting down at last because his heart was out of control. All he could see was Rae. All he could see was all that *emotion* in her gaze.

Worse still, he could feel it. He could feel far too much.

Somewhere inside, he kept taking swings, desperate with it—

His fingers curled into fists. He wanted to batter down whatever he could reach. He wanted to yell, break things, break *himself*—

Still, there was only Rae.

Quiet in the middle of this storm.

Waiting for him.

Slowly, horribly, Riley understood that he didn't have it in him to rage like a hurricane on his own.

And on the heels of that realization came another: they had always stormed together.

Always.

Where he was thunder, she was lightning. Together, they made their own rain.

And that had been the way of things from the start.

It had been true long before she'd lost their baby and kept it to herself.

He remembered, with a sudden rush of embarrassing clarity, shouting matches in high school hallways. Dramatic breakups that ended with one or the other of them getting loud and sloppy in public and private spaces alike. Everything had been high stakes. Everything had always been the end of the world.

In retrospect, none of it had been that bad.

They'd gotten together as teenagers. Married as kids.

And they'd dealt with what came at them with the tools they'd learned. Like kids in a corridor, yelling that no one understood their precious feelings.

There were other realizations hovering there, and his mother's words echoing in his head, but Riley couldn't handle any more just now.

Because the longer he and Rae stared at each other while he battled storms he couldn't control, not without her, he found himself losing his grip on the one thing that had always made him feel powerful in these moments.

Not his control, because he always had precious little of that around her.

But his anger.

He felt it drain away. And Riley didn't understand why he was rooted in place, but all he wanted to do was hold on to it. Get a hold on it however he could.

Because anger was fuel.

Anger was the indignation that had buoyed him for years.

Anger made him drink, and anger made him fight, and anger kept him nice and comfortable keeping his vigil in this house.

Anger meant it was her fault. Anger meant he never had to talk about it, never had to accept any of these heart-breaking realizations, and could keep humming right along on the force of it. Forever.

Feeling it fade away inside his own body felt like losing himself.

And she knew. Damn her, *she knew*.

Riley watched her pull in another shuddery breath, then she covered her mouth with her hands. But not before he saw a tear ease its way out of one eye and slide down her cheek.

And that pulled the plug.

All the rest of it poured out of him. Temper. Anger. Fury. All that outrage he'd been living with all this time, telling himself it was his right as the wronged party. That she deserved every bit of what he might throw at her and more.

He'd made anger his one true love, and when it drained away, for a moment, there was nothing.

Nothing.

Except Rae, looking at him with so much compassion it made everything inside of him a terrible, tangled mess.

"Don't—" he tried.

Riley staggered back a step. And then Rae was on her feet, crossing toward him, and he warded her off with one hand raised.

"Stop."

She stopped. But that didn't help.

Because all of his anger was gone.

And there was nothing for it but to face what remained. Whether he wanted to or not.

It flooded in, filling him, making him feel chopped into pieces, that mess in him—that mess that *was* him— taking him over. Taking him down.

And all the while, Rae stood before him, waiting. As if she knew exactly what demons he was fighting now.

When he would have said his only demon was her.

"I'm so sorry," she whispered. "I hope you know that, Riley. I'm so, so sorry."

And he could have taken a hit. Even now, when he felt so outside himself, so lost, Riley could have risen to the occasion if it were a fight.

But he had no defense for her apology. It punched right through him as if he really were the ghost here. Like he'd been one all this time.

It all seemed to explode inside him then, in a sick kind of slow motion. There was no avoiding any part of it. There was only facing it, like it or not.

God help him, but he didn't want to face it.

"You thought I wouldn't love you," he managed to say, though the words themselves tasted sour. "You thought telling me you were pregnant would be the end of us."

She nodded jerkily, and he could see too many things on her face now. His beautiful Rae, still and always the prettiest thing he'd ever seen. But he could see the fear too. The naked panic.

He could remember it all too well.

More, he could remember his own *certainty*. What he wanted, what he didn't. What his life would look like. What *their* life would become.

He knew she'd had every reason to think that telling him she'd broken one of his rules might be the thing that tipped them over the edge and into a fight they couldn't come back from.

Riley's throat worked. "But you were going to tell me, anyway."

"I was. I really was."

"And then . . ."

Rae nodded, the tears were pouring down her face, and he didn't know whether those tears were for him or her. For them both.

Or for the life they'd lost.

The life they'd created.

The life they'd lived since, bruised with secrets and laced through with anger in place of . . . this.

Sadness. Regret. Longing and loss.

And beneath it all, the reason he felt any of those things.

Love.

Riley found himself lurching forward as if he were drunk and unsteady on his feet. And he held her gaze, this woman who he had pledged himself to long before he'd taken the vows that made them husband and wife. The only woman he'd ever intended to marry. The only woman he'd ever promised himself to, for better or worse, little realizing they would have all these sad and twisted opportunities to explore what those words really meant.

And he was done being angry, but a far sight from grace, and he didn't understand what he saw in Rae's dark, endlessly soft gaze.

He took her hands again. And then they were both moving, or they could no longer stand, and whether it was weakness or want, they were both there on the floor together. Riley wrapped his arms around her, burying his face in her hair.

And he held her while she shook with sobs she didn't let out. He held her the way he should have all along.

"I left you alone," he managed to say. "I left you alone through all of this, from losing our baby to losing us. I'll never forgive myself."

"That's what I came here to tell you," she whispered, then pulled her head back so he could see her face. So she could look straight through him. And into him. So she could see every part of him. "I've already forgiven you. And I hope that someday, you'll see your way—"

And he got it now.

He understood.

"Rae," he said, with all that frustrated, overwhelming love and none of the anger that had been a place to hide it all this time. "Rae. I love you. I've always loved you. You don't need my forgiveness, but you have it. You have everything, and you always will."

And there on the floor of the house he'd built for a different life from the one they'd lived, Riley let go of all those things he'd imagined mattered to him, back when he was young and too sure of himself.

All the frustrations and fears. All the secrets and the lies.

What he'd kept from himself and what he'd kept from her.

He held the love of his life in his arms, and together they mourned their losses, at last.

Because on the other side of loss was life.

And hope.

And the two of them together again, where they belonged.

22

Rae woke up in the dark and, for a moment, didn't know where she was.

But then she did. It was the brush of the soft, flannel sheets against her bare skin. And the pillows that smelled like him. Like love. She reached out her hand to find him, but she already knew that he wasn't there.

Because Riley was better than a furnace, and the bed was only faintly warm, not hot.

She sat up, waiting for her eyes to adjust, but when they did, she didn't see Riley in any part of this large, comfortable room she'd once considered her favorite place on earth.

They had held each other for a long time out there on the floor. Then they'd come in here and had held on to each other as they lay here, twined around each other in that particular interlocking puzzle that had always been only theirs. There beneath the angled skylight that kept snow off and let the stars in, where they'd spent so many of their best nights together.

Rae hadn't meant to fall asleep. She'd forgotten what it was like to sleep here, but climbing out of the sweet, warm embrace of this bed was as hard as ever. She swung her feet out of bed and blew out a breath against the cold. She moved quickly to the chair in the corner and pulled on the leggings and heavy socks she'd worn beneath her boots earlier. She shrugged into her discarded long-sleeved T-shirt and pulled on one of Riley's flannel shirts as a kind of robe.

And it smelled like him too.

It all felt so familiar that she would have cried a week ago. But tonight, it made her smile.

She ignored the mess of her hair, rolled up the sleeves that drooped far below her fingertips, and wrapped the shirt tight around her as she padded out into the rest of the house to find him.

There was a low, smoldering fire in the big fireplace. The woodstove was pumping out heat. Everything was warm and cozy, but there was no sign of Riley.

Rae moved over to the windows and peered outside, her heart kicking at her as she looked to see if he'd gone off somewhere. Driven away to put some distance between them—and she couldn't really hold it against him if he had. Not when she'd done the same thing so many times herself.

But his truck was still parked out front, at an angle to hers—a lot like he was making sure she didn't do any running off anywhere. It made her feel warm inside. It made her grin to herself, like the silly girl she'd always been when it came to Riley Kittredge.

What does it matter where he parks in his own yard? she demanded of herself sternly.

Deep down, however, she could admit it felt like a sign.

And the minute she thought about *signs,* she knew where he was.

She went over to the mat near the door and shoved her feet into her boots. Then she went and climbed up the stairs to the smaller second floor of the house. Riley was using it for storage these days, she saw, the way they always had when she'd lived here. And she was pretty sure that if she looked closely, she'd see boxes she'd put up here herself.

Rae made her way through the maze of boxes, heading toward the front of the house across the wide open space with its high ceiling.

What is this for? she'd asked when they'd moved in, married at last.

If we get sick of the bedroom downstairs, we'll make a new bedroom up here, Riley had said, grinning.

At that point, the very idea that she might get sick of anything involving Riley would have made her laugh. She would have declared it impossible—and she never would have believed that anything could ever get between them. Not for eight minutes. And eight years? No way.

And here she was, all these years later, dressed in his shirt again as if she'd never left.

She'd never felt more beautiful.

She thought briefly of the red dress she'd worn the night before. Or her wedding dress that had made her so happy the first time she'd tried it on that she and Hope and Abby had all burst into tears. Either one was *clearly* more suitable for things like impromptu seductions or saving marriages.

But she and Riley had always been a fact. An inevitability.

Maybe that meant they didn't follow the rules. They made their own and often hurt themselves, but either way, she had no doubt she was doing the right thing when she slid open the window that looked out over the front porch and climbed out onto the sloping roof.

Riley sat out there, a heavy blanket draped around him and his eyes on the cold night hanging there in front of him.

He didn't look up as she came over, already shivering. And she didn't wait to make certain of her welcome. She made a beeline for him the way she would have years ago, expecting him to open up his arms the way he did, then wrap her up in that blanket so she could rest her back against him as if he were a chair.

Funny the things that felt sacred now, so many years after she'd thought she'd given them up forever.

But she didn't really breathe out again until he rested his chin on the top of her head.

"Why are you awake?" she asked softly, burrowing deeper into him as the cold pressed in against her. She hadn't looked at the clock when she'd gotten up, but she'd guess they were in the small hours now. Three or four in the morning, maybe.

Usually right about the time she crawled out of his bed, shaking with guilt and shame, and cried while she drove herself home.

But not tonight.

Though as she listened to his heart beat steadily behind her, and waited for him to speak, she realized some part of her was terribly afraid that this was his version of that same 3:00 a.m. drive.

"I couldn't sleep," Riley said after a moment. "Seems fair enough. I have a lot to think about."

Rae swallowed back her instant response to that. Rapid-fire questions that were all about the uncertainty in her, not him.

She bit her tongue and made herself wait.

The dark didn't get any lighter. The cold didn't get

any warmer. But she was safe in Riley's arms, and that was more than she'd had in a long time.

It felt like everything.

"Tonight, my mother told me I'm just like my father," Riley said eventually. "Not like an insult. She said it like it was so obvious she was surprised it hadn't occurred to me by now."

Rae wanted to hurl herself into that, leaping to his defense—but maybe he didn't need her defense right now. Maybe he needed her to listen. Maybe if they'd tried that out years ago, things would have been different.

"And you know how I feel about my father." Riley made a low noise that could as easily have been disapproval as disgust. "I spent the whole drive back from the ranch house telling myself how wrong she was. She told me I was unforgiving like him. So sure I was always right. So determined because I knew what I wanted and always had. Obviously, I dismissed it all as the rantings of a woman who'd decided to stay married to a man with the humanity of the average rock. But then when I got home, ready to nurse my indignation, you were here."

"Riley. We really don't have to go over this." She snuggled deeper into his arms. "Really."

But it was as if he didn't hear her. "And what did I do? Exactly what I always do. Blame you. Rehash the same things over and over when I already knew there was no answer. And overlook the only fact that should have mattered to me, ever." He took a breath, and it was ragged. Rae could *feel* it. "You were hurt, and I didn't help you."

She turned in his arms then, propping herself against his chest so she could be sure to look him full in the face. "I wouldn't have let you. While you're beating yourself up, please remember that. I wouldn't have let you help me, Riley. I went to great lengths to make sure you couldn't."

One of his hands gripped the back of her neck, holding her still before him where there was nothing between them but breath.

Hope, Rae thought.

"You already forgave me for something I probably wouldn't forgive if I were in your shoes," he said, his voice gravel and heat and her Riley again. *Hers.* "What am I supposed to do with that?"

"We've spent so long doing this," she managed to whisper. "And I really thought the answer was to stop. To throw it all out and start over, because this seemed too hard. Unfixable. It had to be easier with someone new, right?"

He shook his head. "I wouldn't know where to start."

"But I don't want a new person, Riley. I don't want a new marriage. I want a new start." Rae reached forward and ran her hands over the beloved lines of his face. The only face she ever dreamed about. The only man she wanted when she woke up. "With you, Riley. Only with you."

"I don't think I'm ever going to get over how scared you must have been. How alone. And me here with my head up my—"

"Stop." But she whispered it, still holding his face in her palms.

"I owe you so many apologies I don't know where to start," Riley burst out. "I want to tell you that you were wrong to think that I wouldn't accept it if you were pregnant, but I remember what I was like back then, and I know exactly why you thought that."

She looked at him. Really looked at him. With everything she was. "We have to decide, right now, that there's no more going back, or going back is all we're ever going to do."

His mouth curved a little. "My mom said something like that too."

"Your mom is a wise woman," Rae told him. "Maybe your parents decided to keep their marriage private. To take it out of the places where their kids could see the cracks and work it out on their own. Did you ever think about that?" She didn't wait for him to argue the point. "And they don't owe you or anyone any explanations. Neither do we."

Riley shook his head. "My mother thinks I got married early so I could do it better than them. Or what I thought was them. And instead, I became exactly like my father. And worse, I made you the woman my mother used to be. You push, I act like a wall, and everyone comes out of it worse off than before."

Rae laughed a little, and then more when he frowned at her.

"I appreciate you taking that on, cowboy," she drawled. "But I think you're forgetting that I'm the child of a great and glorious lifelong war that's been going on between my grandmother and mother since before my birth. Remind me to tell you how my grandmother didn't speak directly to me for *nine years*."

"Then I shouldn't have—"

She shushed him, grinning when he scowled at her. "As far as I can tell, I don't know love unless it comes with a healthy side helping of fighting. I wouldn't know I felt anything at all unless it came with the opportunity to do battle. You didn't make us who we are, Riley. We built this. Together, you and me. Brick by brick."

There was a gleam in his dark eyes that she didn't

dare believe. His hand around her neck felt like a caress, the way it was supposed to. And between them, that same old sweet heat began to shift into that old, familiar, breathtaking fire.

The way it always had. And always would.

"Baby," Riley said, stars in his eyes when the sky around them was dark and cloudy. "It's time to take those bricks apart."

"Only if we rebuild," she whispered. "Together."

And Rae watched as Riley, the most dangerous of the Kittredges . . . softened.

Just for her.

Only and ever for her.

He leaned forward to press his lips to hers, and it felt better than hope. Better than promise rings in high school or vows in the middle of a hot, ripe summer.

It felt better than explosively stupid fights and hot, incapacitating passion. It was all of those things and more.

It was better than *friends.* Better than *benefits.*

He kissed her like life. Like love.

Like forever.

"I don't deserve a second chance," he told her, the frigid air making their lips cold when they touched, but not when the kiss moved deeper. "I don't deserve you."

"I promise this time I'll trust you with everything," Rae told him in return. "No more secrets, Riley. No more running away. You deserve a wife who stays."

"I'll keep you safe," he promised her. "No matter what."

"And I will love you so true," she vowed. "No matter what happens. There will only be this. Us."

He smiled, there against her mouth. "Rae. I love you."

"I love you, Riley," she replied, her heart so full she was surprised the roof could hold them.

And they made it all new, right there.

One sweet kiss after another.

Over and over again, until the snow began to fall.

They celebrated their reunion energetically throughout what was left of the night, and Rae dragged herself out of bed when her phone alarm beeped at her, already regretting her lack of sleep.

"I hope you're not planning to drive anywhere," Riley muttered sleepily, his face in the pillows. "It snowed again, and your truck is still the same old death trap."

"And yet, it's Black Friday. The Flower Pot can't open itself."

He said a few more things.

She snapped right back at him.

And they were right back on familiar ground.

But unlike all the other times they'd fought over the last eight years, this fight wasn't *instead of* the conversation they'd had last night. This was *in addition* to it.

"In case you're wondering," she panted at him when he tugged her down and rolled her beneath him in that too-hot bed, then found his way inside her with a single, hard, glorious thrust, "I still hate morning sex."

Riley grinned, that wicked, dangerous grin that had sustained her all those long, dark years. "Let's find out."

And it probably should have embarrassed her, how quickly he could have her sobbing out his name.

She shook and shook. And was sure one human body couldn't contain so much joy.

Which was probably why it was so much better shared between two.

By the time she made it out of the shower, he'd fixed her coffee that she was forced to accept right along with the smug look on his face.

"You seemed to hate that a lot," he drawled.

"Marriage is sacrifice, Riley," Rae said piously, and then they grinned at each other as she pressed the mug to her lips.

And it wasn't until he kissed her silly, insisted on driving out ahead of her to the county road to make sure she made it, and beeped twice as she drove off that it really hit her.

They were going to start over.

They'd started over.

She and Riley were going to make it work.

And not because they'd gotten rid of all the tempestuous things that had always made them who they were. That was what this morning had taught her.

They would have that, sure. But this time, they wouldn't have only that.

It was like flowers, she thought later, as she stood in the Flower Pot in her own clothes instead of the dreaded uniform. A flower, standing on its own, could have a certain drama. Even two flowers, or a little nosegay—they could create a bit of theater. They were what they were, beautiful and often doomed.

But take an arrangement instead. The more flowers she wove together, mixed in with live plants, the better it was. From bright blooms to deeply rooted things, all together, they were more than their individual parts. They were beautiful. They were resilient. They made people smile, shined bright, and made happy occasions happier.

And if planted right, they grew.

The way she and Riley had, however painfully, these last eight years.

The way they would going forward.

This time, at last, Rae was sure.

23

A year later, Riley woke up early on a dark Thanksgiving morning after the usual Harvest Gala shenanigans the night before, tended to his usual chores, and found himself out in the quiet of his own yard. Dawn was still a while away, but there were already lights on inside his house. And the chimney filled the cold air with the scent of wood smoke that always said *home* to him.

He took the steps to the front porch at a jump, moving right past the place where that clunker of a truck used to sit. It still sat on the property, but now it was more like a mausoleum, out behind the barn.

Insisting that Rae find herself a safer vehicle had taken some doing. He'd had to wait until he had ammunition.

He eased his way inside and took a deep breath, because his house was a home again, and he still wasn't over it. He hoped he'd never get over it.

Rae had quietly moved back in without a whole lot of fanfare. Riley had packed her up at Hope's, pretended he didn't see the way Hope beamed as if this was all her doing, somehow, and took Rae back where she belonged before the end of that Thanksgiving weekend.

But neither one of them was interested in starting over in the same place where they'd gone off course so badly so many times before. They'd wrestled that bed of theirs upstairs, fought about it and then made up, and then made the second floor—with all its windows to the stars—theirs.

They'd hunkered down for the winter there. And by the time spring came, Riley had not only added another bathroom and opened up the chimney to create another fireplace right there across from their bed, they'd gone ahead and created that ammunition he needed to make Rae take her safety more seriously.

And Riley had loved Rae Trujillo any number of ways. As a distractingly pretty teenager. As his newly-wed bride, half-drunk on the things they could do to each other, and did, whenever possible. He'd loved her long and hard, even through all those angry years. Because none of that had been fun, but they'd sure made up for it night after night.

But he wasn't sure he'd ever love her more than good and round with their baby, cranky and in no way glowing, and yet despite that, still his.

Always and forever his.

As time went on, Riley found they braided together the parts of them that loved to fight with the parts of them that should have been better friends from the start, and the idea of the two of them that they wanted to be this time.

And day by day, they grew together instead of apart.

Anytime he thought he was falling down in one of those areas, Rae was there to pick him up. And anytime she got a little lost in her own fears, he remembered that night on the roof, the snow on their faces, and how he'd promised that he'd keep her safe.

Even if it was from her own head.

At the end of the summer, she gave him a son. They'd had big plans for a hospital birth, but the tiny little creature they'd made together and would soon christen Hunter Donovan Kittredge had other ideas.

He'd come into the world in a fury, scaring his parents half to death, right there in the house where everything else had happened.

And later, after they'd gone into town to make sure everything was as it should be, they took him back home and found themselves standing over his little bassinet. Both of them so strung out by the powerful love they felt for this tiny, scrunched-faced creature that Riley was surprised either one of them could breathe.

It's like he knew, Rae had whispered. *He needed to be born here. To make sure there were no more ghosts.*

Riley knew the truth. Hunter was magical.

For any number of reasons, but one of them was that his appearance had prompted Riley to do the unthinkable and sit down with his father, his son's clearly besotted new grandfather, and lift a few beers.

They didn't talk about much.

But they went ahead and made it a standing thing.

Magic.

Today, he found his wife and child cuddled up in the armchair in the living room when he came inside. And he thought, as always, that Rae could never be more beautiful to him.

Until she was.

Like this morning, nursing Hunter with a tender smile on her face that made him think about the way they'd ended up on the floor right here in this room when they'd found their way back to each other. The way they'd christened that comfortable old couch when it was new and they were too. It made him think about the way she'd looked up at a church picnic a lifetime ago and sent a fourteen-year-old kid who'd thought he was a man reeling.

She looked up and smiled at him, and she was home. His home.

"I love you," he told her, and saw the delight in her eyes and the way it melted quickly into that sweet, hot heat. "God, Rae. I love you so much."

"I love you too," she said. "And I'm glad you feel that way, because there's something you're going to have to face, Riley. It's happening."

He laughed, shrugging out of his cold weather gear. He went over to sit on the arm of the chair and waited until the baby finished feeding. Then he maneuvered Hunter to his shoulder to see about the burping.

"Ignoring it isn't going to make it go away," Rae warned him. She stretched as she got up from the chair, looking sleepy and grumpy and entirely his.

Riley hadn't wanted kids. Maybe the truth was that he didn't want kids in a general sense. He wasn't that guy. But he wanted Rae. He wanted *her* kids. He wanted life with her in all of its variations.

Holding his son in his arms, Riley believed in magic. He believed in love. He believed in the things he and Rae could build together.

Like this beautiful life that they'd been doing together forever. Their way, for better and worse alike.

"It's not happening," he told Rae as she smirked at him. "Whatever you try to do to convince me, I will never sit at your family table and pretend that the carrot soufflé is your recipe. Never, Rae."

But in the shower later while the baby napped, she sank down to her knees, grinned up at him wickedly, and convinced him.

Riley sat at Thanksgiving dinner with her whole family, lied through his teeth, and loved her all the more.

The way he intended to do, day after day, forever.

Keep reading for a bonus novella
from Caitlin Crews!

SWEET NIGHTS WITH A COWBOY

1

If asked, Connor Kittredge would have put his hand on a stack of Bibles and sworn he had paid absolutely no attention to the whereabouts of Melissa "Missy" Minton in all the years since their high school graduation. Not ever. And especially not over the holidays.

Luckily, no one had asked. Because that was a lie.

Not a struck-down-by-lightning lie, maybe, but it wasn't the truth, either. They had dated for most of their junior year, and he remembered the dating part in vivid detail. He could also remember that their breakup had been both theatric and public.

And if he recalled correctly, his fault.

That he couldn't remember whys and hows of their breakup had resulted in Missy—though she'd preferred *Melissa* by then, she'd informed him—laughing at him over her bright and sparkling engagement ring some years back. Right here in this very same bar where he was currently listening to country music Christmas carols over a few beers and was doing his best to keep from noticing that Missy was back in town.

Earlier than usual for her regular Christmas visit, given Thanksgiving had been last week.

Not that he knew Missy's schedule, he reminded himself as he took a pious pull from his beer. Or anything about her actual life aside from the usual small-town stories people told about her that were the lifeblood of a remote mountain town like this one.

But there she was all the same, leaning up against the polished wood bar in the Broken Wheel Saloon. Which was right where it had always been, there on Main Street in Cold River, Colorado, when she was supposed to be some six hours south in Santa Fe, New Mexico. Until at least the twenty-third of the month.

Connor certainly didn't *keep tabs* on her comings and goings, but a man noticed these things when they occurred year after year like clockwork. Always with that enormous ring. Never with the fiancé who went with it. Because said fiancé was a businessman, the rumor mill had reliably informed him, and was much too important for a tiny little cowboy town without a single stoplight.

"Are you *thinking*?" asked his older brother Jensen from across the table, where Jensen was lounging as if he were the king of the world. Because Jensen was always lounging like he was the king of something, even when it wasn't fire season and he wasn't off leaping out of planes into hell.

"Unlikely," drawled Zack, another one of his older brothers. He happened to be the sheriff in these parts and took that as an invitation to underscore his every laconic, lawman word with a smirk. In fairness, he'd been doing that long before he became sheriff.

The only brother missing was Riley, who had apparently taken advantage of the recent holiday to finally reunite with his long-estranged wife. Or ex-wife. Or whatever Riley and Rae Trujillo had been doing all these years—and none of them were talking about that mess after Riley had blown up at the family Thanksgiving dinner table. Prodded by their much younger sister, Amanda.

"I tried thinking once," Connor replied. And grinned, because if he showed any kind of actual reaction, his brothers would see it as their solemn duty to attack and destroy. He knew because he would do the same to them, and happily. It was the entire point of having a big family, in his opinion. "Freshman year of high school. Didn't take."

What followed was a spirited discussion about the various genetic gifts they had each inherited—or notably not inherited—from their parents. And given their various negative feelings about Donovan and Ellie Kittredge and their childhoods in the middle of their parents' once tempestuous and now chilly marriage, it inevitably descended into its own round of cheerful brotherly insults on this cold December night.

Connor quickly had his fill of the same old rounds of who was Ellie Jr. and who was Donovan's clone, because he was the youngest of the four Kittredge brothers. Having two of the older three there to gang up on him was less appealing than Zack and Jensen seemed to think. Particularly when Amanda wasn't around tonight to take her historic place as the one person Connor could roll things down upon.

He opted to cut and run at the first lull in the claims that he, personally, embodied their father's inability to commit to anything or anyone—in the form of ambling on over to get the next round. And without meaning to, necessarily, he chose to head to the end of the bar where Tessa Winthrop was serving drinks.

And just happened to be talking to one Missy Minton.

Missy was prettier than she'd been in high school, and that was saying something. Tonight, she was dressed for the blustery Colorado weather in one of those Nordic-looking sweaters that hung on her like a tunic, but still didn't quite cover the way her leggings clung to her behind, which he'd been admiring from across the room—and across a great many years. She had one winter boot propped up on the brass rung that was set below the bar for that exact purpose, one elbow on the polished wooden surface next to her drink, and her fingers laced lightly around the long neck of her IPA.

When she shifted slightly to look at him, he caught the remains of the laughter she'd been aiming at Tessa. He was struck—as if for the first time—by her eyes, bright and brown. And her dark hair in silken waves, caught tonight to one side of her neck.

"Connor," she said like a greeting, her voice that mix of naturally raspy and lit up with laughter that had pretty much wrecked him when he'd been a teenager.

He was obviously far more grown up and in control of himself now. He hoped. "Missy. Welcome back."

Connor caught Tessa's eye and made a circling motion with one finger to indicate he was buying the next round for his table. Tessa nodded and got to work with her usual efficiency.

Next to him, Missy shifted against the bar. "I'm pretty sure I've told you annually that I've been going by Melissa for years now."

"Maybe out there, you go by Melissa. But this is Cold River." Connor grinned down at her. "You know nothing ever really changes here."

She smiled again, but this time, it didn't light up those eyes of hers the way it normally did. He wasn't sure why he noticed that or why, having noticed it, it . . . got to him.

"You're lucky that as it happens, I've decided to reclaim my old nickname," she said, lightly enough. "But that doesn't let you off the hook."

"I didn't realize hooks were involved."

"That sounds like the Connor I know." Missy rolled her eyes, though it was good-natured. Or it looked good-natured, anyway. "Never sure what the issue is, but sure it's not his fault."

"Are we talking about high school again?"

"This is Cold River, as I was just reminded." She waved her beer in the general direction of all the people enjoying dinner, drinks, and the odd bit of dancing in the Broken Wheel, the much nicer and more welcoming of the two bars in town. "Some folks are still carrying on as if high school never ended."

Connor put a hand over his heart. "I'll have you know that I'm a fully grown adult, thank you. Unlike some people I could mention, who I happened to be related to, I'm not clinging on to high school football teams and the glory I once knew."

"Don't you live at home with your mother, though?" Missy asked, wrinkling up her nose.

And it occurred to Connor that she was teasing him the same way his older brothers did. Perfectly happy to go for the jugular, and not because they'd dated in high school. Or not only because of that. But because she'd known him his entire life. They'd played together as toddlers, something he didn't personally recall but had been reminded of seemingly every five minutes while they'd been dating.

"That's a question with more than one answer, Missy," he drawled, leaning into the bar so he could face her. Not a hardship. "Is it true that I live on the same piece of property where numerous members of my family also reside? I believe you know I do. But you also know that it's a substantial acreage, most of it belongs to the horses, and just to make it perfectly clear, no. I haven't lived under the same roof as my mother since I was about eighteen."

"Sounds like I touched a nerve." She looked delighted at the prospect.

"I understand what it's like for folks like you who moved away from home and claim they're never coming back. All that convenient amnesia and whatnot. I just want to make sure you know where to put me in all your cowboy stereotypes."

She considered. "Do I have cowboy stereotypes? I thought I just knew cowboys."

"Down there in Santa Fe? Living your fancy hotel life all these years?"

Missy looked down and took a swig of her beer. "Yeah, well. Santa Fe has its own magic, there's no denying it."

That didn't sound like much of an answer to Connor, but before he could comment on it, Tessa was there again. She lined up the drinks he'd ordered on the counter, but left them there to go take some more orders down at the other end of the bar.

"Why are you here?" Connor asked, throwing a few bills on the bar to cover the round. "Don't you usually come home for Christmas?"

She tilted her head a little as she looked at him. "It's December, Connor. My mom likes to put up the Christmas tree the day after Halloween. It's been Christmas for a month already as far as the Minton clan is concerned."

Connor wanted to lean in. Ask her more pointed questions. Like why she was being evasive and what it meant, but he knew this was none of his business. Whatever she called herself, whatever magic she believed in, she had a whole life that he only saw a little snapshot of once a year.

If this particular snapshot was going to be a bit longer than usual this year, that was great. He could enjoy it the way he always did and then move on, because there was more than one pretty girl around. There always was.

Off the top of his head, he couldn't think of a single one. But he was sure they were here somewhere.

"I don't *think* Zack and Jensen bite, if you want to sit down with us," he heard himself say instead of telling her it was great to see her and walking away. The way he should have done. "You can join the two of them as they find new and ingenious ways to mock and belittle me at every turn. A family tradition, really."

Missy wheeled around to look at the table behind them. Connor did the same, and saw Jensen telling one of his usually tall tales, complete with a booming laugh of his.

She grinned at him, and this time, it was in her eyes. "I'll admit it. That does sound entertaining."

"If you ask nicely," he said in a tone that was easing a little too close toward flirting, which he should know better than to do, what with her being a long-engaged woman and all, "I might even ask them to call you Melissa."

Missy pushed away from the bar, bringing her beer with her. Then she reached over and grabbed his beer, too, leaving Connor to pick up his brothers' drinks.

"I almost married a man who called me Melissa," she told him, leaning in like it was a secret. Or something shameful, maybe. "I'm kind of over it. But taking this opportunity to settle in and make fun of my high school boyfriend? Count me in."

And then she set off for the table and his brothers, leaving that bomb behind for Connor to sort out—without, he hoped, any of his reaction to the news she was single on his face.

2

Missy Minton didn't know what it was about Connor freaking Kittredge.

Sure, he was a kind of beautiful that only seemed to get better with age and apparent maturity. His hair was more dark than blond, and he had those dark eyes that always looked as if he was thinking about something wicked. And the fact he'd spent his life out in the fields wrangling horses was evident in every inch of the body he'd packed into the local uniform of well-fitting jeans, cowboy boots, and a Henley to make a girl far too aware of the power in his arms.

She was sure he knew it. He'd been a conceited ass in high school, but back then, she'd thought it was her role in life to shock her mother. A conceited ass had been exactly what she was looking for.

Connor had delivered.

Those Kittredge boys aren't likely to settle down, Missy, her mother had fussed at her when she'd been a teenager. *It's not in their nature.*

Riley Kittredge literally married Rae Trujillo five seconds after she graduated high school, she'd replied, as smart-mouthed as ever, and only too delighted to prove Marianne Minton wrong wrong wrong.

I hope you don't think history will repeat itself, Marianne had sniffed. *All that boy will do is ruin your reputation.*

I hope so, Missy had thrown back at her with all the fiery passion of her teenage heart—a move that had gotten her grounded when her daddy came home that night and heard about it.

She still thought it was worth it.

Just like she still thought it was fun to get together with her old high school friends and laugh about the little soap opera of a teenage relationship she'd had with *that boy,* but it was hard to remember all that when she ran into him around Cold River. He'd filled out that lanky form of his, grown a few inches, and held a whole lot more wickedness in his eyes these days.

If she was honest, she thought as she plastered a smile across her face and settled herself down at a seat at the table with two of the other intimidatingly attractive Kittredge boys—who were in no way *boys* these days—seeing Connor every Christmas had been a little balm for her bruised ego these past years. She could admit that.

But she refused to think about Philip in any more depth than that.

She'd declared herself and her new life a Philip-free zone.

Starting from the moment she'd thrown her engagement ring at his head.

"I'll admit that I can't get used to the fact that you're the sheriff, Zack," she said, smiling at the oldest of the Kittredges when he offered her a lazy nod that failed to disguise the shrewd look in his eyes.

"You're not alone," Jensen chimed in with that voice of his that was as big as all his great many muscles.

"Zack claims he's always been law-abiding," Connor

said as he took the seat next to her, sliding his brothers their drinks across the table. "But funny thing, nobody who knows him remembers it that way."

"I'm happy to arrest you all," Zack murmured. "You can debate the finer points of the law and my adherence to it in the county lockup."

"You can always try, big brother," Jensen drawled.

The two of them devolved into a spate of hypotheticals, and Missy found herself a little too captivated by the remaining Kittredge brother at her side.

"What happened to your man?" he asked with a little more intensity than she'd expected from the likes of Connor Kittredge.

Or the Connor she'd known, anyway.

She couldn't decide if she was flattered or irritated that he hadn't let her marital status go, the way a lot of folks had since she'd come home. But then, most of them likely planned to ask her mother instead. Missy doubted Marianne and Connor were on idle chatting terms.

Missy found herself rubbing her thumb over that strange, empty groove where Philip's ring had sat for years. "Oh, he's fine," she said brightly. "Excellent, in fact. He's achieved all his dreams, is the owner and manager of a brand-new boutique hotel right there in the center of historic Santa Fe. But it turns out that when he talked about it being a family enterprise, he had a different family in mind."

She'd been practicing that speech for months now. It had played well at Thanksgiving dinner, since her mother had always hated Philip and her sister, Laurel, had finally confessed she'd only ever found him . . . *slick*. They had been used to him not accompanying Missy home anyway, so it wasn't as if they missed his presence. Not the way they all missed her father, Hank Minton, as if his death took a chunk out of the world every time some-one remembered it. Every time he wasn't seated where he should have been at the family table. Every time he didn't come in at night, his tread on the old wood floors heavy and familiar and comforting.

It had been almost four years now, and it still felt new. Missy figured it always would.

Even if she sometimes thought that it was a blessing that Hank hadn't lived to see what had become of the engagement he'd never *said* he was opposed to. Just like he'd never *said* that he'd been taken aback that Philip had never done him the honor of asking for his daughter's hand in marriage.

It was Marianne who had said that, not Hank.

Philip isn't traditional, Mom, Missy had snapped.

Marianne had sniffed. *Well, sweetheart, your daddy is.*

No one had mentioned any of that. No one would. Missy assumed this was just how it was going to go. Five years of her life, fights she'd waged on behalf of a man who'd betrayed her, an entire future she'd planned out and worked for—*poof.* Gone.

She expected Connor, who as far as she knew had taken nothing too seriously in his entire life, to make a crack. A flippant remark, so they could roll straight on into the usual banter. Bright and meaningless like the twangy carols playing on the jukebox.

"I'm sorry," he said instead, his gaze disarmingly direct.

That was all. No clever joke. No misdirection or attempt to charm her.

And the fact that he didn't gloss over it the way her family had, or act as if she were better off without Philip—no matter how true that might have been—made her feel . . . warm.

"I don't know if I'm sorry or not," she found herself

telling him. *Him,* of all people. Connor Kittredge, who had been an absolutely terrible boyfriend, something he had acknowledged gleefully at the time and years after too. Connor, who had been her first. And she his. And no matter what else had happened between them, the joy and reverence that had marked that particular milestone was what she most remembered about him. Maybe that was why, even all these years later, she felt safe when she was near him the way she had in the back of his pickup beneath a warm spring sky. "It's funny when something is over and when you look back you don't really know why you put up with it in the first place."

Again, he surprised her. Connor didn't look away. He didn't shift uncomfortably or change the subject. "I don't think anybody gets through life without a few regrets. Wouldn't be much of a life if you did."

"I couldn't wait to get out of this town." Missy laughed. "I hated every minute I was here. You remember."

"I do."

"I wanted to shake up the world. I was going to show everybody what I was made of, and I didn't care what names they called me behind my back. It was worth it, as far as I was concerned."

He shook his head. "Missy, you started half the rumors that went around about you."

Laurel had often said such things to her, but Laurel always sounded condemning. Pitying, even, which never went over well. Connor's dark gaze bordered on admiring.

She'd never been able to resist a look like that in this particular pair of dark eyes. "If I recall correctly, Connor, you contributed to the other half."

Her sixteen-year-old self had been so *certain* about everything. So puffed up with pride and attitude and sheer, unfocused determination that no matter what her life turned out to be, it would be different from *this*.

And yet *this* was the only place she'd wanted to be when the life she'd thought she wanted fell apart.

"I never started any rumors about you," Connor protested.

She rolled her eyes. "You told the entire church congregation I was a woman of loose morals."

"I did no such thing. You turned up one fine Sunday in a low-cut shirt that, I won't lie, has haunted my dreams ever since."

Missy remembered that shirt being *shocking*. Her father had been *disappointed in her,* the worst possible punishment, but her mother had been *appalled*. Back then, that was what Missy had lived for.

"It was your fault I wore that shirt."

"I don't remember it as a fault, so much as a gift." Connor lifted his beer, those dark eyes gleaming. "And besides, you didn't have to take the dare."

"Of course I did. And they all believed, 100 percent, that I was scandalous and *flaunting* my low morality for all to see. My mother informs me that to this day, when people ask about me, they call me *that Missy*."

"A fate worse than death," Connor said with a laugh. "The Cold River version of a scarlet letter."

"A scarlet letter?" Jensen interjected from across the table. Missy had forgotten he and Zack were there. "Was that a literary reference? Connor, buddy, are you trying to convince this poor woman that you read?"

"We took English together in high school," Connor replied easily. "She knows I copied off her paper."

Missy felt the urge to rush to Connor's defense. To tell his older brother to be nicer to him when she knew that doing anything like that would be . . . not good.

While inside—and hopefully not plastered across her cheeks—that warm feeling didn't go away.

And later that evening, it seemed almost natural to let Connor Kittredge drive her home from the bar.

"What about your car?" he asked her when they headed out into the dark. "Or did you sled here?"

"Tessa picked me up," Missy said, brightly enough. This was not the time to offer the man a dissertation on how she'd had to trade in the fancy car Philip had insisted she buy, even though she could hardly afford the payments, because they had a certain reputation to uphold. He meant *he* did—and she'd had to default on those payments after he left her and took her job with him, since it was his hotel. That was all a little too much for a happy little December night in Cold River, where there were holiday lights draped across all the Old West brick buildings and the town tree was already bright and shining. "She likes a little company while she's tending bar. And she has to stay until closing, anyway."

Connor drove a much nicer pickup than the one he'd had in high school. But it still felt the same, sitting there on the bench seat in the dark as he took a back road out of town. Not the one that led out to where his family had been breeding horses for over a century but in the opposite direction. Into the part of the Longhorn Valley on the other side of the actual town of Cold River, where people lived on little bits of acreage—three or five, depending—and the farming wasn't any good, so folks concentrated on things like their gardens. Beekeeping. Hiking trails and ATV tracks.

He didn't ask for directions to her mother's house, and that felt good too. He hadn't driven her home in some thirteen years, but he still remembered the way.

"Are you staying through the holidays?" he asked as

he navigated the long dirt driveway that led up to the house she'd grown up in.

It felt a little more intimate than it should have, there with only the light from his dashboard to provide any break from the thickness of the cold Colorado night.

"Yes," she said. And then, because she felt the need to be honest with him, "I don't actually know how long I'm staying. All I know is I'm not going back to Santa Fe."

"No?" She could sense his grin. "But what about all that magic?"

She could feel his gaze on her for a moment. Her cheeks got hot.

"I really did try. But after six months of putting on a good show while Philip and his new, improved fiancée flaunted themselves in my face, I gave in. I'm not proud of it, but I decided it was better to leave them to it."

"You know that sometimes retreat is strategic, right? I don't know why you stayed six months."

Nobody knew why she'd stayed, including Missy.

"Because I thought I was building something. Because I thought that was more important than whatever relationships were involved . . ." She sighed a little as he took the last curve and the house came into view, lights on and waiting for her. "And because, I guess, I still wanted to prove my mother wrong. How pathetic is that?"

And then it all came out of her like a flood. To the most inappropriate person possible, but maybe that was why it didn't feel as crazy as it should have. "My mother hated Philip. I knew she would hate Philip. Just like I knew she would hate my life. *All flash and no substance,* she likes to mutter, because it's hotels and hospitality. Not *honest* work. And I did everything I could to convince myself that she was wrong. I really did."

"Missy." Connor stopped his truck in the clearing below the house and took his time looking over at her. As if he knew she could feel it everywhere. "You don't have to tell me about expectations. There's not one place I can go in this town where people don't know me and figure what they know is the sum total of who I am. I've had the urge to fight against that a time or two myself. Proving your parents wrong is a time-honored rite, in my opinion. It takes guts that you went out there and tried it. And more guts that you weren't too proud to come home."

To her astonishment, Missy felt her eyes fill with tears.

"This is going to sound crazy," she said when she was reasonably sure she could keep her voice even. "And don't read anything into it. But I've been home since last week and this is the first time it's really felt like it."

"I am the man who relieved you of your virginity, as I recall," Connor drawled, heat and laughter in his voice and the dashboard lights making his gaze seem even more wicked than usual. "On command."

A wild burst of joy ricocheted through her like a sudden fire. "On command? Please. My recollection is that your argument was that the whole town already thought my morals were highly questionable, if not downright dubious, thanks to the shirt incident. Why not see what all the fuss was about?"

"It was a reasonable argument."

"It was ridiculous."

"Ridiculous, maybe, but it worked."

"It did work." She felt that same sense of safety again. The way she always had with him because he'd always been like this. Easy. Intense. And somehow, she'd never gotten whiplash going back and forth between the two. "But I still think that in retrospect, I ought to fight you for my honor."

Connor's grin faded into something else. Something

that sent more of that fire spiraling through her. He reached over and tugged on the ponytail she'd fastened beneath one ear, tugging it gently. She found it hard to catch her breath.

And suddenly, everything was bright and hot, safe and *him*.

"We can fight, if you want," he said, his voice low. A sweet drawl that made her feel anything but sweet inside. "But I can think of better ways to welcome you home, Missy."

So could she.

Missy did what she thought she might have been wanting to do for some thirteen years, ever since the day she'd broken up with Connor Kittredge in high dudgeon in the Cold River High cafeteria. Because she'd been so sure she was going places and just as sure that he was staying put. *And* he'd been flirting with that cheerleader.

She leaned over, got her hands on all that strength and heat, and kissed him.

3

Connor hadn't imagined he'd ever have the opportunity to kiss Missy Minton again.

He told himself that was why it haunted him.

Days later, he was still trying to come to terms with what had happened in the front seat of his truck, there in the dark outside her mother's house.

He felt like a kid again.

And then again, not like a kid at all.

Because there were so many things he'd forgotten, or chalked up to the fact that whatever else she was, Missy had been his first. Not his first kiss but his first opportunity to *practice*. They'd gotten together at homecoming and had broken up before prom, and in that time, they'd had long months to perfect their kissing. Something they'd both dedicated themselves to with fervor.

Kissing her again felt both brand new and deliciously familiar.

Just like back then, he'd found himself hauling her into his lap, digging his hands into her hair, and losing himself in the sheer perfection of the way her mouth fit his. The way she tasted. The way she moved against him.

The way she was *Missy* after all these years.

And like back then, he'd found himself laughing against her mouth, then setting her back into her seat again when they were both good and hot.

"Your mama is right inside that house, probably calling in my truck to the sheriff's office," he'd managed to drawl. "I'll remind you that my brother is the sheriff these days, and unlike his predecessor, who mumbled something at me about being a gentleman, Zack will torture me."

"You can handle it," she said in that raspy way of hers that, sure enough, made his entire body ache.

He'd watched her run into the house, and it could have been any night from his junior year of high school all over again.

But he wasn't a kid anymore. He hadn't gone off to college like Missy, then carried on with a fancy life in a far-off city, working in world-class hotels. He was a Kittredge, and that meant horses. Unless, of course, you were Zack—in which case, you thumbed your nose at the family legacy as oldest son and announced that you felt you needed to dedicate yourself to law and order. Or take off every summer to risk death, like Jensen.

It was only Connor and his brother Riley who'd gone ahead and dedicated themselves to the Bar K full-time. Riley was magic with fractious, too-wild horses. Connor had an eye for breeding that had already made him a bit of a name.

He'd always thought it was a gift that he liked where he'd found himself.

Connor liked his life. He liked being a part of the family business and the sweep of history that went with it. He liked living on land that was his, or would be one day. In a house he might not have built with his own hands but had made his own, even if Amanda claimed it looked like a fish-and-game magazine had vomited all over the place. It was his.

He liked the flow of the seasons, he thought one cold morning as he set about his chores. The Colorado Rockies stood sentry over his life, his father's life, and his grandfather's too. His brothers annoyed him half to death, but they were also his best friends, and when he went into town, he was on good terms with everyone he met.

Connor was an easygoing, happy-go-lucky kind of a guy.

Except when it came to kissing Missy Minton. That made him feel just about anything but *happy-go-lucky*— something else he remembered from junior year.

That same evening, he finished up at the ranch, showered off the day in his house, and then headed into town. It was another perilously cold December night, but it was clear all the way up to the stars. The drive from the foothills into town could often be treacherous in winter, but the last major snow had been on Thanksgiving night. Connor found himself driving a little faster than he should. He parked his truck on Main Street, and told himself the sense of anticipation inside him was for the well-earned beer he planned to indulge in tonight. That was all.

He knew himself to be a liar when he walked inside, saw Missy at the bar, and accepted that she was what he'd wanted all along.

"You're starting to look like a Cold River barfly," Connor said as he slid onto the seat next to her.

She threw him a look filled with laughter, and he felt it in places he didn't need to acknowledge while out in public, surrounded by his friends and neighbors.

"It takes one to know one, Connor."

"Fair enough."

He ordered a beer and clinked his bottle to hers when he got it. Then they both sat there, in what he figured was a companionable silence. If he ignored that kiss layered in between them like a shout.

"Settling in?" he asked. Sedately.

When he felt nothing at all like *sedate*.

The look she shot him was as hot as it was amused. "I have an interview at the Grand Hotel here in town. They're looking for a manager now that old Douglas Fowler is thinking about retirement. I also have some feelers out in all the ski resorts. Aspen, Vail. Breckenridge. The usual."

"You don't waste any time."

Connor chose not to pay attention to that strange, curling thing inside him that wanted to tell her in no uncertain terms not to consider Colorado's famous resort towns, all of which were close enough to home. Closer than Santa Fe anyway—but not in the dead of winter. Not when a Colorado snowstorm could make any road impassable in a flash and usually made the passes actively treacherous.

Just like he opted not to ask himself why he was acting like he'd be seeing more of her than a few happy, random, holiday bar sightings.

Missy was playing with tonight's IPA. "I've already wasted enough time. We're thirty, Connor. Most of the people we went to high school with are on their third kid."

"You could have settled down and had kids right out of high school if you wanted," he reminded her. "What was that guy's name again?"

She laughed at that. "You know his name."

He did. "Wyatt Hall. One of *those* Halls."

"Just because a few members of the Hall family have had their skirmishes with the law doesn't make—"

"He was a delinquent," Connor protested with a lot more feeling about ancient history than should have been kicking around inside him, surely. "He still is a delinquent."

"You only think that because he had visible tattoos and that car."

"I have nightmares about that car."

And not because Wyatt Hall, problem kid from a problem family, had rebuilt it and roared it around town like a maniac. But because Connor had hated imagining Missy in that car. Doing with Wyatt what she'd done with him—

It turned out he still didn't want to imagine it.

"Me too, actually," Missy said, grinning. "And before you ask, he was way more interested in driving fast enough to irritate the church ladies than in anything else. As an attempt to annoy my mother, he was great. But other than that? A waste of time. Even if I'd wanted to stick around and have babies, he wasn't going to help with that."

Connor would have to be a sad, sad man to enjoy that bit of information. He told himself he absolutely was not biting back a smile.

"Instead of joining the Hall family criminal organization, I opted for a different road," Missy told him. "I thought it was a freeway. It turned out it was a dead end. Now I have to start over, preferably without the driving metaphors."

He shouldn't have touched her. Especially not here at the bar when anyone and everyone could have been watching. But he leaned closer and pressed his arm against hers. Just a little.

"There's nothing wrong with starting over. It's not a reset button. You get to come to it a little bit wiser."

She shook her head at him, but she didn't move away from the press of his arm. "What would you know about that, Connor? When have you started over?"

It was hard to keep his hands to himself, but he figured their arms against each other was enough. "I'm not just a pretty face, Missy. I have thoughts, no matter what my brothers might tell you. And empathy."

Missy actually snorted. "If you say so."

"I'm not a kid anymore," he continued, feeling not exactly . . . upset. That would be a strong way to put it. But something about the way she looked at him scraped a bit at his honor. Or pride, more like. "I've learned a couple of things in the past thirteen years."

"If you're talking about kissing, you made that pretty clear the other night."

He wanted to argue about how she'd unfairly maligned his character, but not as much as he wanted to talk about kissing her. "Are we talking about that?" Connor about killed himself to sound lazy. Careless. "I got the impression you were going to pretend that didn't happen."

She smiled and her whole face lit up, and he couldn't muster up any defense to that. "I haven't decided yet."

And later that night in the front seat of his truck she threw one leg over him, took his face in her hands, and kissed him so hot and so right that he didn't particularly care if they never discussed it again.

Just as long as she kept doing it.

That was how things went for the next week. December got colder. The snow kicked in when it felt like it, blanketing the valley and reminding everyone that they were only ever one bad storm away from nature taking control.

But Connor didn't care. Every night the roads weren't too bad, he made his way into town, with or without his brothers. And every night, whether she'd bothered to acknowledge him or not inside the Broken Wheel, he drove Missy home.

And indulged himself in nostalgia and a bright, hot new greed there, fully clothed in the front seat of his truck.

"You'll never believe who's back in town," his sister, Amanda, said one Sunday dinner before Christmas, in the family's sprawling ranch house.

Their parents lived there now, and despite the snow today, his grandparents had walked across the pasture from the smaller house they'd built when they were ready to leave the bulk of running the Bar K to Connor's father. It was a full house today, with everyone crowded around the big, wide ranch house table that had been built to seat whoever might show up.

"All kinds of people," Connor said in repressive tones that he knew would be ignored. Because he also knew what was coming. Amanda had been using the story of Missy's low-cut shirt as a weapon for years, which he supposed meant it really had produced the effect she'd wanted. "After all, Christmas is coming. Folks tend to turn up, filled with nostalgia and desperate to escape their—"

He remembered himself.

"To escape what?" Amanda asked innocently.

Connor reminded himself that his baby sister was as evil as the rest of the Kittredges when she put her mind to it.

"Memories of high school, monkey," Connor replied in the same tone, as if he hadn't been about to say *their families.*

"I ran into Marianne Minton the other day," Connor's mother said sedately from her end of the table. "She said Missy has come back home from Santa Fe."

Riley was there with Rae, both of them acting like they hadn't spent the better part of a decade at odds now that their marriage was back on. He frowned. "Missy Minton. Isn't she the one . . . ?"

Amanda drew a line down the front of her shirt.

"Amanda moved out, lived above the Coyote, and served drinks there, which is basically the Cold River version of working at Hooters," he threw out there. "Just to remind everyone."

"Definitely classier than Hooters," Amanda's husband, Brady, said, shooting his wife a look filled with the kind of heat Connor felt it was his duty, as Amanda's older brother, to studiously ignore.

"I didn't realize you had a basis of comparison," Amanda replied tartly.

Brady looked at Riley, his best friend since the dawn of time. "Denver," they said together.

"Connor already knows Missy's back in town," Jensen chimed in then in his *helpful* voice. Which was to say, not helpful at all. "We saw her the other night at the Broken Wheel."

"She wasn't wearing a low-cut shirt," Zack drawled. "Because I know that's the next question. Obviously, as a duly elected member of law enforcement, it would have fallen on me to intervene if there had been any indecent exposure on the streets of Cold River."

Connor schooled himself not to react. It was what

they wanted. Or even if they didn't want it, directly, if he showed any reaction, that would only make things worse.

But that didn't mean his jaw hurt any less as he sat there clenching it.

"I don't think anyone in this room wants their exploits as a sixteen-year-old held up to any scrutiny," Connor heard himself say, despite the clenched jaw and the fact he knew better.

His brothers all stared at him. Brady too.

Amanda grinned. "Not me. I was an angel."

"Accidentally," Brady contributed from beside her.

"Anyway," Amanda said, ignoring her husband, "Missy was in the coffeehouse the other day while I was having a lunch break. She told me she's moving home with her mother until she figures out what to do next. She was engaged, you know." Connor didn't know who Amanda was looking at when she said that, because he was very deliberately studying his plate. "But that ended. She and Tessa Winthrop were talking about how neither one of them has ever been on a real date."

"What are you talking about?" Jensen demanded. "You don't get engaged without dating. And Tessa made it perfectly clear that no one better dream of asking her out unless they want to get shot." He let out a laugh when every pair of eyes at the table turned to him. "Just reporting the facts. If I wanted to ask Tessa out, I wouldn't be afraid of a little shotgun blast."

"I don't think we need to sit here gossiping about that Minton girl, or Tessa Winthrop," Ellie said in her usual sedate way. That every single person at the table knew full well was wrapped around a core of unbendable steel.

Connor didn't thank her directly. But later that afternoon, he found himself driving over to Missy Minton's mother's house to ask her on a date.

A real date.

While the sun was still shining, it wasn't late at night, and there was no pretending he wasn't doing exactly what he was doing.

4

Missy didn't know what she'd expected.

Coming back to Cold River had seemed like such a great idea. Things had changed in town, or so Laurel always tried to convince her. At Thanksgiving, Laurel had waxed rhapsodic about all the new and exciting ways that tiny little Cold River was ushering itself into the present century. As opposed to the way Missy remembered it, which was a town frozen forever somewhere between a John Wayne movie and the gold rush era.

But there were more stores downtown these days. Little boutiques, which Laurel told her catered more and more to weekend and wedding traffic out of Denver. There were more restaurants, even in the dead of December, which meant the proprietors were actually giving the cold Colorado winters a go instead of shutting down until summer. There were new ideas right here next to Old West traditions, and the result was eclectic. Charming.

Missy couldn't help but love it.

But while the actual town of Cold River was changing, other things remained the same.

Like Missy's infamy.

"I don't know what you expected," her mother fussed

at her that particular Sunday. Marianne was bustling around the kitchen as she prepared three separate pot-luck meals for various families in need of a little TLC this week. "I told you at the time that reputations are fragile things."

"Yes, Missy," Laurel said dryly, from where she was slumped at the kitchen table with her phone in her hand. "Your reputation as a sixteen-year-old who wore a scoop neck one day will be the end of you. Might as well pack up your things, go down into town, and beg for work at the old bordello. That's clearly the only option open to you."

Missy bit back a laugh while her mother turned her glare on Laurel.

"I'm not suggesting anything of the kind. But your sister went out of her way to make scenes before she left town. You shouldn't be surprised, Missy," Marianne continued pointedly, "that having stayed away all this time, that's what folks remember."

"I'm not surprised they remember it," Missy said. She wasn't. She had indeed gone out of her way to create a small-town scandal, and she'd known full well that sort of thing haunted a person. Whether it amused her or not depended on the day. "I'm surprised that Lucinda Early felt that it was appropriate to sniff at me about it in the drugstore."

Laurel rolled her eyes. "Lucinda Early will lecture anyone at any time, anywhere."

"Lucinda Early is an elder in this community and de-serves your respect," Marianne snapped. And then sighed. "She might also be the biggest gossip in the Longhorn Valley, I grant you. That certainly hasn't changed."

"Dad used to call her the town crier," Missy said, grinning.

And as with any mention of Hank Minton, they all stopped smiling. Then smiled a bit brighter, because Sundays weren't the same with him gone. He'd always woken them up early, laughing at any expressions of teenage crankiness as he'd rousted them out of bed. He'd made them help him make pancakes with bacon and syrup, fluffy scrambled eggs, and his grandmother's biscuits.

He'd crank up his favorite radio station, and when Marianne would appear, he would dance her around the kitchen, laughing uproariously.

It still didn't make sense that he was gone.

"Want me to turn up the music, Mom?" Laurel asked. Only half kidding, by the look of it. "I can dance too."

Marianne returned to the meals she was tucking away into Tupperware. "Thank you, no. My dancing days are over."

"Don't say that, Mom," Missy said gently. "You have your whole life—"

"I would've thought you'd understand," Marianne said, shooting Missy a baffled sort of look. "Some of us are built to love only once."

The funny part was, Missy didn't think her mother meant that as a slap. Because despite her starchiness and her horror that her daughters had grown up a little too wild, Marianne loved them both deeply. And Missy thought she honestly believed that even though she might not have fully embraced Philip herself, Missy had loved him the way Marianne had loved Hank.

Possibly because Missy had ranted at her parents that she did. That was why she'd chosen Philip, she'd shouted at them. That was why she was marrying him. Because history was repeating itself, and that was all there was to it.

Something Missy had clung to throughout those years when Philip kept coming up with a thousand terrific reasons to postpone their actual wedding. The focus was on the hotel. Building up the hotel. Making sure it ran smoothly. Catering to their steadily growing clientele.

Leaving Missy to defend the endlessly postponed wedding to her family, which she'd done perhaps a little too hotly.

"I guess that makes me the heartless one," Laurel said happily. "I fall in love every Tuesday."

"Oh, you do not," Marianne tutted.

But Missy's attention was caught by the sound of a car in the drive outside. She assumed it was one of Laurel's friends, but when she went to peer out the windows, she saw Connor's truck.

And her stomach flipped over, the way it had when she was still sixteen.

"Who's that?" Laurel asked.

"I wasn't expecting anyone," Marianne said, going to the window to stand beside Missy. Then she stiffened when Connor rolled out of the truck.

And probably not because she was struck by the sight of all his offhanded beauty, the way Missy was.

It was unfair, really. He was dressed in what looked like his Sunday best, which was still cowboy boots and jeans—but nicer jeans. Boots with a little more polish. And a nice plaid shirt, suitable for sitting at his mother's table. Add one of the ubiquitous barn jackets and a cowboy hat, and he was basically a fantasy made real.

A fantasy Missy would have told anyone who asked—and probably had told a lot of people who didn't ask—she'd never had. That was why she'd moved away to a city that trafficked as much in ghosts as it did in dreams of the wild, wild West.

But as Connor started ambling his way toward the house, her body was telling her that no matter what she might like to think, the fantasy was alive and well and kicking around inside of her. It was sending out flames and heat wherever it touched.

Wherever he'd touched, she corrected herself.

And she only noticed that her cheeks were much too hot when she found both her mother and her sister staring at her.

"Oh, Missy," Marianne said in that mix of resignation and disappointment that had been music to Missy's ears when she'd been a teenager. "Not Connor Kittredge."

"Why not Connor Kittredge?" Laurel asked. "He's beautiful. All those Kittredges are beautiful. It's not really fair."

"I would think, after a broken engagement, that you might take this opportunity to stop," Marianne said quietly to Missy. "Think. Figure out what went wrong."

Missy was a grown woman who certainly didn't need to act like a teenager and shout at her mother. Or so she reminded herself then. Even if that meant actually, literally biting her tongue.

"I already know what went wrong, Mom," she said quietly when she was certain she wouldn't give in to the urge to shout. "Philip was sleeping with someone else. For years. He was planning a future with her while he was pretending to be planning one with me. That's what went wrong. The only thing I did was believe in him. And in her, for that matter. She worked side by side with me and pretended to be my friend."

And then she couldn't keep quite as close a hold on herself as she should have. "I understand that you think I brought this on myself because I was a spirited teenager.

But I assure you, I wasn't the one doing the cheating. I was the one being cheated on."

It was into the silence after her announcement that Connor's knock came on the door.

Missy and her mother were too busy staring at each other, too much unsaid—though maybe that was a blessing. Laurel went over to the door, swinging it open and letting the cold air rush in.

"Oh, hi, Connor," she said brightly. "Are you lost?"

Missy jerked her gaze away from her mom and still wasn't prepared for an eyeful of Connor standing in her kitchen doorway. She watched him take in the room. And the tension.

Then he grinned. "Nice to see you, Laurel. Mrs. Minton. And no, I'm not lost. I'm here to see Missy."

Marianne stacked up her Tupperware with what Missy thought was a little too much unnecessary force.

"Good afternoon, Connor," Marianne said primly. "I hope you're aware that it was your influence in high school that led to my daughter being branded—"

"There are no brands, Mom," Missy interjected, her eyes widening in horror as she stared at Connor. Who, for his part, looked wildly entertained. "No branding whatsoever. I don't even have a tattoo, much less a *brand*."

"Her father thought it was funny, but I never did," Marianne continued.

Connor's grin faded. "I know I told you this at the funeral, Mrs. Minton," he said. "But I sure am sorry. My dad doesn't say much at the best of times, but he always told us that Hank Minton was the only lawyer he was inclined to trust."

Missy watched Marianne take that in, blinking rapidly because she knew what a compliment it was, given that a great many members of the community were not inclined to trust a lawyer as far as said lawyer could be thrown. But that had been Hank's charm. He'd been a cowboy first himself, and a lawyer second. All Marianne did was nod and excuse herself, murmuring something about delivering the food.

"I guess it's up to me to ask your intentions, Connor," Laurel said with a drawl, ignoring the glare that Missy sent her. "My sister is not wearing a low-cut shirt today and never can again, thanks to you. Do you intend to further humiliate her—and more importantly, the Minton family name—by forcing her to bare her various body parts around town?"

"Someday," Missy promised her, "I will have my revenge."

Laurel waved a hand. "Bring it."

Connor shut the door he'd held for Marianne, then leaned one shoulder against the doorjamb like he could stand there all day. Like that had been his plan all along. "It was your sister's choice to wear that shirt. I dared her, sure, but she took the dare. I'm not sure the fallout is on me."

"Debatable," Laurel shot back.

Missy looked back and forth between them. "Why are we talking about me like I'm not right here?"

"I know you're here," Connor said. His dark eyes, laced through with laughter, met hers and made her . . . short out. "I heard a rumor that you've never been on a date, Missy."

Laurel's mouth fell open. And Missy felt about as embarrassed as she had that fateful day in church long ago, when she'd sauntered into the congregation in the low-cut shirt that would live in infamy, and had decided to brazen it out.

"What?" She frowned at Connor. "How on earth would you know something like that?"

"My sister said you were talking about it in Cold River Coffee." Connor grinned. "You know that's just as good as taking out a billboard."

"How have you never been on a date?" Laurel demanded.

Missy shot a look at her sister. "Because Cold River has a vibrant dating scene and you're out every night?"

Laurel smirked. "Point taken, but you haven't been living in Cold River for years. You were out there in real places, with real people, and what I assumed were endless single-girl-in-the-city dating adventures."

"As a matter of fact, no," Missy said with as much dignity as she could muster. "Dating wasn't really a thing in college. People sort of hung out, or didn't, but there weren't any . . . actual dates. After that, I was working so much that it was sort of the same. And then, you know. Philip."

Her younger sister was now studying her as if she were a specimen in a lab. "Surely, you had to date him in order to agree to marry him."

Missy wanted to talk about anything else. Anything in the world. Politics, religion, team sports. Anything but Philip and dating him when Connor was *right here*.

Connor, who she'd spent all these nights with over the past couple of weeks. There in the front seat of his truck, all her clothes on as if they were both still in high school. Kissing and kissing until they were both giddy and laughing and entirely too heated up for their own good.

"It never really happened that way," she managed to say. "It was a situation that developed, and then we were together. The point being, I've never been on a traditional date. That's all."

She risked a look at Connor despite her mortification and felt her embarrassment ease a bit. Philip would have been appalled. Disgusted, even, that anyone would be so ill mannered and unsophisticated as to toss ancient history around so cavalierly. But Connor was from here. He had a big, unruly family of his own. He knew small-town ways better than she did, and he didn't look put out at all.

Something inside her eased at that. An old knot she hadn't realized she'd tied so tightly, back when she'd had to navigate Philip's disdain of this place and these people. And everything else she'd held dear.

This was Connor, who would hurt himself to keep her safe.

He'd proved it.

Where that knot had been, something began to bloom as she looked at him.

"You're in luck," Connor told her.

And even though he was grinning, there was all that *intent* in those dark eyes of his. Her heart flipped around in her chest, and she was too warm and too charmed, and it crossed her mind that she might be in trouble with him, after all.

Dates, she reminded herself frantically. *He's talking about* dates.

His grin widened like he could read her mind, and she felt that like his hands, all over her. "I'm going to change that, Missy. One date at a time."

5

And the crazy thing was that Connor meant it.

Missy had laughed, that day in her mother's kitchen. She'd thought that was a cute thing for Connor to say— and she'd still been fighting off her embarrassment—but she hadn't expected much out of it. She didn't have any expectations where he was concerned.

In point of fact, she'd given up expectations right about the time she'd left Santa Fe.

That afternoon, while the light was still waning as the sun flirted with the mountaintops and Laurel was pretending not to both stare and eavesdrop the way she had back when she'd been in braces, he'd asked her if she would go on a walk with him.

It was like falling back through time. In the beginning of their teenage relationship, he'd been forced to turn up on the porch, contend with her father, and then escort her on a walk there in the clearing where Hank could keep an eye on them.

That was what he did that day too. And when they were done taking a long, slow turn around the clearing, they sat on the porch and pretended they couldn't feel the cold even as it turned their noses red.

Because Hank had always explicitly vetoed any blankets.

Hands where I can see them, young man, he'd boomed at Connor from his spot at the window.

"This is ridiculous," she'd said, shivering on the chilly bench. She'd told herself she found it all a lot less fun this time around. A sixteen-year-old was supernaturally impervious to the weather if there was a cute boy around. A thirty-year-old was just cold.

But she didn't go inside.

"It's not ridiculous, Missy. It's a date."

"It's not a date," she'd retorted. "It's a stunt. These weren't dates back in high school, either. Dates require forethought. And an activity. This is what Tessa and I were talking about in Cold River Coffee, by the way, when your sister was eavesdropping. Your high school boyfriend showing up at your house and prancing around the yard—"

"I do not prance," Connor protested.

"—doesn't count. You were making a good impression on my father so that he wouldn't object to you driving me home sometimes, which is where all the good stuff actually happened. But that doesn't make it a date."

"It felt like a date to me," Connor said. "Then and now."

"A date is something that is *planned,*" Missy told him, shivering. "It is something *you* plan, to be more specific. Then you ask me if I would like to join you at whatever it is. I either agree or don't. If I do agree, you have to come pick me up, transport me to said activity, pay for it—"

"I thought a city-girl type like you always insisted on paying your own way."

"If I asked you on a date, of course I would pay. The

asker does the paying, Connor. The asked does not." She shrugged. "I don't make the rules."

"Convenient rules. That's all I'm saying."

"After the date, I may or may not kiss you in the front seat of your truck. I may or may not invite you inside. I won't, because I live with my mother at the moment. But you get my point. *That's* a date. It requires more of you than a stroll around a yard."

"Message received," Connor had said, and he hadn't kissed her, there on the front porch the way he had when they'd both been kids and her father had been looking the other way.

But he had called her later that night to formally ask her on a date.

"A real date," he'd clarified.

"I guess so," Missy had said, trying to sound something other than silly.

"There's that enthusiasm," Connor had replied with a laugh. "I'll pick you up tomorrow night at eight."

And that was how it started.

That first night, Connor picked her up and escorted her to his truck, where he held the door for her while she climbed into the passenger side. Then he drove her down the hill into town and took her to one of the newer restaurants. Where they both laughed over the absurdly hipster menu and were both pleasantly surprised that food like massaged kale with chickpea butter and monk fruit sugar tasted so good.

They lingered over dinner, and when they were done, Connor did not suggest they drop into the Broken Wheel. Instead, he took her home, pulling up in front of her mother's house with a certain flourish. Then he came around to help her out of the truck in the same chivalrous way.

"I didn't realize when you suggested a date that it

would be a very proper date from the 1950s," she said darkly as he escorted her up onto the porch.

"Now you do," he said, though there was that wicked light in his gaze.

And there on the porch, the light felt buttery against the December dark. Connor reached over and ran his thumb over her lips, a corner of his mouth crooking up when she shivered. And not from the cold.

"I object," Missy whispered.

"Then you should probably go out with me again," he said. "On another real date. Who knows what might happen?"

Missy had other things to think about, she assured herself. She had a life to rebuild—or start anew, depending on what level of positivity the day required. She had interviews at different hotels in resort towns all over Colorado, and at this time of year, that sometimes meant overnight stays when the weather stopped cooperating.

But every time she came back to Cold River, there was another date with Connor. He took her dancing in a honky-tonk saloon halfway to Aspen. He took her ice-skating on a crisp, clear Saturday afternoon, up on a lake in the hills that was still filled with giggling high school kids. Like they'd been, once upon a time. They drove up into the woods on Kittredge land and chopped down a Christmas tree that he told her he planned to put in his own cabin.

"What exactly are you doing?" Tessa asked one night. For once, she wasn't working behind the bar at the Broken Wheel. The two of them were enjoying cheeseburgers and fries cooked to perfection on a very relaxed Thursday night, the week before Christmas.

"Eating my cheeseburger," Missy said, pretending she didn't understand the question. "I'm enjoying the cheddar, though I will admit, I'm wondering if I should've gone a little crazy and gotten the Swiss with the mushrooms."

Tessa pointed a french fry across the table. "Mushrooms are the devil."

"Do I have to know what I'm doing?" Missy asked softly.

Two men walked in, and Missy froze. Because they were both tall, gorgeous, more dark than blond with those same impossibly dark eyes—

But it was Riley and Jensen. Not Connor.

Down, girl, she ordered herself.

"No, you don't have to know what you're doing," Tessa was saying. Unaware that there were Kittredges about, clearly. "I certainly don't know what I'm doing approximately 80 percent of the time. But the difference is, I don't do it so . . . publicly."

Missy stopped looking at Connor's brothers and concentrated on her friend. "I don't know what you mean."

"All these dates." Tessa shook her head. "It's cute, but it looks like courting, doesn't it?"

"I don't think so. Mostly because it's no longer the 1800s. People don't *court,* Tessa. You can order sex acts on your phone, for God's sake."

"This is Cold River." Tessa laughed. "Not your fancy sex-act cities. That man has been taking you out almost every night since you came home, and you know how folks are."

"They can't possibly think . . ." Missy shook her head. "They're still talking about a questionable shirt I wore in church a hundred years ago. Believe me, even if they're aware that Connor and I have been going out on dates—"

"Believe me." Tessa's voice was dry. "Everyone's aware."

"—I'm sure they think I'm nothing more than that loose woman he's wasting his time with, part two."

Her old friend looked at her for a long moment. Long enough that Missy began to feel uncomfortable. Her cheeseburger sat in her stomach like a lead weight.

"Is that what you think?" Tessa asked softly. "That you're a waste of time?"

It took her too long to answer. "Of course not."

"I never liked Philip," Tessa said matter-of-factly. "I thought he was full of himself, and he acted like coming from a small town was a fate worse than death. But you always wanted a city guy, and I figured maybe that's what city guys were like."

"You met him all of two times."

"And he was obnoxious both times. Which wouldn't matter if he were good to you. He wasn't."

"No," Missy said on a sigh. "He wasn't."

"People cheat," Tessa said with a shrug. "Life is complicated, and humans do selfish things sometimes. He could have married you and cheated, so I guess doing it before you got married is a kindness, in its way. But what I don't understand is why you're taking what happened as any kind of commentary on *you*. *You* aren't the spineless, gutless liar in this scenario. He is."

"He made a fool out of me," Missy whispered.

"There's a fool in this, sure. But it's not you."

Missy tried to shake it off. "I don't want to talk about him. It's boring."

"We're not talking about him," Tessa said softly. "We're talking about you."

"We can stop that too."

"You broke up with Connor Kittredge our junior year because you were way too in love with him," Tessa said, clear-eyed and very, very certain. "You knew if you didn't, you'd be married to that man and knee deep in babies within three years."

That had seemed like a fate worse than death thirteen years ago. Tonight, it settled in her like spiced wine, rich and warm. Which should have horrified her.

"I broke up with Connor Kittredge because he was flirting with that awful cheerleader whose name I deliberately don't know—"

"You know her name. And she's perfectly lovely, by the way. She and her partner have a goat farm."

"I'm delighted for her, really."

Tessa leaned forward and put her hand on Missy's wrist.

"Is it really the worst thing in the world to admit that maybe you had it right the first time?" she asked softly. "Stranger things have happened, you know. I would have told you Connor Kittredge was incapable of taking anyone on a date, ever, and look. You've been on a million. Maybe you were meant to come back here all along."

"No way," Missy managed to say, trying her best to find her laughter again. And not checking her phone when it buzzed in her back pocket. "Connor and I are having fun, that's all. It's nothing serious."

Because it couldn't be.

6

Connor couldn't have said why he'd started this.

He hadn't liked his family talking about Missy over Sunday dinner. He knew that much. But how that had turned into him deciding to take her on every date he felt she should have had, he didn't know.

And he really didn't understand how somewhere in there, he'd gotten a whole lot more serious than he'd meant to do. He was having some trouble dealing with that—but not when he was with Missy. When he was with Missy, he couldn't think of a single reason he'd ever want to be anywhere else.

When he wasn't with her, however, he remembered that he'd felt this way a long time ago too. And it had ended, anyway.

Funny how he hadn't thought much about that part in all the intervening years.

"What's going on with you and that Minton girl?" Zack asked one morning a few days before Christmas.

It had snowed heavily the past two days, blanketing the valley. And for once, Zack wasn't off in town doing his sheriff thing. He'd come out the night before as part of a sweep through the far reaches of the Longhorn Valley and had stayed over when the roads got bad. Now he was waiting for what little sunlight they expected today to encourage the ice to relax a bit. Meaning, he was on hand to do some ranch work.

Connor had been happy about that, because it was always nice to have company while driving around the fields and pastures to make sure that the snow hadn't done any damage. Riley and Jensen preferred to go solo, like their father, but Connor considered himself far more sociable than any of them.

He was less happy now that Zack was taking this as an opportunity to go all big brother on him.

"Not sure I'd call Missy a girl," he replied eventually, glaring out at the walls of snow all around him. "Since no one's in high school anymore."

"Good misdirection," Zack drawled.

"Is this an interrogation, Sheriff?" Connor asked, doing his level best to keep his wrist draped over the steering wheel carelessly and the same kind of relaxed, easy note in his voice.

"Sure are spending a lot of time with her," Zack observed in the same drawl. "Out on dates every night of the week, as far as I can tell."

"Why are you paying attention?" Connor countered. "Don't you have bad guys to catch and old, rich ranchers to placate?"

"I pay attention to everything that happens in my town," Zack replied. "Especially when it involves my brothers."

"That sounds a lot like a more dramatic way of saying that you're really nosy. Which explains a lot."

"Connor."

There it was. No more older brother. Zack had gone 100 percent sheriff of Longhorn County. Because that was Zack. It was all fun and games until he whipped out his badge. When they'd been younger and he wasn't actually an official of any kind, he'd wielded the power vested in him as oldest to do basically the same thing.

It had been as annoying then as it was now.

"Whatever you're about to say," Connor muttered. "Don't."

"She seems like a great girl." Zack sounded something like philosophical. That had to be a trap. "The Mintons are a nice family. I liked Hank Minton a lot."

"You sound like Lucinda Early."

Zack ignored that. He shifted in the passenger seat and trained that relentless gaze of his on Connor. "But you have to know by now that she's not going to stay here. She left the second she could. And she's only back now because the life she had out there didn't work out."

"I'm aware of her biography, Zack."

"Then you should also be aware that her kind of biography always means the same thing in small-town terms. She's not staying."

Connor kept driving, though he wasn't sure he was seeing the fields in front of him. Much less the unmapped road he was supposed to be following that was little more than a cleared patch of dirt on a summer day. Today, it was beneath the snowdrifts, and really, he should have been giving it his full attention.

But his chest felt tight. And *he* felt . . .

He refused to go there, especially trapped in this vehicle with Zack and the possibility of a ground blizzard every time the wind shifted.

"I'm not sure how you think you know enough about Missy to predict her future," he managed to say.

"I don't." And the worst part was that Zack didn't sound like this was the usual sort of brotherly heckling they all engaged in. "But I do know small-town statistics.

She came home to lick her wounds. Once she's healed, why would she stay?"

"Funny, what I am sure about is that I didn't ask you. Even better, what she does or doesn't do is none of your business."

"Connor. You know what this town is like. There are some folks who stay and a whole lot of other folks who leave. And most of the folks who leave never come back. Not for good. Welcome to rural America."

"Thanks, Mom."

Zack laughed. "Like Mom would ever indicate she knew you had a personal life."

"Why are you?" Connor demanded, slamming a foot on the brakes in the full understanding that the truck would fishtail. And petty enough to enjoy it when Zack had to reach out and brace himself on the dashboard. "I'm trying to imagine any scenario in which you would like it if I rolled up and gave you unsolicited advice about your love life."

Or anything else.

Zack sighed. And obviously wasn't replying to Connor's point, because he couldn't. There was no way it had escaped him that he was out of line here. But being Sheriff Zack, patron saint of his own martyrdom, he would die before admitting that.

And being the relentless jackhole he'd been since the day of Connor's birth, he kept going. "You're knocking yourself out taking this girl on the kind of dates that are guaranteed to make all the ladies in church sigh happily and dream of you dating their daughters. Meanwhile, what do you think she's doing?"

"I know what she's doing, Zack. Because I'm the one who's actually dating her."

"She's interviewing for jobs, Connor." Zack's voice was impatient. And Connor didn't have to look over at him to know he'd likely pulled out that granite face of his too. Useful for quelling rowdy rednecks at a glance. "I heard she's had offers already. And not here in Cold River. You really think you're going to have a long-distance relationship with a hotel manager in Vail?"

"If I did," Connor said, very distinctly, "I wouldn't ask you for a ride. Or for your opinion on it."

"You work on the Bar K." As if Connor had missed that, out here in the fields, like he was every day of his life. "That's not going to change."

"Thank you for bringing up another thing that isn't your business," Connor muttered. "I do work here, yes. You don't."

"I'm literally sitting next to you, right now, working."

"Give me a break," Connor retorted. With more volume than necessary, probably. "Riding around to assess storm damage because the pass is iced over isn't the same thing as working here, and you know it. You didn't want to work here. You and Dad had your thing—"

Zack grunted. "I wouldn't call it a *thing*."

"Because you always think that when it's you, it's different." Connor was gripping the steering wheel way too hard. He forced his fingers to relax. "The point is, you don't need to worry about Missy. Just like you don't need to worry about the ranch. Concern yourself more with picking up bad guys and having discussions with high school kids about forest fires or whatever it is you do all day."

Zack sighed. "You do realize I have deputies, right? A whole department? And that law and order is a real thing?"

"When I want your advice, Zack, you'll know," Connor said. Too intensely, sure. But he wasn't shouting, and that felt like a win. "Because I'll ask for it."

They bumped along in a not exactly friendly silence then, while the minutes stretched out between them. And Connor scanned the fields, now hoping for a structural disaster that he could leap out and tend to, because anything was better than this conversation.

"I just want to make sure—" Zack began again when no disasters presented themselves.

"Is your love life up for discussion?" Connor demanded.

Another silence, and Connor wished—again—that they weren't shut up inside this truck. That he were out there in the elements that he loved so much. Colorado at its best, as dangerous as it was pretty. Cold and snowy on the one hand, but with that bright blue sky up above as if the storm had never happened.

Maybe the truth was he liked women who felt like the land to him. Gorgeous and worth dedicating a life to, but a wise man never turned his back for too long.

"I'm trying to look out for you," Zack said in a low, almost angry voice—as if Connor were being unreasonable. "It's not like I went looking for this information. You know as well as I do that Adaline thinks it's her duty to keep me up to date on every stray bit of gossip she encounters."

"I appreciate that," Connor said, though he didn't. A lot like he'd never appreciated Adaline Sykes, the immovable secretary to three sheriffs so far, because a person who thought their tendency to gossip was a job requirement was always going to be a problem. "And in the unlikely event I need the sheriff, or even my big brother, to sort out my private life, I'll be sure to let you know. Until then? This is all off-limits."

"Understood." Yet Zack was still projecting all that granite at the side of Connor's face. "But for the record, your girl has job offers as far away as Arizona. And *my* love life is fine."

"One more word and I'll make you walk back to the house, Zack," Connor threw at him. "I'm not kidding. I don't care if you disappear into a snowdrift and we don't find you until spring."

He must have sounded serious, because Zack actually stayed quiet for the rest of their tour around the snowy fields. Because he was wrong and he knew he was wrong, Connor told himself. It was older-brother nonsense, nothing more. The usual Kittredge family special—digging all around in people's lives whether they liked it or not.

But alone in his cabin later that evening, with nothing but the bare Christmas tree that stood in the corner and might as well have shouted out Missy's name, Connor was forced to face some facts.

He had gone and gotten too serious. It had snuck up on him, but here he was, and he didn't see how he was going to go about changing it.

And there was no reason for someone like Missy to stay in Cold River. She'd always been horrified at the very idea. She wanted the big, wide world. She wanted bustling cities and a sophisticated nightlife and all the things that went with lives lived outside the confines of this valley.

She wanted things Connor couldn't give her. Things he didn't want to give anyone, because this was where he belonged. This place was who he was. And he didn't need Zack to remind him that women who dreamed of cities never lasted long, or well, far out here in the grip of the land where life was about weather and livestock, seasons, hope, and grit. They all knew the broken marriages, the abandoned spouses, the separations and divorces.

Connor wanted no part of any of that.

The snow was kicking up again. The wind knocked around the cabin, howling and carrying on as the longest night of the year wore on.

Just like it would when she was gone, he told himself, gazing out at the dark and the storm. All winter long without her, like every other winter since they'd broken up the first time, and the sooner he resigned himself to it, the better.

7

On the night before Christmas Eve, Connor picked Missy up and took her out early. He instructed her to wear her cold-weather clothes, so she'd wrapped herself up in enough layers to combat whatever Colorado might throw at them.

And was glad she did when he drove her out to one of the newer ranches—or new to her, anyway—tipped his hat at someone who was clearly a friend, and then treated her to an actual sleigh ride.

"If you want to sing Christmas carols, you should," he told her, snuggled up under a cozy, warm blanket beside her while the prancing horses literally jingled all the way. "I won't tell anyone if you're off-key."

"My singing voice would kill the horses," she replied, filled up inside with something so bright and giddy it almost hurt. "Not exactly the Christmas miracle anyone's looking for."

Connor laughed, his big arm wrapped around her shoulders, and pulled her tighter into his side. And she did her best not to think too much about how easily she fit there, or how much it felt like she belonged.

This was the first Christmas in a long while that she didn't have to work. The first Christmas in years that she didn't have to tend to others no matter what she might be feeling inside. Her only duties this year were to buy gifts for her mother and sister, wrap them up, and stash them under the tree in the living room. She could toy with the idea of baking something, stuff herself with Christmas cookies, and chase everything down with hot chocolate by day and spiked eggnog by night.

All of that was a marvel. She was pretty sure that Connor was the miracle.

When the sleigh ride was done, he drove her back into town, took her out to dinner, and made her laugh the way he always did. Laugh and laugh and laugh. Until she really couldn't tell which part of her was filled with that giddiness and which part of her was made up of laughter.

And after dinner, they walked down Main Street, bundled up against the frigid cold. There had been snowstorms earlier in the week, but tonight the sky was clear. And Cold River was doing its best to outshine the stars far above. There were Christmas lights strung down the length of the street. All the storefronts joined in and the shops stayed open late this time of year, encouraging folks to come spend their money on local gifts and services.

"I forgot all about this," she told Connor as they walked, easing their way through the throng of people. She was glad she'd worn her toastiest boots, as she remembered too well how the wrong pair of shoes could ruin everything in weather like this. "I don't think I've spent any time on Main Street at Christmas since . . ."

"Junior year?"

She grinned at him. "Probably."

"You can depend on Cold River to do it up when Christmas rolls around." And he was still grinning, but it . . . changed then. "We all know it's going to be months of cold and dark. Better shine while we can."

She'd been ignoring it all evening, but that comment seemed to be just as strange as he seemed. Distant, maybe, even while he'd been making her laugh. And even more now.

"That sounds ominous," she said. Lightly.

He was Connor, so his grin didn't dim, but Missy thought she could see a different sort of strain in his gaze then. "Spoken by someone who hasn't lived through a Cold River winter in a good long while."

He was still grinning. She had her arm hooked through his. Why was she looking for trouble in the backs of his eyes? Maybe the prickle down the back of her neck was just the cold.

"I can't argue with that," she said. "And I can't say that I miss the winters, either."

"I don't blame you." And again, all the brightness of the town surrounding them seem to call attention to the fact that he was . . . less bright than usual. But only because she knew him so well. "If I were you, I'd take that job in Arizona. Avoid this altogether."

Something thudded in her chest, hard and a little bit sickening. Missy was terribly afraid it was her heart.

"Arizona?" She stopped walking outside the bookstore that was still open tonight. Part of her wanted to dive inside, ignore anything that didn't feel good. Wasn't that what she'd been doing this whole month? Reveling in Connor. Enjoying all the silly dates that ended in wild kisses but nothing more. Allowing herself something sweet for a change.

How had she lived so long with so little sweetness?

But she could feel that wherever this conversation was going, *sweet* wasn't going to be part of it.

Missy wanted to go inside, but she didn't.

"Did I tell you about that job offer?" she asked. She

knew she hadn't. But she didn't wait for him to answer. "It's a lovely resort, actually. And I've always felt drawn to Sedona. Or, if I'm honest, I've always felt as if I ought to feel drawn to Sedona."

"You didn't have to tell me about it," Connor replied, and this time, she definitely didn't believe that grin. "Look around. Remember where you are. You don't have to tell me a story when the whole town is here to do it for you."

"My dad used to call it *the town telepathy*." Missy told herself that there was a deep, shivering thing inside her because she was cold. Because it was cold out here, no matter how many layers she was wearing. Because Colorado took its winters seriously, and she should too. "I never liked it much."

Connor looked down at her, something too dark in his gaze that she couldn't understand. Or define. She told herself she didn't want to. "Now, we know that's not true. You used it to your advantage."

But she didn't want to joke about her teenage shenanigans. She wanted . . . too many things to name.

She focused on the most immediate one. "Do you want me to go to Arizona?"

And she was kind of horrified when her voice . . . didn't exactly crack. But it wasn't steady, either.

The truth was, Missy had six separate offers for jobs that she was reasonably certain she would enjoy. Each and every one of them. There was that resort in Sedona. Three separate resorts and hotels along Colorado's famous ski town corridor. One offer from as far away as Cape Cod.

And an offer from the Grand Hotel just down the block, which she was sure had the church ladies in a tizzy.

The old Missy would have already made her decision.

It would have come down to the flip of a coin between Cape Cod and Sedona, because neither of those places was Colorado. Missy had always been so firm on getting out of Colorado, no matter what.

The old Missy never would have interviewed at the Grand Hotel in the first place.

And she could tell herself, her mother, and her sister that she was only being practical all she liked. She had.

I'm sure practicality *is really the key here,* Laurel had said, elbow deep in the Christmas cookie batter. *Your sudden potential interest in a job right here in Cold River has nothing whatsoever to do with any cowboys you might know personally.*

Missy had taken to delivering fiery speeches in the shower supporting her *practical* position—that being that she had interviewed at the Grand Hotel but would obviously be going elsewhere. It made sense not to spread herself thin again like she'd be doing if she stayed here and had to juggle family and work. It made sense that she should choose the kind of places that would benefit her career and not let her get sidetracked by some man again—meaning, far away. There were a thousand reasons why she shouldn't stay in Cold River, and most of them had been the very same concerns she'd had when she was a teenager.

But then again, she'd gotten that offer.

"What do you mean?" Connor asked. Lightly enough, but those dark eyes of his were unreadable. Missy didn't like that. The Connor she knew was an open book. Always had been. He was that giddy bubble of joy, nothing deeper. Nothing darker.

But even as she thought that, she knew it was a lie. It had been a lie thirteen years ago. Because they'd gotten intimate, sharing that first time with each other, and then they'd practiced quite a bit. And the more they practiced, the more impossible it had been for Missy to imagine life without him.

It had felt so intense, so much deeper than Missy had even known she was capable of feeling. So much so that when she heard he'd been flirting with another girl, she hadn't waited to see whether or not it was true.

She'd been relieved.

She had stormed down to the cafeteria and broken up with him on the spot.

And now, all these years later, she found herself breathless on a cold street, and in a whole lot deeper than she'd been then.

How had that happened?

"Here's what I know about you, Missy," Connor said, and the way he said her name like that broke her heart. She felt it happen, and felt as powerless to control it as she had that day long ago in Cold River High. She'd opened her mouth and yelled all the things she needed to yell to end it, then made herself walk away, her heart in pieces. "You don't like it here. At the end of the day, this isn't a place you want to stay. And that's okay. It's a big world out there. You should go wherever you need to go."

It was the kind of generous, openhearted thing she should have cheered upon hearing.

But instead, she felt sick and miserable. She wanted to punch him in the stomach. Or the face, she wasn't picky, though he was much too good-looking to bruise.

"So what you're saying is you want me to go. Ten hours away to Arizona."

"I want you to be happy." And though she was sure she could hear an edginess in his voice, his expression was clear. Intent but clear. She hated that too. "All you agreed to was a few dates. I know that."

"A few dates," she repeated. "Right. Just a few, silly, meaningless dates."

"You said you'd never been on a proper date," he said, his voice the kind of rumble that she was terribly afraid would live in her bones forever. "Now you've been on a lot of them. I have to say, Missy. I've always liked being your first."

And that fire that was always inside of her seemed to smolder then. Because he did. Because that was the easiest thing between them, that devouring, consuming heat. It had led to all her bad decisions as a teenager. It had scared her enough to make sure she followed each and every one of her dreams, even when they hadn't all been what she'd imagined they would. And it was still here, all these years later, even though all he did at the end of these dates was kiss her.

"What I don't remember is signing up for the kind of courtship that Lucinda Early would approve of," she said then. It was cold on the street, but everything inside of her was too hot, too loud, too confusing. She moved forward and tilted her head up so she could look him in the eye. "It's almost Christmas. Don't you think you should give me a gift?"

"This is the gift. All month long. You're welcome."

"And it's been wonderful. But I feel like the basic promise of all that flirting in bars over the years was that we would revisit what we do best."

And for a moment, there was so much heat between them, steaming up the windows of the bookshop and de-icing the sidewalks, that she was half-surprised he didn't throw her over his shoulder and make a run for his truck.

But he didn't.

Instead, he smiled down at her. In a manner that she could only describe as sad, somehow.

It made her heart beat harder and hurt more.

"If I were you, I'd wait and look for this kind of thing in Arizona," he told her. That smile of his deepened. It made her want to cry. "But me? I'm better as a memory, Missy. Maybe it's for the best we leave it that way."

8

Christmas Eve morning was spent in her family's usual bustle. Missy told herself she was delighted to be back to take part, and she was. More or less, she was. Marianne and Laurel worked together to create endless tins of Christmas cookies, which they then delivered all over the Longhorn Valley.

"Am I crazy?" Missy asked as she and Laurel braved the slippery roads to drive around their little pocket of Cold River. Delivering tins of love to all the neighbors from the list their mother had prepared.

"I'm going to go with yes," Laurel said from the passenger seat, where she was handling the actual deliveries to doors while Missy drove.

"Very funny," Missy said.

She clenched the steering wheel of her mother's hardy little hatchback, taking the mountain roads possibly a little too fast. That was the trouble with being a local. Because you knew the turns in the road, you figured they couldn't hurt you.

Missy blinked at that. Since when had she started considering herself a local again?

She cleared her throat. "All I mean is, this seems like

a lot of work for a bunch of people who are basically sitting around, waiting for the opportunity to gossip about you behind your back."

Her sister laughed. "Thank you for sharing your contagious Christmas spirit with me today. It really makes all the difference."

Missy pulled up in front of one of the houses on their route. She waited while Laurel threw open the door, charged up to the front stoop, and rang the doorbell. Her sister didn't wait for anyone to come to the door. She started back down the path, waving behind her as the door swung open and there was exclaiming into the cold air.

It was sweet. Missy couldn't deny it.

When Laurel got back in the car, she turned and studied Missy's face. "You don't have to like it here, you know. It's not a requirement. But maybe you could admit that just because it's not the place for you doesn't mean it's not a perfectly decent place."

Missy thought of Connor. She thought of the bright lights down Main Street. All the restaurants she'd been to this month, the activities. The shops and the boutiques and yes, the people.

"I wouldn't say I *hate* it," she hedged. "I guess I don't understand . . ."

"Because you don't want to understand," her younger sister said with a certain matter-of-factness that took Missy's breath away. "You always defined yourself as the one who got away. Maybe it's time you ask yourself what would happen if you were one of the ones who stayed?"

And she didn't wait for Missy to respond to that. She cranked up the music, all peppy Christmas carols, of course, and insisted that everything remained festive during the rest of their deliveries.

Later that evening, after the three of them had their

family dinner—heavy on butter and mashed potatoes, and a lot of very old stories only they knew—Missy found herself alone in the living room. Her mother had gone off to wrap some last-minute gifts upstairs. Laurel had gone out with her friends. And Missy wasn't in the hotel in Santa Fe. She couldn't claim she had a million things to do. A million guest requests to handle.

It was only her, standing in the living room with all the lights off, save for the blazing Christmas tree.

And the tree was so bright it seemed to fill her up from the inside out. She stood by the mantel, staring at a picture of her father while her throat got tighter and tighter.

"I miss you, Dad," she whispered.

And she let herself crumple a little, there in the dark with only the ornaments she'd made as a child to see her.

But when the crumpling stopped, if she kept her eyes shut, she could almost believe that her father was sitting there in his favorite chair the way he always had. That the fire was crackling bright and his favorite music was playing. She was sure she could hear him breathing, or more likely laughing, as he had his drink and read his paper and somehow seem to always know exactly what was going on with each and every one of them.

I don't know what to do, she told him.

You do, he replied. There in her heart.

I made such a mess of things once already, she confessed to him, her eyes squeezed shut. *Now it's Christmas, you're not here, and I'm afraid that if I choose something because it feels good right now, I'll regret it later.*

Baby girl, Hank Minton boomed inside of her. *All you ever have is right now. The future is what you make of it. The past is only as powerful as you let it become. Right here, right now—that's all life ever is.*

And she was so sure he was there, then, that she whirled around. She was positive that she might catch a glimpse of him—

But the chair was empty.

It was her heart that was full.

Right here. Right now.

"What are you doing in here in the dark?" Marianne asked, bustling in with an armful of wrapped gifts and turning on the lamps as she came.

"I don't know," Missy said, blinking at the burst of light. "I almost thought, if I closed my eyes and wished . . ."

Her mother smiled at her as she straightened from placing her gifts beneath the tree. "I know. I feel him too. I like to think he's sitting in that chair—"

"Laughing at everything. Yet always having the best advice."

"Always." Marianne sighed and settled herself on the couch, gazing at Missy. "I realize I'm not your father. But you never know. I might have some good advice myself."

Missy realized it had never occurred to her to ask her mother for advice. In fact, her head went blank as she gazed back at her. For so long that Marianne's smile turned a bit strained.

"I know, I know," her mother said, and it wasn't disappointment Missy heard then. It was something else. Wistfulness, maybe, and that made her heart hurt again. "You and your father were so much alike. He could simply read your mind. I always felt as if I needed a translator."

"Maybe it was my fault," Missy said. She didn't go sit in her father's armchair. None of them did, and they all laughed when one or the other of them pointed it out. But that didn't make any of them take their father's chair. Hank was still here. Hank would always be here. She sat down on the other end of the couch instead. "Maybe I was born angry."

"I don't know about that," Marianne said. "But you did always have very definite ideas. Even when you were small. You couldn't be told what to do."

"I like to think of that as an asset, personally."

"An admirable asset in a grown woman," her mother agreed with a laugh. "But less adorable in a toddler."

And maybe it was Christmas Eve. Maybe it was Hank. Maybe it was just time, but Missy found herself opening her mouth as if she'd been leaning on her mother all her life.

"I don't know what to do, Mom," she said softly. "I have the kind of job offers I always wanted. You know, I never actually meant to stay in Santa Fe. It was only going to be a stepping-stone. To bigger, better resorts. But then Philip happened." She laughed a little, forestalling whatever her mother might be about to say. "I know you never liked him. That's okay."

"I think Philip appealed to the part of you that wanted to pretend you have no roots here," Marianne said carefully. "In the same way that Connor Kittredge appealed to the part of you that never wanted anything but those roots. For the record, I don't think a person needs to choose between the sky and the earth. The world is made of both, Missy. You can't have one without the other."

Missy's heart was beating so loudly she felt as if it might tip her over.

"The future is what you make of it," she whispered. "The past is only as powerful as you let it become."

"Something like that," her mother said. And smiled. "That sounds like something your father used to say."

And all Missy could do was smile.

Later, after Marianne had gone to bed and Missy had

been telling herself to do the same for hours—while continuing to watch Christmas movies on repeat—she couldn't seem to get sky and earth, past and present, out of her head.

That was how she found herself in her mother's hatchback, heading down the mountain to town and then out over the pass toward all that Kittredge land. And as she drove, she challenged herself not to think about all the things she'd felt as a kid here. Not to note each and every house she passed in terms of who had lived there, what stories she knew about them, and how glad she was that she hadn't chosen to live here.

That sounded a whole lot like Philip in her head, if she was honest.

Instead, she thought about how pretty it was. This little town, tucked into the mountains, lit up with all these Christmas Eve lights. She saw friends and neighbors, folks who liked the land that kept them separate but gave back to the community that kept them connected.

And as she drove out into the far reaches of the valley, up toward the foothills, she let the glorious sweep of this wild land roll into her. As if she were a part of it. The sky and the earth, she thought. The stars above, the fields beneath the cover of snow. The small roads that made their way in and around the mighty mountains looming above.

This is home, she kept singing to herself, off-key and happy all the same. *This has always been your home.*

She had only been to Connor's cabin once. He had brought her there on the day they delivered his Christmas tree—and he hadn't let her in.

I don't trust you with my virtue, he'd drawled at her.

Tonight, she found her way deep into the part of Kittredge land that was far away from the stables and the horses and the big ranch house where his parents lived.

He lived up from the river off a dirt road with no name, but she found the grooves in the snow that the tires from his truck had left and followed them. Carefully.

And by the time she made it to his cabin and parked in front, she wasn't sure if she regretted coming all this way or wished she'd done it sooner. She got out of the hatchback and stood there in the little clearing he'd made in the snow. She tipped her head back to look at the stars some more, and when she finished being dizzy from that great tapestry, she looked over to the front porch and found him standing there.

In nothing but a pair of jeans buttoned low on his hips. God help her.

"Merry Christmas Eve," she managed to say. "To me."

"I expected it to be Santa and all his reindeer," Connor drawled. "But instead, look. It's the Ghost of Christmas Past."

"Please. You never read that book. I doubt you know who wrote it."

"I've watched numerous versions of the movie, thank you." But Connor didn't move from where he leaned there in the open door. His smile faded. "And you're a long way from where you ought to be tonight, Missy."

She started toward him, her boots loud against the snow. She climbed the front porch, though it felt perilous, and then she stood there. Right in front of him.

Right here, she told herself. *Right now.*

"It's funny you should say that, Connor." Nothing felt very funny, actually, but she kept going. "I've been thinking a lot about where I belong lately. A resort in Arizona seems to have almost everything I could need or want. A great job, great weather, and an excellent hotel to run with almost no corporate oversight."

"Sounds perfect."

"It has everything," she agreed. She blew out a breath. "Except the one thing I think might be most crucial to my happiness."

He looked indulgent. And still, a little sad. "What's that?"

Like he completely didn't get where she was going with this.

And Missy could admit there was a part of her that was fully a coward. That part wanted to stop.

Before she went too far. Before she showed her hand.

Then again, it was coming up on midnight on Christmas Eve. She'd driven all the way out here without an invitation. Whether he saw it or not, she'd already showed . . . everything.

So why not do what she wanted instead of not doing what she feared this time?

"You," she said, though it made her feel as if she'd tripped and fallen off the side of the world and would never, ever find her footing again. "You, Connor. I need you."

9

Connor felt a roar inside of him, fire and need and a deep, beautiful kind of triumph.

He wanted to haul her into his arms, claim her once and for all, and make like a caveman in every possible regard.

He would never know how he resisted.

Instead, he reached over and took one of her hands. She was already cold, though she'd only been outside for a few moments. Then he tugged her inside, closed the door against the night, and watched her as she walked into the main room.

It occurred to him to worry about how she might react to this cabin of his. After all, his sister had been less than complimentary.

But Missy turned around in a circle, then turned back to him, her eyes shining. "I have to say, this is exactly where I pictured you would live."

"That's not exactly a ringing endorsement."

"It's very masculine, Connor. It looks like there's never been a woman inside these walls."

"How dare you." But he grinned. "My mother, my sister, and my grandmother have all been here, thank you very much."

She looked even more beautiful than usual. Her eyes were so big, and her dark hair was coming out from beneath that cute hat of hers with the pink pom-pom that he found himself dreaming about, crazily enough. Her cheeks were red, and she'd stood there on his porch and said exactly what he most wanted to hear.

But this was Missy Minton.

"The thing about Arizona," he made himself say. "I love that you said that to me, Missy. Really, I do. But we both know that what you really want is that fancy hotel. As for me? I can't tell you how flattered I am, but I'm sure you'll find a dozen like me."

She looked at him for so long he started to feel . . . uncomfortable.

"One of the things I love about you is that you never, ever stand up for yourself," she said, her voice even and her gaze intense. "Not because you couldn't, but because you don't see the point. You let your brothers treat you like you're dumb. You let me act like you hadn't read a Dickens book we literally read together in a class where you got a higher grade than I did. You stand in front of me, right here, acting like there's anyone in this whole wide world anything like you, Connor."

"A cowboy is a cowboy," he managed to get out.

"That's not true. There's only one you, and I know this to be a fact because I'm the one who's been out there. I've gone places you'll never go, met people you'll never meet. And the whole time, no one held a candle to you." She shook her head emphatically. "I'm never going to find a dozen *just like you*. There's only one."

He cleared his throat, not sure what to do with that.

"My brothers don't treat me like I'm dumb," he said. Stiffly. Awkwardly, maybe. "It's their job to poke at me."

"You let them," she said, and he wasn't sure anyone had ever talked to him like this before. As if she saw exactly who he was. It made him feel bigger than his own Christmas tree. "Because you're the youngest, and that helps keep the peace. You never copied off of my paper in high school. You didn't need to. And I would think it was just an act you put on if you hadn't stood here two seconds ago and told me you were easily replaceable."

They were getting sidetracked. Especially when she pulled that hat off her head and ran her fingers through her hair. Then shoved the hat in one pocket, unzipped that puffy little parka, and tossed it on his couch.

Because now the only thing he could think about was getting his hands on her, the way he always did when there weren't enough layers between them. And he'd promised himself that he would treat Missy like a gentleman on all these dates he'd taken her on. The gentleman he sure hadn't been as a teenager.

But his body reminded him that this wasn't a date. And more, that he knew exactly how many steps it took to get to his bed in the back room.

Focus, he ordered himself.

"You need to follow your heart," he told her. "You and I both know that your heart isn't here."

"That's why I came over," she whispered. "Because I think it has been all along."

She moved closer to him. She slid her hands over his chest, making him deeply glad that he hadn't bothered to put on a shirt when he'd gotten out of the shower earlier. He would much rather have her hands on him.

"I think Christmas is getting to you," he said, though it was beginning to cause him pain to argue against his own interests here. "You're not going to feel the same in a few weeks. Let's not even talk about what might happen in spring when it snows again, just to be mean. Which it will."

"I remember high school," Missy said, completely ignoring him. "The more intense it got, the more in love with you I was. The more in love with you I was, the more I was afraid that I would stay here. I had told everyone I was leaving, Connor. I had to go. I didn't want to be stuck here."

He started to say something, but she put her fingers over his mouth. And then kept them there.

"Now it's the only place I want to be," she told him solemnly. "And I know that because this is where I ran when I was done with that big, fancy life I'd built out there. This was the only place I wanted to come to feel better. And I do."

"You need to go right back out there, then," he managed to say, moving her fingers from his mouth, but not letting go of them. He could only do so much. "You should."

"Connor. Stop trying to be noble." She laughed. At him, he was pretty sure. "I'm going to take the job at the Grand Hotel. I'm going to stay in town. I guess what I'd like you to tell me is whether you want to keep dating me while I do that."

"Missy . . ."

"You're going to have to think about it pretty carefully," she told him, smiling up at him as if she already knew what his answer would be. As if she could see straight through him. And he found he loved that she could. "Because I can't guarantee that when I'm feeling a little wicked down the road, I won't pull out a low-cut shirt and march right into church again. I have that in me."

"Amen to that," he managed to say.

"Well?" she asked. And he saw, then, that she wasn't

as confident as she was pretending to be. Her eyes were a little too bright. And he could see her pulse in her neck, beating wildly. "Have you decided?"

Connor took his time. He ran his hands up her arms, then down her back, pulling her close to him and holding her there. Letting her feel exactly how much he wanted her, and how much he'd been holding himself back.

"Missy," he said, because her name was a meal. And his favorite. "I don't want to date you."

He heard her indrawn breath. "You don't?"

Connor dropped his head, until his mouth was right there, so close to hers.

"No," he said as if it were a love word. Because they were all love words. "I want so much more than that."

This time when he kissed her—there in front of the Christmas tree he had every intention of decorating with her, year after year—it felt like the first time.

Better.

Because this time, it was forever.

10

Six months later, Missy Minton lived up to her scandalous reputation by moving out of her mother's house at last and shacking up with that Connor Kittredge.

Everyone was appalled.

In the sense of being delighted, that was, because there wasn't much folks around Cold River liked better than two hometown kids finding their way back to each other in the end.

Connor was pretty fond of the story himself.

"You know I have every intention of marrying you," he said the day she moved in, after he carried her inside, laid her out on the bed, and removed every article of her clothing. By way of christening the cabin that was now theirs.

And which she'd already put her stamp on, so it was more cozy and less . . . fish and game.

Her smile was wide and bright and all his. "I know."

"I'm happy to marry you right now. I love you, Missy. I think maybe I always have."

"I love you too," she said. "I know I always have. I'm so glad you were here when I was finally ready to come home."

And for a long while, there was only that.

Loving her, with his mouth and his hands, his body and his personal commitment to finding every last bit of that fire that had always raged and raged between them.

Much later, they lay side by side in that bed that was now theirs.

"You can't ask me to marry you for at least a year," she told him.

"If this is about your ex," he began, feeling remarkably less calm than he had a moment ago.

"What? Never." She scowled at him, tucked up in his arms. "Please do not defile our home by mentioning him. What's the matter with you?"

"You're the one who said we need to wait a year to get married. What other reason do we have to wait?" He sighed. "You should know I've spent some time in the graveyard, having discussions with your father. It's taking some work, but I think I've talked him around."

He wasn't kidding. And it was worth every time he'd felt silly while he stood there, laying out his case to a gravestone, because her eyes got soft and wide.

"Have you really?"

"Of course," he said gruffly. "Hank was the kind of man who would appreciate being asked for his daughter's hand."

"He was," Missy whispered. "And he would have loved telling you no a few times, just to keep you honest."

"He would have made me very, very honest." He pushed her hair back from her forehead. "But if even he approves, why do we have to wait?"

"Connor. Please." Missy smiled at him, big and wide and wicked, the way he'd always loved her best. "What's the point of living in sin if you don't do it for long enough to horrify as many people as possible?"

He laughed. "Somehow I don't think you're taking to small-town life in quite the way you should."

The truth was, whether she was reacclimating to small-town life or not, she was fantastic at her job. She'd been working at the Grand Hotel since right after New Year's, and Douglas Fowler had been heard to say—in as close to emotional terms as a man like him was likely to get—that it was almost like having a family member taking over. That was how good she was, in his estimation. She was deserving of his highest possible accolade.

Connor wasn't surprised at all.

"I told you," Missy said then, rolling over on top of him and sliding her body against his. "I have no intention of ever forgetting who I am."

They would never be conventional, Connor understood. They would do some things out of order, do other things solely to please themselves, and make the old ladies like Lucinda Early tut at them.

Truth was, Connor couldn't wait.

"I wouldn't let you forget," he told her, kissing her again. And then again, because she was his, and he was hers, and everything flowed out of that and always would. "I love who you are, Missy Minton."

And he had a lifetime to show her.

So that was what he did.